Voyagers

The Sleeping Abductees

Volume I

By Ashayana Deane,

formerly published as Anna Hayes

Second Edition

Voyagers

The Sleeping Abductees

Volume I

of the
Emerald Covenant CDT-Plate Translations

Second Edition

By Ashayana Deane

Information Transcribed from the Guardian Alliance
regarding Extraterrestrial Visitation, the Extraterrestrial Agendas,
Keylontic Morphogenetic Science, and the Mechanics of Alien Contact.
These transcriptions are NOT derived from channeled sources.

Wild Flower Press

Library of Congress Cataloging-in-Publication Data

Deane, Ashayana 1964-
Voyagers : the sleeping abductees / by Ashayana Deane
p. cm.
ISBN 1-893183-24-6
1. Human-alien encounters.
2. Spirit writings.
I. Title.
BF2050.H38 1999
001.942--dc21
99-23148
CIP

The Voyagers series
Volume I second edition

Cover Artwork and internal illustrations: Anhayana Deane
Cover design: Pamela Meyer
Manuscript editors: Brian Crissey, Pamela Meyer, Julie Sherar and Susan Westhoff
Indexer: Brian Crissey, Ph.D.
Printed in the United States of America.

Address all inquiries to:
Wild Flower Press, an imprint of
Granite Publishing, LLC
Post Office Box 1429,
Columbus, NC 28722 U.S.A.
828/894-8444

Granite Publishing, LLC., is committed
to living lightly on the Earth.

Dedicated to
The Guardians
of all Races and Realities

And to
The Guardian Alliance
for their patience and wisdom
and for the creation of this book.

In Recognition of the
Eieyani Indigo Children,
Past, Present and Future

Voyagers I Table of Contents

Table of Contents

Introduction

ALL THINGS CONSIDERED—
OTHERWORLDS, ORIGINS AND EVIDENCE

Voyagers is a set of books best approached by asking the question: *What do we really know about the nature of reality?* Many of the ideas presented in this book are different from the old belief paradigms through which we have been taught to view reality, they do not negate the old, but rather challenge old ideas to evolve. I suggest that the reader take an open-minded approach to the information contained in this book, in order to receive the benefits of the *Voyagers* material. The greatest benefit of the *Voyagers* perspective is the gift of an uncommon knowledge, through which some of the mysterious aspects of reality can be comprehended and the majesty of personal existence may be rediscovered.

Challenges inspire growth and *Voyagers* is a challenge, it is a book to grow with in your quest for understanding. *Voyagers* is not the average book, its implications are so intrinsically profound that at times it seems unbelievable, but this is not a fiction story. It is not just a book of ideas. It is evidence of a most intimate journey through personal events that can be described as nothing less than extraordinary. This book is not about my personal experiences, it is rather the result of those experiences. If the book is approached with flexibility of mind and a keen intuition, its message can be enlightening, its implications transformational.

Confronted with extraordinary experiences, I found that the integrity of my being was on the line and I was not about to write myself off as mentally deranged until I had fully examined other possible explanations for the events I had encountered. This confrontation finally led me to question what we really know about the existence of other worlds, our origins and the nature of reality itself. I began to question the facts of contemporary belief paradigms to see if there were other possible perspectives that could rationally explain my experiences. Through my questioning I came to realize that the facts were not carved in stone, they were simply assumptions about the nature of reality that many people accepted as fact. My questioning ultimately created enough reasonable doubt regarding mainstream reality interpretations that I could consider the ideas presented in *Voyagers* in a more objective framework, rather than simply dismiss them because they challenged what I had thought I knew about the nature of reality. I became receptive to the *Voyagers* material.

The need to validate my mental integrity was much less important than my need to understand the truth. As I explored the mysteries of human nature I realized that the *Voyagers* material could quite possibly represent a good portion of the mysterious truth about humanity that is presently unrecognized within our modern culture. I began to take the *Voyagers* material seriously. Only then did the profound implications of *Voyagers* really hit me, as I realized that, if this information is valid, we are in a most significant time period. We are approaching an evolutionary crossroads and through our choices the course of our collective future evolution will be determined. I became grateful for the *Voyagers* material as a potential tool through which effective action could be taken. *Voyagers* is not the entire truth of human reality, it is not the end of the story through which all mysteries will be solved. This book represents a beginning point, through which we can start to comprehend the incredibly complex framework within which human reality takes place.

Comparative analysis between contemporary beliefs and those presented in *Voyagers* led me to realize the potential validity of the new ideas. Once holes in the logic of the old paradigms became apparent, it was much easier to identify the potential logic of the ideas presented in *Voyagers*. The perspectives offered in *Voyagers* were equally as rational as those promoted through contemporary belief paradigms. I made peace with the *Voyagers* material. Peace came as a result of understanding how the ideas in this book could literally be possible and in realizing that this possibility implied that humanity's evolution had a greater purpose, meaning and cause than we presently suppose. I hope the reader may understand the evolutionary promise implied by the *Voyagers* worldview. It is a promise that reminds us of the majesty of our Divine nature and reaffirms our connection to a sacred Creation.

In the remainder of this Introduction I will share some considerations concerning contemporary belief paradigms, that helped me to recognize the potential validity of the *Voyagers* perspective. It is not my intention to challenge or negate the validity of popular assumptions, but I hope to offer some additional insights into these assumptions and to provide possible alternative perspectives through which the facts can be viewed. The following Considerations and Conclusions represent my personal perspectives; I do not ask you to accept my opinions as your own, but only to consider them as potentially interesting points of view through which greater understanding might be gained.

THE ORDINARY EXTRAORDINARY

In our contemporary world we are progressively presented with more and more experiences and occurrences of an extraordinary nature. Over the past 20 years alone it seems as if the extraordinary has taken on a life of its own. People now routinely report extraordinary experiences, such as psychic phenomena, Out-of-body-episodes, Near-death-experiences, hauntings, channeling of disembodied spirits, visitation by angels, sightings of UFOs and abductions by aliens, to name a few. All of these events share a common implication of the existence of Unseen Worlds, or Otherworlds, as I like to call them. Never before in recent history have these events reached such mass proportions. It is difficult to label such experiences as aberrations of a disturbed mind when masses of perfectly normal people begin reporting extraordinary encounters. Perhaps the current increase in extraordinary events will inspire us to reevaluate our perspectives on reality. If we look toward history for answers, we may find more explanations than we might suppose.

OTHERWORLDS - REEVALUATING THE PAST

Consideration 1: Do ancient records suggest the presence of Visitors from other worlds? Throughout the mythologies of ancient cultures, from indigenous tribes to ancient Sumerian, Egyptian, Greek and Roman civilizations, we are presented with accounts of extraordinary visitations by *gods* and demons from other worlds. The Visitors-from-elsewhere were both feared and worshipped by ancient man and the foundations of most ancient cultures were built upon a literal acknowledgment of unseen worlds. In contemporary times we have dismissed ancient recorded accounts of other-worldly visitations as the superstitious folly or imaginative fantasy of a primitive peoples, much in the same way that we attempt to invalidate the extraordinary experiences of people today, by viewing them as mental aberrations. Our scientific communities tend to view the Otherworld beliefs of contemporary humans and ancient cultures in symbolic terms, considering them to be representations of psychological archetypes of the times, rather than as valid evidence for human contact with other worlds.

Conclusion 1: It is quite possible that ancient records included both symbolic and literal representations of reality. Our contemporary interpretations of ancient records may not fully reflect the actualities those records were intended to describe and our potential misrepresentation of ancient events may cause us to misinterpret the extraordinary events of today.

What if the ancient mythologies were, at least in part, a colorful presentation of literal events? In our current societies we record and capture the essence of our cultural events through various media, from news reports, to drama, comedy, fiction and non-fiction, to the arts. Ancient peoples might have been doing precisely the same thing when they etched out odd flying craft and helmeted visitors in their cave drawings or wrote of their elaborate dramas with angels, creator gods and Visitors from Otherworlds. It would be easier to remain complacent within our interpretation of these ancient events as imaginings of the primitive mind, if we were not presently being confronted with precisely the same type of extraordinary encounters within our contemporary society.

Consideration 2: Is the belief in the literal existence of Otherworlds a minority perspective? Growing numbers of contemporary humans are reporting events of Otherworld contact. Over the last 40 years contemporary New Age culture has emerged, with much of its emphasis placed upon the spiritual worlds. New Age spiritual development frequently includes communication with channeled spirits and contact with ETs. Native American, Aboriginal and many other tribal cultures have always interpreted Otherworlds in literal terms. The majority of our ancient races left evidence suggesting that contact-from-elsewhere served an integral role within the very structure of their sociological organization. From the polytheistic, pantheistic, pagan and monotheistic religions of the ancients, through the rich historical tapestries of cultural mythology and up to the religious traditions we hold most dear today, humans have demonstrated awareness of the existence of other inhabited worlds. The names, locations and attributes assigned to the Otherworlds differ between cultures. Christianity and Judaism refer to Otherworlds in terms of heaven, *hell* and purgatory. Ancient Grecian myths described them as Olympus - the abode of the Gods. Tribal cultures and New Age ideologies identify the Otherworlds in terms of various dimensional levels and sometimes as identified planetary systems in our known galaxies. Regardless of the terminology and categorization used, the common belief in the literal existence of other inhabited worlds remains the same.

Conclusion 2: The majority of collective humanity has validated within their belief paradigms, the existence of unseen worlds inhabited by intelligent beings that periodically interacted with human culture. Within the traditional, New Age and indigenous religious communities of the present day and throughout the ancient civilizations of historical record, the collective majority of humanity has always acknowledged the literal existence of the unseen Otherworlds and the reality of Visitors from elsewhere. Whether the

Visitors are viewed as angels, demons, spirits or ETs, the underlying implication is that mysterious Visitors from Otherworlds interact with Earth and human culture.

Consideration 3: How did the ancients know of Otherworlds if contemporary science has yet to prove their existence? Our contemporary scientific paradigms attempt to refute the existence of other inhabited worlds, based upon two primary assumptions:

1. Conditions supportive of evolved biological life have yet to be found within local planetary environments and

2. Planets showing evidence of past or present civilization have not been found. While the scientific communities refuse to publicly validate the possible existence of inhabited Otherworlds, until they can tangibly prove this reality, the majority of humans on Earth and throughout history have known that the Otherworlds exist.

Conclusion 3: Knowledge of the Otherworlds did not come to our historical masses through technological validation, scientific hypotheses or mathematical calculation. It is possible that this knowledge may have come as a result of direct contact with Visitors from Otherworlds and through humans interfacing directly with the realities of other-dimensional systems. Ancient peoples did not need technology to prove the existence of the unseen worlds if this reality was validated through direct experience. Otherworld knowledge may have been passed down through generations, following periodic instances of ancient physical contact with non-terrestrial Visitors.

The skepticism toward the idea of Earth visitation from Otherworld inhabitants that is presently promoted by the majority of our scientific communities, represents ideas held by only a small minority of humans, primarily those who accept the assumptions of the contemporary scientific community. Modern science may be missing the fact of Otherworld realities, which the human majority has known all along, through failure to consider a broader range of criteria when formulating their hypotheses. First of all, the hypothesis that non-earthly environments supportive of evolved biological life have not been identified is built upon the assumptions that all forms of evolved biological life require the same environmental conditions and that science has identified all possible forms of evolved biological life. The fact is, there may be types of highly evolved non-carbon based biological life forms (such as silica-based biology) of which science is unaware and other types of biology may require other types of environmental conditions. Planets assumed to be uninhabitable could actually support subterranean, surface or etheric civilizations of evolved life forms that are not yet known to exist.

Secondly and of most importance, the hypothesis that evidence of past or present civilizations has not been found on other planets is built upon two unlikely assumptions:

1. All planets and galaxies in the universe can be perceived, located and identified through modern technological instrumentation.

2. The existence of all possible worlds can be theorized through contemporary mathematical computation.

Our scientists have not yet seriously considered the possibility that inhabited Otherworlds may not only exist on other planets in other star systems, but that they may also reside within other-dimensional reality fields that differ from our own, within unrecognized parallel universe systems or that visitations could occur through inter-time structures that allow interface between various periods of space-time. Quantum physics theory presents new possibilities for validating the existence of parallel, interdimensional and inter-time worlds, but our scientific understanding of such realities is in its infancy.

The facts are: Otherworlds, supporting advanced civilizations, may appear *unseen* from today's scientific perspective because they exist in dimensions (or fields of frequency) unknown to contemporary science. They may exist in parallel universes (which Quantum physics theory is only beginning to suggest.). Non-terrestrial Visitors, reported throughout history, could originate from these unseen worlds or may visit Earth via time travel through unidentified inter-time structures. Contemporary mathematical computation may not possess the sophistication to factor multi-dimensional reality systems into workable theories, from which clear hypotheses as to the locations of Otherworlds can be drawn.

These possible explanations for the apparent invisibility of other inhabited worlds are equally as valid as the scientific assumption that such worlds cannot exist simply because science has yet to discover them. Otherworlds may not exist for science, but they have always existed for the general human collective.

BLINDED BY SCIENTIFIC INTERPRETATION

Consideration 4: Does scientific dogma distract us from other potentially valid reality interpretations? We often fail to see other potentially valid perspectives regarding inhabited Otherworld existence because of our contemporary acquiescence to the dictates of scientific expertise. Blinded by the shining accomplishments the sciences have achieved, we tend to overlook the larger body of subject matter that science has yet to comprehend. In western culture especially, we have allowed the glamour of the scientific dynamic, (with its nasty habit of negating the reality of anything it cannot yet define, dissect, reduce to mathematical computation or place under a microscope), to create our belief paradigms for us. Too often we accept the assumptions of the scientific experts as fact, even if those assumptions are incomplete or serve to negate our personal experience and understanding. Contemporary humans have allowed themselves to become conditioned to blindly accepting the hypotheses of the scientific community, when the scientific community itself often negates its previous assumptions with the discovery of new insights. In the world of science the facts frequently change, yet the general public often accepts scientific fact as absolute truth.

Conclusion 4: We have placed our sciences on a pedestal and in so doing we have disempowered our own abilities to assess conditions of reality and to scrutinize the value of scientific hypotheses. As long as we place the reality interpretations of the scientific machine above our ability to think for ourselves, we will remain blind to other possible interpretations of reality, which may have equal or superior value compared to the assumptions of the scientific majority. Science has its place within an evolving culture, but if it is allowed to become the ruler, dictator and governing force of the private mind, the wisdom that comes to us by way of the Soul may be extinguished.

(Scientific paradigms traditionally do not recognize the validity of the soul. Readers of a scientific persuasion may substitute, in the above sentence, the concept of the Super-conscious Mind, for the term Soul, as the modern science of psychology is beginning to recognize this idea. In truth, the Super-conscious Mind and the Soul represent the same level of higher identity and there are levels of identity that exist beyond this point.)

We have accepted the scientific assumption that ancient recorded accounts of Otherworld contact represent the symbolic folly of a less developed primitive mind and thus we discount the possible implications of those ancient records. Through this acquiescence of perspective to scientific dogma we have lost touch with the possibilities of our creation and have become blind to the realities of which our ancient ancestors might once have been aware. Invalidation of the unseen worlds and denial of the evidence that supports their existence represents a specialized digression rather than an evolution of our conscious awareness. We have achieved simple scientific and technological prowess, while sacrificing a greater cognition of ourselves, the cosmos and the Divine; awareness our ancient ancestors might very well have possessed.

Consideration 5: Were ancient human cultures more evolved in Mind Technologies? Under the influence of popular scientific ideology we have learned to view ancient human races as primitive compared to our own, because they apparently lacked sophistication in externalized mechanical technology. We rarely consider the possibility that some ancient peoples might have possessed a higher level of evolution regarding Mind Technologies than that which is presently demonstrated in the contemporary human. Many present day experiences of an extraordinary nature are categorized as mental problems, when in truth they may represent evidence of a more evolved consciousness that was ordinary during ancient times.

Conclusion 5: It is perhaps a greater sophistication in technologies of mind and resulting attributes of perceptual expansion that allowed the ancients more open dealings with Otherworld inhabitants. Many of the rituals and spiritual practices of old could represent intuitive comprehension of the direction of subtle energy and hidden forces—an art that contemporary science is only beginning to hone through the use of the rational mind and external technologies. If we viewed ancient cultures with more respect for their inherent mental integrity, we might discover the logic behind some of their spiritual beliefs and practices and realize that such practices might have advanced scientific validity at their core. If we begin to validate the contours of the ancient psyche we would begin to comprehend more about the workings of the contemporary mind and would perhaps not jump to the conclusion that people are mentally disturbed simply because they have extraordinary experiences. We might discover that extraordinary experiences are the result of perceptual evolution. Once we collectively advance to a more evolved state of consciousness, extraordinary experiences, such as contact with inhabitants of Otherworlds, might become quite ordinary.

GODS AND VISITORS

Consideration 6: Have Visitor agendas influenced human evolution? When less developed cultures encounter members of more advanced civilizations they frequently view the more evolved beings as gods due their advanced knowledge and seemingly magical abilities. If our ancient cultures were indeed visited by members of more evolutionarily advanced races from Otherworlds, it is quite likely that such Visitors would be considered as gods. Ancient polytheistic and pantheistic religions could very well have been built upon the dramatic visitations of advanced interstellar, inter-time or interdimensional races, that literally took place within the life experience of our ancestors. Such visiting cultures could have laid the conceptual foundations for ancient spiritual belief, reducing their advanced spiritual and scientific comprehension into simple terms more easily understood by a less developed civilization. Monotheistic religious traditions, which remain strong within our culture today, could likewise have been brought here by advanced, visiting races from the Otherworlds. The Visitors may have depicted themselves as gods in order to establish an attitude of reverence, obedience or subservience among ancient populations or to bring to us their own spiritual and scientific knowledge in ways that we could understand.

Perhaps the great theological discrepancies, still apparent within contemporary religions that have their roots in ancient ideologies, have resulted from diversification among ancient Visitor races. Each race, having a worldview of its own, may have at different times dispensed teachings that reflected their particular understanding of the cosmos. Through the passage of time the original teachings were propagated within various aspects of human culture, laying the foundations for the great spiritual and theological perspectives that have molded our civilizations up to the present day. It is quite possible that ancient cultures and the direction of human evolution itself have been directly influenced by a Visitor presence and that such influences continue today through discrete Visitor involvement. This contemporary influence may have a direct effect upon the course of our future evolution.

Conclusion 6: Visiting representatives from Otherworld cultures may have directly influenced the evolution of human culture on Earth. Our religious belief systems of today may have their roots in Otherworld cultures. The development of our present scientific paradigms may also be influenced from behind the scenes by contemporary Otherworld Visitors. It may be no accident that scientific paradigms have evolved in a way that attempts to negate the possibility of Visitor presence. Perhaps Visitors allow us to evolve primarily on our own, observing from afar while periodically influencing the direction of our evolution. Some Visitors may have agendas toward the human populace that depend upon our ignorance to their existence. If we were being covertly manipulated or directed toward a hidden evolutionary goal, it could be to the benefit of the Visitors to remain undetected. If Visitors are concerned about the course of human evolution a motive could plausibly exist for them to influence through covert means, the evolution of our scientific and religious ideologies. Scientific and religious organizations form the foundations upon which our mass cultural belief systems are built. If our scientists and clergy were secretly guided, (via various means of covert Visitor infiltration), to follow specific perspectives about our origins and the nature of reality, perspectives that lead us away from considering the idea of Visitor involvement with Earth, Visitors could direct the course of our evolution while remaining invisible to our people. Covert Visitor influences may have existed from the time of human beginnings on Earth, continuing discretely up to and including our present time.

If the Visitors are benevolent in nature, then such evolutionary guidance might have our best interests at heart. But if some Visitors held malevolent motives, our continued survival could be at stake. This interpretation of human evolutionary history is not often promoted through present day scientific or religious culture, but the Visitor Influence theory is potentially equally as valid an interpretation of human evolution as those offered and endorsed by the contemporary expert majority. There is no proof to the contrary and historical records themselves serve as potential evidence of Visitor influence. The possibility that ancient cultures were directly influenced by Otherworld Visitors and that the course of our evolution up to the present day might have been directly guided by a covert Visitor presence, is a potential of our evolutionary history that our culture has barely explored. It is no less an intelligent approach to exploring our evolutionary history, than to assume that ancient peoples independently and imaginatively created elaborate depictions of Otherworld involvement due to the *ignorance* of the primitive mind and that contemporary people experiencing contact events are simply mentally unstable.

We may have been covertly guided, throughout various portions of our evolution, to negate the possibility of Visitor presence, or to worship Visitors in terms of conceptualized Gods, so our race would remain open for manipulation and direction by Visitors from Otherworlds. It may do us well to consider this possibility now, as instances of extraordinary Visitor encounters make a resurgence within contemporary society, because the intentions of all Visitors may not have the best interests of human evolution at heart. As long as we negate the possibility of Visitor presence, we will not explore the implications of how such a presence might affect us now or through the course of our future evolution and we will be completely unprepared to handle ourselves effectively in the face of Visitor encounter.

VISITORS AND HUMAN ORIGINS

If we view ancient records in terms of a potentially literal (albeit colorful) interpretation we can see the plausibility of the Visitor Contact theory. If Visitors were present throughout our history, perhaps they have indeed charted, guided and influenced the path of human evolution all along. This possibility leads to **greater considerations.**

Consideration 7: Is there a Genetic Connection between humans and Otherworld Visitors? If Visitors interacted with us periodically and influenced the course of our evolution throughout history, it would seem that the Visitors had a vested interest in the development of the human lineage on Earth. One plausible reason visiting races would be interested in our development is that our races were somehow connected. This connection could be genetic. What if the truth of our origins on Earth is not the accidental collision of elemental space dust and its resulting evolutionary progression, as suggested by some scientific schools of thought? What if the Father-god created man on Earth theory, that is promoted by most monotheistic religious doctrines, is a simplification of a greater creation dynamic? (For all we know the Father-God of our monotheistic creation stories could have been a biological ET or a non-terrestrial etheric Entity from Otherworlds, who gave us our creation stories to help us understand our inherent spiritual connection to the cosmos). What if we were put here to evolve, by an Elder Race of interstellar, inter-time or interdimensional Visitors, as the propagation of their genetic heritage?

Conclusion 7: Human lineage could very possibly have originated through an older race of **extraterrestrial (ET)**, other-dimensional or inter-time Otherworld Visitors. If our true ancestors are non-terrestrial in nature and are more highly evolved than contemporary humanity, then our genetic heritage may be richer then we have imagined and our evolutionary potentials may be greater than we suppose. Our original home and the purpose for our existence may exist within the Otherworlds.

Considering the possibility of non-terrestrial human origins does not negate our beloved spiritual teachings, but rather suggests that our creation stories fit into a larger picture. Otherworld origin does not imply that we have been created by other races alone, it suggests that we may be the continuation of Elder Races who were also created through a Divine Source. It would simply imply that our Divine Source had created greater diversity of form than that which is apparent on Earth. God's creations would thus include the ET, OD (Other-dimensional) and IT (Inter-time) inhabitants of the Otherworlds, as well as human and other life forms on Earth. The idea of non-terrestrial origins does not intrinsically conflict with our religious teachings. Visitor seeding as the origin of Earth humans is equally believable, if not more so, than the scientific assumption that we emerged by accident rather than by design, through the unintended spontaneous collision of elemental forces. The possibility of non-terrestrial genetic origin does not negate our intrinsic connection to a Divine Source but may imply that our concepts of God need to expand. We often assume that God is created in the image of man, when in truth it may be that our intrinsic creative consciousness, our spiritual essence not our bodies, were created in the image of God. Otherworld inhabitants, regardless of their manifest appearance, may equally represent expressions of the image of God, sharing with us the Divine Creative Essence.

ORIGINS, SCIENCE, EVIDENCE AND INTERPRETATIONS

Consideration 8: Did we evolve from early primates or primitive man? Presently large numbers of our populations do not seriously consider the possibilities of non-terrestrial genetic heritage or Visitor involvement with

Earth, because our scientific paradigms have moved our attentions in other directions. In the recent past the theory of human origins promoted by the scientific community was that of the primate-evolutionist model. Applying the natural selection theory (survival of the fittest) of 19th century Charles Darwin to the human origins question, for a time it was believed that the *Homo sapiens* represented the cumulative evolutionary product of progressive genetic adaptation of early primate species. Our lineage was said to have its identifiable beginnings as early primates, to have progressed via evolution through various stages of primitive man, arriving at its present superior form in the *Homo sapiens*. Certain genetic similarities were detected between some primates, early man and the *Homo sapiens* human, but an irrefutable genetic bridge confirming the progression has not been established. In more recent analysis apparent genetic discrepancies and missing links within this hypothetical model of progression have discredited the potential accuracy of the primate-evolution theory and this model of origins is no longer viewed with the scientific enthusiasm it once inspired.

Conclusion 8: The primate-evolution model simply represents a possible theory of human origin, it is by no means a paradigm carved in stone. The truth of the matter is that our scientists are still guessing, they do not yet know the facts of human origins and they can offer us only assumptions using their present body of knowledge.

Through genetic analysis and archeological discovery the sciences have unearthed various pieces of evidence related to the evolution of early human culture. The facts of historical evidence of our origins are simply these: we have certain genetic similarities to various early hominid and primate species, remains of primitive man have been found during periods when *Homo sapiens* was not evidenced on Earth and *Homo sapiens* remains are evidenced after species of primitive man had apparently disappeared. These facts can be interpreted in a variety of ways, from attempting to fit them into the primate-evolutionist model, to considering the possibilities that the *Homo sapiens* and primitive man species were independently seeded here, at different times, by visiting races from Otherworlds. Genetic crossbreeding between an earlier Otherworld *Homo sapiens* race and earthly primate forms could easily account for the genetic similarities between certain primate, primitive hominid and *Homo sapiens* species. We may not be the descendants of primitive man, we might very well be its progenitor.

This fact remains: a concrete answer to the question of human origins has not yet been adequately determined and the existing evidence can be interpreted in a variety of ways. If we add to the equation a literal interpretation of ancient historical records, depicting Otherworldly contact, (some of which include stories of the *gods* coming down to interbreed with human females), the cumulative evidence points more strongly to Visitor involvement with our lineage, than to the hypothesis that we are the product of primate-evolution.

MYSTERIES

Consideration 9: Could Otherworld Visitors be responsible for some of our unsolved mysteries? Visitor presence could account for some of the ancient and contemporary mysteries we have yet to solve. The emergence of sophisticated early Sumerian culture. The astronomical knowledge possessed by the primitive Dogon Tribe of Africa, whose contemporary descendants claim their ancestors received this knowledge from ET Visitors from the Sirius star system[1].The obvious mathematical and architectural achievements embodied within the Great Pyramid of Giza, Egypt. (Did primitive humans really devise the sophisticated mathematical relationships of form that are demonstrated in the pyramid's construction, were they able to calculate measurement with such precision that stones are fitted together tightly enough so as to rival the abilities of modern technology? Did they really carve and haul those massive blocks of stone by hand, with only the aid of primitive building technologies?) The ancient Nazca lines of Peru[2]. Each of these mysteries presents evidence of advanced knowledge, knowledge that is inconsistent with evolutionary levels of development that we assume apply to the peoples of ancient times. How did ancient cultures come to possess this knowledge? Why do certain indigenous people of today, including some Native American tribes, claim that they have always known they were descendents from the stars? What ancient peoples had flying technologies that would allow them to create the aerial art of the Nazca drawings? Where do our contemporary crop circles and UFOs come from? Why are contemporary reports of ET and angelic contacts on the rise? These and many other mysteries may share the common element of Otherworld Visitor presence.

Conclusion 9: If we include the appearance of ancient oddities within the problem of deciphering the truth of the human drama, oddities which demonstrate inconsistent evolutionary advances and mysterious architectural achievements, yet another variable is added to the equation. Our evolutionary equation already contains many ancient records of reported Otherworld visitations (including ancient cave drawings depicting flying aircraft and helmeted stick figures), the records indicate that entire cultures were built upon

---

1. The Dogons knew about the star Sirius B, in the Sirius star system, long before modern science *discovered* it.
2. huge, ancient drawings etched into the Nazca desert depicting geometrical and animal forms, that can only be clearly identified from an aerial view.

the literal acknowledgment of the existence of Otherworlds. There is a lack of conclusive knowledge concerning our species origins or the reality of its evolutionary progression. Reports of Otherworld contact (such as angelic visitations, Near-Death-Experiences, spirit communications, ghostly hauntings and alien abductions) have existed as part of our *folklore* throughout history and reports of such contact have drastically increased over the last 50 years. Documented records and photographs of contemporary UFO sightings, crop circle formations and unexplained cattle mutilations continue to expand. Traditional and New Age religions of all varieties, despite their obvious theological conflicts, fully acknowledge the existence of inhabited unseen worlds. Native American, Aboriginal and other tribal cultures have always validated the unseen worlds and many have acknowledged the star people as progenitors of the human lineage.

What about the bodily scars and scoop marks apparent on some people claiming to be alien abductees or the circular impressions left on the ground that are occasionally reported following UFO sightings or abductions? Recent medical revelations have included the surgical removal of physical implants from the bodies of several people claiming to have had ET encounters; implants created through an advanced technology not yet available on Earth. Are physical implants the product of imagination? Perhaps the mysteries of the massive Stone Heads on Easter Island, the technical artistry of the Mitchell-Hedges Crystal Skull and the Face on Mars NASA photo also fit into the category of Visitor evidence? The Great Pyramid of Giza and the Sphinx (with its curious resemblance to the Face on Mars) might also represent remains of a Visitor presence. Along with this persuasive physical evidence, we have records from ancient times throughout our known history indicating Otherworld contact and we have literally thousands, if not hundreds of thousands, of contemporary eye witness accounts of UFO sightings and Visitor contact or abductions.

How can we expect to solve the equation of the human drama while blatantly ignoring the body of evidence that suggests Otherworlds and their Visitors do indeed exist? How can we rationally ignore this cumulative evidence and assume that all of the cultures throughout history and all people experiencing extraordinary phenomena today, just don't know what they are talking about? How can we ignore the potential connections between various elements of physical evidence and the correlation between the physical evidence and the subject accounts of witnesses throughout the ages?

Why would we want to ignore or deny this information?

It is illogical and irrational to ignore this evidence.

Many people assume that there is no evidence to support the theory of Otherworld Visitor contact. This is an erroneous assumption, for the fact is that quite a bit of evidence exists to support the Contact theory. The idea that no evidence exists could be part of a propaganda program, orchestrated via covert Visitor infiltration into human culture, that is intended to conceal Visitor manipulation and activities from human view, by convincing the masses that Visitors cannot and do not exist. This is a scary thought but it should be addressed, as we explore the possibilities and implications of Visitor presence. There is no more concrete proof to support evolutionary theories that negate or ignore the possibility of Visitor presence than there is for the Contact theory. Substantial evidence is lacking in either case, but when existing evidence is viewed collectively, its many pieces placed side by side, a convincing picture of probable contact emerges. Many people may challenge the idea of Visitor Contact with a *prove-it* attitude, using scientific or religious perspectives to refute the Contact theory. The truth is that both contemporary science and religion cannot prove their own origins theories, precisely the theories they use to negate the possibility of contact. The argument is a stalemate and will remain so, until we irrefutably discover life on other planets or the Visitors make their presence on Earth undeniably known.

MISSING EVIDENCE, PARTICLE TRANSITION AND TIME

Consideration 10: Why isn't there a greater amount of physical, archeological evidence of ancient Visitor contact? It is possible that remains of an Elder *Homo sapiens* race or evidence of ET, IT (inter-time) or OD (other dimensional) Visitor presence have not been found on Earth due to destruction of evidence through geological Earth changes, such as pole shift or other cataclysms. It is also possible that the evidence is here but has not yet been discovered. Another reason we haven't found physical remains other than ancient records and mysteries, could be that members of visiting races returned to the Otherworlds from which they came. Before leaving they may have made an effort to destroy, remove or conceal evidence of their presence, in order to keep their activities hidden from the general human populace. It is rumored that this tactic is certainly used today in regard to Visitor involvement with covert human governments. Perhaps the Visitors held agendas toward human development throughout history, which required concealment of their presence from all but a few. One plausible reason for the seeming absence of archeological evidence supporting *contact* has not yet been considered. It is the most likely reason for the absence of evidence, but it is also the most difficult explanation to understand. It is a scientific dynamic known as Particle Transition, a dynamic which is not presently understood within the scientific communities of Earth.

Particle Transition is part of the natural evolutionary cycle of planetary bodies and can be understood through advanced applications of Keylontic Morphogenetic Science, as further detailed in the latter portions of this book. In brief, a planet evolves through a fixed multi-dimensional frequency scale, following certain Time Cycles and Time Continua inherent to its dimensional system. In Earth's evolutionary cycle, a 26,556-year Time Cycle holds six smaller Time Continuum cycles of 4426-years each. Earth's progression through this fixed structure of time is synchronistically intertwined with the evolutionary cycles of Earth's anti-particle double/parallel Earth. During the six Time Continuum cycles Earth passes through in its larger 26,556-year evolutionary cycle, Earth and its double literally trade places. Our particle Earth spends two Time Continuum cycles within the anti-particle universe, while during the same period, parallel anti-particle Earth spends two continuum cycles in the particle universe. (This is done through complex dynamics involving the reversal of electromagnetic polarity and shifting of the angular rotation of particle spin).

During the two continuum cycles when the planets switch places within their respective universes, any matter constructions created on those planets will be composed of particles or anti-particles inherent to the universe within which the planet is stationed. Objects and biological remains of civilizations taking place on Earth while it is in the anti-particle universe will be composed of anti-particles. As Earth passes back into the time continua cycles of the particle universe, most matter constructions and remains from Earth's parallel universe period will remain within the anti-particle universe. Remains of activity taking place on the anti-particle parallel Earth while it is in the particle universe, will likewise remain in the particle universe. As the planets simultaneously transition back to their *home* universe, the remains of one planet will appear within the physical particle base of the other planet. This implies that remains found on our Earth, that can be dated to the periods when Earth was in the parallel universe, are actually the remains of activity that took place on parallel anti-particle Earth while it was in the particle universe. Our Earth's remains from that period would not be found here, they would exist within the particle base of parallel Earth in the anti-particle universe. Otherworld races visiting Earth while the planet was in the anti-particle universe would leave evidence of their activities within the grounds of parallel-Earth. We would not be able to unearth these remains until our particle Earth passed back into the anti-particle universe, following the successful completion of its 26,556-year evolutionary cycle.

In the present 26,556-year time cycle, Earth passed into the parallel anti-particle universe in 13,474 BC, remained there for two time continua cycles (8852 years), then returned to the particle universe in 4622 BC. Our Earth's archeological remains from the time period of 13,474 BC through 4622 BC, would not be found on our Earth; they would exist on parallel Earth. Archeological remains found on our Earth, that can be dated to the period of 13,474 BC to 4622 BC, would actually represent the remains of civilizations and life forms that existed on parallel Earth during this period of time. The Particle Transition process of multi-dimensional planetary evolution is very complex and utterly *alien* to our scientific communities, yet it is a cohesive model, consistent with the structure and mechanics of 15-dimensional physics that are introduced in Volume II, *Voyagers: Secrets of Amenti.* If this model accurately illustrates the hidden dynamics of planetary evolution, the seeming absence of Visitor or Elder Race evidence on Earth can be easily accounted for; the remains exist, but most of them are contained beneath the soils of parallel Earth. Remains that *vanish* when Earth transitions back into the particle universe, can be rediscovered when Earth once again passes into the anti-particle universe, at the completion of its 26,556-year time cycle. Within Earth's natural time cycle passage, the present cycle would end in 4230 AD, at which time various types of missing remains would become available for discovery. Due to events described in Volume II, the opportunity for some such discoveries may present itself between 2000 and 2017.

This is a very brief review of the basic concepts involved with the Particle Transition theory; the mechanics involved are much more sophisticated than I have described. I don't fully understand these dynamics, but I find the theory absolutely fascinating. It is the most intelligent hypothesis I have come across to account for a lack of physical evidence supporting ancient Visitor involvement with Earth. This theory would completely revolutionize our studies of archeology and ancient history. Our mythologies regarding advanced early civilizations, such as Atlantis and Lemuria, could depict actual realities as well. The remains of pre-4622 BC Atlantis might be hidden beneath the waters of parallel Earth, perhaps awaiting our discovery between 2000 and 2017.

Conclusion 10: Whether non-detection, natural destruction, intentional concealment, Particle Transition or a combination of all of the above are responsible for the apparent lack of ancient physical *contact* evidence, much evidence is still available if we begin to view ancient records with a bit more integrity. Mysterious cultural advancements of the ancients also support the validity of the Visitor contact theory. The information from the past, coupled with the growing phenomena of extraordinary experiences today, offers a convincing body of evidence to support the idea of the existence of Otherworlds and the premise that Visitors from elsewhere have periodically interacted with Earth throughout history and into the present. Evidence to the contrary is no more conclusive—it is only more popular, due to the old interpretations of our scientific and religious communities. Evidence to support the premise that other inhabited worlds exist throughout the cosmos and that Visitors from these worlds have interacted directly with Earth, can be found through closer examination of our past and through objective observation of the extraordinary events that are presently unfolding within our contemporary global culture.

HYPOTHESIS

Through analyzing the evidence upon which our contemporary belief paradigms are built I was able to see some of the illogical conclusions negating the possibility of Visitor presence that have been traditionally drawn from existing evidence. I have become aware of other potentially valid interpretations of this evidence that support the idea of past and present Visitor involvement with Earth. My ultimate conclusion is that Otherworlds do exist, so do the Visitors and they are beginning to make their presence known in our contemporary world. I believe that some of the Otherworlds exist within physical solar systems that are part of our observable galaxies, but that the majority of them exist within parallel, other-dimensional and other-time reality systems that our scientists have yet to discover. I have grown to accept the theory that we are not alone in the universe and never have been, as evidence suggests that Visitors from more advanced cultures from Otherworlds have interacted with human evolution from the time of our inception on Earth. It will be quite some time before the scientific majority endorses this perspective, but regardless of their skepticism the reality of extraordinary events and Visitor contact will continue to take place around us. We have a choice, between blindly accepting the incomplete conclusions offered to us through the expertise of contemporary science and religion, or to open our minds and venture forward to explore the unknown realities on our own. We have a right to explore available evidence, to interpret that evidence in our own way and to draw our own conclusions. If we expect to understand what is really taking place on Earth and how contemporary events are connected to our ancient past, the right to explore becomes a personal responsibility to do so. If we wait for science to draw the conclusions for us, or allow overly restrictive authoritarian religious doctrine to dictate the answers, we may be leaving ourselves vulnerable to the influences of the unknown worlds and we may never know the real truth of the human evolutionary drama.

Until scientists and clergy discover that the universe is constructed upon an ordered model of multi-dimensional reality, (in which physics and spirituality/evolutionism and creationism co-exist), they will be unable to prove or disprove the existence of the Otherworlds. We are living in extraordinary times. The new millennium is a time for closure and a time for new beginnings. It is a good time to purge ideas that reduce us and to embrace those that set us free. In this book you will find new perspectives on the human condition, perspectives which challenge old ideas to evolve. You will discover a worldview filled with potentials and challenges that you may never have dreamed possible. Voyagers is a doorway into the world of the extraordinary. It offers unique perspectives on history, science and humanity's evolutionary purposes and it offers a glimpse into the realities of the contemporary Visitor phenomena. But of most importance this book offers us a practical analysis of the extraordinary circumstances Earth will encounter during the next 18 years and provides educational tools through which we can effectively prepare for Earth's passage into the Golden Age of Enlightenment. If we can open our minds to the potential validity of the *Voyagers* material, we will use the opportunity to employ these educational tools for our evolutionary benefit. I hope the insights I have offered will help the reader to become more receptive to the possibilities and potentials *Voyagers* presents. These insights helped me to grow from skepticism and self doubt to realization and self-renewal. Perhaps for you they will do the same.

The Golden Age of Enlightenment is dawning and it offers us a golden opportunity to reevaluate our reality, to reinvent ourselves and to come full circle, reuniting contemporary knowledge with the wisdom of our ancient ancestors. It is a time when the past and present come together, the result of which will decidedly direct the course of our future evolution. *Voyagers*, by its very nature, is an extraordinary series of books. It does not merely contain the speculations of a human mind, but rather offers us a unique perspective on the human condition as observed from an objective birds eye view. I was quite relieved that, in analyzing available evidence, I was able to convince my skeptical, rational mind to validate the existence of a Visitor presence. If I hadn't been convinced, if there was not enough evidence available to override my personal disbelief, I would have misinterpreted a lifetime of extraordinary experiences and negated the integrity of my personal perceptions. The evidence was there, only the pieces needed to come together. The information contained in this book is further evidence of an active Visitor presence on Earth today. The production of this book is the result of a 27-year physical and communicative relationship that I have been privileged to share with members of an organization of Visitors from the Otherworlds, who refer to themselves as the Guardian Alliance.

CONTACT

Intruders

In 1969, at four years of age, I had my first conscious initiation into the contemporary world of extraordinary events, as I was physically abducted from my driveway in broad daylight by a small gray being with large black eyes. It soon became apparent to me that Visitors from elsewhere were far more than creative expressions of the imagination. Following this event I endured three years of ritual abductions in which I was physically taken from my bed at night and transported to a silent spacecraft, escorted by a trio of identical gray beings. During my encounters with the Greys I was subjected to frightening experiences and medical procedures that I did not understand. Aboard the alien craft I learned that the Greys worked in subordination to various other types of nonhuman beings. In positions of authority were ominous creatures that resembled large, upright insects, similar in structure to spiders and wingless moths. The administrators who directed the activities of this menagerie were tall, black robed beings with heavily boned faces and deep blue skin.

Many years later I would understand that this plethora of zoological wonders represented various sub-species within an ET/interdimensional race based primarily in the Orion star system. In their dealings with Earth they are known as the Zeta Reticuli, their primary race strain being the blue faced Zephelium, the administrators and directors of the lower ranking sub-species of Zeta. In recent times the Zeta races began interacting with Earth around World War I and by World War II they had established covert treaties with both the Nazi and Allied governments, through which they were entitled to abduction-experimentation rights on the unwitting public, in exchange for their weapons technologies. Since the 1980s the Zeta have joined forces with their ancient adversaries, the Dracos, a reptilian hybrid race whose ancestry is also traced to the Orion star system. Both the Zeta and the Dracos races share a common hidden objective of claiming sovereignty over the territories of Earth. Collectively I refer to legions of the Zeta-Dracos alliance and any other Visitors from elsewhere who hold agendas that are detrimental to the evolution of humans, as the Intruders. Between the ages of four and seven years I did not understand such things, nor did I comprehend why this malevolent group of beings had invaded my life, striking terror into my heart. I would never have come to understand these events had it not been for the intervention of another group of benevolent Visitors that collectively refer to themselves as the Guardian Alliance.

Guardians

I first met representatives of the Guardian Alliance when I was seven years old. While I played alone one afternoon in my Grandmother's yard I was physically approached by yet another gray being, but this one had bright blue eyes, rather than the standard-issue black-eyed Greys I had encountered during three years of repeated Intruder abductions. Unlike the other Greys, this being demonstrated kindness and I was told that I no longer had to be frightened of my malevolent abductors because another group of Visitors would insure my protection from this point forward. Following this event the rate of my nightly Visitor abductions increased, as the intervening group began taking me to Children's Circles aboard their spacecraft, where my education into the world of the extraordinary began.

The Zeta Greys were not in charge of the organization called the Guardian Alliance. Many members of the GA appeared to be quite human, but they possessed knowledge and abilities far beyond conventional human development. Other members of the GA included: the regal Lyran-Sirian Whites, an Elder, pale-skinned hominid Sirian race frequently called the Founders; the Aethien, large, white graceful beings of high spiritual development, which resembled upright preying mantises; the Rhanthunkeana, tall, thin light-emitting beings with translucent white skin, almond-shaped eyes of various hues and *kinky* white hair; skilled shape-shifters and highly advanced spiritually; the Breneau, advanced beings from the highest-dimensional worlds that appear as tall, luminescent figures with elongated heads and large eyes, when they physically manifest; the Queventelliur, large, long-haired apelike beings of great intelligence and sensitivity, who are occasionally glimpsed on Earth as they monitor Earth's environment for guardian purposes; and the Turaneusiams, tall, beautiful humans with elongated heads and skin/hair colors representing all of those apparent on Earth plus some in pastel hues. The human lineage evolved out of the Turaneusiams, the Elder Race, primarily immortal. There were many other species involved with the Guardian Alliance, from the various hybrids created through intermixing of these species, to the vast, formless, sentient conscious entities who direct the Guardian Alliance, entities that exist beyond the scope of dimensionalization. The Zeta members affiliated with this organization represented defectors from the Intruder Zeta groups that had been given political asylum by the GA, in exchange for their commitment to honor and uphold GA agendas and to follow GA protocol. I learned that the GA was a co-operative organization through which an enormous variety of different interstellar, multi-dimensional and inter-time species and races worked together, to assist in the evolution of developing cultures throughout the multi-dimensional universe. The GA represented a smaller, specialized group within a greater guardian organization called the Interdimensional Association of Free Worlds.

During my childhood I did not understand the complex political dramas taking place between the various races of interstellar Visitors and I was not informed about the various Earth agendas held by Guardian and Intruder races until I was well into my adulthood. Throughout my childhood the GA repeatedly took me, via consensual nightly abductions, to educational facilities aboard their mother-ships. There I was exposed to a variety of educational subjects, such as 15-dimensional physics, bio-energetic healing modalities, the Elder Race human history, spiritual teachings of the Law of One and I was trained in the rudimentary dynamics of Keylontic Morphogenetic Science. I was trained to become a bio-physical translator of the universal symbol-code language known as Keylonta. During my years of education with the GA I was treated with the utmost of kindness, respect and unconditional love and I grew to admire their members for the incredible wisdom, knowledge and spiritual grace they demonstrated in all of their activities.

Interaction with the GA became my secret life that I was not permitted to speak of during my usual human interactions. The Guardians explained to me that, due to present human ignorance about the presence of Visitors from elsewhere, I would be persecuted and misunderstood should I try to share my knowledge of the GA. Until I was of an adult age I was to remain silent about my contact to protect myself from the interference of a well-meaning but ill-informed psychiatric community that was not in the least bit prepared to handle cases of Visitor involvement effectively. I understood the warnings of the GA and knew that if I began speaking about my experiences I would be mislabeled and *diagnosed* as having psychological problems, because our culture does not yet possess the knowledge through which these experiences can be rationally understood. I was consciously aware of my contact experiences throughout childhood and into adulthood, I have never been placed under hypnosis to retrieve memories of these events. My childhood memories of contact events still remain quite clear.

My memory of visitor interaction during adolescence is still somewhat fuzzy. I do remember numerous episodes of contact but it seemed that the Intruder Visitors had once again appeared on the scene. Some of my adolescent memories involved abductions by humans dressed in military garb, in which I was forcibly taken to underground military-like facilities and subjected to interrogation and rough handling. This period of my life was very confusing due to obvious gaps in contact memory and the seeming reemergence of the Intruder Visitor presence. Through the GA I have learned that during my adolescence the Intruders had attempted to reclaim their specimen, once again subjecting me to forced abductions, experimentation and memory repression and mind control technologies. The GA continually intervened. During this period in my life I did not understand that I had become an unwitting pawn in a game of ET politics. The mind control technologies used by the Intruder forces and their human cohorts made clear sequential memory of the adolescent encounters nearly impossible and also affected my ability to clearly remember contact with the GA during this time. In January of 1983, at age 18, I had a Near-Death-Experience, following which clear contact with the GA resumed and the Intruder presence once again vanished. I have since learned that during the NDE event the GA had removed Intruder implants from my body and bio-energetic field and once again released me from Intruder manipulation tactics.

Later in 1983 the Intruder group that had been involved with my prior abductions had, along with numerous other Intruder groups, defected from the Zeta Alliance, seeking political asylum with the GA. Asylum was granted and the Intruder group involved with me was assigned to off-planet GA re-education facilities. The GA no longer had to contend with this Intruder group interfering in their relationship with me, and my reluctant involvement with the Intruders and the Secret Government had come to an end. After the NDE, I was able to receive direct, remote telepathic communications with the GA, as well as contact through the dream-state. The instances of direct physical contact with the GA dwindled as the lines of direct subtle communication progressively opened. Telepathic dialogue with the GA was soon replaced by a strange form of contact through which I would receive large bodies of communicated text, that would open up in my mind like a form of psychic e-mail. These dry data communications did not exhibit the type of live, person-to-person communication that was characteristic to telepathic dialogue, but I was able to receive thousands of pages of instructional information from the GA through this mode of communication. Through subsequent *live* encounters (some physical) the GA explained that the dry-data communications were made possible through my childhood training in translation of the universal Keylontic Symbol Code language.

The GA was able to pre-record information for me, in the form of digital data packages called Keylontic Symbol Codes. The GA would *program* the Keylontic Codes into my bio-energetic system via remote electronic transmission. Once the encoded data had been programmed into my bio-energetic field, it would process through my neurological structure in the form of electrical impulse. Through the natural bio-chemical and electrical translation processes inherent to the human biological form, the electronically encoded information would translate into my native language and appear in my mind as direct cognition, formatted into either word text or image pictures. I did not hear the words in my mind, as no audible sound was involved, a stream of worded information would simply flow through my mind and I could feel the words as electrical impulse patterns. Image translation came in the same way, no mental pictures, but rather clearly felt electrical impulses that carried complete images. My mind just knew the audio or visual content of the electrical impulses, as if the impulses bypassed sensory translation and appeared as direct cognition. Later I learned that this mode of data exchange is called Keylontic Communication—an electronic, bio-neurological language that represents only one rudimentary application of Keylontic Morphogenetic Science.

Introduction

For 16 years I have been involved with translating Keylontic Communications from the GA. Most of these communications provided spiritual teachings on the Law of One (the perspectives of interdependent universal brotherhood and co-creative evolution, practiced by advanced races who understand the interconnections between all life forms and reality systems). Through these teachings I experienced personal growth to self-actualization and began my personal journey toward spiritual awakening. Since the age of 18 my communication with the GA has been almost a daily phenomenon and since that time I have also experienced numerous physical encounters and visitations, though such episodes are not nearly as frequent as they were in childhood (for GA members, communications require much less effort than do physical encounters). In December of 1996 the GA asked me to go public with my story and to bring forth a message from them to the people of Earth. The GA explained that they had withheld a great deal of information from me regarding the greater picture of Visitor involvement with Earth. They had focused upon teaching me things that would assist in my personal spiritual growth so that I would eventually be mature enough to handle the information they were withholding.

In 1996 I was not aware of the mass ET drama unfolding on Earth. I knew nothing about the Secret Government-ET agendas and I was not at all involved with our contemporary UFO community. I agreed to go public on behalf of the GA because they had indicated that their message was very important to the continued well being of human populations. I did not know what their message entailed until 1996, when I began translation of this message. The message of the GA was delivered via Keylontic Communication, which has been translated verbatim from their remote transmissions. (Keylontic Communication is not channeling, it is the remote transfer of electronically encoded data. Channeling involves merging the personal consciousness with other portions of personal identity, the energy identities of beings from other times, places or dimensions or the direct absorption of electrically encoded data from the crystalline universal memory matrix. In Keylontic Communication the personal consciousness remains within its usual conscious focus as a communicator from elsewhere intentionally transmits electronically encoded data to the receiver via remote projection of frequency.)

The GA organized their message in the form of a book that was completed between late 12/1996 and late 2/1997. On 10/25/1997 the GA orchestrated a physical consensual abduction through which new information on the Bridge Zone Project was provided. On 6/26/1998, due to events that are explained in the Volume II, the GA added nearly 200 pages of new information to their original message. The first two volumes of the *Voyagers* series, *The Sleeping Abductees* and *Secrets of Amenti*, are the compilation of the 12/1996 and 6/1998

GA Keylontic transmissions. It represents the first official GA message to the people of contemporary Earth. It is their message, presented in their format, using their words. I do not claim authorship for this book, as I served only as translator of information that originates with the GA. Translation of this information has been an educational journey for me and I am frequently in awe of the breadth of information the GA provides. In the fourth volume of this series, *Voyagers IV: Visitors through the Portals of Time*, I will describe, in my own words, what I have learned and experienced through contact with the GA. But of greater importance is the message of the GA and hence their books must appropriately come first. The human evolutionary story is not complete without the inclusion of multi-dimensional reality and the facts of ET, Other-dimensional (OD) and inter-time (IT) Visitors' involvement with Earth. Neither the dynamics of such visitations nor the mechanics of human evolution will be understood until the multi-dimensional framework within which all manifest realities take place is acknowledged. As a child I did not choose to believe in ETs, but they made their presence known to me quite without my prompting, and the reality of their existence was undeniable. I am convinced that the presence of ET, OD and IT Visitors has been an on-going, yet relatively hidden part of the human story since our earliest beginnings on Earth. Groups such as the GA have always been aware of this fact and they are quite familiar with the myriad of different interdimensional space-time locations from which Visitors may come.

When I asked the GA about their location in space-time they explained that their organization spans many different planetary, space, time and dimensional fields. Membership within the GA reaches from the matter-based galaxies and universes of the lower dimensions, to the unfathomable cosmic reality fields of pure consciousness that exist beyond the Metagalactic Core, free from dimensional structure. However, they also indicated that the GA members directly involved with me have their primary physical base of operations within a space-time location that represents future-time from our contemporary Earth perspective. Many of my GA contacts reside within the reality fields of pure consciousness, having evolved beyond the confines of space-time and matter-based forms. But those who appear in human biology (and some of the ETs), are physically based upon a planet called Tara, in the year 6520 AD, within our linear progression of time. From their position on Tara, members are in contact with GA legions throughout the cosmos. In the past history of my Taran GA contacts, Tara was known as Earth. Though the GA has many members of a truly ET nature, unrelated to Earth, many of my GA contacts are quite terrestrial in origin, they are time travelers from a future version of Earth that we may one day evolve to become. The two groups that oversee the Taran GA membership are the Priests of Ur and the Priests of Mu, ancient immortal humans of the Elder Race, that have always been involved with the evolution of our species. (These priesthoods are not gender based—female, male and androgynous members equally serve and facilitate teachings of the Law of One). In my dealings with the GA it has become quite apparent that the universe is much larger and much more diverse than we have yet ventured to imagine. Many of our ancient earthly ancestors were quite aware of this fact.

I am grateful for the knowledge and education I have gained through my relationship with the Guardian Alliance. I am comforted by the thought that members of the GA, our Elder Race and our galactic and cosmic neighbors, cared enough about humanity to inform us about conditions that will directly affect the quality of our evolution. What we choose to do with this information is entirely up to us, personally and collectively. The Guardian's message, as contained within this book, is not the end of the story, it is only the beginning. This book provides the background setting through which the saga of continued human evolution unfolds. I personally believe that events on Earth are occurring as the GA has indicated. The GA and other pro-human Visitor groups are here to help us understand and successfully maneuver the challenges our planet will face during the next 18 years and they hope to lead us gently to a realization of our multi-dimensional heritage. They are also here to teach us to protect ourselves today from Intruder Visitor races that do not have our best interests at heart.

It is often said that realization is always personal. One day our race will collectively realize the truth of our rich multi-dimensional heritage. Until that time realization of this reality is right and the responsibility of the individual.

I am privileged to introduce the message of the Guardian Alliance.

—Anna Hayes, January 1, 1999
   now publishing as Ashayana Deane

The Azurite Temple
of the Melchizedek Cloister, Inc.

Sarasota, FL, USA, United Kingdom and Europe
Non-Profit Corporation

The Azurite Temples MC are non-denominational, egalitarian, spiritual service organizations and Temple-Churches founded upon the principles of unified spiritual and scientific paradigms. Azurite Temple spiritual teachings are based upon the "Law of One," which acknowledges the value, interconnection and interdependence of all components of reality and the living God or Spirit alive within all things. Azurite Temple scientific teachings are based upon advanced Universal Unified Field Physics, ancient Light-Sound-Scalar-wave and Merkaba Mechanics and Matter-Template Science. Through teachings of unified spiritual-science, the "Christos Within" and Esoteric Metaphysical Order, Azurite Temples MC provide state of the art Spiritual Development and Holistic Healing Programs, through which greater integration of the physical and spiritual aspects of the human condition can be gained. Azurite Temples are dedicated to providing cutting-edge information, teachings, services and community outreach programs for Spiritual Discovery, Consciousness Expansion, Life Empowerment, Holistic Healing, Personal Enrichment, World Peace and Planetary Stewardship efforts. We offer pro-active, affirmative action, personal and global healing perspectives focused upon expansion of consciousness and educated enlightenment, through which the ideals of reverence, respect, love and cooperative co-creation are fostered within the global community. Azurite Temples MC serve the international community through Educational Workshop Tours and Local Events, Prayer-Meditation Services and Educational Resource Publications. Azurite Temple MC of Sarasota, FL currently offers Baptismal, Nuptial, Renewal of Vows, Burial Rites and MC Ordination services in the "Law of One," Melchizedek Cloister spiritual tradition.

Executive Directors: Reverends Michael and Ashayana Deane, Ekr.MC

About the Author

Ashayana Deane Ekr.MC (formerly published as "Anna Hayes") is host of the **Life Empowerment Workshop Series**, founder of the **Kathara Healing Institute** and the **Azurite Temple of the Melchizedek Cloister, Sarasota FL.** Ashayana is author of the **Voyagers, Kathara and Emerald Awakening Series** books, the **Kathara Bio-Spiritual Healing System™**, the **Tangible Structure of the Soul Accelerated Bio-Spiritual Evolution Program™** and the **Amenti and Life Empowerment Series Videos.** Ashayana experienced **"Conscious Birthing"** as an **"Indigo Child,"** with open Fetal Integration memory (soul entering fetal body) and reincarnational remembrance since birth. She encountered 28 years of **ritual physical contact** and training with the **Emerald Order Melchizedek Cloister ("EOMC") Priests of Ur.** The EOMC Priests of Ur are living members of the original pre-ancient Oraphim-Turaneusiam-"Indigo Children" Angelic Human **Grail Line**, formally referred to in ancient times as the *Eieyani (pronounced "E-yon'-E")* through which the human lineage was originally seeded 560 million years ago. (Note: **"Ur" means "light,"** in reference to **serving the agenda of enlightenment for all**). In contemporary times, as they have done since the pre-ancient past, the Eieyani Priests of Ur continue to serve as representatives of the **Guardian Alliance ("GA")**, the primary task force of the **Interdimensional Association of Free Worlds ("IAFW")** universal service organization.

During childhood, Ashayana was visited many times and escorted to Eieyani learning centers for short periods, by members of the Eieyani Priests of Ur, who initiate contact from the island of **Kauai, Hawaii.** Throughout adolescence, Ashayana kept numerous appointments with the Eieyani Priests, in which she was physically transported by means of interdimensional spacecraft and Merkaba, to an Emerald Order base near the island of Kauai. Escorted by members of the Eieyani, Ashayana experienced physical **"wave-riding,"** a term used to describe physical teleportation through space-time portals via Merkaba Field activation, from the Kauai location to an Eieyani educational facility called the **Center for the Advancement of Interdimensional Communication ("CAIC").** The CAIC physically exists on Earth on what is now the Kauai, Hawaii site, but in the future time period that translates into **6520 AD** Earth time. (Quantum Physics theory will eventually validate the reality that *time is simultaneous* in nature, and that universal order is multidimensional; facts that presently elude contemporary Earth scientists but stand as common and demonstrable knowledge among the Eieyani and within other advanced inter-time nations.) For her protection, the Eieyani required Ashayana to take a **Vow of Silence** regarding her contact experiences, until she reached adulthood. On numerous longer adolescent visits to the CAIC, which on various occasions extended over several days, Ashayana was reported "missing" and thought by family to be a "run away"; a family perception she allowed to remain to account for the extended periods of time in visitation with the Eieyani Priests.

Following a **Near-Death-Experience** (NDE) at 18, Ashayana received final training and Ordination in the Emerald Order Melchizedek Cloister Priesthood-Order of the Yunasai, through the Eieyani Priests of Ur. (See "*Melchizedek Priesthoods,*" *Voyagers Volume-2.* Melchizedek "initiations" and Cloister "ordinations" are not the same thing—there are 12 Initiation levels for every Cloister Ordination Degree). Born in this life incarnation as a **Regent** (Level-3 of 6 Ordinate Minister) of the Melchizedek Cloister Priesthood, Ashayana completed her **Consummate** Level-4 Ordination at age 27, **Elder Consummate** Level-5 Ordination at age 30 and final Eckatic Level-6 Ordination at age 33. In completing Level-6 (of 6) Melchizedek Cloister ordination under mentoring of the Emerald Order Eieyani Priests of Ur from the GA, Ashayana was commissioned as a **6th-Degree Melchizedek Cloister Ordinate Eckar**, an incarnate Priest of Ur and Emerald Order representative and **Speaker**. Since the time of her conscious Fetal Integration, which resulted from accelerated activation of the 4th and 6th DNA Strand Templates that is often characteristic to the Indigo Child Grail Line genetic code, Ashayana understood that she had incarnated in this lifetime to serve as a member of the Eieyani Priests. She is known among the Eieyani Priests of Ur as *Aneayhea Kananda Ashayana-Tu Melchizedek.*

Through her progressive experiences with the Priests of Ur, and personal validation through conscious reincarnational memory since infancy, Ashayana understood that what our society calls "ETs" are not the "sci-fi aliens" our contemporary culture depicts them to be. Contemporary "visitors" responsible for the phenomena of the **New Age and UFO Movements** are the ancient races of interdimensional, inter-time **Angelic and Fallen Angelic legions** that have been reported throughout human history as the angels, gods, devils and demons within every ancient spiritual tradition. **Eventually science will reveal that such characters of ancient human mythology are in fact part of a greater life-field of biological beings, whose physicality is characteristic to the levels of matter density and dimensional reality fields from which they emerge.**

Receiving little religious training as a child, Ashayana's validation of the existence of Angelics and Fallen Angelics came from direct, early experience with contact and from extensive memory of humanity's dealings with the same visitor races throughout many different time periods of human evolution. The **Angelic Human** races of the Eieyani Priests of Ur, who are capable of sustaining full physical manifestation on Earth or altering their biological orientation at will to engage interdimensional time travel or dimensional ascension, assisted Ashayana in her Fetal Integration process and later in her NDE. Though the Eieyani Priests are capable of, and often utilize, remote subtle interdimensional contact, the majority of Ashayana's childhood experiences with them, and numerous contacts in adulthood, were fully **physical in nature**, involving her physical transport to their learning facilities rather than simply "astral body travel."

Since the age of 7, and cumulatively for over 29 years, Ashayana has received private training from the Eieyani Priests of Ur, in the teachings of the **Emerald Covenant** and in translation of the ancient *Cloister-Dora-Teura Plates* or **CDT-Plates**, the **12 Pre-Atlantian Holographic Disc Records** from **246,000 BC**. Information pertaining to the CDT-Plates was under high security categorization of the GA until November 1999, when the last missing disc of the 12 CDT-Plate set was finally retrieved by the Eieyani Priests from Earthly Illuminati forces. Ashayana was permitted to release data on the existence, content and history of the 12 CDT-Plates as of May 5th, 2000. The CDT-Plate discs have been in protective custody within the **Azurite-EOMC Eieyani Priests of Ur** family lines since a cataclysmic event that took place on Earth in 208, 216 BC. At that time, 2 of the 12 discs had fallen into the hands of Illuminati family lines on Earth. The 11th disc was recovered by the Azurites of the GA in the 1600s AD, the 12th disc in November 1999. In many physical encounters of childhood and adolescence, during which she was being trained in CDT-Plate translation, the Eieyani Priests permitted Ashayana to hold the **small pale silver CDT-Plate discs** in her hands, which confirmed for her the tangible physical existence of these pre-Atlantian technological artifacts. As her abilities in physical translation of data from the discs grew, she was then trained in **remote translation** of the CDT-Plates. Remote translation of the CDT-Plates would allow Ashayana the capability of frequent CDT-Plate translation in adulthood, without the need of the Eieyani Priests continually relocating her to the storage facility where the CDT-Plates are kept in protective custody. (See "CDT-Plates, Emerald Covenant and the Mass Drama" on page xli.)

As is customary when CDT-Plate translations are initiated on Earth, **three individuals** are chosen by the Eieyani Priests to hold one of three "**CDT-Plate Speakers Contracts**," through which translations of the CDT-Plates are returned to the human collective. Ashayana was chosen, by the Eieyani Priests of Ur, as the **First CDT-Plate Speaker** and **mentor** to the later Second and Third CDT-Plate Speakers in contemporary times, due to her reincarnational history, much of which she had conscious memory from birth and of which the Eieyani Priests are fully aware. In the "Christ Drama" of 2000 years ago, Ashayana, then an Essene woman named **Miriam** (born 5 BC-37 AD), had served as the Third CDT-Plate Speaker. Miriam served this role in collaboration with two

Essene men historically known as **John the Baptist** (31 BC-34 AD), then First CDT-Plate Speaker and **Jesheua Melchizedek** (12 BC-27 AD), then Second CDT-Plate Speaker and leader of the Essene "Christian Movement" (known as "Jesus" in the Bible). Prior to her CDT-Plate Speakers Contract as Essene Miriam, with others incarnating from the Eieyani collective, Ashayana had served as CDT-Plate Speaker and Eieyani Priest numerous times during early Lemurian, Atlantian, Hindu, Celtic-Druid and Egyptian historical periods. The history of Ashayana's recent reincarnational involvement with CDT-Plate Speaker Contracts on Earth began with her incarnation as *Ashayana-Tu Melchizedek*, an EOMC Eieyani Priest of Ur born on Earth in **246,041 BC**, during the "Middle Cloister Race Period" of human evolution (500,000 BC-208,216 BC). During this period Ashayana served as a member of the original EOMC Eieyani Priests of Ur *Azurite Universal Templar Security Team*, the GA collective responsible for reinstating the Emerald Covenant peace treaty on Earth and providing the CDT-Plates to the Urtite human Cloister Race in 246,000 BC.

The Templar (Star gate) Security Team EOMC Eieyani Priests of Ur have incarnated on Earth at various times to assist in human evolution and protection of Earth's **Halls of Amenti Star Gates**. The EOMC Azurite Universal Templar Security Team has been progressively incarnating on Earth over the last 100 years, especially since 1955, through the Eieyani Grail Line genetic lineage, known in contemporary times as the **Indigo Children.** (*See "GA Signet Council-6, Sirius B, Indigo Children And 'Christiac Grail Lines'" on page 171*). Presently there are approximately **550,000 Indigo Children** physically incarnate on Earth, just beginning the DNA Template activation cycle through which they will "awaken" to remember their higher aspects of identity and Templar Security Team commissions; many more will be born between 2000-2012. In her present incarnation Ashayana was born as an **Indigo Child Type-1**, incarnating as an original member of the EOMC *Azurite Universal Templar Security Team*; for this reason she was chosen and trained since childhood by the EOMC Eieyani Priests of Ur from Kauai, Hawaii. As per pre-birth agreements with the Eieyani, Ashayana was trained to serve as the First CDT-Plate Speaker, 6th-Degree Melchizedek Cloister Eckar, organizer of Azurite Universal

Templar Security Teams presently incarnate on Earth and public representative of the Eieyani Priests, Interdimensional Association of Free Worlds and the Guardian Alliance.

Through over 29 years of frequent physical contact and remote telepathic communication with the Eieyani Priests and the GA, Ashayana was trained in a wide variety of subjects including: *Melchizedek Cloister Law of One Spiritual Actualization studies. Keylontic Morphogenetic (matter template) Science. 15-Dimensional Unified Field Physics. Primal Creation Mechanics. Advanced Merkaba-Kundalini-DNA Bio-Regenesis Ascension Mechanics. Kathara Core Template Healing. Planetary Templar Star Gate Mechanics. Pre-ancient History, Founders Races and Angelic race evolution. Higher Sensory Perception and OOB Travel, and remote translation of the CDT-Plate Holographic Discs.* Following her NDE at 18, Ashayana redirected her original interests of pursuing a degree in psychology to continue intensive study with the Eieyani Priests. The mother of 3 Indigo Children, she worked in commercial printing and theater management and accepted professional commissions as a fine artist-painter, while pursuing Masters studies with the Priests of Ur. In 1996 the Eieyani Priests of Ur and GA released Ashayana from her childhood Vow of Silence, and requested her services as the First CDT-Plate Speaker, for which she had been trained. In 1997 Ashayana translated the Eieyani Priests first chosen introductory dispensations of CDT-Plate teachings, which were published in May 1999 as the **Voyagers Series**, Vols. 1 and 2.

Following first release of the Voyagers Books in May 1999, Ashayana continued further translation of CDT-Plate dispensations in a series of workshops called the **Life Empowerment Workshop Series**, the most expedient method of making the CDT-Plate teachings available to the public (available on video). In November 1999, upon request of the Priests of Ur, she founded the **Azurite Temple of the Melchizedek Cloister**, a non-profit spiritual service organization, presently with over 200 Ordained Melchizedek Cloister ministers in the US and abroad. In February 2000 Level-1 of 12 of the **Kathara Bio-Spiritual Healing System™** holistic core template healing and DNA Template Bio-Regenesis program was translated from the CDT-Plates, and the **Kathara Healing Institute** and **Kathara Alliance ("KA")** of Kathara Healing Facilitators was added as a department of the Azurite Temple. Since May 2000 the Eieyani Priests of Ur and Ashayana have worked to awaken and organize groups of the Azurite Universal Templar Security Team and Amenti Planetary Templar Security Team Eieyani Indigo Children. Since January 2000, Ashayana and members of the Templar Security Teams have orchestrated global healing endeavors called **Planetary Shields Clinics** or "PSCs." During PSCs, the Eieyani Templar Security Teams utilize Masters Planetary Templar Grid Mechanics from CDT-Plate translations of the "**The Book of Maps and Keys**," one of the "**lost books of the Bible**" translated from the CDT-Plates by Essene Jesheua Melchizedek in 10 AD. (**This and other related Essene books were intentionally "lost" in 325 AD at the hands of the Church of Rome's Council of Nicea**).

PSCs are being initiated by the EOMC Priests of Ur and races of the Emerald Covenant, with assistance of the incarnate Templar Security Teams, to assist Earth through, and prevent pole shift during, the star gate opening cycle of 2000-2017. The last full star gate opening cycle, called a "**Stellar Activations Cycle**" or "**SAC**," occurred in **208,216 BC**, resulting in cataclysm, pole shift and de-activation of Earth's Templar (star gate and core energy grid system.) PSCs of 2000 have taken Ashayana and Templar Security Teams to **Egypt, Peru** and **England** and various other regions; further PSCs are scheduled for Hawaii, England, Peru and Tibet in 2001-2002. Respected for her in-depth insights on New Science, Spiritual Development, Esoteric Studies, Pre-ancient History and Extra-ordinary Phenomena, Ashayana has been interviewed on various radio programs such as Janet Russell's "Beyond the Unexplained," the Jeff Rense "Sightings" show and SHINE. She has frequently appeared as a speaker on the US Expo Circuit during 1999-2000. In October 2000 Ashayana was united in marriage with fellow childhood Priest of Ur contactee, CDT-Plate Speaker and EOMC Eckar (6th-Degree MC Ordinate Minister) **Rev. Michael Deane M.Sc.** of England, founder of the **Azurite Temple UK and Europe**.

Together Michael, Ashayana and the Eieyani Priests continue the work of CDT-Plate translation and PSCs, and are presently preparing a **Personal-Planetary Studies Masters Course** in Spiritual Development, DNA Bio-Regenesis, Merkaba and Advanced Planetary Templar Mechanics. The Masters Course will be offered as private classes in Florida and on video through the Azurite Temples and Kathara Healing Institute in 2002. Currently residing in Florida, Michael, Ashayana and Ministers of the Azurite Temples offer non-denominational community support services of **Ministerial Ordinations, Baptisms** and **Marriages** in the ancient **Law of One** Melchizedek Cloister "Inner Christ" spiritual tradition. They periodically offer, Spiritual Development, Bio-Regenesis, Kathara Healing and Planetary Healing workshops at home and abroad. In order to make the CDT-Plate teachings more easily available to the public, in January 2001 Michael, Ashayana and the staff of Azurite Temple began organization of the **Azurite Educational Resource Library** correspondence programs, currently featuring over 40 audio, video and book products drawn from Ashayana's 1999-2000 workshops. As Azurite Temple MC does not solicit donations, proceeds from the Azurite Educational Resource Library fund continuing Human Potential, Spiritual Advancement and Holistic Healing educational outreach programs progressively under development through Azurite Temple.

While preparing for the PSCs Planetary Healing Expeditions scheduled for 2001, Ashayana is continuing work on the following upcoming books based on continuing CDT-Plate translations, scheduled for publication in 2001-2002:

- Voyagers Series-*Granite Publishing*; Vol. 4 ***Voyagers- The Angelic Dossier: Intro to the Angelic Rosters and Lost Books of Enoch.***
- Kathara Healing Series-*Granite Publishing*; Vol. 1 ***Kathara- Introduction to Bio-Regenesis Healing.***
- The Emerald Awakening Series-*Granite Publishing*; Vol. 1 ***Return of the Emerald Order-Secrets of the Emerald Covenant***
- The Christos Series-*Azurite Press*; Vol. 1 ***The Maharata-Book 1 –The Christos Within: Reinstating Personal Divinity***

The **Maharata** is the ancient Sacred Text translation of the Founders Race CDT-Plates from 246,000 BC, which originally contained **590 volumes**, and over **500,000 pages**, of non-dogmatic, egalitarian, **Sacred Spiritual-Science Teachings** covering every aspect of mastering personal and cosmic reality. Before intentional editing and distortion at the hands of Fallen Angelics and **corrupt human power elite**, the teachings of **every traditional religious belief system on Earth**, from Christianity to Buddhism and Indigenous Tribal Oral Tradition, **originally emerged from re-translations of the Maharata Texts and CDT-Plates**. The Founders Races, via the Azurite Universal Templar Security Team, IAFW and GA, are beginning to return the Maharata Texts in contemporary times in fulfillment of the promise of the *Emerald Covenant*.

Since release of *Voyagers Volumes 1 and 2* in May 1999, to the time of this writing in January 2001, Ashayana has conducted over a dozen 6-18 hour public workshop presentations in the US and abroad, each based upon a progressive level of new CDT-Plate translations, many including written handbooks. The *Tangible Structure of the Soul Accelerated Bio-Spiritual Evolution Program* audio course, *Kathara Bio-Spiritual Healing System* certification program, Volume-3 *Voyagers Keys to the Secrets of Amenti* and *Angelic Realities-The Survival Handbook* books were also produced. Also during this period of less than 2 years, Ashayana founded the *Azurite Temple* MC and *Kathara Healing Institute*, ordained over 200 MC Ministers, conducted Planetary Healing Intensives to Egypt, Peru and England, attended numerous other speaking engagements and organized the *Azurite Educational Resource Library* correspondence programs. Due to this excessive and constant workload, preparation of an official **web site** for greater public accessibility to the GA work has been thus far impossible to achieve. Dedicated to making the teachings of the CDT-Plates readily available to all, Ashayana, Michael and Azurite Temple staff are currently working to create the *Azurite Temple MC-Kathara Healing Institute* web site, intended to go on-line by Summer 2001.

CDT-Plates, Emerald Covenant and the Mass Drama

The information contained within the Voyagers Series Books, Kathara Bio-Spiritual Healing System, Tangible Structure of the Soul Accelerated Bio-Spiritual Evolution Program, and related materials produced through the 3 legitimate GA Speakers, represents translation of ancient records. These ancient records exist in physical form as a set of 12 Silver-metallic discs called the Cloister-Dora-Teura-Plate Libraries or "CDT-Plates." The 12 CDT-Plates are holographic recording, storage and transmission devices that hold massive amounts of data in encrypted, electromagnetic scalar-standing-wave form. Translation of data from the CDT-Plate Libraries is accomplished through initiation of specific frequency transmissions, through which the discs activate to release their stored data in the chosen form of holographic, audio, visual or digital translation. The 12 CDT-Plates were manufactured from a form of striated-selenite-quartz crystal organic to the Density-2 planet Sirius B, surrounding a radioactive isotopic core, encased in a "hybrid-metal" silver-alloy compound organic to Earth.

The CDT-Plates were manufactured by the Taran Priests of Ur and Maharaji Sirian-Blue Human "Holy Grail Line" races of the Council of Azurline, often collectively called the "Azurite" or "Eieyani" Races, on Density-2 Sirius B, GA Signet Council-6 and guardians of D-6 Sirius B Star Gate-6 in the Universal Templar Complex (see: Voyagers, Vol. 1). In 246,000 BC, CDT-Plates were presented as a gift to the Urtite Human Race, the Seed Race of the contemporary human lineage, by the Azurite Races Sirius B, in honor of the Urtites entering the Founders Races, Emerald Covenant Co-evolution Agreement peace treaty. The CDT-Plates contain massive encrypted tomes of practical physical and spiritual evolutionary advancement teachings, presented to the races of our 15-dimensional Time Matrix by the Density-5 (dimensions 13–15) Elohei-Elohim-Emerald Order, Seraphei-Seraphim-Gold Order and Braha-Rama-Amethyst Order Melchizedek Cloister Breneau, the 3 Prim Founders Races in our Time Matrix.

The teachings contained in the CDT-Plates cover the full evolutionary history of life evolution in our Time Matrix since the last life-wave was seeded 950 billion years ago up to the present. Time is simultaneous in nature; past-present-future exist as multiple sets of interconnected cycles of evolutionary development that form manifest probabilities of possible experiential action. The CDT-Plates also contain "future records" of the many various paths of evolutionary development of human and inter-dimensional, inter-galactic, inter-time races, which emerge from free-will choices rendered in our present space-time continuum. (Of the existing "probable futures," or Primary Time Vectors of evolutionary development that exist as "future" experiential potentials, our present moment choices determine which line of probable evolution we will perceive in manifest form as a future continuum of time emerging from our present space-time coordinate.)

Most valuable to our present time, the CDT-Plates contain extensive educational records pertaining to Founders Race Creation Mechanics, "Universal Unified Field Physics," and "Law of One"—"Inner Christ" Sacred Spiritual-Science "Ascension-Merkaba" training. The CDT-Plates also contain the history and details of the Founders' Emerald Covenant Co-evolution Agreement peace treaty, humanity's historical relationship to the Emerald Covenant. As designated by the Emerald Covenant restatement of 246,000 BC, the CDT-Plates contain the teachings of Masters Templar Mechanics (Planetary, Galactic and Universal Star Gate mechanics), DNA Template Bio-Regenesis and Kathara Core Template Healing technologies. These masters' teachings were originally provided to the Angelic Human race of Earth in order for humanity to fulfill its original "Creation Commission" as guardians and keepers of the Universal Templar Complex.

The CDT-Plates have served as an intrinsic part of human evolution on Earth since they were given to the Urtites in 246,000 BC. The first written translation of part of the CDT-Plate library was rendered by the Urtite human race of Earth, upon receiving the CDT-Plates in 246,000 BC. The first written CDT-Plate records were a collection of large books, collectively called the Maharata (pronounced "Ma-ha-ra-ta"; translates into the "the Inner Christos" dispensations"). The Maharata text was a collection of over 500,000 pages of condensed text transcription, spanning 590 volumes. The Maharata transcriptions were hand-written on a form of durable textile-paper resembling crisp, semi-translucent vellum that was in common use at this time among the Taran civilizations of Density-2; the volumes of the Maharata were compiled in large-format, embossed-leather-bound books through a hand-rendered process that resembles contemporary "perfect binding." The original Maharata Books were transcribed in the Anuhazi language, the first spoken-written language form of the Density-4 Emerald Order Elohei-Elohim-Anuhazi (Feline-hominid)

Founders Race, out of which all other external language forms in our Time Matrix emerged. The 12 CDT-Plates were kept on Earth in the protective custody of the Urtite human lineage, until the Temple Wars and resulting pole shift of 208,216 BC. Just prior to the 208,216 BC pole shift and decimation of the Urtite human culture, 10 of the 12 CDT-Plates were retrieved by the Sirius B Azurite Races and placed under Azurite Universal Templar Security Team protection.

The CDT-Plates have always been coveted by many interstellar races, not only for the practical knowledge they contained, but also due to their dual purpose in relation to obtaining manual access to the 12 Primary Star Gates of the Universal Templar Complex. The 12 CDT-Plates are part of a larger apparatus that included 12 corresponding, larger silver discs called the Signet Shields. The 12 Signet Shields, manufactured at the same time as the CDT-Plates, are a technology through which the 12 Primary Star Gates of the Universal Templar Complex, which span the dimensional fields and galaxies of dimensions 1-12, can be manually activated and opened. The 12 CDT-Plates, designed for interdimensional frequency transmission capacity, can be used to manually activate, from remote locations, the Signet Shields and their corresponding Universal Star Gates; the 12 CDT-Plate discs are the Activators for the 12 Signet Shields. In the wrong hands, the CDT-Plate-Signet Shield technology could bring universal devastation to this Time Matrix, and so the CDT-Plates remained under the highest security possible. On behalf of the Emerald Order Melchizedek Cloister Elohei-Elohim Breneau of Density-5, and their primary Guardian Universal Service organizations (the Azurite Universal Templar Security Team, the IAFW, and the 12 Signet Councils of the GA), CDT-Plate-Signet Shield protection had been commissioned to the Azurite Races the Sirius B Council of Azurline. The Urtite human lineage of Earth was entrusted with protection of the CDT-Plates and Signet Shields in 246,000 BC, when humanity was officially appointed as active co-guardians of the Universal Templar Complex through the Urtites entry into the Emerald Covenant restatement.

The GA Signet Council-6, Council of Azurline from Sirius B reclaimed 10 of the 12 CDT-Plates under their protection in 208,216 BC. Two of the 12 CDT-Plates and all 12 Signet Shields fell into the hands of various competing human and Fallen Angelic Legions on Earth during the course of human evolution since this time. In the 1600s the Azurites secured one of the missing CDT-Plates. In November of 1999, the last of the 12 CDT-Plates, once called the "Tables of Testimony" by the Knights Templar races, was retrieved by the Azurites from a contemporary Freemason family line through which possession of the CDT-Plate had been passed from Atlantian generations. The 12 Signet Shields still remain buried in various hidden locations on Earth. Since the times of the 208,216 BC cataclysm, the Azurite Races of the Sirius B Council of Azurline have periodically offered dispensations of knowledge translated from the CDT-Plates to the evolving human cultures of Earth. Translations of the CDT-Plates were the first foundations of ALL legitimate spiritual teachings among ALL races of Earth, before the genuine CDT-Plate translations were repeatedly compromised, destroyed and distorted into "religious control dogmas" by competing factions of corrupt human power elite and Fallen Angelic visitors. Each time the Azurites offer return of CDT-Plate translations, three CDT-Plate Speakers incarnate through the Maharaji race line Council of Azurline from Sirius, into the human "Indigo Child" Grail Line on Earth (See "The IAFW, Azurite Security Team and the MC Eieyani Master Council" on page 162.), to serve as the three CDT-Plate translators or "Speakers".

The First CDT-Plate Speaker is trained for the position from childhood through physical contact with the Azurite Races and Priests of Ur, and serves as mentor for CDT-Plate Speakers Two and Three. The three CDT-Plate Speakers are always contemporaries and work closely and cooperatively together, collectively presenting on Earth the translations of the CDT-Plates to which they are commissioned over a 12-year period of time. The tradition of selecting only three CDT-Plate Speakers who are entrusted members of the Emerald Order incarnate in human form is a security measure that has always been employed by the Azurite Races in order to protect the integrity and intended purity of CDT-Plate translations. In Atlantian times, the most commonly known Third CDT-Plate Speaker was a Nibiruian-Anunnaki-Atlantian by the name of Thoth. In 22,340 BC, Thoth was entrusted by the Emerald Order Melchizedek Cloister and Azurite Races to bring oral translation of parts of one CDT-Plate into specific segments of Atlantian culture. During this time, Thoth defected from the Emerald Covenant in favor of Nibiruian-Anunnaki dominion agendas, translating portions of the CDT-Plate into written form, in a text that became known as the "Emerald Tablets of Thoth." Thoth presented the Emerald Tablets to the then-corrupt Annu-Melchizedek Priesthood of Atlantis, which culminated in the final destruction of the Atlantian Islands in 9558 BC, and subsequent chaos of human evolution since the colonization of Sumerian culture. In 2040 BC another attempt to bring translations of the CDT-Plates to Earth was rendered through an individual by the name of "Enoch," who served as Second CDT-Plate Speaker in that time period. Enoch's CDT-Plate translations consisted of three volumes of history that were once contained in the Maharata; the Book of Amenti, the Angelic Rosters and the Book of the Dragon.

In 10 BC, three Essene CDT-Plate speakers known as John the Baptist, Jesus Christ (Jesheua Sananda Melchizedek, born 12 BC; see: *Voyagers* Vol. 2), and Miriam, collectively translated nine additional books from the CDT-Plates, creating the original foundations of what was intended to become the legitimate Christian doctrine. These books included Jesheua's Six Books of Process, detailing self-generated Ascension Mechanics, Core Template Bio-Regenesis and the Book of Maps and Key—the technical manual for Earth's Halls of Amenti Star Gates and Planetary Templar Complex system. The translations of Miriam were the three Books of the Cloister, once translated in the Maharata texts, detailing cultural structure built upon the Founders' Emerald Covenant model. The Templar Mechanics books of John the Baptist were not completed, as he was murdered prior to completion of CDT-Plate translation. The books of Enoch, Jesheua and Miriam represent 12 of the 15 "Missing Books of the Bible" that were originally part of the legitimate Essene "Grail Line" teachings. The Essene teachings were intentionally edited and distorted in 325 AD, by the Council of Nicea and the Church of Rome, to create the control dogma religion presented as the Canonized Bible. The Cathari of Southern France held some of the original Essene records of Jesheua and Miriam until the Church of Rome ordered extermination of the Cathari in 1244 AD. Before their demise, the Cathari hid portions of the genuine Essene records, along with one of the 12 Signet Shields that had been in their possession. These relics will be eventually discovered in contemporary times to validate the teachings of the three CDT-Plate Speakers of present times, once these individuals have completed their current commissioned translation of the CDT-Plates.

Other CDT-Plate translations of ancient times were dispensed through Speakers born into Hindu, Chinese, Tibetan, African, Egyptian, Mayan, Incan and Celtic-Druidic Grail Lines. Since pre-ancient times, all CDT-Plate translations seeded into every earthly culture have suffered the same fate of destruction or distortion. Since 208,216 BC, translations of the CDT-Plates were repeatedly given by the Priests of Ur Azurite Races in order to prepare Earth humanity for the next scheduled Star Gate Opening Cycle (called a "Stellar Activations Cycle, or "SAC"; see: *Voyagers* Volume 2). During the next SAC to follow the failed SAC of 208,216 BC, the Angelic Human race of Earth would be called upon by the Azurites and guardian races of the Emerald Covenant, to assist in healing Earth's damaged Planetary Templar Complex. When the next SAC arrived on Earth, humanity would also be asked to peacefully assist Guardian Angelic Nations in protecting Earth's Halls of Amenti Star Gates from Fallen Angelic race dominion. Since 22,346 BC, all interdimensional races knew that the next probable SAC on Earth would occur between 2000-2017 AD. The Emerald Order Melchizedek Cloister Founders Races, Azurite Races and Nations of the Emerald Covenant are again returning translations of the CDT-Plates to humanity, in preparation for their intended mass visitation that will occur if Earth can be safely guided through the now-commencing 2000-2017 SAC. The three CDT-Plate Speakers of contemporary times will continue to release their commissioned translations of the CDT-Plate teachings into the public domain between 1999-2012. Between 2007-2012, if cataclysmic Earth changes can be prevented on Earth during the progressing SAC, Jesheua Sananda Melchizedek, the Second CDT-Plate Speaker of 10 AD and the man known as Jesus Christ in the Bible, will again enter physical human incarnation through the Sirius B Council of Azurline. Any beings or interdimensional visitors emerging into Earth's drama that claim to be Jesheua Sananda Melchizedek or Jesus are misrepresenting themselves for the purpose of human manipulation; Jesheua is returning to incarnation as an "*Indigo Child*" *infant* through the Sirius B Council of Azurline, as he did in 12 BC. Jesheua's scheduled return is intended to herald the beginning of open contact with the inter-galactic Guardian Angelic races of the Emerald Covenant and humanity's long-awaited graduation into the interdimensional, inter-galactic communities through officially delivered invitation into another restatement of the Founders' Emerald Covenant Co-Evolution Agreement universal peace treaty. Open contact with interdimensional, inter-galactic, inter-time Guardian races will occur through opening of Earth's Halls of Amenti star gates, if cataclysmic Earth changes can be prevented during the 2000-2017 SAC.

In preparation for the 2012 opening of Earth's Halls of Amenti Star Gates, Jesheua's 2007-2012 foretold "Second Coming," and the mass Angelic Nation contact that these events are scheduled to precede, Jesheua's contemporaries of 10 AD, Miriam and John the Baptist, are already incarnate in human form. The present-day incarnations of Miriam and John are currently working closely together to fulfill the First and Second CDT-Plate Speakers Contracts, which are now being progressively translated for public access. The individual holding the Third CDT-Plate Speakers Contract is a woman in the USA, who has also previously served as CDT-Plate speaker during Hindu, Egyptian and African incarnations of ancient times. All CDT-Plate Speakers work closely together through the established Azurite Temple of the Melchizedek Cloister, FL, an organization created in 1999 at the request of the Emerald Order Elohei-Elohim of Density-5, the Priests of Ur Azurite Races of Sirius B and the many IAFW-GA races of the Emerald Covenant. The three CDT-Plate Speakers are presenting foundation teachings of the Emerald Covenant CDT-Plates to assist the Azurite Universal Templar Security Team, IAFW, GA and Founders Races in preparation for the scheduled 2012 opening of the Halls of Amenti star gates. If Earth changes can be prevented through the 2000-2017 SAC, these events will culminate into humanity's intended graduation into the long-awaited and foretold "New Age of Unity, Love, Freedom and Enlightenment."

Administrative Levels of the
Emerald Order Melchizedek Cloister
and Races of the *Founders'*
Emerald Covenant Co-Evolution Agreement Peace Treaty.

(In **descending Order of Administration**. *All* EOMC organizations are egalitarian co-operatives and **do not work under authoritarian hierarchical order**, but rather through **co-creative agreements** based upon principles of **Law of One communion**, and genuine **non-patriarchal Melchizedek Cloister** *Maharata*-**Inner Christos teachings**.)

THE YUNASAI
"Central Point of All Union- Eternal Consciousness of the One-All." Also called Great Spirit, Source, or God.

YANAS
Eternal Collectives of Consciousness projected by Source-God to form the **3 Primal Sound Field**—the *Khundaray,* of the **Energy Matrix**, beyond our 15-dimensional Time Matrix, from and through which the conscious life field of our Time Matrix is seeded. Last seeded the current life-wave into our Time Matrix 950 billion years ago. Also called "**Geomantic Entities**," "**Ultra-terrestrials**," the "**Cosmic Trinity**," (legitimate) "**Ascended Masters**" or collectively the "*Melchizedek Cloister Order of the Yunasai*," **Melchizedek Cloister Eieyani Elder Council**" or our "**Cosmic Family of Consciousness**."

- <u>Grandeyanas</u>- Yanas of the First Primal Sound Field, the **Eckatic Level** of the Energy Matrix-**first individuation of Source**. Also called the "Emerald Order Yanas" or "**Blue Flame Yanas**."

- <u>Wachayanas</u>-Yanas of the Second Primal Sound Field, the **Polaric Level** of the Energy Matrix-**second individuation of Source**. Also called the "**Gold Order Yanas**" or "**Gold Flame Yanas**."

- <u>Ramyanas</u>- Yanas of the Third Primal Sound Field, the **Triadic Level** of the Energy Matrix- **third individuation of Source**. Also called the "**Amethyst Order Yanas**" or "**Violet Flame Yanas**"

BRENEAU ORDER FOUNDERS RACES

Three Eternal Gestalts of Consciousness projected by the Yanas to form the 3 Primal Light Fields-the *Kee-Ra-ShA*, of dimensions 13, 14 and 15, in our 15-Dimensional Time Matrix. The **Density-5 Antematter** Spherical Thermoplasmic Conscious Light Radiation Fields of the Kee-Ra-ShA are the point of consciousness entering manifestation in the form of Light Radiation. Also called "**Rishi**," "**Solar Rishi**," "**Meta-terrestrials**," or collectively the "**3 Founders Races**" of consciousness, our "**Universal Family of Consciousness**" or the "**Universal Trinity**."

- <u>Emerald Order Elohei-Elohim</u>: First Light manifestation of Source consciousness, projected from the Blue Flame **Grandeyanas Eckatic** Energy Matrix Sound Field. Seeded *Anuhazi* **Feline-hominid Elohei-Elohim** *Christos Founders Race* 950 billion years ago on Density-4, D-12 Pre-matter planet **Lyra-Aramatena** via Universal **Star Gate-12**. "*Royal House of Aramatena*" **Eieyani Grail Line** and **Oraphim-Turaneusiam-Angelic-Human Grail Line** Primary Founders. **Density-5 MC Eieyani Master Council** appointed by Yanas as **Primary Guardians of our Time Matrix**. Founders of the 15-dimensional **Interdimensional Association of Free Worlds, Azurite Universal Templar Security Team** and **Guardian Alliance** universal service organizations and the **Emerald Covenant Co-Evolution Agreement** of 950 billion years ago. **Fallen D-11 Anyu Feline-Aquatic-Ape hybrid line** of D-11 planet *Lyra-Aveyon* became the **D-11 Annu-Elohim Fallen Angelic Race** line 250 million years ago, creators of the many **Anunnaki Fallen Angelic** "*Anu Avenger*" races of the Sirius star system, including **Pleiadian-Nibiruian-Anunnaki**-hominid and "**Bipedal Dolphin People**" of Sirius A.

- <u>Gold Order Seraphei-Seraphim</u>: Second Light manifestation of Source consciousness, projected from the Gold Flame **Wachayanas Polaric** Energy Matrix Sound Field. Seeded *Cerez* Avian ("Bird People"), *Aethien*

Mantis, Insect-Reptile-Dinoid Seraphei-Seraphim Christos Founders Races 950 billion years ago on Density-4, D-10 Pre-matter planet **Lyra-Vega** via Universal **Star Gate-10.** *"Royal House of Vega"* **Eieyani Grail Line** and **Oraphim-Turaneusiam-Angelic-Human Grail Line** *Secondary Founders.* Appointed by Yanas as **Secondary Guardians of our Time Matrix.** Charter Members of 15-dimensional **Interdimensional Association of Free Worlds, Azurite Universal Templar Security Team** and **Guardian Alliance** universal service organizations and the **Emerald Covenant Co-Evolution Agreement** of 950 billion years ago. Appointed as **custodians** of **Fallen Drakonian** race rehabilitation efforts. **Fallen D-10 Omicron "Dragon-moth"** and Odedicron **"Reptile"** lines of D-10 planet Lyra-Vega became the **D-10 Drakonian Seraphim Fallen Angelic Race** line, creators of the *Drakon, Zephelium-Zeta, Dracos, Necromiton, Azriel, Dinoid, Reptile* and *Insectoid* **Fallen Angelic** races, centered in the Orion star system.

- <u>**Amethyst Order Bra-ha-Rama:**</u> Third Light manifestation of Source consciousness, projected from the Violet Flame **Ramyanas Triadic** Energy Matrix Sound Field. Seeded *Inyu* **Cetacean "Whale People,"** Aquatic **Dolphins,** *Pegasai* ("Pegasus") **Avian-Horse-Deer** and *Yonei* **Aquatic Ape Bra-ha-Rama** *Christos Founders Race* 950 billion years ago on Density-4,   D-11 Pre-matter planet **Lyra-Aveyon** via Universal **Star Gate-11.** The **legitimate** *"Royal House of Aveyon"* **Eieyani Grail Line** and **Oraphim-Turaneusiam-Angelic-Human Grail Line** *Contributing Founders.* Appointed by Yanas as contributing **Secondary Guardians of our Time Matrix. Charter Members** of the 15-dimensional **Interdimensional Association of Free Worlds, Azurite Universal Templar Security Team** and **Guardian Alliance** universal service organizations and the **Emerald Covenant Co-Evolution Agreement** of 950 billion years ago. Appointed as **custodians** of the **Fallen Annu-Elohim/ Anunnaki** race regeneration efforts, many of which are orchestrated by the **Great White Brotherhood."** Fallen Bra-ha-Rama race lines hybridized with both Annu-Elohim and Drakonian-Seraphim Fallen Angelic races.

IAFW—INTERDIMENSIONAL ASSOCIATION OF FREE WORLDS
Massive Universal Service Organization assembled by the Yanas and Breneau Founders Races **250 billion years ago** upon **restatement of the Founders *Emerald Covenant*.** Under the direction of the **Density-5 Emerald Order Elohei-Elohim Founders** and their **Density-4 Anuhazi** Feline-hominid **Christos Founders Race,** the **Gold Order Seraphei-Seraphim** and **Amethyst Order Bra-ha-**

Rama rallied their Density-4 **Christos Founders Races** for restatement of the Emerald Covenant. The Elohei-Elohim **Anuhazi,** Seraphei-Seraphim Avian **Cerez** and **Aethien** Mantis, and Bra-ha-Rama **Pegasai** and **Inyu** Cetatean **Christos Founders Races** organized the IAFW, creating a unified collective of **Guardian Angelic Nations.** The IAFW was created to **protect our Time Matrix** from Fallen Angelic race dominion, to **restore the structural integrity of our Time Matrix** that was damaged by Fallen Angelic warring and to offer **Melchizedek Cloister Bio-Regenesis** rehabilitation and ascension programs to the Fallen Angelic Legions in our Time Matrix. The Founding Races of the IAFW created the **Azurite Eieyani Grail Line** race strain and the **Azurite Universal Templar Security Team 250 billion years ago** and the **Guardian Alliance 570-568 million years ago.** The 15-dimensional IAFW and its over **25 billion** interdimensional **Guardian Angelic Nations** have served as the **Primary Guardians of our Time Matrix** since the Founders creation of the IAFW **250 billion years ago.**

DENSITY-5 MC EIEYANI MASTER COUNCIL

Sometimes called "**Sirian Council**" or "**Azurite Council.** " The *Melchizedek Cloister* ("**MC**") **Eieyani Master Council** is a specialized collective of **Emerald Order Elohei-Elohim Breneau** from the **Density-5** (dimensions 13-14-15) Primal Light Fields. They were appointed by the Yanas **250 billion years ago** following the Density-4 **Lyran-Elohim Wars** as the **administrative council** for the **Azurite Universal Templar Security Team,** the mobile branch of the IAFW. Members of the MC Eieyani Master Council incarnate into Density through the **Sirius B Azurite** *Blue-skinned Feline-land-water-mammal-Avian-Hominid hybrid* **Azurite Eieyani Grail Line** lineage. Following creation of the Oraphim-Angelic Human 568 million years ago, they also incarnate through the **Oraphim-Angelic-Human** *Indigo Children Type-1 Eieyani Grail Line*. The MC Eieyani Master Council serve as the **Primary Liaisons** between Yanas Collectives in the Energy Matrix and Guardian Nations in our Time Matrix. They oversee all **IAFW activities** from Density-5 and incarnate into **Azurite Race** lines for crisis intervention.

1

AZURITE UNIVERSAL TEMPLAR SECURITY TEAM

Created by the **Founders Races** of the **IAFW** upon the organization's assembly **250 billion years ago.** The **Azurite Security Team** and **Azurite Eieyani Grail Line race** were created to allow the members of the **Eieyani Elder Council** from the Energy Matrix to incarnate directly into the Densities in our Time Matrix, for **Crisis Intervention.** The Azurite Eieyani Race line has a full **48-Strand DNA Template**, which allows for direct incarnation into Density from the **Eckatic Energy Matrix.** The Azurite Race line is the **originator of all Eieyani races** in Density. The Azurites are the **forefathers** (with the Anuhazi Elohei-Elohim Feline-hominid Christos Founders) of the **Oraphim-Angelic Human, Sirius B Maharagi,** the **Taran MC Eieyani Priests of UR** and the **Magi Azurline Priests of UR Christiac** ("Jesus Christ"-Jesheua Sananda Melchizedek) **Eieyani "Indigo Child" Grail Line on Earth.** The Azurite Security Team serves as the **mobile unit of the IAFW,** its Azurite races stationed near each of the **12 Primary Star Gates** of the **Universal Templar Complex** within the 4 Density Levels of matter in our Time Matrix. The Azurite Race line was commissioned to **restore and maintain the structural integrity** of our **Universal Templar Complex.** The Azurite Security Team also serves as **Overseeing Guardians of the 12 Primary Star Gates,** and is commissioned to promote the **Emerald Covenant Co-Evolution Agreement peace treaty,** the **Melchizedek Cloister Ascension** and **Bio-Regenesis** programs, and **Law of One** Founders Race spiritual-science **Inner Christ teachings** to advance evolution for all in our Time Matrix.

GA-GUARDIAN ALLIANCE

Created by the IAFW 570-568 million years ago, during the **restatement of the Emerald Covenant** during which the *Oraphim-Angelic Human* lineage was created. The GA was formed as a **TASK FORCE** to **increase security** in our Time Matrix when the Annu-Elohim Fallen Angelic Legions created the **Anunnaki race line** 568 million years ago to destroy the Oraphim-Angelic Human lineage and races of the Emerald Covenant. Specializes in propagation of the Emerald Covenant and serves as the governing body of over **10 million Emerald Covenant Star League Nations** within 4 Densities of matter in our Time Matrix. The GA is **directed by** the **Yanas**, Density-5 **MC Eieyani Master Council** of the **Elohei-Elohim Emerald Order** Breneau, **Christos Founders Races** and the **IAFW.** The GA is the **administrative body** of **12 GA Signet Councils.** Each of the **12 GA Signet Councils** is appointed by the **Yanas** and **IAFW** to serve as the **Primary Guardians of one of the 12 Universal Star Gates (SG's)**in the **Universal Templar Complex.** Each of the 12 GA Signet Councils is composed of **2 Master Command Committees, 2 Subordinate Command Committees** and many other smaller organizations. GA Signet Councils 10, 11 and 12 represent the **"Lyran High Council"** races, as they protect the star gates of the **"Cradle of Lyra"** in Density-4, the passageway into and out of Density for seeding incoming creation and for ascension out of our Time Matrix.

- **GA Signet Council 12-** The *Council of Aramatena*-**Lyra. Emerald Order** Elohei-Elohim **Anuhazi** Feline-hominid **Christos Founders.** Guardians of **D-12 Lyra-Aramatena-SG-12.**

- **GA Signet Council 11-** The *Council of Aveyon*-**Lyra. Amethyst Order** Braha-Rama **Pegasai** and **Inyu** Cetacean **Christos Founders.** Guardians of **D-11 Lyra-Aveyon-SG-11.**

- **GA Signet Council 10-** The *Council of Vega*-**Lyra. Gold Order** Seraphei-Seraphim **Aethien** mantis and **Cerez** Avian-hominid **Christos Founders.** Guardians of **D-10 Lyra-Vega-SG-10.**

- **GA Signet Council 9-** The *Council of Mirach*-**Andromeda. Emerald Order** and **Amethyst Order** races from the **Andromeda Star League.** Guardians of **D-9 Andromeda-Mirach-SG-9.**

- **GA Signet Council 8-** The *Council of Mintaka*-Orion. **Gold Order** Seraphei-Seraphim **Aethien** Mantis, **Emerald Order Anuhazi** Feline-hominid and **Emerald Covenant** races from the **Orion Association of Planets.** Guardians of **D-8 Orion-Mintaka-SG-8.**

- **GA Signet Council 7-** The *Council of Epsilon*-Arcturus. Also called the "**Sirian-Arcturian Coalition.**" Crisis Intervention administration of **MC Eieyani Master Council** and **Azurite Security Team,** oversees **Emerald Covenant** races from the **Arcturian Federation of Planets.** Guardians of **D-7 Arcturus-SG-7.**

- **GA Signet Council 6-** The *Council of Azurline*-Sirius B. **Maharagi** "Blue Human" Azurite-Oraphim **Emerald Order MC Eieyani Rishi Grail Line.** Council from which *Jesheua Sananda Melchizedek-"Jesus Christ"* incarnated in human form in **12 BC.** Guardians of **D-6 Sirius B-SG-6** and the **Halls of Amorea D-6 passage.** Presented **Urtite** humans of Earth with **12 CDT-Plate Holographic Disc records** of the Emerald Covenant-*Maharata*-Inner Christ teachings in **208,216 BC.** Present **custodians** of the **12 CDT-Plate discs. Progenitors** of the contemporary **Eieyani "Indigo Children Types 1 and 2" Grail Lines** of Earth.

- **GA Signet Council 5-** The *Council of Alcyone*-Pleiades. Guardians of **D-5 Pleiadian-Alcyone-SG-5.** *A Council in crisis.* **Emerald Order** Taran **MC Eieyani Priests of UR** and **Anuhazi** Feline-hominid, **Gold Order** Seraphei-Seraphim hominid-avian-Oraphim **Serres** and **Amethyst Order** Bra-ha-Rama Cetacean **Inyu** co-governing body. **Governing Command Committee** is **Emerald-Gold Order** *Ashalum Command.* **Second Command Committee was** *Ashtar Command,* which is made up of Amethyst Order Bra-ha-rama overseeing rehabilitating **Anunnaki races** that entered the Emerald Covenant. Once included **Sirian** and **Nibiruian Anunnaki** organizations participating in **Bio-Regenesis** through the Emerald Covenant. **Anunnaki branches** of the Alcyone Council are referred to as the "**Ruby Order Annu-Elohim and Anunnaki.**" Ruby Order groups include the **Nibiruian Councils of Nine, Twelve and Twenty-four,** the **Pleiadian-Nibiruian-Anunnaki, Galactic Federation,** "**Archangel Michael**" collective, **Ashtar Command** and the **Annu-Melchizedek** legions. Many Ruby Order Emerald Covenant **defectors,** including **Galactic Federation, Ashtar Command,** the **Archangel Michael Matrix, Annu-Melchizedeks** and the **Pleiadian-Nibiruian Anunnaki** were responsible for **manipulation and digression** of the earthly Angelic Human lineage since **25,500 BC.** These groups **temporarily rejoined the Emerald Covenant** during the **1992 Sirian-Pleiadian Agreements,** and entered the Guardian's **July 5th, 2000 Treaty of Altair.**

On **September 12**[th], **2000 the majority of these groups defected from GA Signet Council-5 Alcyone Council** to join the **United Resistance** with Drakonian Fallen Angelic Legions in **promotion of the Earth pole shift agenda**. Some groups accepted **Amnesty Contracts** from the GA and IAFW, **remaining in the Emerald Covenant**. It is **very difficult for humans to detect what agenda affiliation these groups may now have; caution** is advised in **contact** or **channeling** communication.

- **GA Signet Council 4**- The *Solar Council*. **Intended** Guardians of **D-4 Sun Sol-SG-4**. **Guardianship** entrusted to the **Nibiruian Council of Nine** by Alcyone Council in **148,000 BC. In 25,500 BC Nibiruian Council of Nine defected from Emerald Covenant** sharing Sol-SG-4 control with the **D-11 Annu-Elohim Fallen Angelic Legion**. The *Solar Council* **Fallen Angelic Legions** have **progressively infiltrated Earth culture** since 25,500 BC. In **22,326 BC** the MC Eieyani **Magi Azurline Priests of UR** from D-6 Sirius B-SG-6, attempted, but failed, to secure Sol-SG-4 under guardian protection. **Pleiadian-Nibiruian-Anunnaki** Fallen Angelic Legions intend to use **Sol-SG-4** and **Battlestar Nibiru** to create **pole shift** between 2003-2008. Emerald Covenant Guardian Angelic races will **attempt to secure Sol-SG-4** from Nibiruian dominion to **avert the pole shift "Armageddon"** drama that the Fallen Angelic Legions desire to manifest.

- **GA Signet Council 1, 2 and 3**. The *Amenti Planetary Templar Security Team* and *Inner Earth MC Priests of UR*. Universal Star Gates **D-3 Earth-SG-3, D-2 Inner Earth-SG-2, D-1 Parallel Earth-SG-1** and Earth's **Halls of Amenti** star gates are under guardianship of the **MC Eieyani Master Council** of Density-5, directed through the **Sirius B Maharagi** *Council of Azurline*, the *Lyran High Council* (GA Signet Councils 12, 11 and 10) and the *Inner Earth* **Breanoua and Melchizedek Cloister Human race, Shambali** and some **Rama** Mixed-Cloister Human races and the **Eieyani Grail Line races of Inner Earth**. Inner Earth is presently caught up in the surface Earth drama. **United Resistance** is focusing most of its attentions on attempting to **seize the Inner Earth protected star gates** from Guardian protection. The outcome is yet to be determined, and will be greatly influenced by humanity's participation in the drama.

Intruders, top to bottom:
Sirian Anunnaki, Dracos (Drakon and Human Hybrid), Zephelium
(Administrators of Zeta), Zeta Grey-Rigelian,
Rutilia (Zeta and Dracos hybrid, or EBE)

Some Types of Guardians, top to bottom:
Zionite, Aethien, Lyran-Sirian Elder, Queventelliur,
Turaneusiam-1 (Azara), hybrid Zionite-Human, Jonathan (One of the
Priests of Ur), Dralov (Arcturian), Amera Zeta Grey, Rhanthunkeana.

1

UFOs, Visitors, and the Interior Government

INVESTIGATING THE UFO

We shall begin this discourse with the subject of **UFOs** or Unidentified Flying Objects. We are referring here to those reported sightings of seemingly mechanical-type vessels of transport that have no apparent terrestrial origin. In this category we shall also place other airborne phenomena of related characteristics, but those which lack the elements of mechanical type vestiges. The latter are usually described as **Light Formations**, reportedly witnessed both at close range and great distances. Both types of UFOs have at times appeared in radar tracking, as well as having many eyewitness reports of sightings or encounters with such yet unexplained phenomena. Photographs and film have at times captured images of both types of UFO presence.

In attempting to explain the origins of such phenomena it is necessary to broach the issue of human physics. Some understanding of the nature of time, matter and perception is required if sense is to be made of these events. In regard to the solid object UFOs often witnessed and documented, suffice it to say that these objects are existing (at the time of encounter) within the range of perception of three-dimensionality. That is, these objects are functioning within the same time-space continuum as other objects within the earth's objectively perceivable and measurable reality. So, as our first point of interest, we shall say that any such three-dimensionally perceivable UFO is (at the point of encounter) functioning within the laws and mechanics of physics as your culture presently understands them. Having determined this obvious fact of corresponding time-space sequence, the next question to address is that of the origin of the object being perceived. The question of "what it is" is directly related to the issue of "where it came from," for you cannot answer one question without answering the other. If you desire to elicit intelligent answers as to the nature of these phenomena, it is necessary to ask intelligent questions. In order to ask intelligent questions, it is necessary that you expand the framework of reference out of which these questions are drawn.

Official investigation into the nature of three-dimensional mechanical-type UFO events centers around *explaining these phenomena using the current premise of scientific thought*. The core assumption or root belief within the scientific dictum is that the objectified Earth field of three-dimensional reality is the "only real reality that exists." Phenomena must be explained within this terrestrial-based scope of perception. Underlying and interwoven with this core assumption are the ideas that the human species is the only "real intelligent life form" in the universe, and that the three-dimensional Earth field of perceivable reality is the only "real" reality and thus all things must be explained *within the perceivable confines of that reality*.

In researching UFO phenomena the officials tend to look for data and correlations that will *prove their own theories and assumptions*, rather than investigating the phenomena as an active reality from which there is *knowledge to gain*. More effort is put into disproving the reality of the phenomena than is applied to investigating *what information the phenomena is presenting that will add to the understanding of how reality works*.

In regard to three-dimensional mechanical UFO sightings the first series of intelligent questions that should be asked involve how the object behaves in relation to the known laws of physics as they are presently understood. Does the object exhibit behavior consistent with those laws, or are there anomalies in its exhibited characteristics that seem to contradict or push beyond the scope of those "laws" as they are presently known? If more attention is paid to such questions, the phenomena themselves would lead researchers to add information to their present bank of laws.

Time, space and perception are intimately intertwined. Science and physics have already lent credence to the "theory" that time is not linear in nature as once thought. The mechanics of quantum physics present a solid argument for the curvature of time and the possibilities of "times" coexisting in overlay formation...one sequence of events being superimposed over others and each functioning within their own "coordinate pattern" or frequency band. Within these "theories" are the realities that will give your science the ability to expand its framework of understanding enough to begin asking the right questions in regard to three-dimensional UFOs.

We are presenting this information to you because it is time for humanity to "take its head out of the sand," and face the realities that are everywhere presenting themselves.

The appearance of three-dimensionally perceivable UFOs of the mechanical type should lead first to questions of whether or not the object *behaves in accordance with known physical laws* or whether it exhibits properties not consistent with laws of "solid matter." Did it display erratic movement patterns or maneuvering abilities seemingly superior to those of known vessels of transport in the earth system? When such events are encountered it is usually assumed (if the sightings' reality is given any credibility at all) that the UFO must be a *physical* vessel of transport, made of solid matter and possessing a mechanical technology advanced in comparison to your own. *This is not always the case.*

Some three-dimensional mechanical-type UFOs are indeed solid vessels. Some are quite terrestrial in nature and are born of the secret scientific societies that exist within the Earth's governmental structures; we call these covert constructions **the Interior Government.** In sightings involving this group the government will *not* "own up to" its flying devices, as to do so would require revealing that it is in possession of technologies that are superior to what it has led the public and general scientific communities to believe. It is easier to allow such sightings to fall "between the cracks" and join the ranks of other UFO sightings or unexplained phenomena, rather than to incite individuals to begin asking the right questions. Much is being withheld globally by such government underground, including many developments concerning your own technologies as well. Your sciences and physics are far more advanced than you have been led to believe, and this cover up of information has been a consciously orchestrated deception emanating from the highest places within your governmental hierarchies. You have technologies and knowledge presently within your culture that could literally wipe out most of the maladies you experience on a global scale, but this knowledge is being kept from you by segments of your own populace. The knowledge in the possession of the underground elite would literally disintegrate all the present cultural structures as you know them, from science to health care, economics and religion. So do not expect the governments to "own up to" even their own witnessed UFOs unless they are hard pressed for an alternative program of disinformation. They will use whatever tactics necessary to squelch the expansion of the knowledge they hold. We will provide more information on the Interior Government in later writings. However, some three-dimensional mechanical UFOs are not simply covert developments of the technologically elite, they are far more.

Some such UFOs are indeed "space ships" or vessels of transport belonging to other intelligent species within your galactic sector. Yes, you are being visited, watched and studied by various other cultures of intelligent beings that you are not yet, as a whole, aware of. And yes, some of your UFO sightings involve solid-matter vessels piloted by such life forms. Many of these visitors are indeed from "outer space" as you think of it, and some of these groups are in active workings with your Interior Government. But not ALL of your three-dimensional UFOs fit into these aforementioned categories.

There is quite often much more to the UFO than "meets the eye," as you will soon discover.

DECIPHERING UFOS

You must begin to realize the truths hidden within your mathematics and geometries, for in the mechanics of these sciences the existence of multiple worlds (parallel Earths) and dimensions is indicated and will one day be proven as fact. There are **Parallel Earth Systems** and there are *portals through time* that link your world with others and with *other versions of itself*. Some of these other worlds (Earths) have a more advanced technology than your own. Some know how to use the **Time Portal System** and explore your reality just as you might explore life upon another planet, if you had the ability and knowledge to do so.

Many of your sightings of mechanical-type and light-formation type UFOs emanate from these other systems. At times objects (and people) from these parallel systems interface briefly with your system, and they can appear in a variety of different forms. What you might see as a "cigar-shaped object" hovering in the sky in your reality may in actuality be a house, a car or a weather pattern from a parallel dimension interfacing with your time-space coordinate accidentally. Such phenomena are not necessarily "vessels" or "travel craft" at all, but common objects from a parallel system that *appear in different form* when they interface with the electromagnetic frequency bands of your dimension. In your photographs they may appear as discs or craft, but in such cases that would be an illusion created by **dimensional distortion**. Not *all* discs or UFOs fit into this category either but it will serve your research well if you are aware of this possible explanation, for many of your sightings are just this phenomenon in action.

Other discs and vessels are actual solid-matter transport devices but these will emanate from within your own dimensional system, either from human-related sources or from sources of an extra-terrestrial nature. To further this point a bit we will add that many of your "naturally occurring" biophysical phenomena (such as ball lightening) are *also* sightings of the interdimensional kind. Sightings so common that your scientists consider them part of the organic operations of planetary physics. These common interdimensional phenomena (lightning, thunder, magnetic variations, etc.) are actually the residual effect of action taking place within other dimensional fields.

As you may now see, when addressing the issue of UFOs you are not dealing with events that have only one explanation. All of the proposed explanations do apply but it is up to you to discover which one you are dealing with in each case.

For your information, the US government does possess three-dimensionally solid wreckage from various craft not of human manufacture. This wreckage has come from two primary places, and some of it is not wreckage at all. There have been vessels of transport from parallel dimensional systems that passed through the time and dimensional portal structures and emerged within your system. These craft are not equipped to deal with magnetism as it exists within your dimension, and they most often crash or incinerate upon entry. There are four such wreckage fragments presently in the possession of the US government. Two of these originate from systems parallel to your own and two have come from third-dimensional systems outside of your Milky Way galaxy.

The wreckage of these four aforementioned vessels is the least of which your government is attempting to hide. There exist *several hundred* other vessels of advanced technology harbored by the US government alone (many more globally), but these were not the result of reconnaissance. The vessels and instrumentation we speak of were traded...*presented as a gift from those whose culture created them*...a culture your government has been aware of since 1926 and actively involved in negotiations with since 1934.

Wake up humans! If you continue to believe without question the information concerning UFOs and extra-terrestrial life presented to you by your government and media, you will effectively render yourselves blind and powerless over the true reality within which your lives are couched—a reality that you need to be aware of before you allow yourselves to fall victim to the disinformation that has been hand fed to you for generations. If you think that your human species is alone and superior within the universe *you are in for a rude awakening!* Within the next 50 to 60 years of your time the reality of which we speak will become painfully obvious to many of you, even to those who choose to keep their heads in the sand and pretend away the existence of extraterrestrial and multidimensional reality. Your awakening does not have to be painful—not if you are prepared, not if you are informed. And so we seek to make available to you the information you will need in order to make a smooth transition into multilevel inter-galactic consciousness—the next stage of growth upon the pathway of human evolution.

TYPES OF UFOS

The three-dimensional mechanical-type UFOs we have discussed thus far can be placed into the following four categories:

1. those belonging to covert government operations who will maintain a policy of non-disclosure and denial regarding sightings of their crafts.

2. those representing interdimensional anomalies from parallel systems that appear as vessels but in actuality represent other phenomena as they appear when interfacing with your system.

3. actual craft from other dimensions that emerge through the Time and Dimensional Portal Systems.

4. actual craft belonging to human or extra-terrestrial cultures that emerge through the Time Portal System from locations within the third-dimensional universe.

In all of these cases the craft *appear* physically solid, some having material wreckage left behind as validation of their existence. There have been photographs, film, radar and eye-witness accounts of all such phenomena, though rarely are your sightings researchers able to make distinctions between these categories unless obvious *visitor* presence is indicated.

There are other categories of UFOs related to these which need to be addressed. Quite often there are reports of encounters with UFOs that do not have the characteristic physical vessel structures as mentioned above. Often reports of "paranormal" activity also fall into this category. Frequently sightings of this sort are dismissed as naturally occurring atmospheric anomalies or mental aberrations. We are referring here to the sightings and encounters of phenomena that appear as **light-form manifestations**. There is a wide variety of such displays ranging from simple "flashes" or "sheets" of light (witnessed both indoors and outdoors) to large appearances of spherical light forms, singularly or in group formation, that appear as three-dimensional energy forms. Often when these are photographed they appear as UFOs though usually a vessel or solid-mass source of light emanation cannot be found. Some encounters involve the appearance of such light-form activity which then manifests into a solid-mass vessel sighting or an odd experiential journey on the part of the witness.

These light-form sightings are much easier to discount as insignificant as they breach the boundaries between the "seen and unseen"…the physical and ethereal…the "real and unreal." There are many more accounts of such encounters than you realize, but most often they go unreported or easily discounted by scientific and governmental communities. Witnesses themselves frequently discount their own perceptions as quirks of vision or imagination. Though some light-form activity can be explained in terrestrial terms as naturally occurring or psychological phenomena, many of these encounters are not so easily explained. We would like to "shed some light" on the subject for you.

Previously we described the type of UFO in the solid matter category that was in actuality *a manifestation created through the interface of your system with a parallel or adjacent dimensional world.* Some being actual vessels, and others only appearing as such as they passed through your system's frequency bands. Not all of these interdimensional phenomena appear as solid objects when they are within the electromagnetic patterns of your world. More often than not *light* (flashes, forms, pulsations, movements) will be the indication that an interdimensional interface has occurred.

Again, as with the solid object sightings, not all of these represent an intentional "visitation" by some intelligent force. Many are simply part of the mechanics of physics as they operate within a multi-dimensional reality system such as your own. (Physics your scientists are just beginning to discover and are far from comprehending). However, just because some of the interdimensional manifestations are not purposely directed by sentient life forms does not mean that all of them are accidental and intrinsic to natural laws. Some such interdimensional phenomena are indeed directed purposely by intelligent beings from other systems, both of human and nonhuman origins.

Some of these manifestations involve the **Interdimensional Time Portal System** directly and allow humans in other dimensional worlds or time-space coordinates to interact with and study your system. In these cases your UFOs are actually human "earthlings," but they have their home in a dimension closely adjacent to your own. Some would be from your *past*, some from your *future* and some from *alternate presents*. But not all such visitations would be from those in *human* form.

EXTRATERRESTRIAL VISITATION

There *are* other highly intelligent non-human species residing in your universe; for your comfort we suggest that you get used to this idea as soon as possible. Of the light-formation sightings we mentioned most do not fall into the two groupings we have discussed. Most are not accidental dimensional interface phenomena or natural atmospheric anomalies nor are they intentional interdimensional probes sent by sentient life forms in other dimensions. Though some light-formation sightings do fall into these categories most fall into a third category—a category you might loosely call "alien visitation."

In choosing this term we are implying that most of the light-formation sightings witnessed in your times are the direct result of extraterrestrial involvement with your planet. Within your own universal structure, in your three-dimensional band, there exist an enormous variety of sentient, intelligent life. Your scientists will not find much evidence of these cultures until they break the primary codes of your three-dimensional time structure. There are time zones within your universe, as well as multiple dimensions of those time zones. Though the mechanics of these two systems are intertwined they represent two separate areas of study.

The **Time Portal System**, as we call it, involves a system of interlocking passageways that keep in motion a set of "locks" or "gates" between time elements in your linear time structure within your three-dimensional frequency band. The **Dimensional Lock System** differs from the Time Portal System in that its mechanics operate and maintain the dimensions and frequency bands themselves linking multi-dimensional universes not just time zones within the same universe/dimension.

THE VISITORS

In terms of your "alien" visitors, or extraterrestrials, we are referring specifically to those visitors who approach your reality from within the Time Portal System. That is, they are not interdimensional so much as they are inter-time, emanating from different time coordinates within your three-dimensional interstellar system. So most of your light-form UFOs are indeed extraterrestrial intelligence interacting directly with you.

Zeta Reticuli

There are seven cultures (world cultures and their various sub-cultures) within your three-dimensional Time Portal System who possess the knowledge and technology necessary to interact with Earth in such a way. Two of these cultures are primarily responsible for all such visitations (light formation, solid mass and crop circle events). The remaining five are not involved with your planet or galactic system. Of these two world cultures one group is more advanced than the other in terms of brotherhood. One group has presently been identified in your culture, and within the inner circles of those who investigate such visitations, this group has become known as the "little greys" or **Zeta Reticuli**. Others call them the "lizzies," referring specifically to the Rutilia sub-species of Zeta that have a more reptilian-like appearance when manifesting within your system. Though technologically and intellectually astute the Zeta generally do not possess the spiritual development necessary to forge strong bonds of brotherhood with other life forms. Like humans, the Zeta also are evolving.

The Zeta are indeed real, and physical in terms of biological form. They are not from your planetary system, but they have a working knowledge of the Time Portal System in your dimension. It is the Zeta and affiliated groups, such as the reptilian Dracos, that have been in contact with your government and are responsible for much of what you have come to call the "UFO/alien abduction" phenomena.

Little Grey

The Zeta represent more than just the **Little Greys** (those small greyish beings with large black eyes). There are various sub-species of the Zeta prototype, some more "hybrid like" in appearance, some resembling other forms not at all organic to your system. There are lizard-like Zeta in numerous colorings and sizes. There are Zeta that more closely resemble your insect kingdoms, particularly that of the arachnid (spider-like) though somewhat larger than your earthly versions. Other types of Zeta have been described by your witnesses as "blues," "browns," and "silvers," all of which possess some human-like or dwarflike characteristics, and who represent a group of Zeta mutations created through their experiments in genetic engineering. The blue-skinned Zephelium are the administrator caste of the Zeta, governing all lower-ranking Zeta castes. The Zeta are a fragmented species and their customs and policies differ widely among the various groups.

Aethien

Often seen appearing with the Zeta (especially with the "greys," "browns" and "blues") are the tall skeletal-like beings that upon closer inspection resemble in structure your earthly preying mantis insect. These beings are usually whitish or golden in color and can stand up to twelve feet tall. These beings are known in some circles as the **Aethien.** Aethien are not of the Zeta species but often work with them and assist humans in their encounters with the Zeta. They also work with those from other dimensional systems.

The Aethien are not organic to your three-dimensional frequency band, nor are they from parallel or adjacent Earths. Rather they originate from galaxies existing within the dimensions of adjacent Earths, which places them in our interdimensional/extraterrestrial category. Aethien work with humans and other sentient life forms both in your dimension and in others, and throughout the Time Portal Systems in those dimensions. They represent a species superior to that of the Zeta, and come as emissaries of peace and growth toward brotherhood for all species.

The Aethien always work as teachers. When they appear with the Zeta or other three-dimensional extraterrestrial groups the Aethien are with them but not of them. Only Zeta groups who have agreed to work in brotherhood with all life will be accompanied by the Aethien.

At this point in your species evolution you need to begin to understand how vast is your playing field of three-dimensional reality and what other players are alive within this drama. We are not trying to frighten you with this information, but rather we are hoping to give you the framework of intelligence needed for you to understand your reality and cope with it effectively.

The Zeta groups come to you for numerous reasons, some of them to benefit humankind (the more spiritually advanced groups) and others to study you for their own purposes (these are mostly responsible for your reports of "negative" or harmful alien encounters). Both groups possess technology and operational knowledge of reality systems far superior to that of the human race at this time. They understand multidimensionality to a large degree and are avid users of the Time Portal Systems of the third dimension. Their sciences are built upon this knowledge, and thus there is much humankind could learn from the Zeta.

The Zeta possess physically solid three-dimensional vessels, but only the smallest ones have ever approached Earth's atmosphere. However, as they know the mechanics of the Time Portal System they are able to place their vessels just outside of the frequency bands that constitute your three-dimensional system. They are able to establish "holding patterns" between dimensions and thus can become invisible to your system at will. The Zeta also have the ability to use the Dimensional Lock System to some degree and are able to appear in some of the adjacent dimensions. But the Zeta originate from your three-dimensional system in a different time continuum than your present reality.

Though possessing knowledge far superior to your own, the Zeta do not have a full understanding of the Dimensional Lock System, nor have they mastered the Time Portal Systems of adjacent dimensions. Both humans and the Zeta have much to learn.

The second group of extraterrestrial cultures from your three-dimensional system presently working with you are those whom we call the **Rhanthunkeana** (ron than con' a). Some refer to them as the **Ranthia**. They are from the distant stars in terms of your universe, but they have full mastery over the Time Portal System. (They are responsible, in part, for many of your "crop circles.") The Ranthia are more advanced technologically and spiritually than are the Zeta, and they have been involved in your Earth culture since its beginnings. They have been your guardians in many ways and have helped protect your species and planet from interference both multidimensionally and galactically.

Rhanthia

The Ranthia also possess the ability to "park" between dimensional frequencies so as to appear invisible to your world. Like the Zeta, the Ranthia often appear in your system as light formations, especially those that manifest in spherical form. Unlike the Zeta, however, the Ranthia are not fully "matter based," biologically speaking. They possess the ability to manifest in physical form within numerous dimensions when desired, but they are not confined to a reality with matter densities as strident as your own. They are "masters of hologram" as are the Zeta, but the Ranthia have superior abilities in this regard.

The physicality of the Ranthia could be compared to what in your system appears as water. That is, their "organic form" has the properties of fluidity you associate with the element of water. They can take on many forms because of this fluidity of form, yet they are a conscious, sentient, intelligent race of beings.

Many of the visitors presently involved with Earth, both interdimensional and those of the Time Portal System, have the ability to bend the laws of physicality as you know them. Many of them are "shape-shifters" and can modulate the dimensional frequencies and time portals sufficiently so as to manifest to you in whatever form they desire. The Zeta and Aethien use this ability quite often in dealing with humans, taking on animal forms, human forms or those of solid objects. Zeta are the least skilled in this area as they lack certain bioenergetic characteristics (the "emotional body" energies) that are required to fully master the art of transmutation. They can link forms and partially transmute, but to do so causes excessive drain upon their own biological systems. Most often the Zeta will remain physical and use simple frequency modulation tactics to "scramble" the brain wave patterns of those viewing them[1]. They are there, but they can interfere with the human's bioelectrical system sufficiently enough to make themselves appear invisible, "ghost-like" or disguised in other forms. We will discuss this "perceptual interruption" tactic in greater detail within the pages to come.

---

1. "Odd odors" in association with the Zeta often reported by witnesses or contactees indicate that such "scrambling" tactics are in use. The odors result as the distorted perceptual data is processed through the human brain and neurological structures.

THE OLD ZETA AGENDA

There are a large number of Zeta involved with research upon your planet, and some of them possess agendas you need to become aware of so you do not fall into their plans as they desire. Your Interior Government has been working with the Zeta on some of these agendas but even they do not realize what is being orchestrated. The Interior Government itself is being tricked and used manipulatively into facilitating the Zeta plan.

The "Zeta Agenda," as we call it does not simply involve your dimensional system alone. As we have explained, the Zeta have limited access to interdimensional passageways. Your three-dimensional Earth system is not the only system the Zeta are interested in exploring. The Zeta are a driven race, driven by a vision and a purpose which stem from their home planet. This planet's name is insignificant to you as its location cannot be charted within your time-space continuum using the mechanics you presently have available.

On their home planet the Zeta evolved within their own time continuum to a point of technological sophistication superior to your own. Their cultures were not originally structured like human culture, as they possessed a more *centralized* community model. They did not think *independently* for centuries of their evolution, but operated as individual units of a **collective mind.** The Zeta mind was exploring methods by which they could break through the **Dimensional Lock System,** hoping to expand their reality and knowledge by consuming (draining energy from) parallel and adjacent versions of their own planet and combining these reality fields with their own. They had mastered the three-dimensional Time Portal System and wanted to "expand their territory." They did *not* realize, however, that using the methods they employed would *destabilize* the time portals and dimensional bands of their own system. They were *partially* successful in *blending dimensions* in their world but they did not realize the consequence of these actions until it was too late.

The Zeta did not *originally* possess the small grey forms you have come to know. This form resulted from a *mutation* in their genetic code caused by the frequency blending to which they had subjected themselves. This mutation intensified over numerous generations, the form weakening, losing strength and agility, losing power, until the time came when they could no longer tolerate the atmospheric conditions of the planetary home for which they had been intended. (The *original* Zeta prototype was a larger white-colored being possessing bilateral symmetry and having certain characteristics resembling those of the early human, but with a greater number of appendages. The wide variety of Zeta forms now existing are the result of uncountable genetic experiments. There are many similarities between your Earth reptiles and the original Zeta form, particularly those of the early reptiles that roamed the Earth.) As each successive generation paired they progressively lost the ability to naturally procreate their species. They became genetically neutered. The dimensional merger that they had forced also caused irreparable damage to their planetary structure. They had set in motion the death of their planet and its dimensional counterparts.

These events, from the perspective of your time continuum, are occurring in what you would perceive as your *future*. The Zeta then have "gone back in time" to your time continuum (and others) in hope of finding answers and solutions to their dilemma. Part of their own Time Portal System collapsed because of these events, so they are unable to access their own portals directly. (They cannot thus access the "past" of their planet before the destruction as they had originally hoped). The Zeta entered your time continuum because of the proximity of Earth's time portals to their own and also because the Earth has certain environmental elements the Zeta need for survival. (Oxygen-based air systems, water systems and the presence of elements such as zinc, plutonium and iron-based minerals.) However, the carbons in your environment proved to be toxic to the Zeta, and those interacting with your system found themselves in accelerated states of deterioration.

ORIGINAL ZETA AGENDA AND THE WORLD WARS

We have given you information about the Zeta so that you may begin to understand their motives for involvement with you. Their *original* purpose involved *accessing other dimensional versions of their planet and time continuum* by going through your time portals, as they had destroyed their own. If they could move through the dimensional portals of Earth and into a parallel system, then access their own "past" planet and time continuum from there, they hoped to *reconstruct* the pathways to their own three-dimensional time continuum—*to reattach their three-dimensional zone to the interdimensional grid*. They had not planned to interact with you for any period of time

Their plan was good in *theory* but *not* in *application*, as the Zeta soon discovered. Though they possessed much knowledge of how the time portals worked in a three-dimensional system, they did *not* have such mastery over the time portals in *other* dimensional systems. Large groups of Zeta became "*trapped between dimensions*," and *stuck* in your time/space continuum. They "leaped into" your system from the third dimension, moving *backward* in time. They accessed certain other versions of your continuum, but were *unable* to "leap" from there into their own other dimensional time continuum. The Zeta were a dying race trapped in time very far from home.

The Zeta began to look for other alternatives. They became involved with experimentation in your Earth dimension and in some others. Meanwhile the health of the Zeta was suffering. The carbon-based elements present to some degree in *all* of the Earth dimensions was rapidly declining their species.

On your planet the scope of the Zeta involvement accelerated just after your First World War. The environment was being *speculated* at this time. Attempts were made at raising the Zeta's biological tolerance level to the carbon elements but these experiments were met with little success. By the time of your Second World War the Zeta had devised a plan of **genetic cross-breeding**. They became interested in creating a **Zeta-human hybrid**, a **mutation**, in the hope that such a form would allow the continuation of their species within the three-dimensional Earth and adjacent systems. At first other life forms were studied (cattle, rodents, lizards, birds, etc.), other Earth species, but these experiments were not successful and produced a variety of sorry creatures that the Zeta later destroyed. Finally the human species was approached as a last resort (there would obviously be more difficulty with experimentation involving humans directly). For a period of time corpses were used for these experiments as they attempted to link the human DNA with that of the Zeta. These experiments also failed.

During your Second World War the Zeta came into communications with humans directly. (*They are in part responsible for the final activation stages of the atomic bomb*). You must recall, we explained that the Zeta were capable of "**shape-shifting**" to some degree, and they specialized in the art of "**perceptual interference**," being able to alter human perceptual frequency enough to appear in whatever forms they chose. Using these tactics to establish contact and to infiltrate the human governmental systems, agreements were formed between the Zeta and the US, British and German governments. The Zeta were not particularly concerned at the time with the outcome of World War Two, they "sold out to the highest bidder" so to speak.

The Zeta had great interest in the Nazi experimentation with genetics and were supportive of their agenda of creating a "superior race." The Zeta would let the humans help them create a genetically superior human prototype which they would then use to create the Zeta-human hybrid. Zeta interest in the Hitler regime began to dwindle over disagreements concerning the Nazi's anti-Semitic policy. Like the Nazis, the Zeta viewed the Jewish peoples as a *race*, not simply a religious grouping, but unlike the Nazis, the Zeta believed the Jewish race to be *superior* genetically, and they were *not* interested in a human prototype that did not carry the coding particular to the Jewish race. (More will be given on the Zeta perspective of the Jewish people in other writings). The Zeta interest then began gravitating toward the opposing factions. They were beginning to take interest in the *outcome* of the war as they had a vested interest in keeping those of Jewish lineage alive and well. The Zeta wanted this genetic strain protected at all cost, so they began negotiations with the allied governments.

Around this time the aforementioned Aethien (*mantis-like beings from a universe within a parallel dimension*) began interacting with the Zeta in other dimensions, with the intention of teaching the Zeta better ways to fulfill their purposes without violating the human populace. The Zeta remaining in the three-dimensional Earth system were of the last to accept guardianship from the Aethien. But the Aethien are committed to assisting the Zeta in their spiritual growth toward brotherhood, and so maintain an open invitation for assistance to Zeta in *all* dimensions.

During the time of World War II the Zeta in your system approached certain elements of government in the allied forces, using the guise of human form. Remember, they were adept at "perceptual interference" and so were able to place themselves in key positions to be heard when new ideas were most needed by the allies. *The Zeta themselves set in motion the structures for what has become your global, covert Interior Government.* Using their human guise they were able to offer certain strategic and technological advancements to top military groups. They also began preparing the humans for direct contact with the Zeta in their true forms. Great meetings were orchestrated in which the human covert elite were introduced to the Zeta and certain aspects of their technology.

The Zeta came under the guise of wanting to help humanity and of being concerned with world peace. They used their advanced technology and knowledge of universal physics to seduce their human cohorts into believing they were far superior to humans and came as "**angels**" or **planetary guardians**. The Zeta play upon the core religious beliefs of the people and their fears to create the *illusion* of themselves as "saviors" so as to foster human dependence—a covert method of gaining human cooperation with their agenda. Much effort was put into building human perception of Zeta as saviors and helpers.

Only later, after the "debt" involving the outcome of World War II was "incurred," so to speak, did the Zeta begin to demonstrate their desire to have *favors* exchanged for their services during war time. Military, medical and communications knowledge was given to the Allies during this time. The humans, easily enthralled by the sophistication of the Zeta technology, had no idea just how much knowledge the Zeta withheld from them. Nor how the knowledge that was given was used to direct and manipulate the humans for Zeta purposes.

The individuals *presently* involved in the Interior Government *still* have no idea of the degree to which they have been and are being manipulated. To those of you involved in these covert activities (you know who you are) we suggest that you *wake up now*! Take charge of your destiny and break free before that choice is no longer available to you. The Zeta are not "evil monsters" out to get humanity, they are simply a species trying to solve their problems. But so much like humans the Zeta often do not realize the harm and violation they bring to other life forms in their quest for growth. Both humans and Zeta need to *evolve spiritually* into a working knowledge of universal brotherhood.

Old Zeta Agenda and Personal Growth

Currently your visible world government leaders know very little about the workings of the Interior Government. Most know of its existence but they have been misinformed and misdirected so they will not receive adequate information about the true operations of this community. The individuals who *do* have direct knowledge of the covert group have agreed to perpetuate the debunking activities set in motion by the covert group at the Zeta's insistence in hope that they will be "let in on the secrets." The Interior Government has proposed to certain individuals within the official government that great advances in power, economic strategies, and healing modalities will be given at an appropriate time if these officials will cooperate with them now. These individuals in the official government are led to believe that the Interior Government and the Zeta are working with them and for them. When in truth the plan has been since its beginnings to undermine and take control of the official positions when the appropriate mass control devices have been set in motion.

All of this might sound a bit far fetched to you but this is only because you have been brainwashed for so long. Your official governments are not responsible for the activities of the Interior Government nor are they working in cooperation with them *as they think they are*. The official governments are fast becoming "puppets" to these interior forces and will eventually find themselves at their mercy if they do not wise up and *change their public disclosure policies*. Your governments presently are ignorant to the reality going on around and within them, and will remain so as long as they allow themselves to be blinded by arrogance, elitism and the quest for power. To the "common" people, please see these frailties of those to whom you give your power. They are like children playing with dangerous toys. Individuals, have the courage to begin *asking the right questions!*

The idea of an Interior World Government may come as a surprise to many of you because you have been conditioned *for centuries* into the blind adherence to the dictates of an *outside authority*. Though at one time this conditioning may have been in the best interest of human development, as your species learned to work within a group collective, this tactic of learning is no longer appropriate to the well being of the species or to the individuals within the human collective. For it is precisely this conditioning that is being used to

16

manipulate and misguide you. Along with awareness comes the *responsibility* of using that awareness effectively. We have given to you now the *gift* of awareness concerning the activities taking place within the infrastructure of your power-elite. For many of you the burden this gift will carry may seem too much to bear. After all we are suggesting that you begin to *think for yourselves*, to question the very authorities to whom you have always turned for guidance and security. We are compelling you to begin *looking within yourselves* to the core of your private being, to begin looking for answers from the whisperings of your *heart* rather than accepting *programmed responses* from the confines of your logical mind. A heavy burden of responsibility indeed for those who have become complacent within the pre-programmed illusion of "official" reality that has been hand fed to you through government, media and religious dogma.

We cannot urge you enough to begin *looking within*, to discover the wisdom and brilliance of your inner self—a portion of your own identities that you have been programmed to discount, negate, and fear. For it is through this disowned self that lives within each of you that your own *truth* will be discovered. It will be from this place within you that you will be enabled to find your own answers. And those answers may very well put you at odds with the official reality program you have been fed. Taking the time to look at the beliefs and ideas that constitute your moral, ethical and perceptual codes will be well worth the investment, as then you will gain *mastery over the contents of your conscious mind*, rather than allowing that mind to be directed by the whims of those outside of you—those who may or may not have your best interest at heart. As you temporarily sacrifice the sense of false security and pat answers given to you by the *"official program"* you may take comfort in knowing that you are gaining the priceless acquisition of self-sovereignty. Through self-sovereignty *true personal security and clear answers will be found*.

In relation to subjects such as Interior Government, ET life, "paranormal" phenomena or self empowerment you will not find a great deal of support for your interest from the "official" viewpoint. Indeed, the official program presently in place within your mass reality *depends* upon the *negation* of these very aspects of human reality. The brainwashing program has been so well orchestrated through your *subconscious* beliefs that even your friends and family may stand against you when you begin to *ask the right questions*. They have been taught *not to question*. They have been programmed to follow the program and to perceive as a *threat* anything that *questions* the motives or applications of that program.

THE PROGRAM

You may be wondering now what we are referring to when we speak of the "brainwashing program," so we will provide a bit more information concerning the "official reality program" presently operating in your world system. You do not *feel* "brainwashed," you may be having a difficult time grasping the idea that you have been brainwashed, and you most likely do not think that there is anything amiss within the ideas and beliefs propagated by your official outside authorities (government, the medical experts, the economic experts, the defense experts, the scientific community, the religious experts, etc.) The very structure of your daily lives *seems* to depend upon those "experts" figuring it all out for you, telling you "how it is" and what is the "*right* thing to do." Through these seeming authorities you are taught *not to think about the bigger picture*, about what reality really means, about the *purposes* your existence may hold.

You are taught to believe that such questions are *unimportant* or perhaps *unanswerable.* You are taught to "follow the rules" as dictated by the majority, to think as your parents had thought, and they as their parents thought before them. This is the *program* of which we speak and presently for most of you, it operates on a *subconscious* level. Where did this program of disempowering the individual originate? Did it emerge accidentally as a quirk of human belief evolution? How did it come to be that this program of ideas now *defines* reality for you and urges you to *never* define reality for yourselves? Who has trained you to believe that humans are the *only* intelligent life forms in the universe? Where did your species get the idea that the only real reality was that which could be defined through the five known senses? You have been trained to believe that "this is just the way reality is," and most of you still accept that premise. *This is the program!* Where do you think these ideas have come from? (You may not ever have considered this query, as to *ask that question* is *not* part of the program).

This program of ideas did not come to you accidentally, nor as a quirk of evolution. And this official program that now serves as a **reality filter** for you does not give you a clear or accurate picture of how reality "really" is. *Who* do you think benefits from your believing that ET life is not reality? Who do you think might benefit from humans being locked into a world of five sense perception? Who do you think would most benefit from teaching generations of humans not to question authority or the ideas upheld by that authority?

Until you begin to *open your eyes* and realize that ET and other-dimensional intelligence play a *significant* role in human evolution, and *have been involved since the beginnings of your species time on planet Earth*, it will be difficult for you to define the "who" or the intelligence behind and within the program. The Zeta are *not* the only species of intelligent beings aware of and interacting with Earth. Extraterrestrial involvement has been a reality since far before your recorded history. Some groups of these visitors worked in behalf of human evolution, others worked for the *exploitation* of the race. And now, in your present point of evolution these factions still exist. Some working *toward* your enlightenment, others working to enslave your energies for their own purposes

In this section we have given you information on some of the covert activities currently taking place within your reality. Though the official reality program you are living within will not assist you in becoming aware of these events, as it is primarily orchestrated *by those factions interested in exploiting your resources* (they depend upon your ignorance and disbelief to protect their covert agendas), there are other sources of information from which you can draw perspective. But if you cannot pull yourselves out of the program enough to realize the existence of these helpers, there is little we can do to assist you in becoming informed.

You are responsible for your own awareness and for the choices you make that will either expand that awareness toward enlightenment or plunge you into darkness and fear. We highly suggest that you pull yourselves out of the program and begin, as individuals, to ask the right questions concerning your planet, your government, your "experts," and the beliefs you have accepted regarding the true nature of reality.

The information we provide regarding the Zeta and the formation of the Interior Government is intended to inspire you to ask *who is pulling your strings* as individuals. The greater amount of information you have at your disposal the better able you will be to make informed decisions and wise choices. We are *not* suggesting an overt rebellion against authority as you know it, but simply the use of a *discerning* eye when being presented with views by those authorities. In *looking within yourselves* and beginning to explore the portions of your identity and knowing that live within, you will discover alternative perspectives to choose from. You will have more information from which to draw your conclusions, and you will find many more questions to ask that the program itself cannot provide answers for. By *asking the right questions* you will begin a personal spiritual odyssey that will lead you above and beyond the program into the rightful enlightenment that is your next stage of evolution as a human.

THE RANTHIA

Now that we have given you a basic rundown on the Zeta presence and agenda, and the "official reality program" as it presently operates within your system, let us return to the discussion of UFOs that appear in the form of light manifestations. The Zeta are not the only three-dimensional ET forms capable of manifesting in this manner. Though Zeta are skilled light manipulators, the aforementioned group the Ranthia (Rhanthunkeana) have superior ability in using these mechanics. Whereas Zeta usually create manifestations of form in conjunction with light phenomena the Ranthia

19

regularly make their presence known through light phenomena alone. That is, the Ranthia most often do not create illusions of three-dimensionally solid forms.

The Ranthia also greatly interact with humans during the human dream state and altered states of consciousness. They are aware of the Zeta agenda, and like the other dimensional Aethien, are attempting to teach humans, Zeta and others, ideologies and technologies that will help these collectives work toward the peaceful evolution of all concerned.

The Ranthia originate from a three-dimensional time coordinate in which the matter density is far less than that of your Earth system. They are highly evolved both technologically and spiritually from a three-dimensional standpoint. They are able to see the far-reaching implications of what is now transpiring within your system. The Ranthia now come to offer their knowledge and assistance, and to intervene in the Zeta plan if possible. The Ranthia are also masters of illusion, and they understand the workings of the human bioelectric circuitry and the electromagnetic mechanics of the planet. They will provide information and assistance to those who desire to learn.

Unlike the Zeta, the Ranthia must be asked to intervene; they cannot impose their assistance or contact upon humans or others without invitation. This is part of their own ethical code, which honors the free will of all life, and they will not violate this premise. Not all beings have reached this level of spiritual maturity.

Some Zeta groups who have agreed to accept the teachings and guidance from the Aethien are now being led into agreements with the Ranthia. The Ranthia and Aethien are attempting to shift the Zeta paradigm and agenda to a model more conducive of peaceful evolution by offering enlightenment and alternative solutions. Humans are being put in the precarious position of having to take charge of their own destiny and learn what is needed to play their part in working toward enlightened brotherhood. Presently the masses are ill-prepared to fulfill this leadership role effectively. The Ranthia and Aethien desire to work with humans, to educate them and teach them what is necessary for fulfilling their part in this multidimensional/intergalactic/inter-time scheme. But it is often quite difficult for these helpers to interact with humans as the present belief structures perpetuated by the "official program" render their attempts at communication void, or suspicious at best. In your culture little is understood about the nature of interdimensional and inter-time communications. The methods by which these events take place are largely misunderstood, and so it is this issue we will next address. What is the method by which such communications come to you and from whom do these communications emerge?

2

Keylonta Science and Abduction

INTERDIMENSIONAL COMMUNICATION

In your present culture there is much fear and misinformation surrounding the occurrence of multidimensional communication. Superstition and science both have added their share of negative interpretation of events of this nature. Popular consensus would place such events of communication into the categories of *intentionally contrived hoax* or into that of *mental deficiency* on the part of those receiving such communications. Religious factions, on the other hand, most often place such events under the category of "demonic" activity or attribute such communications to the work of some "evil" force. These ideas and misinterpretations are a *direct result* of the "official reality program" and its brainwashing. So much effort has been put into devaluing and negating the *method* of communication of knowledge that the true *value* of the knowledge is lost. This is unfortunate, as it leaves the majority of the human populace thinking that such communications do not really exist as such, or that if they do exist they are of some "evil" or mal-aligned source. This makes it quite difficult for other dimensional and other time helpers to offer their assistance to humans directly, *as so few of you are receptive to the method by which that assistance is offered.*

It is our hope that in providing you with information about the true mechanics of multidimensional communication that you will be able to step outside of "the program" enough to put your prejudgments aside and learn something new and quite valuable. In your present time certain terms have been used to describe this process of information exchange: "telepathy," "mediumship," "automatic writing," "channeling." All of these terms give you a very vague conceptual understanding as to the true dynamics of this phenomenon. If you do not understand the mechanics of the process then it will be difficult for you to decipher the source from which the phenomena emerge. Just as is the case with UFO sightings, "what it is" cannot be discovered using only one explanation. UFOs can be a variety of things. So too can be what appears to you as multidimensional communication.

Not all UFO sightings imply *live* contact with other life forms, though some *are* indeed precisely such contacts. In the event of multidimensional communications, again, not *all* such communications imply *live* contact with other-dimensional or inter-time beings, *but* some of these communications are indeed genuine contact with beings from systems other than your own. Learning to *differentiate* between the various possible explanations is necessary before an accurate assessment of the phenomena can be achieved in studying both UFOs and multidimensional communication.

Some instances of **subtle communications** (we will use this term henceforth to replace the rather lengthy phrase of "multidimensional communication") can be attributed to conditions existing *within the mind* of the receiver, and others are indeed intended "fakes." Still other such events are quite legitimate occurrences of subtle communications with a "live" source, be it inter-dimensional, inter-time, intergalactic or originating from within your own Earth system. The latter you most often call "telepathy," or "mind-to-mind" communications, but there is much you do not yet understand about the workings of telepathy alone. The important thing for you to understand at this time is that in all such cases of communication you are dealing with far more than the simple "linking of minds" as your term "telepathy" suggests. You are dealing with a highly sophisticated form of communication that is in itself a *language*. It is the language of light, sound, symbols and energy, that in our system is known as **Keylonta**. In our system Keylonta is the foundation for all other forms of learning, and it exists as a highly technical science and creative art form.

THE LANGUAGE OF KEYLONTA

Keylonta is not merely a language *as you think of it*, but a tool, communications being one of its applications. Its dynamics are used in teaching and healing, but also in the literal formation of reality constructions where it serves as the *structure upon which manifestations are built*. The codes of the Time-Portal System and the Dimensional Lock System are found within the workings of Keylonta, and it is also the method used by those wishing to communicate with your world *through those systems*. We will provide you with much more information on the language of Keylonta and its applications in other writings, but for now we simply desire to familiarize you with this dynamic so that you may begin to evolve your ideas about the nature of subtle communications. The point we would most like you to understand is that Keylonta, like any language, is a *tool*. In and of itself it cannot be judged as "good or bad," "godly or evil," helpful or detrimental to the human collective. It is a tool which can be used to convey meaning. The *intention and skill* with which that tool is used will determine its value. It is time that you put your fears and superstitions aside and begin learning *the language of the stars*—the language of your ancestors, the language that will allow you to evolve into multidimensional beings who possess technologies and wisdom beyond those now available to the visitors presently interacting with your Earth system. *Do not let the "official program" rob you any longer of the knowledge that is your birthright and inheritance.*

Now that we have given you some information on the method by which the helpers (and others) communicate with you, we will offer some insight into why this method of contact is presently selected, as opposed to other alternative means of contact such as mass landings of spacecraft. For reasons that should be obvious to you, those wishing to assist or make their presence known to you cannot viably set a mother ship down upon the lawn of the White House and schedule a press conference! Indeed, if the visitors were able to hold off the Zeta and the Interior Government (not to mention your "official" government) long enough to stage such an event, their message and intentions would be lost amidst the panic and hysteria that such an event would generate within your ill-prepared masses.

The Interior Government, Zeta and official governments have done such a good job at programming the masses into *fear and disbelief* reaction patterns that it would literally be useless to the visitors to attempt to reach you as a collective. The public has been brainwashed into *denying the validity of their own perceptions* and those of their fellow humans. For this reason visitors (both of the helpful and harmful kinds) attempt to contact individuals or small groups of individuals that show some sign of receptivity to their intended contact. (*The non-helpful visitors will often choose those whom they believe are easily manipulated through the Keylonta codes.*)

For centuries your people have been taught to subjugate their own authority and have delegated their ability to perceive clearly to objective authority structures such as government and religion. All of you have a *right to know the truth* about the conditions that directly affect you. Unfortunately for you, your governments do not agree with this premise. So as a collective you are quite certainly ill-prepared to meet directly ET visitors, no matter how benign their agenda may be.

Part of the reason that many advances have been withheld from the general scientific and public communities is that this knowledge would give individual citizens *the power to better direct their own lives, their health, their economic standing and their own protection.* If the public had access to such abilities the governments could no longer use such tactics as fear and intimidation to illicit blind obedience. They would lose control over their people and their peoples resources as the people gained control over themselves. So the "official program" *lie* has been created and perpetuated to keep each of you in the dark, fearful and dependent upon the approval and support of outside authorities. You have been brainwashed and betrayed, and that *also* applies to those of you who think you are responsible for creating and maintaining the official program. Most of you have lost sight of the fact that alternative perspectives exist. Most of you have lost sight of what you have lost in succumbing to the program's *tunnel vision.* Some of you, in reading these words, will *know* the truth as these ideas move through you—you will *simply know.* And at first you will probably find anger, and beneath the anger—fear. For if what you have been brainwashed into believing is not truth, then *what is true?* It will feel as if you are upon a precipice overlooking an endless abyss, and you will not know where to turn, or whom to trust, or where to look for answers. Looking within (perhaps for the first time?) to the core of your own spirituality will be the light that leads you through this darkness.

Many of you will reject this data, perhaps heatedly, for that is seemingly far easier than facing the raw fear that can be generated by seeing the truth for the first time. Not all of you are ready to see the truth, for within the lies there existed the *illusion* of safety and comfort, and an innocence to the loss of freedom and integrity that the official program has created. You may choose to take the stance that "what you don't know won't hurt you." Indeed, if it is hurtful it *will* hurt you, but in choosing blindness you may not be aware of the harm being done. You may not realize the sacrifice you have made until it is too late and death or disease have overtaken you.

We care for all of you. And we hold all of you in high enough regard to offer you the option of viewing your reality as it exists, so you may make your choice *consciously* as to what you will believe. We exhibit far more personal respect and honor for you than do your governments and religious organizations who employ codes of discrimination, elitism, secrecy and the withholding of knowledge and resources. Knowledge is intended for the many who are open to receiving it, not for the few who seek to use it to control, disempower, and manipulate the many it was intended to serve. Many humans within positions of power need to learn this simple lesson. It is the gift of knowledge that we offer you—can you accept the gift?

And so we have explained to you some of what you are up against in your evolution toward enlightenment. We have given you an idea of who the players are, where they come from, and what agendas they hold. Now we will let you know the rest of the story about the *greater realities* taking place within your present time, for those who are *ready*—for those who chose to know what is taking place within the universe around them.

SUBCONSCIOUS SYMBOL CODES

We have explained to you how the Zeta, Aethien, Ranthia and other time-portal and interdimensional groups are able to create "perceptual interference" or "sensory interruption" in humans, and how these tactics are presently being used in regard to some of your "UFO abduction" experiences. The aforementioned Keylonta codes, which govern the activities of the *subconscious symbol codes* contained within human DNA, are used to implant and orchestrate these sensual deceptions. All of these groups are capable of creating such events because they understand the mechanics of the human bio-electric system and its operations within the living organism. If they did not understand the relationships between form and energy they would not be able to use such technologies, nor would they be able to maneuver within the Time-Portal and Dimensional Lock Systems. If they did not know the language of Keylonta they would be trapped within their own reality and time-space systems just as your species is presently trapped within the three-dimensional Earth system. They are able to traverse other reality systems and to direct their own biologies because they know things that you and your scientists do not yet know.

Because such cultures possess this knowledge that yours presently lacks they are able to manipulate your biology and your perceptual field and thus your consciousness. Literally all of the groups mentioned use this knowledge to interact with you, some for the purposes of *helping* you to grow, others to keep you from evolving into your full potentials. The human biology speaks a language quite different than that of the "conscious mind" (as you understand that facility). It is a language that you have consciously forgotten, the language of energy relationships—Keylonta. It is the foundation upon which all of your languages and modes of perception are built. We have come to refresh your memory and to remind you of your "native tongue," so that you may once again begin consciously using the language contained within your cellular structure. The language of living knowledge is contained within every molecule of your three-dimensional, matter-clad world. You had help in forgetting this language, and so now it is appropriate that you should have help in remembering.

THE ZETA AGENDA

In order to understand the Zeta agenda and the dramas unfolding within your universe you must have some idea of the workings of Keylonta. It is the language of the *symbol codes* ("subconscious" from your perspective), the intrinsic, interior geometric-electric and magnetic structures that create the foundations for all form and structure within the dimensional systems, a language of light, sound, pulsation and vibration of energy. And the method by which form is created and maintained within your system. It represents the *living codes of matter* and all biologies built upon them. The Keylonta codes set everything from the *type of body* you will manifest through the genetics of your biology to the very chemical, hormonal and energetic functions which keep that body in motion. *It is the key to your known and unknown universe.*

The Zeta, as well as the helping ET groups, are aware of these codes and how they can be used in relation to the human organism and the Earth system. The Zeta have, *from the beginnings of their interaction with you,* used the Keylonta codes to *direct and manipulate* human perception. It is through these codes and an active knowledge of their usage that the Zeta are able to manufacture the perceptual interference and sensual interruption previously mentioned.

We are not trying to frighten you, but if you do not soon take responsibility for mastering the mechanics of your own biology, you *will* be "sitting ducks," so to speak, for those who do understand these workings. We do not recommend waiting until your governments, scientists or official medical communities figure out how to do this for you, because they may be one of the last to know the mechanics of the inner workings. Their inherent belief structures are prejudiced against the very methods that will bring this knowledge to you. *Responsibility for biological mastery lives with the individual,* each individual, for only the intrinsic life force within each organism has full access to the code combinations unique to its form. You can learn to master your own biological codes by *working through your own consciousness* and greater identity, but no objective organization will be able to decipher the intimate balances upon which your biology is built. There are practices which can assist you in your quest for biological mastery, and we will offer some of these in other writings, when we explore in greater detail the language and applications of Keylonta.

Through Keylonta mechanics your cellular structure can be altered. Your bodies can be healed, your consciousness expanded. The mysteries of your three-dimensional system can be unraveled. Through Keylonta enlightenment will one day belong to your species. But until that day Keylonta can be used in ways that do not benefit your development, used by those who have the knowledge but who do not as yet possess the wisdom to use these gifts as they were intended—those such as the Zeta.

These codes are presently being used in a number of ways by various time-portal and interdimensional groups (such as ourselves, as we communicate with you). Keylonta is *the* language for communicating through the time and dimensional portals. Though you receive these communications in the language most familiar to you, and in the linear progression of thought and word that is characteristic of your time-space coordinate, the *true* communication is passed on first *to your cellular structure.* It is placed into your DNA codes as minute electrical signals. We transmit our communications through the interdimensional portals then "fine-tune" our transmission through the time-portals into your time-space coordinates. We are able to transmit large amounts of data into a vast area in this manner. This information is then translated to your level of perception through those individuals whose *bodies* have the ability to pick up and synthesize advanced (compared to the average operational frequencies of your present time) electrical impulse patterns. All of you have translation abilities to *some* degree, but some of you are more *genetically predisposed* to this ability.

Our communications come to you from another dimension, through a time-portal system of an Earth that exists parallel to your own. Our culture lives within that parallel system, but in its own time-portal frame it is placed within the future of even that Earth version. These Keylonta transmissions, coming from this distant place, will reach those in various dimensions and time coordinates who are ready to translate them. *These communications will become available to those who are in need of the knowledge contained within them.*

It is our hope that if you can become aware of Keylonta mechanics enough of you will be enabled to develop the *tools* you need to counteract the harmful ways this knowledge is presently being used to manipulate you and keep you blind. We cannot "win the game for you" in relation to your deal-ings with the Zeta and other groups, but we can offer the tools of knowledge you will need to effectively direct your own destinies.

Now we will explore how the Zeta and other self-interested groups are using Keylonta to mislead you.

PERCEPTUAL INTERFERENCE

Keylonta is the *means* by which the Zeta are able to create **perceptual interference**. They have the power through these mechanics to literally cre-ate **mass hallucinations**. We do *not* favor this word of your English language but instead prefer to use the word "**hologram**" for its meaning is closer to the actual reality that is taking place. The term **mental hologram** may give you a better idea of the concept we are trying to convey.

Through manipulating the **impulse codes** intrinsic to the human biology literal "reality pictures" can be created for the unsuspecting human to per-ceive. We are not speaking here of mental images or simple hallucinations, but rather actual **three-dimensional reality overlays** that emerge into the surrounding objective environment. These contrived "reality pictures" can be coded to emerge as past memory or as present time three-dimensionally objective experience. Unlike a simple hallucination the "reality picture" not only affects the individual or group that is being altered, but will *also* affect anyone coming into the encoded perimeters of its boundaries. It is as if someone created a "virtual reality" picture for you to walk through, and its contours are so seamless compared to your "real" reality that you do not realize anything has changed. Events can be manufactured *for* you in this way, without your conscious knowledge or permission. In such cases "what you don't know" could very well hurt you, and you might not be aware of what harm is being done. We refer to these "reality pictures" or "experiential overlays" as **holographic inserts**. It is time that humans became aware of the existence of such technologies, *for they have been used throughout your history to alter and bend the nature of your historical development.*

HOLOGRAPHIC INSERTS

Holographic inserts work in a number of ways. First of all, in order to create them a working comprehension of the relationships between biology, energy and perception is required. Humans in your system presently do not have such a working knowledge.

When the **mechanics of energy** are understood (as they are by groups such as the Zeta), it is quite easy to impulse the base DNA codes of humans to carry an altered or contrived "program" or electrical imprint. As the base DNA code is electrically altered the entire *physiology* of the individual on the chemical and hormonal level is altered. The neurological structure then processes this *altered* code and, through the intrinsic mechanisms of bodily matter, brain and senses, a literal hologram is manufactured. This process may be difficult for you to understand as your sciences do not as yet realize the rudimentary mechanics of how the illusion of three-dimensionality itself is created through the human organism. The human body has not as yet been identified as the living "holographic projection mechanism" that it is in actuality. Though these understandings would be helpful to you, they are not necessary for you to begin working with Keylonta codes. Even if you do not fully understand the "how" of these mechanics you can benefit by learning technology that will better allow you to direct the result of these energy manipulations.

As the neurological structure processes the altered codes, the individual will perceive *outside* of himself, as three-dimensional matter the images and events or "reality pictures" that were programmed into his DNA. Some of these codes can be contrived to become "permanent" additions to the original DNA base code. This process can be used to assist humanity in reaching great levels of spiritual enlightenment, physical health and beauty, and mental and emotional expansion. But it can also be used to create horrific traumas upon the human biological organism and the consciousness that depends upon this organism for its three-dimensional life.

Holographic inserts are presently being used *against you* by the Zeta and other groups. If you can learn some of these mechanics (through Keylonta) you can stop them from manipulating you. *You can protect yourselves and keep your perceptions clear. And you can grow.*

Events have already been set in motion to begin using holographic inserts *on a mass level.* This is part of the aforementioned Zeta agenda. Individuals have been tested and experimented upon for some time as the appropriate processes were fine-tuned. The Zeta are now ready to begin using holographic inserts on a mass level, starting with small groups and later moving into whole collectives. The Interior Government has long allowed such experimentation to take place, and they themselves have been the greatest test subjects for the Zeta; *they succumbed to the very tactics they were trained by the Zeta to employ against other humans.* Do not be surprised if in years to come you begin to see more and more reports of odd happenings witnessed by masses of people appearing in your news media and tabloids. Many of these will not be "made up" by overzealous reporters, but will mark actual events of holographic inserts in operation.

Next we will discover how holographic inserts have been used in relation to what you call the "UFO abduction" phenomena.

MECHANICS OF VISITOR ABDUCTION

We have explained to you in the beginning of this writing the different categories into which UFO phenomena may fall, some being benign manifestations of natural phenomena, others being intentional or unintentional contact with sentient beings from your or other systems. We have explained to you that what *appear* to be solid-matter physical objects are at times illusions created as other dimensional phenomena interface with your three-dimensional system. If one were able to control and direct the movement of an object through dimensions or time portals, and were familiar with the different forms that object takes within the various dimensions, it is possible that alterations could purposely be made to objects by moving them through dimensions. That is, the *form* of an object in one dimension could be changed by *moving it into another dimension* for alteration, then returning it to its original dimension where the other-dimensional alteration would appear as a change in form. This process is called **transmutation of form,** and it is accomplished through **dimensional transmigration.** Familiarity with this concept will facilitate your understanding of the nature of the **UFO abduction** phenomenon.

If an object existed in the form of a rock in your dimension, let us say, this rock could be moved into another dimensional frequency, altered there, and then returned to its original dimension where the alteration would then manifest as form change in terms characteristic of that dimension. Your rock for example, could be taken to an adjacent dimension and altered, then reemerge as a tree when placed back in its original system. How do these mechanics apply to abduction scenarios? Quite simply, the human "object" (which is what many Zeta view humans as being) is temporarily *neutralized* using the Keylonta codes—perceptual interference is orchestrated. During this sensual interruption the human mental awareness ("mental body") becomes momentarily disengaged from the biological structure. The mind or "mental self-awareness" is placed in a temporary state of suspended animation. It is put "on hold" within the three-dimensional frequency, while the biological organism is taken into a different dimensional frequency or through a time portal. This part of the process is what creates the experience of a seeming "separation of bodies" often reported in abduction cases. It seems as though an **astral body** is being pulled out of a physical body, the same experience known as **astral projection.** (Not all abduction episodes contain this particular feature, but many do). And it is here that many abductees become confused as to whether their experiences were "really real" physical events or whether they were mental events, hallucinations, dreams or excursions into the "astral plane."

The reality of what is occurring is that the energy field of the mind and that of the cellular pattern of the flesh are being put on "different speeds" (different rates of vibrational oscillation). The mind-field is accelerated, its rate of oscillation increased, which creates the sense data of the lessening of density. Meanwhile the energetic field of the molecular structure is *decelerated*, its rate of oscillation *slowed*, creating the bodily-sensed data of an increase in density. The oscillation rates of both of these energy fields are held within a certain interval or within a particular *ratio*, which temporarily disengages the connection between them. The mental awareness and the body consciousness thus are *split*, placed within two separate **frequency bands.** The mind is held at a frequency *higher* than that of the third dimension—its oscillation rate is increased. While the mind is accelerated and tuned into a higher frequency pattern, the body is decelerated, its oscillation rate slowed, tuning it to a lower frequency. In greater terms this maneuver constitutes moving the mental awareness into the "future" while placing the cellular consciousness in the "past." After the particular ratio between body and mind speeds is reached, the body is then quickly accelerated in oscillation, enabling it to "leap" through a time or dimensional portal. Thus by manipulating the speeds of various aspects of the bio-energetic field a **window in time** is created, which enables the body-matter to move through portals without its form being destroyed.

In abduction cases that utilize the above manipulations the physical body is taken, but it is **shape-shifted,** literally turned into light formations within another time and dimensional frequency. It is first taken backward in time to its pre-matter form, then catapulted from that condition into the future of that form where the desired manipulations are made, and then moved from that future perspective backward toward the present where it is then re-engaged to the mental energy aspects that had been "put on hold" to await the body's return. Alterations to the body are actually carried out while the body is in a non-solid form existing as light and sound patterns, but upon the integration of the body with the mental facility these alterations then take on the symbol codes that give the illusion of form. The alterations of light appear in memory as the **medical experiments** so often recalled in abductions. To the body and mind these events will indeed appear as if they had taken place physically, and in one sense they have, for the physical sensory imprint is valid within the present moment focus of the consciousness. The remembered events were real but they took place within the future where matter-solidity had not yet caught up with them. When intersecting these future events with a conscious mind focused in the present the events will immediately be translated into the codes of the mental body, thus giving solidity of form to the remembered events. *Memory is stored within the body cells and DNA*, and so the events experienced in a future time are recorded there, but they will be remembered consciously only as the mental body grows to the point where it is able to translate that stored data into symbols. The mental body can only translate impulses that fall within its range of frequency, so within abductions of this kind the remembered events will unfold "over time" as the mental awareness grows and expands its frequency rate to translate a greater variety of "impulse packages."

Alterations that take place during such experiences may take the form of **physical manipulations**, as well as that of remembered events. *Scars* may appear upon the body as the organism reintegrates the cellular and mental codes, **implants of devices** may be located within the body, fetuses may be found *missing. The body will translate into physical reality the events it has encountered and that are stored within its imprint*, whether those events occurred in the past or the future. (In present time you may fall and immediately your body produces a bruise which seems to be the result of the fall. In greater reality what you are seeing is a complex interplay of **electrical impulse manifestations.** The "result" appears to your conscious mind to have been created through the "cause." The actual manufacturing of the result and cause together elude you as they take place within frequencies not within your range of translation. The *illusion* of what you perceive as "cause and effect" is a primary base code of the three-dimensional system, so what you perceive three-dimensionally will appear to follow that pattern. In greater terms both cause and effect exist at once as part of a whole pattern, and what you see as this relationship is simply that pattern viewed "in pieces." Because of the alignment of what we call your **Genetic Time Codes** you will perceive one part of the pattern first, what you know as the "cause." And the other part of the pattern, what you know as the "effect", following it in time. The bruise and the fall exist at once as part of the same pattern, though it appears as if the fall created the bruise. In terms of greater reality it could just as easily be said that the bruise created the fall, as each exist as part of a whole pattern in which the existence of one implies the existence of the other. You will see the "cause and effect" as dictated by your Genetic Time Codes, rather than the true construction of the entire event and the process of its manifestation.). In regard to the manifestations of alterations conducted during abduction experiences, the "result" (implant, scar, etc.) exists as part of the whole event of the process of the alterations, but you perceive it "in pieces," where as the abduction seems to have taken place in the past of your present and was responsible for the creation of the effect. What in truth has taken place is that your consciousness, in its present moment of focus, has participated in action taking place within frequency bands that are both higher and lower than those of your present moment frequency. All of these frequency bands exist at once in the ever-present *now*, but you perceive them strung out in linear fashion because of the arrangement of your Genetic Time Codes. As your consciousness is fragmented into the various frequency bands, then reassembled into the frequency of your present moment focus, the Genetic Time Codes sort and organize this electrically coded experiential data into a pattern that your conscious mind can synthesize into linear, sequential reality. The other frequency (which is conceptually synonymous with "other time") events are translated, through the biology, into "remembered action" and the "result of that action", which sets in motion the body's **innate sensory-projection mechanisms** that create the physically observable manifestation.

The important thing for you to realize is that such abduction experiences are quite *real* and *valid, just as real as any seemingly "normal" event within your three-dimensional reality*. Both types of events, however, employ mechanics that you are presently unaware of, but in the case of the abductions you get a little more of a glimpse as to how these mechanics operate. To understand the nature of abductions you will begin to find a greater understanding of the nature of three-dimensional reality.

Not *all* abduction cases involve the transmigration (movement) of the physical body through other frequency bands/time zones/dimensions. Not all human bodies are able to withstand such process, some would be destroyed or damaged by this type of manipulation. In cases where this transmutation process *is* employed the *mind* will *at first* have *no* recall of the events, **missing time** is experienced as the *body and mind reharmonize their respective rates of oscillation and build the necessary neurological and chemical structures that will allow the "flow" of energy between them to be reestablished*. It takes time in your system for the conscious mind to "catch up with" the altered bodily imprint.

At first the new imprint alterations "do not compute" within the mental body and a "mental blank spot" is left until the organism re-balances itself. When the mental facility integrates the new imprint "flashes" of memory will then come into conscious awareness, most often "triggered" through the associative process. That is, a sensory perception (sight, smell, noise, etc.), will trigger the release of the new memory into awareness. Such memories can also be found through techniques like **hypnosis**, where the conscious mind is slightly disassociated from its focus within the present moment and is encouraged to traverse cellular memory. Often there will be memory of an odd event ("missing time", a UFO sighting, or uncharacteristic emotional or behavioral reaction, etc....), surrounding the event which has not yet surfaced into conscious memory. Hypnosis would then serve to assist the mind to translate and integrate more of the new imprint, bringing it to the surface of memory. The event of **sequential memory** of the abduction returning to the abductee marks the point of integration of the new cellular imprint; the "mind has caught up with the experiences of the body" so to speak. It constitutes the return of the full consciousness (which was fragmented during the event) to the focus within the present time, or the *return of consciousness to its original frequency band*.

To integrate the full imprint of such a **multi-time event** the human organism literally manufactures new, minute neurotransmitters and nerve networks to accommodate the altered DNA imprint. Your three-dimensional instruments presently cannot record most of these activities as these instruments are "keyed" or "tuned" to only the three-dimensional time coordinate in your particular frequency. You may eventually be able to chart the "results" (the portion of this activity that *does* take place within the three-dimensional frequency) of such base code manipulations, but you will not find the "cause" as it exists *outside* of the three-dimensional frequency band in which *your instruments have their being*.

Abduction episodes following the format just described would be considered **clear-cut abductions**. They are orchestrated in a *straight-forward manner, transmutation and alteration of form through the process of transmigration*. Not all abductions are clear-cut. Clear-cut manipulations are carried out upon those who possess a biological organism that can withstand the rigors of transmigration. Most of your population, at the present time, cannot biologically endure such manipulation. Some abduction cases involve partial use of transmigration in combination with tactics of perceptual interference, whereby holographic inserts (as described in previous sections) are used to "cloak" the abductee's perception of the abduction event prior to the "splitting" of awareness and transmigration. In these cases you will often find "cover memories" that will emerge in place of or in conjunction with actual memories of the abduction event. Abductees may remember seeing wolves, owls, or humans instead of "aliens and spaceships." The *emotional reaction* to these **cover images** will seem out of place, however, over-reactive to the seeming content. This is a clue to the possible application of cover memories and holographic inserts. This tactic is most often used to distract the subject long enough to instigate the splitting of awareness; it is a more delicate procedure in some subjects and takes more time to achieve. The inserts create a diversion from the actual events that would, of themselves, cause panic or hysteria, two conditions that can have dire effects during the "splitting" process.

Still other types of abductions utilize holographic inserts exclusively. They are often used to create present-moment or remembered experiences of "traveling aboard a spacecraft" to distract the mental awareness of the abductee while **electromagnetic alterations** (using Keylonta) are performed on the body while it remains within the three-dimensional frequency. Here transmigration would not be involved. This type of abduction usually occurs when the subject's biology cannot tolerate the transmigration of dimensional movement. (Such as is the case with cattle and most other animal life indigenous to Earth. Some of your reported "cattle mutilations" occurred as a result of this type of experimentation.)

There are two primary reasons that "alien abductions" occur:

1. *For abductee training:* Though it may be difficult for you to believe, many humans have *willingly agreed* to participate in visitor projects. Most often these agreements were entered during the human's dream state through the subconscious facility. Many such agreements were arranged *prior to birth*, whereas the *soul awareness* of the incoming infant chose to accept as a possibility the fulfillment of a contract with souls who would not be manifesting in human form. (And yes, dear humans, for those of you who are unsure, you do indeed have a **soul** or an identity greater than what can be held within the confines of your matter-form.) We refer to these contracts as **Soul Agreements.** Abductions of this kind are not intrinsically intrusive but they may *seem* to be to the conscious personality who has not remembered the agreement or who has *blocked the awareness of soul.*

Abductions involving soul agreements have many purposes. Most often the human is given *information and lessons* during the experience which will then be used to assist the abductors in the greater plan upon which all have agreed. The majority of these encounters serve to *assist in the positive evolution of humanity.* Though the abductee may never consciously remember what has been learned, the information and training will motivate him/her on the *subconscious* level toward fulfilling the greater purposes for which the soul had incarnated.

2. *For study, experimentation and genetic seeding by self-serving groups* such as the unenlightened Zeta. Though the abductors in these cases are not *delib-*

erately initiating harm against their human subjects, neither are they operating under a contract of consent. Many abductors view the human in a manner similar to how the human views the animal and plant kingdoms. *They simply do not consider the human as an intelligent life form, but rather as a natural resource that can be used and exploited for their own purposes.* Humans who have worked to build the *conscious connection to soul* and who have a healthy flow of the souls energy running through them will *usually* not encounter such events. Often the human soul will *allow* for the event of violation to take place so that the individual will begin to reach for that soul connection. Humans have free will and do not have to follow the impulse of soul, *though it is in the human's best interest to do so.* The soul and subconscious awareness will often allow for tragedies from the personality's perspective if the personality has become so immersed in its finite identity that it blocks out cognition of and cooperation with the soul.

Abductions that occur without soul agreements are a *violation* to the human subject. These events can be quite traumatic. (You might begin to speculate about how your laboratory mice might feel at the hands of your human scientists.) The human is viewed as a thing rather than a being with needs, desires and *feelings.* Human genetic material is quite valuable to some ET groups, and there are interspecies breeding experiments underway, particularly within the Zeta factions. The Zeta have had some success with this hybrid race and their experimentation continues. *Self awareness and soul awareness are the human's greatest protection from abduction violation.*

The abductee-training encounters are usually perceived by the human as traumatic *until the personality moves through the fear of the unknown* and actively pursues answers, support and validation of the experience. Once fear subsides further conscious contact is usually initiated by the teacher abductors and the human embarks upon a path of accelerated spiritual growth and awakening to the soul identity. Some abductees will begin to remember the soul agreements they had made and center the rest of their lives around fulfilling those agreements.

In the abductions that involved violation of the human subject there is usually great *fear, anger and a feeling of helplessness* on the part of the abductee. Many such abductees will never have recall of their abduction experience, but may manifest *psychological or emotional difficulties* as the intrusion has registered on a *subconscious* level. Others will find recall and will be faced with trying to find a perspective on what they have experienced. Very little support exists for people who suffer this type of trauma. If they turn toward the government or authorities for answers and assistance they most often find their character attacked and their encounter invalidated. The medical and psychiatric professions presently offer little help to such people, as a general rule, because the *possibility of the experience being valid does not fit into their belief paradigm.* As more and more abduction cases come into public awareness and more abductees speak out about the encounters, a greater support network is emerging. (*The Interior Government will resist this movement at every turn.*)

The most terrifying aspect of alien abduction for both groups of abductees is that no one seems to have any answers. Even if they can find the support network most within that network are uncertain as to what they are dealing with in terms of the abductors. Comfort may be found in sharing that uncertainty, but peace and understanding may still seem quite elusive. It is for this reason that we have brought this information to you, hoping to reach those of you who need it most. Those of you who need to understand the reasons and purposes behind the alien abduction experience—we bring to you information that is new to your time, but it is indeed timely. We hope to inspire you to learn more about the nature of your reality and the very real aspect of your reality called **alien abduction.**

3

Human Origins and Hybridization

HYBRIDS

In order to learn more about alien abductions you must first realize that in most reported cases the events are quite real and *deserve validation*. Quite literally you have been taught, or programmed, to "not believe in aliens." The mainstream view still sees the idea of ET life as a joke or product of romantic fantasy. Once upon a time in your history the masses viewed airplanes in the same way. *Once upon a time only "lunatics" believed the Earth was round.* It is time for individuals to begin looking beyond the small scope of their global reality and begin wondering of what greater community might it be a part.

Your governments and sciences have been manipulated into debunking and invalidating abduction and UFO sightings experiences *by the very beings whose reality they proclaim does not exist. The Zeta and others would like to see humans remain ignorant to their activities, for in so doing they can direct humans in any way they choose.* Some Zeta factions are still involved in creating a hybrid race whose ultimate purposes would be to *compete* with humans for the Earth and her resources. These hybrids *already* exist, but their strain is not quite strong enough, their masses still too few. If this experiment was to progress unchecked, these beings would misuse the resources of the Earth and violate its inherent integrity, much as the Zeta have violated the integrity of the humans they study. For this reason, and the potential *future consequences* within the third dimension, there is much assistance being offered to humans, and to the Zeta themselves, for finding better solutions. The greatest threat to Earth and to human life at this time is not a "pole reversal," self-imposed nuclear holocaust, depletion of natural resources or over population. The greatest threat to your well being is that of *manipulation and exploitation by forces that you do not even yet know are real.*

The Zeta have successfully interbred with human females. There are hybrid babies and children, or what would *appear* as Zeta-human hybrids if they were within the three-dimensional system. They do appear as such when they are brought into the third dimension to have contact with their human mothers. The hybrids presently cannot enter the third dimension fully; their biology is *not yet adjusted* to the concentrations of matter density within which the third dimension is cloaked. They originate from and exist within an adjacent dimensional band of Earth. The Zeta are cultivating them within those coordinates, *not* within the present coordinates of your three-dimensional Earth structure. The hybrids are being cultivated to engage in an intersection with your Earth at a time point *400 to 500 years in your future*.

There are various strains of these Zeta-human hybrid beings, each designed to fulfill certain roles within the Zeta plan. Some appear as large, thin white beings with wispy hair, usually white in color when in maturity. These represent the first-born strain of the race, and these possess the capacity to *understand human emotion*, as you understand it, better than the more sophisticated strains that have emerged from them. They are the "closest to human" in terms of biology and psychological orientation. Other strains have been sighted in your times during abductions. The small, dwarf-like creatures you call the **blues** and also the **browns** are hybrids, but they were specifically created as the "worker" strain. These are not simply Zeta-human hybrids, but represent a conglomeration of genetic material derived from other dimensional species as well as from human DNA. Unlike the Zeta-human hybrids the blues and browns do not possess a high degree of intellectual or intelligence capacity, nor do they harbor within their gene structure a large scope of evolutionary probabilities. They are linked through a hierarchy of centralized minds and are "programmed" or contoured to serve the needs of those higher up on the evolutionary scale. These beings will often be found in proximity to the **whites** (the Zeta-human hybrids), serving as guards or general **soldiers**.

ZIONITES

Many experiments continue to be carried out within the Zeta factions, some combining Earth animal aspects with Zeta and other dimensional life forms. There is one other category of Zeta created hybrids that we would like to mention. These represent the highest strain and they are also **conglomerates**, created through the genetic fusing of Zeta, humans and other dimensional ET life forms. We have mentioned previously the mantis-like beings called the Aethien The Aethien being highly evolved teachers commissioned to assist the Zeta, the humans and many others through out your dimension and others. The Aethien have agreed to assist those Zeta who have made a commitment to non-violation of other systems. The Aethien offered their expertise and some of their genetic material to assist the Zeta in continuation of their species through genetic mutation. Out of this agreement yet another strain of hybrid was formed, the Zeta human-Aethien strain that we refer to as the **Zion-ites.** The Zionite strain constitutes a master race of beings whose abilities and powers reach far beyond the present moment of your Earth history. Indeed, this race was created by "splicing together" the best of the human strain with other highly advanced genetic material from other systems. The Zeta drew genetic material from the distant past of your species, and they also sent matured hybrids back in time to directly interact with humans. The past we speak of involves advanced civilizations that existed in your past historically but of which you presently have no record.

Zionite

The Zionites are cultivated time travelers. Though their species came into being through the genetic experimentation of the Zeta in conjunction with the Aethien, their strain is unique in its abilities of maneuverability through time. From their points of origin in a dimension of Earth adjacent to your own, and running along a time continuum parallel to that of your present, the Zionites have fanned outward in time within your third dimension and also within other dimensions. There are planets within your universe upon which Zionites can be found, and

there are large groupings of them working with the Aethien in their home systems. Though in your present terms they could be considered a "fledgling race," you must realize that (because of their inter-time abilities) they are also a fully matured race simultaneously. They exist as a part of your future in your three-dimensional world, but they are also a part of your past. Through the Zionites involvement with your ancestors they are also part of your heritage as humans, and they have had a tremendous effect upon the development of your species.

TURANEUSIAM

Prior to your recorded history there did exist upon the Earth civilizations of humans that would be considered *superior genetically* to your present human strain. These beings had interaction with others "from the stars" in your terms. The original human prototype contained genetic materials gathered throughout the galaxy. The human prototype was *not* of Earth in its original construction. Humans originated on Earth's fifth-dimensional counterpart planet Tara. The Zionites were one of the "star groups" whose genetic material was supplied to create the original human prototype. The race of humans of which we speak is called the **Turaneusiam.** Their biologies emerged 560 million years ago (YA) from combining various species of animal-like life forms indigenous to Tara during those times with other, more advanced genetic strains from other planetary and other dimensional systems. Tara was viewed as a "nursery" of sorts, where this new human hybrid could develop and gain sovereignty over the life forms upon the Tara. *The human prototype was intended to become the custodian and guardian of Tara, and to enjoy open intergalactic and interdimensional exchange with many other civilizations.* For a period of time this development occurred and the new species (humans) evolved graciously. There came a point in time however in which the species began a path of **de-evolution**. The humans (Turaneusiam) began interbreeding with the other indigenous life forms. Their genetic strain became more and more animal-like, *which progressively reduced their ability to carry the higher intelligence for which they were intended.* The species digressed, falling into more and more behaviors characteristic of the less developed life forms. Some of the humans left Tara and joined with their interstellar brothers. Others remained upon Tara while genetic diversity began to fragment the human species. Many attempts of reeducation were made by the cultures who had seeded the original prototype, but the digression became too great. *The humans who had originally been intended as Tara's guardians were losing the ability to fulfill that role.*

The Turaneusiam had originally possessed great power and knowledge. As the genetic digression continued distortions in their knowledge began to manifest in *instinctual behaviors*, within which *abuse and misuse of power was prevalent.* Tara's resources and other life forms were more and more abused and misused. The creators of the Turaneusiam, after a millennium of attempted reeducation, finally decided to allow the species to continue its digression into its natural end—the *self-termination of the species*, which nearly occurred during events of 550 million years ago. The prototype was preserved *through those Turaneusiam who had retreated underground or resettled in other systems within the three-dimensional universe.*

The legends now common in your culture involving **Atlantis** and **Lemuria** have emerged through the genetic memory into your times from that prehistoric reality. Though "Atlantis" was not the actual name of this civilization the drama your legends associate with it are actual translations of some of the events that occurred during this period of original human creation.

TWELVE TRIBES

Several thousand years again passed during which time there were periods of relative stability and instability as Tara rebalanced and realigned its magnetic grid. During this cycle it was decided by the creators of the Turaneusiam that yet another experiment would be tried—they would *again seed their humans, this time into the* Earth *system.* This time it would be done more slowly—*the genetic imprint of the original prototype would be broken down into sections or sub-imprints.* Each imprint would be used to create a "smaller" prototype, or subspecies of the original Turaneusiam. The genetic package was broken down into *twelve* units, each containing two primary attributes of the original pattern. The original pattern possessed twelve strands of DNA. The twelve were separated into individual packages and then polarized. Each of the twelve sub-species was assigned on a genetic level to re-bundle their polarized strand into one complete unit. As each of the twelve groups of beings or **tribes** overcame the duality coded within its genetic structure, it would be brought into alignment with the tribes that had done the same. Through this process the human genetic strain would, over time, *evolve into the wholeness of its original pattern.* The digressive elements that were mutated into the strain from its animal interbreeding would slowly be mutated out, leaving behind *the pure code of the human prototype.* It was and is a plan that would take several hundred-thousand years to complete, *if* the species was able to evolve rather than fall into de-evolution once more.

Your Biblical stories of origins and of **the flood** emerged out of this drama. The "fall" in Biblical terms represents the digression brought on by animal interbreeding, the resulting mutation of form, and the cataclysmic events that nearly terminated the species 550 million years ago. The version of that story popular in your times has been twisted and contrived away from its original symbolic meaning. The "flood" within your story represents the period of time *when the twelve sub-species of humans were reseeded upon the Earth.* The Sodom and Gomorrah drama is a retranslation of the "Atlantean/Lemurian" events that occurred on Tara before the flood, these two elements being combined into a new version carrying the same theme but restructuring the time context. "Adam" and "Eve" were *symbolic* personages representing the polarization of the sub-strands of DNA and the birth of duality of consciousness. The symbolic story of Adam and Eve was itself twisted from its true meaning, which in allegorical form stood for the *polarization of the twelve single strands of the subspecies.* Your version promotes the idea that "Eve was created out of the rib of Adam," which symbolically implies that man was created first. The polarization of the DNA, and the resulting birth of duality of gender, occurred *simultaneously.* It further encourages you to believe that woman was created to *serve* man, to be "lesser" and to play a subservient role. *These distortions were purposely given to you to keep from you and suppress the power and wisdom held within the female form and consciousness.* Through this distortion the polarities or duality within each of the twelve sub-species could never be overcome, and thus the completion of human evolution into its original exalted form could never be actualized.

Just as the original creators of the human prototype desired to see the ful-fillment of the species as guardians of the Earth and Tara there also exist forces of great power that do *not* wish this plan to succeed. If humans are able to fulfill their evolutionary blueprint, the Earth and many other reality fields will *no longer be free for exploitation*. They will become protected by a species equal in power and greater in knowledge than those who wish to misuse these realities. It is from this interdimensional conflict that your concepts of "good vs. evil" and "God vs. devil" emerge. One group of advanced beings wish to see humans *evolve into wholeness, equality and co-creatorship,* while another group of beings desires to *stunt the evolution of humanity* so it can continue to utilize its resources for self serving purposes. The latter group has come to rep-resent the **dark** or **evil** forces within the collective human unconscious, while the former has emerged into your mythologies of the **gods**.

Because of this "cosmic conflict" so to speak, attempts have been made by both sides throughout your history to train the evolving humans. One set of teachings will lead humans to *evolve*, the other to *digress*. The ploy of distort-ing the helpful teachings has been used repeatedly throughout your species development by the forces that do not wish you to succeed. Much of your present teachings are so contaminated by these distortions that the *true meaning of the original teachings has been lost,* or applied in a way that creates the opposite effect for which the teachings were originally intended. During your recorded history much information was given to assist humanity's devel-opment. Your speculations about **ancient astronauts** bringing knowledge and technological advancements to Earth cultures are *quite accurate*. This method of assisting your culture was indeed employed often in your historical devel-opment. Certain cultures were able to interact directly with the travelers from other systems. One such group is the **ancient Egyptians**, another is the **Melchizedeks**, the group that has fragmented to become those affiliated with the Christian and Jewish faiths. The predecessors of your Celtic and Druid lineages also had involvement with interstellar teachers, as did many others. At one time or another the teachers interacted with all human sub-groups, helping to form the basis for their mythologies and creation stories, their psy-chologies and their technologies. The group of teachers we would like you to become familiar with are the aforementioned *Zionites*

THE SILICATE MATRIX

The Zionites interacted directly with your ancient Egyptian cultures, and prior to this they were heavily involved with **Sumerian** culture. Not only were these cultures gifted with *knowledge* but they were also imbued with the gift of *interstellar seeding.* Zionites would often interbreed with the humans, adding the potentialities of their genetic code into that of the evolving humans. Certain groups of these "special" humans were seeded, and that genetic seed was dispersed among the races through further interbreeding within the twelve human tribes. The Zionites traveled back in time giving to your species the code of transmutation. We refer to this "genetic package" imbued by the Zionites as **the Silicate Matrix** or the **Crystal Gene**. The Silicate Matrix contains the original twelve-strand DNA code structure of the original Taran-human prototype (the Turaneusiam). It presently exists within a number of humans as a *latent genetic code sequence* that must be brought into activation. Once activated, it allows for the *progressive transmutation of form*. Not *all* humans carry this code, and not all code carriers can endure full activation, but those who carry this matrix (contained within the cellular material you currently call **junk DNA**) have the potential ability of *accelerated evolution*. *They possess within their genetic makeup the latent ability to transmute cellular structure, which will one day allow them to traverse the time portals and interdimensional passageways without deterioration of their biological form.*

Though there are other **teaching races** that have had similar involvement with the human populace, none of these possessed the genetic combinations needed to allow for this advancement in human biology. Those carrying this strain have a predisposition to multidimensional perception, interdimensional communication and UFO abductions of the Soul agreement kind. The Zionites are working from your future as well as from your past, leading their **chosen ones** to the fulfillment of their genetic imprint, through which these humans will assist in setting the codes for the *advanced evolution of the species*.

Though the Zeta were in part responsible for the creation of this master race, many of them now live *in fear of them*. Their "children" became far more wise and powerful than the Zeta themselves, and went on to join interstellar groups far beyond the scope of the Zeta's perceptions. Those Zeta who bring harm or violation to humans, and who have not agreed to work in brotherhood find themselves up against a formidable adversary. The Zeta working toward peace view them with respectful awe. *There will be a time in your Earth future when direct contact with the Zionites is orchestrated.* Many of the abduction experiences in your present time are geared toward assisting the human populace in preparing for that encounter. This future event is the purpose behind the genetic experiments presently being carried out by the Zeta, Aethien and humans with soul agreements. The hybrid human-Zeta beings, ("whites," "blues," "browns" and others), serve an instrumental role in making that introduction successful.

HUMAN HYBRID PREGNANCIES

Human females that have subconscious soul agreements to provide the human egg required to foster the hybrid embryo most often *do not remember* their abductions. These mothers have a genetic code that would *not permit them to engage in interdimensional transmigration.* They fit into the group whose biologies would be *destroyed* by such activity.

They do not carry the **gene of transmutation** (Silicate Matrix or "Crystal Gene") from the earlier Zionite encounters. The eggs from such women are used to create the "whites," as previously mentioned. Male sperm is also used to create a variation of this strain. The "whites" cannot interact fully with the three-dimensional system for any prolonged period of time.

These human females are the **egg donors**, but will not have the experience of pregnancy in regard to the abductions. Most of them *will never remember* their encounters with alien forms consciously, but most *will if techniques such as hypnosis are employed.* Usually the trauma of the experience registers on an emotional level where it then becomes *buried within the symbol codes.* Some instances of these experiences emerge to the woman as recall of sexual abuse or violation, where the psyche then puts on **cover memories** creating a form of "false memory" of childhood or adolescent assault. The trauma is real and has occurred, but it is "cloaked in human clothing" so to speak. Not *all* cases of repressed-memory sexual assault are due to abductions, but many can be attributed to such encounters. Instances in which the physical facts and circumstances of the alleged assault *do not easily coincide with actual historical aspects of the case* can be a *clue* for investigators to look deeper into the possibility of alien abduction.

Some women donors are being used by Zeta that are *not* in cooperation with the peaceful brotherhoods. These abductees experience *violation* at the hands of their abductors and are often used *repeatedly* for their services. The more frequently the abductions occur in these cases the *closer to conscious recall* will be the memory of the experience. Most women experiencing donor abductions do so under the contract of *soul agreements. They may feel violated until the actual memory and agreement has been brought into conscious awareness.* Hypnosis by skilled practitioners can be therapeutic in either case, but validation of the experience is necessary if healing is to take place. **Donor abductions** are only one form of encounter presently experienced by humans. Women who have the abduction experience of **missing fetuses** or **vanishing pregnancies** fall into another category. These women are not simply "egg donors" but serve as surrogate mothers for another version of the "white" hybrid.

Women who have been selected to carry an embryo or fetus are those who carry some trace of the Silicate Matrix within their latent genetic code. Their bodies are able to endure some degree of transmutation, even if it is only the small amount of acceleration in body vibrational rates needed to accommodate the hybrid fetus. Like the donors, these women usually experience abductions that take place within the third-dimensional field, in which holographic inserts, perceptual interference and "cover memories" are utilized to distort or block memory of the event. However, because of the trace of the Silicate Matrix within their gene code *they are able to sustain the beginnings of pregnancy involving a hybrid fetus.* The hybrid fetus develops in its early weeks and months in the same way as the human fetus would mature. It carries a *slightly higher cellular oscillation rate* than that of a human, but this difference is so minute that the fetus would appear to you as no different than that of a human.

As the fetus develops certain *vibrational patterns within the genetic base code* begin to change, making the fetal pattern more and more incompatible with the body resonance of its host. At some point the fetus *must be removed and transferred to another dimensional frequency where its development can progress.* Mothers who have carried such pregnancies, only to find their fetuses missing, have undergone such fetal transplant *in order to protect the integrity of their own bodies as well as to secure the development of the fetus.* It would help for these women to know that the *children are not being stolen from them.* If the hybrid fetus were allowed to mature within its human host either the mother's body would miscarry the fetus, treating it as "foreign material," or more often, the fetus itself, in its thrust for life, would quickly deplete the body and energy of the mother. Only **Hybrid** fetuses are ever taken, those produced through human conception are *never* used in relation to the enlightened Zeta ("Stealing human fetuses" is not a tactic often employed by the abusive Zeta factions either, as their interests move in other directions.)

Carrying the hybrid fetus beyond the first trimester (or slightly into the second trimester in rare cases) would disrupt the hormonal balances within the female. Muscle tissue would rapidly deteriorate, as would bone structure and certain vital elements within the bone marrow. The developing fetus would act as a cancer within the woman's body, *rapidly destroying cellular integrity.* The hybrid fetus is *hardy,* the human body of its host far more fragile, so the continuation of a pregnancy involving the hybrid would end the life of its mother. Great care is taken during soul agreement abductions to protect both fetus and host.

The duration of these pregnancies is a clue to the degree to which the Silicate Matrix has been found present within the mother's genetic code. The longer pregnancies imply a greater presence of this trace gene and thus a greater ability on the part of the mother to engage in interdimensional transmutation. *Mothers involved in the longer gestations are those often taken later to visit with their hybrid offspring.* Having the Silicate Matrix present within their genetic structures allows for the mothers to undergo the dimensional transmigration necessary for such visitations to take place. As infants or children *none* of the whites can be brought into the third dimension for any period of time without suffering potentially irreversible damage to their biological structures. For this reason visitations are arranged "between dimensions" or within certain contrived "frequency modulation zones," whereas the human mother and hybrid child can meet within a temporarily neutral atmosphere. Though visitation with the human mother is usually in the best interest of the *child's* development, the meetings are arranged *only* when to do so would also *benefit rather than traumatize the mother. As more human surrogates learn of what is taking place within their abduction experiences and "make peace with the process" so to speak, more mother/hybrid-child visitations will be offered.*

Women abductees who feel they are ready can request such a visitation by making their desire known *just prior to sleep.* The visitation may take place during the dream state or another "consented abduction" arranged in which the mother's wishes can be carried out. *The enlightened Zeta have no desire to create trauma for human females, and they are willing to assist these women in understanding the purposes behind their encounters.* The women *must take the initiative* in this regard, and let their Zeta acquaintances know they are receptive to such communication and contact. Again, requesting contact prior to sleep or during practice of meditation or focused solitude are the most effective methods of communicating this intention. Abductees are continuously monitored by the Zeta and the request will be observed and acted upon *if appropriate to the needs of the woman.*

Male humans have also participated in this interbreeding and many have progeny within the race of whites. It is *rare*, however, that visitation between human father and hybrid child is arranged, as human males tend to react more aggressively and exhibit less receptivity toward peaceful contact. The males *usually* have less biological bonding with the child, as they have not had the opportunity to feel its life within their biology. (We notice that many human males exhibit this same lack of bonding toward their own human progeny, whereas they often do not feel the emotional connection to their children as readily as their female counterparts.) Human males tend to view children as the *propagation of lineage*, taking the possessive stance of authority over them rather than viewing their children as individuals with whom they are to build sustaining emotional bonds. Such bonding usually takes place later in life, after the child has grown, if it takes place at all. Not *all* men view their children in such a way, and many more emotionally aware males are quite able to establish bonds with their offspring, even from conception. These more matured males are more likely to be offered the opportunity to visit their hybrid progeny than are those who exhibit bonding difficulty or overly possessive attitudes toward their children. Many women share these attitudes as well—we are not simply "picking on" the males of your species. But because human women have developed a greater emotional sensitivity, as a general rule within your culture, (because of the gender-related beliefs prevalent in your times) the women are more often able to cultivate attitudes that are more accepting, trusting and conducive to nurturing. There are exceptions in either case, and "attitude is everything" when it comes to parental visitation between human parent and hybrid offspring.

BORENTULISUM

Borendt

The hybrid whites created through fetal transplant have the ability to enter into the three-dimensional frequency bands for *short* periods of time. They carry a stronger **human imprint** than those derived from egg-donor conceptions, which allows for certain advantages. These beings possess the strongest emotional imprint of the hybrids and are thus better able to understand, interact and utilize telepathic communications with humans. They will one day serve the role of *intermediaries* when Zionite contact is made with the human populace. They will also serve as *teachers and helpers* to those humans who agree to assist in the accelerated evolution of the human species. The hybrid whites born of fetal transplant, who are capable of limited interdimensional transmutation and transmigration are referred to as the **Borentulisum** (bor en thul' is um). Those whites born of egg donation and non-biological insemination, who cannot usually endure interdimensional transport are known as the **Borentasai** (bor en' thas i). Both hybrid strains are highly intelligent, with a strong mathematical leaning and great ability to comprehend the workings of universal physics and advanced sciences built upon that comprehension. Both represent *pure strains of Human-Zeta hybrids*, those two races being the only contributors to their genetic makeup. Their base strain was formulated out of the genetic materials of the "little grey" Zeta and the human genetic imprint, used in various combinations. (Other Zeta-human hybrid strains utilizing the Zephelium-Zeta genetic code are presently being constructed.)

Both strains of the **Borendt** (bor en'), (as they are called collectively), have the ability to **link minds** directly with human contactees, using the aforementioned Keylonta Codes. They are thus able to interact with humans during the human dream state or during times of altered states of consciousness, such as those that occur when practicing certain *meditation* techniques. Often they will leave "pre-recorded" imprints, packages of communicated data in electrical form, within the base codes of the human DNA, that will one day be retrieved by the human and translated into conscious communication or cognition. For those humans who are ready and able to receive such communications directly the Borendt are willing to begin sharing information and creating conscious relationships. They *can* be trusted, as you will not find the Borendt present with Zeta groups who are working in violation of the human species. On the rare occasions that Borendt accompany unenlightened Zeta, they are either held captive via mind control or work covertly as guardian infiltrates, in either case they hold pro-human sympathies at heart. The Borendt were *created out of your lineage*, and are aware of this fact, and so *they view the human race with great compassion and a parental sense of responsibility.* One day they will be welcomed and respected among those humans working toward universal brotherhood. The Borendt have much to teach your race, skills and knowledge that you need to make your evolution easier and more fulfilling, both for the individual and the masses.

We would like you to understand that the Zeta are *not* "evil monsters" desiring to destroy or misuse humanity. Rather, *they are a fragmented race, many of whom live in fear of extinction*—a race trying to create solutions for themselves using the only methods they possess. As is the case within the human species, some Zeta are more aware, enlightened and spiritually mature than others. *The groups bringing harm to humans are guilty of the crime of ignorance. They do not believe non-invasive methods of interspecies cooperation exist.* They have observed that humans quite often cannot treat even those of their own kind with compassion, understanding and tolerance, so they have little faith in the idea that a cooperative relationship could be developed between the species. The Zeta factions working against a positive human evolution believe *they must take what they need before it is taken from them.* The resources of Earth, *upon which they are progressively coming to depend, are viewed as the subject of interspecies competition, and humans as the objects or obstacles that need to be overcome to protect their interest in Earth's resources.* They do not really understand the human emotional reactions of pain and anger that so often meet them. They do not understand that in "neutralizing their competitors" they are *violating human reality and spiritual integrity*, any more than many humans understand how they have plundered their indigenous plant and animal kingdoms that "stood in the way" of human progress. To the unenlightened Zeta, humans stand in the way of their progress toward cultivating alternatives to their pending extinction. They have a "vested interest" in the development of Earth, so to speak.

It would be very helpful to the human experience if you were to view these unenlightened Zeta as fellow beings, facing some of the same challenges your species faces, rather than seeing them as potential enemies with whom you must do battle.

You are *not* equipped, technologically or mentally, to do battle with the Zeta. Such endeavors would prove fruitless to your race at best. *The unenlightened Zeta, as well as the unenlightened humans need to grow, to develop concepts that promote brotherhood and cooperation rather than segregation and competition.* They need to be taught a better way, by example. *Enlightened humans have a responsibility not only to their own species but also toward those within other species, be they the plant and animal forms indigenous to Earth or the visitors from elsewhere who come to Earth as they evolve within their own line of development.*

We will explore the Zeta-human relationship more fully as our writings progress.

4

Hidden Motives and Mechanics

LEARNING DRAMAS

We have talked about the Zeta involved with humans at this time who act in *violation of universal law,* which dictates *brotherhood and cooperation.* You exist within a *free-will universe* and because of this freedom there is much greater leeway of experience than in other systems that operate upon a formatted structure of predetermined action. But in a free-will zone there are also drawbacks, from the perspective of security, conformity and "playing by the rules." There are "rules" in operation within all universal structures. These "rules" serve as a primary set of agreements which allow for the contours of a chosen reality to unfold into a platform upon which life dramas (and the experiential learning they allow) can take place. In a free-will zone one of the "rules" or base agreements is that participants within that reality have the choice to "play by the rules" or to ignore them, creating their own versions as they go along. *The rules within your particular system prescribe brotherhood, cooperation and harmony between all portions of reality.*

But the rules also have designed for you a polarized universe, where in all things exist within a duality of perception. It is this feature of your system that allows for the experience of "free will" to take place. Duality allows you the choice of breaking the rules or following, of working with the flow of natural evolution or against it. Each choice will provide for you a consequence of action, or seemingly so from your focus of perception. In greater terms each choice will show you a manifest translation of the ideas you entertain. If those ideas move with the flow of evolution you will experience a perceived state of ease, feelings of lightness and pleasure and you will expand or grow into ever greater reality fields. If you are moving against the flow of evolution you will experience the opposite of these conditions; tension, heaviness, displeasure and contraction, as you digress into ever smaller fields of reality and identity. Both "paths" exist simultaneously; one implies the other. They exist together as parts of a greater whole that is dimensional reality. Your choices

50

will determine experience while you are in a polarized system, and thus you learn to make better choices.

The Zeta who inflict their experiments upon humans without consensual agreements from the soul identity of the human are making a choice to move against the flow of evolution, just as those humans who violate the free will and birthrights of brotherhood of their co-inhabitants of Earth are choosing to digress. Violation ultimately breeds the same, though the "action/consequence" ratio may be spread out over time, where the balance of universal law is not easy to detect. **The Law of Reciprocity** or "What goes around comes around" is *one of the rules* within your universe. It applies directly to all that you do and all that you experience, but in your present state of evolution most of this balancing takes place upon a subconscious level. Because of this many things may seem "senseless" to you. You may witness violation of yourself or others and wonder at the seeming unfairness of the universe or "God." Many of you view death as the ultimate victimization, especially for those who appear to be victims of an untimely or unjust demise. You are seeing the surface of events, and without knowing the greater dramas those surface events are linked to it can often appear that they are without cause or purpose. In viewing from the surface only you may easily misunderstand the seeming "rules" (or lack of them) that allow such apparent violations to take place. Three-dimensional reality can seem quite threatening, unjust and chaotic when viewed from the surface perceptions provided by your five known senses.[1] This is an illusion, very real from your perspective, that seems to be true because the true justice, purpose, reason and order behind events, and the true mechanisms of universal law, are hidden from your view. You do not have "all of the puzzle pieces" to use an analogy, and so it is difficult to "make sense out of the picture." As your race evolves and its perceptual range expands more "puzzle pieces" will be found, and as you grow you will begin to see a very different picture of the universe than the one you presently hold. You will discover the order behind the chaos, the justice within the injustice and the reality behind the illusion.

One day you will come to master the experience of three-dimensional reality and will no longer find yourselves trapped within its confines. But until that time you are dealing with duality, free will, choice and the responsibility of learning how to direct your choices wisely.

The Zeta and all others within the dimensionalized systems are learning these basic lessons, in their own way and through their own path of develop-

---

1. The human organism, in actuality, has twelve senses, five of which you have consciously identified, the remaining seven working subconsciously from your personality's perspective.

ment. Learning can seem difficult when moving against the flow of evolution, or it can be achieved with ease when moving within the flow. Zeta and humans share many of the same lessons, and they will play, within your three-dimensional drama, great teachers to each other and will eventually learn the consequences of maneuvering within the structures of universal law. The consequences can be a great delight or they can seem quite treacherous. Either way learning takes place, and that is why the soul awareness allows for consequences to be experienced. When identity becomes integrated and the human (or other biological being) grows to encompass the soul awareness the need for treacherous outcomes declines. Souls, as groupings of identities, are also learning and reaching for integration of the greater identity structures of which they are a part. The greater the amount of integration of awareness that takes place the less treachery is experienced

All life forms share a common goal of growth and expansion. Impetus toward growth is one of the primary rules within your universe. Growth into comprehension of the mechanics of brotherhood is a "rite of passage" all will eventually pass through; when the interconnectedness of all things is recognized as one of the basic universal laws the cognition and practice of brotherhood will be achieved. Though the Zeta generally are advanced in intellectual growth and technological achievement compared to the human, many of them possess no greater spiritual awareness than the average human of your time. Many Zeta fall behind humans in regard to true spiritual cognition for they do not possess the biological systems that allow for the characteristic you call emotion.

Emotion is far more than you realize. You use this term to describe the perceived result of a subconscious process organic to your form, but you rarely glimpse the reality of that process in energy terms. Emotion is the "product" of the Seventh Sense, which can be called "Cellular Absorption." (We will detail the mechanics of this sense in other writings). It is the ability, present on a cellular level, to filter energy and frequency, create energetic imprints of that filtered energy and translate the imprints into "packages of perception" that are then used to feed information to the other senses. All body mechanisms are regulated through this facility within the human organism, and it allows for the development of tremendous potentials within the human species. The Zeta biology is set up differently. As we previously described the Zeta presently involved with your system are mutations from their original form. That mutation occurred as a result of their experiments in dimensional blending. Originally they did possess a sense facility similar to that of the human emotive structure, which allowed them greater freedom to connect with the universal energy-grid structures that support the third dimension. With the mutation they lost this ability. They became trapped within their own biology and their soul identities became severed from the greater structures from which they had been created. The Zeta were, in essence, cut off from their central power source. Their species became disconnected from the *Soul Matrix*.

THE TREE OF LIFE

All beings within the dimensional systems enter those systems through a web work of interconnected energy strands. There is a precise pattern to systems entry, just as your computers have precise codes of access to their operations. If you imagine the structural growth pattern of branches upon trees you can get a rough visual representation of the energy web work we describe. The tiniest bud is connected to the whole through a system of intricate relays or branches. Nourishment is sent to the bud via this pathway, replenishing and sustaining all of the many buds that grow upon the tree. The energy web work of which the soul (and all of its personalities) is a part can be compared to the network of branches in the trees energy distribution system. Like the bud, the soul exists as one expression or aspect of the greater network out of which it grows. The personalities or incarnations of the soul can be compared to the leaves emerging out of the bud. They are birthed, grow and die only to be replenished and born anew within the next cycle of the seasons. As the leaves exist as part of the tree, each taking up a different placement in space but existing together simultaneously following the cycle of the seasons, so too exist the personalities of the soul. Viewing placement in time for the personality as you view placement in space for the leaves and tree will help you to understand the nature of time and identity. It will also help you to better understand your distorted concept of reincarnation. Humans are connected to a soul that exists as part of a greater network of life. We refer to the entire network as the **Energy Matrix.** The "world within which the tree grows" in our analogy. The tree in our analogy would represent in energy a structure we call the **Time Matrix.** As the tree exists within a world, the Time Matrix exists within the Energy Matrix. The leaves on our tree exist within and emanate out of the bud, just as the personalities exist within and emanate out of the soul. In our analogy the bud would represent what we call the **Soul Matrix** or **Dora Matrix.** Just as the leaf implies the existence of the bud and tree, the fact of your existence implies the existence of a Soul Matrix and Energy Matrix System.

The Zeta are also part of such a "tree of identity." Their species, like your own would represent a bud upon a cosmic tree, in terms of our analogy. We explained before how the Zeta inadvertently collapsed the time portal system surrounding their home planet. You could compare their portal structure to a branch on the tree. If a branch is dismembered from the tree upon which it grows, not only will the branch wither and die, but so will the buds and leaves that depended upon that branch to transport nourishment and life force energy from the tree. There is an intimate connection between the time portal system and the genetic code of all life forms within it. When the time portals are damaged the genetic imprint of biological life is altered, mutated from its original pattern. When the Zeta disengaged their time portals from the main grid of the Time Matrix it caused their mutation. Their biology no longer carries the appropriate codes to allow them to link into their Source. They lost the ability to experience emotion to a large degree, and the emotional facility can be compared to the branch systems of our tree. The Zeta are able to draw energy from their souls, but their souls can no longer draw energy from the Time Matrix, Energy Matrix or Source. Once the leaves fall the bud can no longer renew itself if it cannot draw energy from the tree.

The Zeta are as leaves and buds stunted upon a withering branch that has been severed from the tree. A dying race unless they are able to once again mutate their biological strain into the Time Matrix and the Energy Matrix System. Through genetics they are attempting to create what could be compared to a "splice," taking their fallen branch and reintroducing it to another tree in hope that the "splice" will "take." Their "home tree" exists within another "forest," an area in the galaxy they can no longer return to as the road of transit has been destroyed.

If you can understand a bit more about the nature of your own reality and the Matrices we have mentioned you will be more prepared to comprehend the plight of the Zeta and why they have interest in your race. Perhaps you will be able to forgive them of their violations against you if you can realize it is ignorance and desperation that drive them to use methods that go against the flow of evolution. Just as forgiveness and reeducation are the most appropriate means to deal with fellow humans who cause others violation, so it is too when considering the Zeta. Violation is caused by ignorance to universal law, period! And its only true remedy is growth to awareness and enlightenment. Some Zeta have grown to higher understanding working with the aforementioned Aethien and other groups such as the Ranthia. They have agreed to work in brotherhood under policies of nonviolence and have committed to serving the flow of evolution, for all species, not only their own. These enlightened Zeta are beginning to see how the Law of Reciprocity operates. As they extended fairness, compassion and the desire to cooperate with other forms of life, they found the same gifts being extended on their behalf.

GUARDIAN INTERVENTION

The Aethien and some other advanced interdimensional races agreed to assist the Zeta in creating mutations in their lineage through genetic engineering. Aethien are masters in this regard and with the Zeta they created a plan that would serve the good of all species involved. Previously the Zeta groups attempting to form Zeta-human hybrids were aiming for a being that would function, like humans, within the three-dimensional Earth system. If they were successful in creating such a hybrid yet another species would be entered into the Earth in competition for its resources. This plan was bound to fail and create hardship for the Zeta, the humans and the Earth itself. It would create a battle zone which was not in the best interest of anyone involved. This plan would also create the disaster foretold by your visionary Nostradamus. If the original Zeta plan had been allowed to unfold you would have experienced your own version of "star wars," right upon your Earth. The visions of nuclear holocaust many of your seers "picked up on" came from the future event in which the Zeta invaded Earth because they felt the humans were not capable of working cooperatively and there was no other option but to take the space and resources they needed. This event would have indeed "marked the end of time" as you know it.

We have mentioned before that other intelligence has been watching over your planet since its beginnings. The events of the pending Zeta-human clash were observed by some of these groups as the potential for that probable event moved closer to fulfillment. In the mid 1980s a decision was made by the observers. It was agreed that humans had shown enough growth toward brotherhood and had evolved to at least a minimum degree wherein the scheduled event was worthy of outside intervention. The "watchers" as we will call them, decided to help, as many humans had requested this assistance. Humans who knew some of what was brewing, knew that something dangerous was approaching. The watchers set in motion an alternative plan, enlisting the help of the Aethien, Ranthia, Ashtar and other groups. Some were assigned to helping the humans accelerate their spiritual evolution so they would not react with malice when encountering the Zeta. Others were assigned to assisting the Zeta, and to finding other alternatives for them.

The Aethien and the Ranthia began to work closely with the Zeta. They formulated a plan in which hybrids would be created using human genetic material but this could only be done if the soul identity of the human was in agreement. As the Zeta already possessed some abilities in multidimensional acclimatization an environment better suited to their biology and needs was found. An Earth existing within another dimensional band adjacent to your Earth, but not within the third dimension, was chosen. Certain adjustments would have to be made to the hybrid strain they were developing so as to assist in its transplant to the new environment. The Aethien knew how to orchestrate these alterations. So with the help of numerous groups the Zeta agenda was shifted away from the pending holocaust and toward a peaceful, co-creative, cooperative plan that would open new options for growth for both the human and Zeta lineage. Humans do not presently realize what great times are upon them, nor do they comprehend the scope or meaning of the tragedy they just barely avoided. You, as humans, do not yet realize what gratitude is in order. The majority of Zeta in your system now work toward brotherhood, and with the Aethien, Ranthia and others offer whatever assistance they can to humans on the quest of enlightenment. Most Zeta can be trusted, but it is difficult for them to convey this sentiment to those humans they interact with because they are so often met with fear, anger and violent reactions due to human misunderstanding.

Even though most Zeta can now be trusted in their dealings with humans, there are certain factions of the race who have not yet agreed to the new agenda. We refer to these factions simply as the "unenlightened Zeta." The unenlightened ones are those responsible for numerous abductions in which pain was caused to the human; not merely frightening encounters and mild testing, but actual physical or mental harm. We are not happy to inform you that quite a few of your mentally ill population became impaired as a result of the activities of the unenlightened groups. Because soul agreements are not involved in such abductions the Zeta responsible had little clue as to what tactics were useful, and what was harmful. They experimented randomly, such as your scientists do with laboratory rats.

Some of your "missing persons" cases are also caused by these intrusions. For a time the unenlightened ones did not comprehend the genetic orientation of the human, and did not know of the aforementioned Silicate Matrix within some of the populace. They assumed that all humans could undergo dimensional transmigration. Numerous subjects were lost in attempting to transport them into craft stationed beyond the third-dimensional frequencies. Some were actually lost in time, thrown into the past or future of your time continuum, because the relationships between the time portals and the human genetic structure were not understood by these groups. Certain cases (but not all) of "spontaneous combustion" reported in your present time occurred at the hands of Zeta, abduction attempts that "went wrong."

These travesties took place (and still occasionally do) because of Zeta ignorance to the human structure, and because no attempt was made by them to contact the soul identities of the human subjects. Like many humans, many Zeta do not understand the reality of their connection to soul, and because they do not comprehend this reality in themselves they do not validate it within other life forms. The enlightened Zeta are learning of these things from the Aethien and Ranthia. Those who are willing to learn, and there are many, are being trained in contact procedures that do not violate the integrity of the human subjects. The groups who are working toward brotherhood can be easily identified as there will always be among them the Aethien, Ranthian (who sometimes take on human guise during working with humans) or Zionite (as previously discussed) guardians, serving as hosts, advisors, teachers, healers or in positions of command.

It is important that humans become aware of the Zeta presence, and learn to distinguish between the enlightened groups and those that may bring them harm. One tactic of differentiation that is useful during abduction encounters is that of holding in mind (Zeta can see your mental pictures) the image of one of the guardian races (see Guardian images, page lvi). If you are dealing with an enlightened Zeta you will be greeted with a response of curiosity and positive acknowledgment. If it *is* an unenlightened Zeta the reaction will be one of tension and a "hands-off" stance, as the Zeta who are aware of the guardians and have chosen not to cooperate are intimidated by them. When dealing with Zeta who do not know of these overseers, you may still hold the image in mind and request assistance. Zeta still have a strong link to the collective Zeta mind. Though they now operate independently you can still reach the collective by projecting your thoughts through one of its individual members. The impression will be picked up by one of the helping groups if it is strong enough. Zeta manipulate through the mind, and humans must learn to do "mind-to-mind combat" and to redirect the harmful Zeta rather than attempt to destroy them. They cannot be fought successfully by humans, but they can be redirected to haggling it out with their own kind. The enlightened Zeta and the groups working with them are the humans best allies in protecting themselves from the harmful Zeta. The enlightened groups are doing the best they can to redirect their strayed brethren to the new benign agenda. Humans engaged in encounters with the tormentors are urged to assist in this redirection. Reactions of fear, anger and panic will do nothing to protect you, but staying centered in your own identity with the intention of redirecting the abductors will prove well worth your while. In helping yourself you will be helping others also, a universal law in operation. Humans are being called upon to pass on this vision of hope to those who need it most—the abductors who have yet to learn the wisdom of co-creative brotherhood—and their fellow humans who are learning the same lessons.

ZETA CONSPIRACY

The Zeta following the old agenda believe themselves to be desperate. They are weakening—their bodies and abilities are failing. Though the majority of Zeta have transferred to the new agenda there are still several hundred thousand following the old plan, both in your dimension and in those surrounding it. Collectively they still represent quite a force, a force that can impact your future adversely if it is allowed to go unchecked. They are presently trying to orchestrate, through the workings of your Interior Government (previously discussed), a travesty upon your species. The humans involved in this scheme are blinded by the pursuit of power and domination. And it is because of their involvement and willing participation that the old agenda still looms as a potential threat to your system. Though much assistance is being offered to your species from the guardian races the events you encounter will still be the consequences of your choices, individually and collectively.

How many of your numbers will blindly follow the dictates of leadership, a leadership that unknowingly grows more and more influenced by the presence of the Interior Government? How many will have the courage and ability to poke their heads above the programming enough to begin asking the right questions? How many will dare to believe stories such as this, that challenge everything the program has taught you to believe? How many humans will embrace the value of their personal essence and follow it into spiritual awakening? The answers to these questions will determine what reality awaits you as you proceed into the 21st Century.

Presently your Interior Government thinks it is manipulating the Zeta (it has been working with them on the old agenda for several decades). These humans have as their human agenda a quest for world power. These humans think nothing of betraying their own people (as they have done in the past and continue to do), seeing "lesser" humans (in their minds) as expendable resources and Zeta as tools through which they can bring about their plan of global dominion. You would be frightened if we told you of some of the things that have been and are presently being done. Many of you would not believe us so conditioned have you become to unthinkingly accepting what "authorities and experts" tell you. *Choosing to think and question* is a *choice*, and like its opposite, will have consequences.

The Interior Government factions plan to continue to "cooperate" with the Zeta, allowing them to take what they desire from the human populace in return for technological and genetic advancements (this group of humans would love to "live forever," since they have little true spiritual comprehension—death is viewed as their greatest defeat. They are nearly obsessed with techniques, genetic or otherwise, that will prolong life span and deter biological deterioration. Advantages they are seeking to horde for themselves, of course.) They employ UFO debunking and witness character assassination tactics, (and occasionally witness assassination) to provide a cloak of secrecy for the Zeta following the old agenda. They are dangerous people, (as our translator may find when our books begin to circulate), with many resources, but they are a minority. There is no safety in blindness, only blindness. Safety comes from awareness and making appropriate choices, informed choices, and that is precisely what the Interior Government does not want the masses to be capable of doing. They prefer to keep you distracted, and will create all sorts of political, economic, and environmental strategies aimed at fueling controversy, internal conflict and other preoccupations so the public does not have time or energy to notice that information on many things is being withheld and misrepresented. Be aware of the tactics being used, for they are employed to sidetrack you from the covert agenda that will affect every one of you more than you know. Does availability of money affect you? Does personal security for yourself and loved ones affect you? Does your biological and psychological health affect you? For these are the specific areas through which they plan to manipulate you on a mass level. The old agenda is much larger than you suspect, and it has been progressively employed in stages. This plan is still being carried out by those involved. On the surface you may see "still waters," or perhaps a little ripple here and there just so things look natural enough, but did you ever think of what might lurk within the murky depths of the collective world government infrastructure? You have probably been too busy with "more important things," just as you have been programmed to be.

The Interior Government has approximately 100,000 key members globally at the time of this writing—no small enterprise. We are referring here to its human members. Many others are involved but do not consciously know what they are submerged within. Once in, members rarely get out...alive. This may sound like some sort of plot from a communist regime, but it is in operation beneath the democracies of the world also. At least within the dictatorships the common people know they are not free and can make their choices accordingly. But in the democracies of the world the people believe in the freedoms provided by their constitutions and judicial systems. They believe they are free, and in one sense they are—free from knowing that they are being compromised by an Interior Elite. Free from knowing what they are being subjected to at the hands of these hidden directors. Free to think that they alone are controlling their own destiny as they struggle to evolve within the status quo. Who do you think would benefit the most from having the public believe that UFOs were hoaxes and aliens imaginary? The public? Do you really think your national or personal security is being protected by having the public kept in the dark about the fact that humans are *not* the only *or* most intelligent form of life in the universe?

Wouldn't you rather know the truth? Why do you think the truth is being kept from you? Who would benefit most? Questions you might choose to ponder if you ever have time for such things.

These statements may anger many of you, those of you who love your free countries and the liberties they stand for. It would reduce you to tears if you knew the truth of what goes on behind the back of your official governments.

So preoccupied are your people with the surface issues that few look deep enough or far enough to begin to see the scheming that takes place "underground and behind closed doors." Those who get close often "disappear," meet with a "terrible accident" or decide to conveniently "kill themselves." We are not joking. We are not exaggerating. Does this sound like democracy to you? In our opinion it is an indignity to the concept and a desecration to the good-hearted people who would put their lives on the line to uphold their country's virtue. And so we tell you of some of the truths you may not want to hear. Now we will tell you more; for those who desire to understand.

The Interior Government plans to use the Zeta they pretend to co-operate with for their technology and knowledge, and when they feel confident enough in using these new acquisitions they plan to overpower the Zeta in their weakened condition. Then they hope to further implement their plans of directing and controlling global resources. The Zeta, however, are far better at this game of strategic manipulation, and have been covertly manipulating the human element within the Interior Government since the beginning of their involvement.

HOLOGRAPHIC INSERTS

One type of technology that is presently being shared by the Zeta is the artificial creation through mechanical means of **Holographic Inserts** (See page 27). (Zeta are able to initiate this tactic using mental applications and without mechanical devices. They have not divulged these methods to the humans but instead convinced them that human biology was not equipped to create that level of implementation, which is only partially true.) This covert Zeta and human team is planning to utilize this technology to manipulate and direct large masses of people. And they are orchestrating it in a way that will "hit home" with the gentlest of souls. Holographic Inserts depicting religious personages and dramas have already been employed in small doses, as test runs for the greater applications. Faking "miracles," appearances of saints and holy ones, the return of deceased loved ones, all of these personally sacred subjects are fair game to the exploitation of holographic inserts. Plans are in the making to stage dramas using the traditional as well as "new age" belief systems. True "miracles," and visitations will also be occurring as this century closes and will continue well into the next. How will you know which events are real and which events are being manufactured to manipulate the populace? How will you know who or what to believe when you won't even be able to fully trust what your five senses are telling you? Is there a way to detect a holographic insert or to protect yourself from being victimized by them? We will address these questions and more in the following sections.

If our perspective seems radical to you, upsetting and unsettling, we apologize. It is hoped that you can understand the concern and indignation on your behalf from which we speak. There are many beings, both human and otherwise willing and able to assist you in your growth and spiritual development. There are many positive agendas taking place within your external government, scientific and religious communities that provide needed assistance, growth opportunities and support to the public. And there is a wealth of kindhearted, just, spiritually aware people throughout your world whose dedication, love and wisdom serve to uplift and inspire your species toward fulfillment of its vision of brotherhood. These positive forces, combined with a treasury of support "behind the scenes" from within the multidimensional and multi-universal systems, continue to move humanity forward in its evolution despite the efforts of the Interior Forces to thwart them. You are progressing well in your development toward enlightenment, and we commend you.

If we did not fully believe that humans were capable of fulfilling the role for which they were created, the role of Earth guardian and conscious co-creators of reality, we would not labor to bring you information you will need in your journey to success. Unlike those who attempt to hold you back, we do not underestimate your intelligence, your fortitude and your ability to become responsible for the direction in which your destiny unfolds. We believe in your innate goodness and honor you for the noble beings that, in truth, you are. Let us remind you of that nobility so that you may rediscover the beauty of your race and allow that beauty to burst forth into the universe renewing all that it touches. May you, yourselves, be renewed in resurrecting the majesty of your multidimensional being.

Next we will explore the current Interior agenda of holographic inserts and how these will be used in an attempt to direct you away from the truth and integrity that live within you.

FREQUENCY FENCES

The technology of the holographic insert holds great promise for furthering the development of your species. This ability, even if it was mechanically created would revolutionize every aspect of your society. It would also begin to open your abilities to traverse your localized time portal system. The Zeta have not provided the data necessary for the time portals to be activated. They do not want the Interior Government or any other humans to have access to a working knowledge of these systems. Instead they have provided some information to the Interior forces, to appease them, but this data is distorted and incomplete. So the Interior as well as the exterior scientific communities still struggle with "sending things back in time" and "making them disappear" (Some progress has been made in the case of the latter). The Zeta are utilizing the Interior's greed for power. They are helping to orchestrate the utilization of holographic inserts on large masses of people. Though the Interior Government thinks the Zeta are assisting them to put in place certain mass "frequency control devices" that will eventually have the power to "scramble" selected human brain wave patterns, thereby blocking out frequencies coming from sources outside of government control (such as those transmitted by ET and other dimensional groups, and also the frequency patterns emanating from the personal and collective Soul Matrix) but the Zeta are in actuality working toward orchestration of a different plan.

Zeta are helping to create this "frequency fence" but not in order to assist the Interior Government in creating a docile and obedient populace. The Interior desires to control the mental and emotional forces within the populace in order to use individuals and masses to do their bidding. They are interested in creating a form of "Super Soldier" that will be able to easily neutralize simple human armies. By setting itself up as the "Invisible Big Brother" they will not only be able to horde and control the distribution of Earth's resources, but they hope to be able to "explore and conquer" new territories once the time portal codes are activated. Their purpose is to plunder for personal gain and for the "thrill of the kill" in bringing others under their dominion. Other abusive forces that do exist within the universe watch them with amusement, as the Interior is playing right into their hands.

As the Interior moves silently forward with its plan of dominion their Zeta "helpers" are using them to help fulfill their personal agenda. The Interior is more concerned with keeping people distracted, fragmented and confused, so they do not notice that their freedom is being stolen out from under them. The unenlightened Zeta have something else in mind. These factions of the Zeta race, resigning themselves to the probability that they would reach extinction before finding a way to return to their own planet and time continuum decided to opt for the "next best solution." If they could cultivate hybrids acclimated to the Earth environment they would be able to repopulate the planet. There is one small obstacle in the way of this plan, however—the presence of the human race. Other species could easily be dominated and integrated into a Zeta regulated society. But humans will not be easy to subdue, and the Zeta know this. The Zeta acknowledge their present dependence upon the species for the provision of genetic material. They have a plan of segregating the global population into those possessing desirable genetic qualities and those who do not have qualities they care to reproduce. The humans chosen as breeders would be utilized to create a work force to supply Zeta needs and the "best among them" genetically would be used to create various strains of hybrid beings to strengthen and re-colonize their settlement on Earth

Humans presently do not have the power to successfully ward off the Zeta through force. The planet would be plundered in the attempt to do so. Humans greatest defense is becoming aware of what is taking place and uniting their energies with those willing to assist in the name of universal brotherhood. The renegade Zeta must not be permitted to fulfill their plan. Though this plan is still in its early stages within your three-dimensional Earth system, this is not the case in several parallel and adjacent systems. One adjacent system in particular has been fully infiltrated and those controlling that reality have their sights set upon expanding into your three-dimensional Earth system at a time coordinate that exists within your future. Humans that enjoy their present levels of freedom within the democracies of Earth and those who believe in the liberties of a free society had best take heed of the events now occurring within that adjacent system as the groundwork for its interception is presently being set within your global community by the Interior Government forces. We will elaborate upon this adjacent Earth system in sections to follow, but for now we will return to our discussion of holographic inserts and how they are presently being used to direct the perceptions of your people.

Previously we mentioned that holographic inserts using themes popular within your traditions were being used in "test runs" of the project. Most of these tests were orchestrated using individuals or small groups of people, in which scenarios pertinent to these subjects were created and the emotional reaction patterns of the participants were studied. Attention is paid to perceptual range of the human subject as the Zeta are aware that are great variations among the populace in regard to perceptual ability. They are attempting to find a consensual mean of frequency through which they can broadcast the holograms and hope to use the frequency fence to block out frequency bands that do not fall within that average range. In this way large masses of people can be "tuned into" the particular range of the holographic insert and blocked from receiving frequency that would create sense data that was in contradiction to the illusion of the insert.

The inserts are being designed to engage the emotional facilities of the human. Themes deeply engraved within the minds of the people are being contrived into distorted interpretations of events that have basis in reality for the subjects. As Zeta have time portal access they have been able to monitor some of the activities of the other ET, interdimensional and guardian groups who are planning to create encounters with humans for purposes of helping the populations to grow and evolve successfully.

Though the Zeta will not be able to stop these helping groups, or halt the implementation of the events they plan to create, they are able to scan the intended events and create distorted versions of them through the holographic inserts. Over the next twenty years alignments of certain key time portal structures are occurring, following the cycle intrinsic to your planetary placement within the galactic grid. These alignments make it easier for data to be entered into your system from other times and other dimensions. Many of the helping groups intend to use this opportunity to introduce new information and technologies that will assist in the evolution of your species. The Zeta and the Interior are aware of this and they do not want this information to be made available to the masses as it is intended. They are planning now to "raid" certain of the positive agendas creating misleading holographic inserts that will direct the perceptions and thoughts of the populace away from the applications of the positive agendas.

The Zeta are using images, scenarios and personages held sacred to the traditional religions to divert the people into submission, subservience and blind obedience to the official and covert governments. Philosophies that rely upon congregational following of authorities, in which people are taught to trust the leaders interpretation of spirituality above their own spiritual comprehension (a practice coloring most of the world's traditional religions), are primary targets for manipulation using holographic inserts. The Christian and Jewish faiths, along with some Eastern practices and traditions popular within the South American continent have been singled out as primary testing grounds for the implementation of holographic inserts on a mass level. People who blindly follow the dictates of these traditions and those who lead them are especially vulnerable to holographic manipulation. David Koresh and the Waco, Texas, Branch Davidians and Marshall Applewhite and the Heaven's Gate group are two such organizations that have been manipulated by the unenlightened Zeta through holographic insert technology. The inserts have been and will be used to lead people away from the true divinity that lives within them and from any true spiritual connection.

The desired result of this manipulation is to sever the actual energetic connection of the individual to the personal Soul Matrix and reconnect the individual to a "group mind" network existing within another dimensional structure. The Zeta are well aware of the multidimensional operation of the **Collective Mind** as their own species existed for centuries under such a structure. Though the mechanics of this endeavor are complex, the concept is simple. All people exist as individualized embodiments of a greater energetic identity. This greater identity can be viewed as the portion of their conscious awareness that is too large in energy volume to "fit into" the limited confines of the body structure. The body, and the consciousness focused within it exist within this greater pool of energy, and it is this energy that creates the body, sets the autonomic body processes, and continually feeds the body life force energy.

There are certain structures that link the body, mind and emotions to this Soul Matrix of energy. (See "The Tree of Life" on page 53.) It is possible, for those who understand how to manipulate the subtle energy bodies, to "splice" an individual from one Soul Matrix into another matrix, and disconnect the bio-energetic circuitry from the original soul. This process can be used to assist individuals under certain conditions, but it can also be used to disable them from connecting with their greater identity and innate spiritual connection. When used in negative applications you could view this process as "soul robbing," as the physical embodiment is "stolen" from its original Soul Matrix. This is precisely what the Zeta have in mind as part of their agenda. By linking those selected from the human populace into a "false matrix:" (part of the original Zeta Collective Mind Matrix), humans would be easily controlled as the false matrix would continually sustain certain holographic inserts making them appear as "permanent" features of reality. Any sensually illusional reality could be sustained in such a way, and the humans involved would have no idea or memory indicating that anything was out of order.

As the individual becomes disconnected from its original soul matrix all memory contained within its DNA and cellular pattern is wiped away, as it is the Soul Matrix that acts as the programming device and storage house for human memory. When the human is fully connected to the false matrix, the original connection to the soul can then be disengaged, and the new matrix will program the DNA and "download" the "memories" purposely programmed into the false matrix. At this point in the process there would be a brief lapse of all memory, and a minor disability in short term memory functions, while the cellular code begins to process its new set of instructions. There may be trace memories from the "original soul program" that arise to awareness in "ghost image" form, which will occasionally create severe mental disturbances for the human subject. Pieces of memory from the old program may emerge spontaneously from cellular residue and interface with the operational "instructions" from the new program, distorting the electrical impulse patterns to the brain, as well as the chemical balances of the human biology.

In severe cases the individual will be unable to hold a consistent present-moment focus in time, and will "flip back and forth" between a multitude of "identity fragments" that represent pieces of memory from both residual traces of the old Soul Matrix (not only memory bits from the individual but also from the entire bank of identities stored in the Soul Matrix) and fragmented pieces of the new program and the entire contents of the Zeta Collective false matrix. The human biology is not designed to assimilate such an onslaught of inconsistent electrical data and will be biologically unable to process the memory fragments into a coherent focus of identity in time. Should the unenlightened Zeta

65

plan from the old agenda reach fulfillment your populace would literally be robbed of its individual and collective memory, creating "biological puppets" that the Zeta could program in any way they choose. In this way they will be able to take advantage of certain "desirable" strains of humans while easily controlling them by directing the contours of their individual and mass identities.

The complexity of orchestrating a "mental takeover" on a species level is vast, but it has been done before at different times within all of the dimensions. The aftermath of such a project is always disastrous in the long run, for the planet and local galactic structure as well as for the life forms existing within those systems. There are areas within the intergalactic and multidimensional grid that at different times have literally been blown out of the grid and cut off from the reality fields of which they were a part. Like humans and other biological individuals, planets and galaxies also possess a Soul Matrix, of which the Soul Matrices of all the systems inhabitants are a part. All of these grids or matrices are created through and connected to the Time Matrix. (See "The Tree of Life" on page 53.) The Time Matrix is the energy distribution system which carries life force energy from Source into the dimensional systems.

When a planet or galaxy is "blown out of the grid" of its Soul Matrix, which directly connects it to the Time Matrix and thus perpetual energy supply, its energy and its evolutionary potentials become finite. The system falls into digression, and as its finite energy quotient is expended the system has no way to replenish its supply. The existing energy is recycled within the system, but will eventually become negated as the recycling continually reduces the "thrust" or power contained within its particles. The matter forms within such a system deplete, atrophy and eventually (sometimes over hundreds of thousands of years) implode, their "blueprint" (and thus the possibility of regeneration or replication) fragmented into unorganized units of energy and consciousness. This fragmented energy is the state of being indicated by your concept of *oblivion*. It is the condition your religious concept of **Hades** or **Hell** was intended to depict, in symbolic form. (Your concept of **Purgatory** describes the experience of living within a system that was cut off from the grid, before its pending implosion. It has also been used to indicate the state of being for the personality who has become severed from its own Soul Matrix.)

ZETA PLANET DESTRUCTION

All within the Time Matrix grid is interconnected, and when a planet or galaxy is blown off the grid a *hole* is left within the grid "fabric." This hole affects everything within the area of activity surrounding the hole, as energy flowing around the broken grid lines hits "blank spots" or breaks in the pattern. The grid lines within the Time Matrix represent **Time Continua**, or "passageways of linear time sequencing." When energy approaches the hole in the fabric of the Time Matrix it is magnetically pulled into the hole. Once it enters the hole the time sequence organization that it originally carried as part of the Time Matrix becomes scrambled and the energy is no longer able to reenter the Time Matrix from the position in which it first entered the hole. This "energy" can take the form of an individual in biological form, a personal Soul Matrix or "soul," a planet or galaxy or the entire galactic Soul Matrix. When one element from within a given time continuum enters the hole, its own sequential program will serve as a "beacon" for all other energies possessing that particular coding. This beacon not only "broadcasts" its signal back into the Time Matrix through its electrical particles (which act as transmitters) but it also begins to draw in like energy through its magnetic particles (which act as magnetic receivers). The element lost within the hole then pulls in more and more energy from its home system. The "holes" we are referring to are, of course, the phenomena you describe as **Black Holes**.

As described in previous sections, the Zeta originally entered your system as they searched for solutions involving conditions that occurred upon their own planet, Apaxein Lau. The "conditions" the Zeta hoped to remedy are precisely those described above. Through their experimentation with dimensional frequency blending they created a situation in which a minute hole was ripped into the "frequency pattern" of the regions involved in the dimensional merge. The intended merger of dimensional fields was not successful as the hole would not allow the area of frequency blending to stabilize into a consistent particle code pattern that would allow for a stable linear time sequence to take hold. The blended-dimension reality field was kept open for several hundred years before the Zeta became aware of the hole. A great amount of energy from this blended region "fell into" the hole and systematically pulled in more and more energy.

Black Holes will pull in first those forms that possess energy coding that is consistent with the coding of the particles that exist at the site of the hole. That is, the items to first disappear are those who's particle structures are in the continuum, or "grid strand," where the break in pattern has occurred. In the Zeta incident this particle compatibility emerged within certain elemental components of the outer atmosphere of their home planet. Over centuries there became an obvious depletion of this elemental component within their atmosphere, which is what led the Zeta to suspect that there was a problem with their dimensional blending project. The hole was finally located and identified by observing the rate and form of depletion of controlled samples of the outer atmosphere. The depletion rate was accelerated when the samples were placed in various locations upon the planet. They were able to pinpoint the hole by observing particle movement and "following the path" of accelerated particle depletion for the element in question. They were able to "follow the beacons" emitted by the particles within the hole but only to a certain point at which the beacons (minute electrical emissions) would disappear. It took several generations to discover that these particles were pulling in an exponentially expansive quantity of matter. The particles would disappear as the "scrambling" of their base time code structure occurred. The original code was unraveled, its elements disbursed within the reality fields of the black hole.

The Zeta realized that this condition was a result of the dimensional blend, and so they hoped that by "undoing" the blend and closing the mediation zone between the dimensional portals that had been forced open, that they could effectively disengage the black hole. What they did not realize is that once a hole is created it will continue to exist until all energy that passed through it is reclaimed and restored to its original time sequence organization. They were able to close the mediation zone effectively, and when they observed the area where the hole had been the hole was no longer there. The Zeta assumed that they had closed the hole when they closed the mediation zone territories in which it had existed. This was not the case. The mediation zone had been created by merging certain frequency patterns of the third-dimensional and other dimensional versions of their planet. The frequency patterns of each were "bent" slightly until they came into range of each other. Then an artificial "frequency splice" was added to serve as a bridge between the two frequency bands. This bridge forced open an existing dimensional portal and kept it open as long as the bridge was in place (this is a manipulation process that goes against universal law, as it throws the entire time cycle of which it is a part out of synchronization with the Time Matrix). The black hole was still encoded within the frequency patterns of both dimensions, and when the bridge was closed the hole pattern fragmented, changing location within the outer atmosphere of both planets. Again it took generations to rediscover the continued existence and new location of the hole, and by this time the genetic mutations that this project had initiated began to show themselves.

Knowing that the hole was responsible for their declining species, they hoped to retrieve and reorganize the lost energies so as to reverse the genetic mutation and restore health to their species. Though they had the technology to *seal off* the hole and stop it from pulling energy, they did not do this because the hope of reversing the mutation was within retrieving the energy from the hole and permanently closing the structure. The Zeta could no longer reside within their planet's atmosphere and so they decided to evacuate and temporarily relocate to another planet within an adjacent dimension to their own, where they could continue with the project of retrieving the energies from the hole. They had not planned on anyone "raiding their project," but that is what took place. Other, more advanced groups within the surrounding galaxy knew the danger of keeping the black hole opened. It was pulling energy at an alarming rate and posed a serious threat to the entire Time Matrix coordinate that was home to the Zeta and many others. The black hole was *sealed*, a process which took time, and accelerated its magnetism. The Zeta home planet and it dimensional counterpart were "sucked in," leaving only a small portion of the planetary Soul Matrix behind within the Time Matrix. It is through this event that the Zeta became trapped within your system, and the others to which it had migrated. Literally homeless and rapidly declining, they had no choice but to seek other solutions.

We hope that this little story about the Zeta will serve as education to your scientists who play with small particle mechanics before they have the knowledge to understand the consequences of their actions.

HOLOGRAPHIC INSERTS AND MATRIX TRANSPLANTATION

Now we will resume our discussion about the Zeta plan to use holographic inserts and matrix transplantation to orchestrate a "mental takeover" of the human species. When a "soul robbery" or forced matrix transplant occurs (when the human is removed from its connection to its organic Soul Matrix and connected to another, for example) the "cord" of energy that once connected the human to the Soul Matrix is "left hanging," so to speak. This cord spews energy from the Soul Matrix, just as your finger would spew blood if the tip was severed. If this energy leakage is not stopped the Soul Matrix itself would become depleted, as well as the energy structures that feed it, and a large buildup of energy would occur within the planetary grid. This energy buildup would follow the path of the particles carrying its code. The human who had been "transplanted" to another matrix structure would be natural receiver of this energy. As the biological structure of the human is "close circuited" into the new matrix, the energy would then be drawn into the other dimensional Earth version, or "parallel universe," and to the individual residing in that system who represents the implied counterpart to the human living within your system. We will not go into the mechanics of universal physics in this transmission, so it is enough that we say here that you have a "reflection," "double," or "doppleganger" (as some in your system call it), residing within a parallel system, that represents the "antiparticle" to your "particle." This double is often called the "light body" in your times, or sometimes the "shadow." Both terms can be misleading so we will use the terminology with which we are familiar. We refer to the double as the **Dolar Imprint** or **Dolus** for short. In other writings we will elaborate upon the Dolus and its counterpart. For now, what you need to know to follow our discussion is that the Dolus will be the recipient of that "spewing" energy from the forced matrix transplant.

This errant energy will emerge within a portion of the double's "subtle energy bodies." Humans (and other biological organisms) are connected to the Soul Matrix by "strands" or "cords" of energy. The cord runs from the core unit of identity for that person as held within the Soul Matrix, and extends outward to a "sac" at its end. Some in your time refer to this sac as the "tissue capsule"; we call it the **Nadial Capsule** or the **Nadis**. The Nadis is a literal "sac" of energy that surrounds your physical body. It contains all of the life force energy you will use in one lifetime as a single incarnation in time and space. The process of growth, in your terms, is the process of bringing the energies from within the Nadis through into the biological form, *thus expanding that form.* As energy leaves the Nadis and enters into the body it must first pass through the two inner layers of the Nadis. These inner nadial structures are known in your time as the **Mental** and **Emotional Bodies**, and they give to you the qualities of being you know as mental awareness, or "thinking," and emotional cognition, or "feeling."[2]

The errant energies spewing from the severed cord are rechanneled into the Dolus, (other dimensional double) through its center point. (The excess energy stimulates the opening of the center point within the Dolus). These energies then become a part of the "subtle energy bodies" of the double, first entering the mental area then filtering into the emotional body. If the physical body of the double does not rapidly expand (which it cannot do if blocks in the mental body are present) to accommodate the new energy this energy will build up within the emotional body of the double as erratic electrical impulse which will throw the emotional balance "out of whack" and with it the chemical and hormonal balances within the physical body. If left unchecked this condition will cause acceleration of the aging process as the erratic patterns block the clear flow of energy from the Nadis. If the double is able to reactivate the center point (located near the heart region in the physical body, somewhat to

---

2. As energy moves from the Soul Matrix to form the Nadis it "starts at the center" expanding the Nadis outward from that central point. The body forms within a certain portion of this expansion and the center point "closes." The growth process involves bringing in energy from the expanded regions of the Nadis. When the full supply is used outer layers of the Nadis collapse, chemical and hormonal patterns shift, and the body begins the "aging process," using up the Nadial energy now stored within the mental and emotional bodies and cellular structure. Natural death occurs when there is no longer enough energy left within cellular structure to sustain the body mechanisms. However, if the center point is activated new energy can be brought into the Nadis and it can be expanded beyond its original form. This renewed energy will pass from the center point into the mental then emotional bodies and into the physical body, then outward into the Nadial Capsule. We will deal with this subject more fully in another transmission/book.

the right of the heart, and often called the **heart chakra**), opening the channel for new energy from the Soul Matrix to flow in, the new soul energy will reorganize the errant patterns, if it can get through the mental body patterns. "Expanding your mind" is no joke—it is a very important energy process. The soul energy will then regulate the flow of the errant energy into and through the body, in a way more harmonious to its rhythms The energy will then pass into the Nadis where the body can draw from it within its own rhythm pattern. If the double cannot reactivate the center point, and "connect with soul" (open its energy systems to that of the Soul Matrix) the double will experience emotional distress and imbalance which will lead to disease of the body and early death. In this case, there will be energy left within the Nadis that the body was unable to process. The double in the other dimension (the one who received the forced matrix transplant) is no longer available to receive the energy, and so the energy becomes trapped within that dimension, where it must wait until the time cycles allow it to reintegrate with its Soul Matrix.

The identity (individual human, for example) and its Dolus (double) exist as one "identity package" within the Soul Matrix. There are twelve such identity packages within one Soul Matrix, each being extended into different time/space continuums within the dimensional system.[3] All of these "identity packages," which we call "aspects" or **Tauren** exist at once within the Soul Matrix and Time Matrix, each experiencing its own line of linear development within its respective time-space location. This group of twelve constitutes the Soul Family, and the existence of one aspect (person) implies the existence of the other eleven aspects. The soul family, which we call the **Dora** moves in cyclic fashion within the Time Matrix. Within those cycles each aspect has its own smaller cycle that constitutes its passage through time, or its life span. There is a sequential relationship to the aspect or Tauren cycles, which implies a correlation between the births and deaths of its incarnates (Tauren/aspects). In the case of "soul robbery" through forced matrix transplant, the early demise of the double/Dolus affects the entire Soul Matrix cycle (we call the cycles of the Soul Matrix the **Aundanct Cycles** and the smaller aspect cycles the **Tauren Cycles**). All of the Tauren are accelerated in their rhythms and all will reach depletion of cellular energy sooner than they would have otherwise. All will thus leave residual nadial energy within their respective dimensions which will become trapped there unless at least one of the Tauren are able to activate the center point and accelerate their physical body enough to allow the residual energies of all of

---

3. Your somewhat distorted concept of "reincarnation" is an attempt to describe this relationship and its dynamics.

the other Tauren to be expanded into their own nadial field. If one is able to perform this feat and complete its own nadial composition, then the Soul Matrix can move out of the dimensional bands involved. The Soul Matrix can evolve in this case. The Soul Matrix cannot leave the dimensional octave it is in until all of its residual energies are pulled back into the Soul Matrix. So you can see, if the Zeta implement their plan of forced matrix transplant upon large numbers of humans, a vast number of other individuals *and soul* Families/Dora/Soul Matrices will be adversely affected. They will become stuck within their positions in the Time Matrix and unable to evolve until those trapped energies are released.

Perhaps now you will be able to comprehend the serious nature of our communications. Much is at stake within this human/Zeta drama, most of which humans do not understand. The events and practices we have mentioned in this section all have direct bearing upon the future of your system, and the plan to begin the aforementioned "mental takeover" is now beginning to emerge within your three-dimensional Earth system. We have explained some of the methods by which this takeover will be orchestrated, from its inception through holographic inserts to its culmination in the Zeta Collective Mind link up through forced matrix transplant. This is the plan that humans can help to redirect, by making a strong, genuine connection to their own Soul Matrix/Dora and learning to handle themselves within holographic inserts and Zeta abductions. These things are already going on around you, whether or not you are aware of them, whether or not you choose to believe that it is true. Those who understand can do a great deal to assist themselves, their Soul Families and their fellow humans if they are willing to grow, expand and learn.

You might wonder how such a massive "mental takeover" could be pulled off "behind your backs" so to speak.

It is more so being done "over your heads" literally, as the manipulations involved are being conducted, to a large degree from dimensional frequency bands that are higher than the range of your perceptions. This is a plan that will take time to implement, so the sooner you are aware of these events the sooner you will be able to redirect your future

In the following sections we will cover methods by which you can protect yourselves from being brought under the control of the aforementioned "frequency fence." We will offer suggestions as to how holographic inserts can be maneuvered and also some clues to look for that will allow you to watch the progression of the events of which we speak.

In closing this section let us leave you with one final example of how this plan will be implemented, an example that may illustrate the power of the holographic insert to persuade human perception.

What do you suppose might happen if ten thousand devout Christians suddenly saw "Christ" float down upon a cloud (or a spaceship). The skies tremble and open and the savior, in the flesh, levitates down and begins to touch the heads of his beloved. Then he says "Come with me to the promised kingdom," as a brilliant set of "pearly gates" appears behind him. "Follow" he utters as he turns and begins to walk through the gates. *Do you think most of those devotees would say "no"?* And who would be the wiser, (except those creating the holographic insert), if those masses passed beyond the gates in ecstasy only to be marched through a dimensional portal. A portal their biological forms are not prepared to encounter. Who would mourn those people as they entered the portal and were incinerated upon contact, their bodies destroyed and their consciousness fragmented into the ethers while onlookers watched them move joyfully through the gates of heaven?

A rather ingenious way to evacuate a planet of "undesirables" to clear the real estate for resettlement. Even those who did not go would not believe that anything bad had happened. The masses simply "went with Christ to the promised lands," as had been foretold. *This is what a holographic insert can do!* And some of the Zeta, the unenlightened ones following the old agenda, are quite capable of this type of travesty. Not only are they capable of this, this is precisely the type of holographic drama they have planned once the "frequency fence" is in place.

If you find security in the concept of being "sheep," then please, *make sure you know who your shepherd is!*

5

Awareness, Emotion, and Intuition

AWARENESS

In presenting this material we are not trying to frighten or mislead you, but we are trying to help those who are ready to become *aware*. Your true "salvation," protection and power will come through *awareness*, not through subjugation of self to illusions of outside authority. It takes courage to become aware and choose to look beyond the pat answers your culture has offered you for so long. Many of the problems presently facing humans are not created by humans alone. You have been left blind to the outside involvement that has influenced your development throughout history. Involvement of races of beings from other dimensions and other galactic origins. You presently have little idea of how drastically this involvement has influenced your evolution or how fully you have been manipulated. As long as you are unaware you will not remember what has been stolen from you by certain of these visiting groups (the Zeta being only one member of a larger force), and that is precisely how they would like to keep the situation. Those who care about your evolution, who desire to see your species reach the freedoms, joys and power shared by many within the universe, realize the time has come for you to be informed. And so we offer to you the information you need in your growth to awareness.

Holographic inserts are a reality. This technology has been used to direct your race many times since its rebirth upon the planet Earth. Some of your historical "facts" are actually records of the dramas staged through holographic inserts. In the last section we discussed the use of "forced matrix transplants." This idea may seem strange to you, perhaps impossible when viewed from your present state of disinformation. It might surprise you to know that this tactic has been used upon your species in the past, and is partially responsible for your present state of unawareness

Both holographic inserts and matrix transplants can be used to assist you. In your distant past, after certain mal-aligned ET forces began disrupting the genetic code of your developing species, other well intended interstellar groups decided to intervene on your behalf. Certain Soul Matrices or soul families agreed to birth into your three-dimensional system and take on human form so that the digressive genetic code could be redirected back toward its original pattern. Through these highly evolved beings entering your system new probabilities for development were given to the human species. The period of time we are referring to involves a segment of linear history about 5,509,000 years ago. During this time there occurred events of which you have no record. These events did not involve a human strain of biology, but rather numerous others from your star system and others. We refer to these events as the **Electric Wars**.

THE ELECTRIC WARS

The Electric Wars lasted in your terms about 900 years. These events were orchestrated by certain factions of interstellar cultures who desired "possession" of the Earth territories. Some wanted it for observational purposes, others for exploitation. The beings who originally created the Turaneusiam race (first human prototype) wanted these territories protected so that their experiment could again be attempted. In order to secure the Earth territories for the rebirth of the Turaneusiam race its creators had to make agreements with certain Interdimensional forces who possessed the power to reclaim the Earth territories. The Electric Wars began when pro- and anti-human ET factions fought over humanity's continuing right to evolve on Earth. Other-dimensional forces were brought in to resolve the drama. These were not forces of a biological nature but rather "pure beings" of power and awareness. Some refer to them as the "Solar Lords," others call them the "Great White Brotherhood." We know them as the **Breneau**. We cannot describe to you the nature of their reality for you presently do not have the conceptual basis for this understanding.

The Breneau agreed to assist certain factions of the group who had created the Turaneusiam prototype. The creators of the Turaneusiam were a large, diversified group from your universe and also from other dimensional universes. Some had more involvement in the Turaneusiam-12 tribes experiment than others. Two groups from your galactic co-ordinate had greater interest in the experiment because of their proximity to Earth. Being part of the same intergalactic structure as Earth, their own realities would be affected by what transpired upon the planet. Knowing this, these groups petitioned the Breneau for assistance in protecting the planet for further development. The two groups we are referring to here are associated with the galactic coordinates you know as the Sirian and Pleiadian star systems. In exchange for the assistance granted by the Breneau these two cultures agreed to allow the

75

Breneau to intervene in the 12-tribes experiment if they did not approve of the developments that took place. The Breneau are concerned with the successful evolution of all life throughout the entire Time Matrix and interdimensional systems. They granted their assistance under the agreement that the Sirian and Pleiadian cultures would step in on their behalf and allow the experiment to be redirected should it at any time pose a threat to the intergalactic/interdimensional structures. These cultures agreed to play this role allowing the Breneau to work as overseers of the project.

About 20 million years ago the new strain of Turaneusiam was entered into Earth and began to develop and again digress, and the Breneau petitioned the Sirian councils for intervention in the project. They did not desire to see a repetition of the previous Taran-Turaneusiam experiment, which caused the digression of Tara's planetary structure. At first the Breneau wanted the experiment to be ended, the species destroyed and the sub-prototypes put out of operation. But the Sirians, on behalf of the Taran Turaneusiam from the first experiment, who had evolved well in other systems, requested that instead of ending the strain the Breneau assist them once more in redirecting the strain into a more productive pattern of evolution. Many in the multidimensional structures petitioned for this intervention, and so the Breneau agreed to work with them in cultivating a species that possessed greater potentials.

The Breneau made further agreements with certain Soul Matrix families that existed in dimensions more closely related to the Breneau. These groups were asked to join the experiment taking place on Earth and to assist in restructuring the genetic imprint of the species. These groups entered into different time coordinates within the Earth structure and began seeding a higher mutation of the genetic code. These groups were used as the catalyst for *matrix transplant*. Large numbers of humans were led, through *holographic inserts* into training programs that would allow for the development of intellect and greater self awareness. Many of these early humans had already digressed to the point where their original Soul Matrices had become fragmented and cut off from the Time Matrix grid. In order for these beings to evolve out of their digression, a matrix transplant was used to "re-power" their diminishing Soul Matrices. The soul families agreed to allow for this, so these were not forced matrix transplants. The Soul Matrix families themselves were also transplanted to other Matrices that had their organization and energies intact. There were numerous Host Matrix families involved, all of them from other dimensional bands. Each of them had their own orientation and methods, and brought their own unique perspectives and energetic coding to the experiment. The human strain would have been lost to digression and self-termination if it had not been for this intervention. You would not be "who you are today" had these events not transpired.

During these centuries of re-training and genetic reorganization the humans evolved. Some were unable to make the transition successfully and became "extinct" in your terms. Those humans who had interbred with the animal presence indigenous to Earth had the most difficult time with reorganization. Their biologies could not undergo the transmutations involved in the development of intellect as you know it, and so they met with demise, usually due to changing environmental circumstances. Other humans, whose strain had not been overly diluted by animal interbreeding were able to make the transition successfully. The perceptual quality you know as intellect was born during the first Seeding of the 12 tribes, between 20 and 25 million years ago.

Though the Breneau involvement did preserve the species, and the majority of Soul Matrix transplants were successful, these events also created other challenges for the developing species. As mentioned in the previous section, Soul Matrix transplants create a variety of "side effects." One such effect being the clearing of organic memory, or removal of the information stored in the original Soul Matrix. With this loss of memory there is often the re-emergence of trace or "ghost" memory imprints as the biological cells still hold residual electrical impulses from the original pattern. Your species is presently suffering from these effects, induced by subsequent Soul-Matrix transplants that occurred thousands of years ago in terms of your time. As the species evolved it was necessary for the new Host Matrices to "create a remembered past" for its newly acquired aspects in time. The genetic material that had once linked these aspects to their original Soul Matrices remained disassembled within the cellular structure of the body, while the Host Matrices manufactured "new memories" and new ideologies that were appropriate to the times and stage of development of the species. All of your major world religions were seeded into your culture during this time of transplanting and reorganization of the genetic code. The problem of "ghost" impressions or fragmented bits of original cellular memory required some framework of explanation to the developing intellect of the species. Some groups handled this problem by making these impressions "off limits" to the human, teaching that these images and impressions were "bad "or "evil" and must be avoided.

The intellectual facilities of the digressed human species at that time was not ready to understand concepts of genetics, thus they were not ready to comprehend the truth of their origins. By leading them away from the old memory imprints and into a focus upon the new program that the Hosts were trying to instill, the humans were allowed to develop a clear linear focus of identity in time, so as to become functional within linear, present-moment reality, while developing a sense of consistent linear progression of identity through time. At that time exploring the "ghost" images that were surfacing from the dismantled DNA would have created such bleed-through from the old Soul Matrix that development of intellect would have been impossible. So in the early teachings things were put simply. Gods, "demons" (the ghost images emerging from cellular memory), laws and punishments. Portions of the truth, in diluted and symbolic form were given to the species as self awareness grew. Humans of the First Seeding evolved under host matrix transplants until the outbreak of the Electric Wars 5,509,000 years ago. Matrix transplants were also used successfully during the Second Seeding after the close of the Electric Wars.

CREATION MYTHS

The religions were given to you by the Host Matrix families, according to their particular orientation. **Creation Myths** were provided and orchestrated through *holographic inserts*. Though divergent in content these seed religions all shared practical information for day to day behavior that would assist the species in its evolution. Originally all of the "sacred teachings" addressed the reality of the Soul Matrix family, the universal teachings of the **Dora-Teura** as they are often called. Each of your present world religions has its common root in the ancient teachings of the Dora-Teura. The original plan for the species, as dictated by the original Turaneusiam creator groups and their Breneau allies, was the evolution of the species and the growth of intellect and intelligence to the point where the truth of origins could be understood. Once the new human sub-species evolved to comprehend their origins they would be able to reassemble the dismantled DNA within their cellular structure, reorganize the actual original memory imprints, and with the help of interdimensional teachers *reconnect to their original soul matrix families*. For only through this connection to their original Soul Matrices could the species re-bundle the 12-strand DNA of the first Turaneusiam prototype. If the 12 sub-species of humans seeded after the destruction of the Taran-Turaneusiam race could fulfill their genetic imprint the biological transmutation of the species into that original "Super Human" Turaneusiam race could be achieved.

Throughout time, teachings have been given to your race to assist its evolution toward that greater purpose. The teachings presently available to you contain some of the original information, but all of them have been purposely manipulated, edited and rearranged. While there are many within the universe and the other dimensions who desire to see the fulfillment of your genetic potentials, and who are ready to welcome you as the new bearers of the Turaneusiam strain, there are also some who do not wish for you to achieve this. If you will recall from earlier in this section we discussed the "Electric Wars." There were numerous groups in competition for the Earth territories at that time and it was only because of the intervention of the Breneau that the Earth was protected as a forum in which the Turaneusiam could be reseeded and evolve. The original Taran-Turaneusiam had been created as a *guardian creator species*. Their purpose in maturity was to become conscious co-creators with other universal cultures and to serve as guardians and overseers for the evolution of the life forms upon Tara and also for the planet itself.

Can you perhaps understand why some of those groups who had interest in Earth and Tara for their own purposes would *not* want you to evolve back into the original grandeur that once belonged to you? If you succeed in your transmutation into your original form, *the planets and their destiny will be in your hands. You will be the protectors of these territories, and it is you who will stand in the way of the other forces that desire to utilize these planets.* The Breneau originally chose to assist in your evolution because, if success was achieved, the best interests of the planets and their local galaxies would be served. The Breneau were not supportive of the agendas of these other groups as they were primarily self serving. If your experiment is a success, the other groups will not have access to Earth and Tara. And some of these groups cannot accept that decision. If your experiment fails, and your species proves itself unable to fulfill its role as Guardian Creator, the Breneau have agreed to withdraw their involvement. This would open the Earth and Taran territories to other potential guardians. Though this would not be in the best interest of the evolution of the planets and their other life forms, this would be allowed, as Earth and Tara exist within a free-will universe. Much hangs in the balance within your evolution, and your species has matured enough to begin to understand the truth of its lineage and the role it is intended to play.

The teachings that have been given to you throughout time are intended to assist you in your evolution. Those who desire to thwart your progress, who desire to keep you within the role of unaware, subservient workers, have time and again invaded the sanctity of those original teachings. Holographic inserts have been used throughout your history to distort the teachings and confuse or mislead the species. And other attempts at forced matrix transplant have been orchestrated. We have mentioned before the concept of a "frequency fence." Now we will elaborate upon this idea, explaining how it has been used to create the present state of chaos, confusion and fragmentation within your species. Then you will begin to get an idea of what has been stolen from you, how you have been robbed of your birthright and enslaved to do the bidding of other dimensional and galactic groups that have little interest in your well being.

A frequency fence is a technology possessed by those who have a working understanding of universal physics. Through the manipulation of sound wave patterns and cycles many things can be created, for the energy you identify as sound serves as the "glue "that holds together matter-patterns within the Time Matrix. Those who are adept at manipulating sound have great power at their disposal, much greater than you can imagine. Sound directs matter, and thus anything "cloaked in matter" can be directly influenced by sound. The human DNA functions within a very specific pattern of frequency. This frequency directs all of the bodies processes and thus the type and range of perception that can be experienced through that biological organism. If one desired to direct the focus of human perception, a knowledge of **Sound Genetics** would be needed. We have previously referred to these "sound genetics" as "the language of energy, light and sound," the language of *Keylonta*. (See page 22.) "Sound genetics" are part of this language, and they have great bearing upon the human condition.

What we call the **Keylonta Codes** exist within the cellular pattern of your biology, and also within the literal strands of DNA. They represent the specific sound patterns that combine to form the frequency bands of your biological matter, and thus set the base frequency codes within which your conscious focus will take place. Depending upon the arrangement and activation of these codes, you will have either a great range of perceptual and experiential freedom or a very limited range of focus while you are within a matter-based form. When your species experienced the Soul Matrix transplants thousands of years ago the DNA held certain Keylonta Code patterns that were set by the Host Matrix families. They carefully disassembled the original codes within your DNA and replaced these "electrified sound patterns" with those from their own Matrix organizations. Like the interior of your cells, the Soul Matrices and the Time and Energy Matrices are composed and directed by these organizations of "electrified sound particles." These particles are composed of **Units Of Conscious Energy**, and they serve as *carriers of identity* as well as carriers of the blueprints of matter.

The patterns of your original Soul Matrices were left in disassembled form within the cellular pattern, but were not directly attached to the newly implemented DNA organizations that took place through the processes of the Soul Matrix transplants. Your original Keylonta Code patterns were left within the cellular imprint so that once your species had evolved into cognition of its true lineage you would have with you the original codes needed to reassemble your connection to the original Soul Matrix. Once your species became aware of these realities it would be able to draw these patterns out of their latent and disorganized state and re-integrate them into the active DNA strands. This process of re-integration would take several centuries to complete, but in keeping the old codes stored in your cells you would have the tools needed to begin this genetic healing. Certain key codes that would link and organize the latent codes to your active DNA structure were removed and stored within the Host Matrix families. In reaching a certain level of development, physically, mentally and spiritually, the Host Soul Matrix would then set a path of instructions for you to follow, as individuals and groups, which would lead to the retrieval of these stored key codes.

Some of these instructions emerged throughout your history within the sacred texts of your major religions and belief systems. As you were led through certain progressions of Earthly dramas you were led closer and closer to the frequencies that would allow you to access the key codes and begin your process of re-integration of the latent Soul Matrix particles. A portion of the disassembled codes from your original Soul Matrices has been recently identified by your scientists, who have labeled this sub-particle phenomenon **junk DNA**. This is "no junk"! But instead part of the heritage that will one day led you back to the wholeness of your identity. The key codes of access that were removed and placed in storage were kept separate from the base imprint of your DNA (and thus out of your perceptual range) by the employment of a *Frequency fence*. This frequency fence was created through "splicing out"' certain configurations within the stored key codes, then linking together those portions that were taken out, disconnecting them from the stored key codes. This created a *literal barrier in minute sound particles* that kept your base DNA from picking up the contents of the "electrified sound signals" that were stored. This is a frequency fence. It is created by "editing" and "splicing together" specific portions of a frequency band, that serves to "remove the receivers" on one end of the wave pattern and "quarantine" the other portions of that band, whereas the new wave pattern generated through the splice "overrides" the original wave structure, sending portions of it "riding above" this artificially created wave pattern. It is a form of frequency modulation, and when applied to the base tones (base sound units of the Keylonta Codes) of the human DNA effectively creates a "perceptual block" by altering the electrical impulse patterns and thus the chemical and hormonal operations within the biological structure.

The original frequency fence employed by the Host Soul Matrices was used to allow you time to develop as a species, without disabling your physical bodies through excessive frequency input. The matter particles of which you were composed had to expand through time before they would be able to hold the amount of energy contained within the key codes. So as your intellect developed so did your physical structure. A "natural progression to enlightenment" would have occurred had there not been uninvited intervention on the part of the groups who desire to see you fail in your evolutionary mission. If things had gone well you would have developed more rapidly, and you would be well on your way to fulfilling your Turaneusiam imprint. But instead there were set backs. About one million years ago, during the Second Seeding, certain of the disruptive groups began to visit your planet in hope of figuring out a way to divert your progression. Some of these beings were related to the Zeta Reticuli, and carried various types of reptilian form. They were highly intelligent but not well suited to the Earth environment.

DRAKONS

Drakon

The group that created the most disruption within your genetic imprint was a group known as the **Drakon**. The Drakon originated from a different planetary system in your universe. When they visited your planet during several periods of the First, Second and Third Seedings, they created certain strains of their own species that could live comfortably within the Earth environment. Combining certain strains of reptilian life present upon your planet they integrated their own coding into these hybrids. Your "dinosaurs" were originally vegetarian and quite docile in temperament. Through the Drakon experiments hybrids were created, carrying the more aggressive tendencies of that race. These were the original prototypes of your carnivorous reptiles. The Drakon used their reptilian hybrids to monitor human development from their home system.

About one million years ago, when the Drakon had gained enough information through these observations, they began mutating captured humans, seeding the women through rather painful inductions carried out during their frequent visitations. The hybrids that resulted were not what the Drakon had hoped for, as they could not survive within the Earth environment and had to be taken to the Drakon home planet. The Drakon-Human hybrids are known as the **Dracos** reptilian race. Through experimentation upon these hybrid creatures the Drakon were able to access some of the Keylonta Code particles that held in place the original human frequency fence. They "poked holes in" the existing fence (having no idea of the potential results of their actions), which began a process of "information leakage" from the Host Soul Matrices. The human mind and body were not yet mature enough to assimilate these code fragments effectively, and the fragments began to set in motion activation of the stored original Soul Matrix codes ("junk DNA"). This created havoc within the developing human biology, as a resurgence of the "ghost" cellular imprints began. It was during these times that the aforementioned Zionites (time traveling Zeta-human-Aethien hybrid from "the future" time co-ordinates), first intervened, in hope of accelerating the biological evolution of the species by creating hybrids among a select group of humans. These humans were chosen randomly throughout the 12 tribes, and were imbued with the Silicate Matrix from the Zionite code. This allowed them to synthesize, through a course of several generations, the Host Matrix code patterns that had "leaked" through the holes in the frequency fence. During this time the humans were taught the technologies need for them to begin their migration underground, in preparation for the Drakon presence extermination program that was scheduled to take place.

About 956,500 years ago, the cycles of the Earth pattern were approaching a time of shift, where the magnetic grid poles would partially reverse. Aware of the problem of the Drakon upon Earth, the Breneau agreed to accelerate this cycle slightly so the Drakon monitors would be destroyed by the climatic changes that would occur with the magnetic grid shift. For several hundred years prior to the shift populations of the Earth were moved underground, the humans as well as numerous forms of plant and animal life. (Eventually you will find evidence of this historical period). When the pole shifts and resulting weather changes occurred the Drakon-monitor hybrids were destroyed, and the Drakon could no longer monitor and manipulate the human frequency fence, as they had depended upon their Earth extensions to carry out this manipulation. Through subsequent events, the Dracos race was banned from Earth by Guardian forces, temporarily removing the Drakon problem from the course of human evolution. Through these events the original plan of human evolution was accelerated as the Zionite "Crystal Gene" made its way into the human genetic pool.

Your Biblical stories of "Adam and Eve" bore the symbolic coloring of these events, as "Eve eating the apple at the seduction of the serpent" symbolically represented the Drakon forced interbreeding with the human females, and the resulting opening of the Host Soul Matrix, the symbolic "tree of knowledge." It was indeed the opening of this bank of knowledge that birthed into human perception the exaggerated duality that is your lineage. The duality of perception created by the fragments of the original Soul Matrix memories and the new memory fragments emanating through the "leaked" Keylonta code fragments from the Host Matrix families. Two sets of memory imprints directing one body. This is part of the challenge humans of your time face in gaining sovereignty over your genetic heritage. While you remain unaware of the contents and processes within your genetic makeup you will remain vulnerable to those who once again wish to manipulate you away from the true purposes for which you have come.

INTENTIONAL DISTORTIONS OF SACRED TEACHINGS

We will now address the issues involving the Zeta, their plan for using holographic inserts to orchestrate the "mental takeover" of forced matrix transplants in hope of gaining dominion over the Earth territory, and the need for humans to become aware of these events and learn how to conduct themselves within them. This "invasion of mind" has been planned by the Zeta and others for many, many years. You have been cultivated toward its success. Numerous attempts have been made throughout your history, by various groups, to divert you from your successful path of evolution. As we have said, Earth is a valuable piece of property in universal terms. The teachings, as seeded by the Host Matrix families have been heavily distorted. Much information was removed from these writings in order to keep you unaware. Humans themselves, under the direction of these mal-aligned forces, have twisted and withheld key aspects of these teachings throughout your history, and there is not a single religious text within your times that has not been subjected to these manipulations. For this reason much new information is being offered, but even with contemporary translations you must watch for these intended distortions.

Through the distortions in your traditions you have been taught to disown personal power, to deny your perceptions and to perpetually distract yourselves from looking inward to the knowledge that lives within your connection to the Host Soul Matrices that now serve as the organizational structures for your fragmented genetic code. These distortions in teachings have served to further rob you of the ability to link with the Soul Matrix and instead have cultivated you to adhere to the dictates of outside figures of authority. As we have said, your species has been cultivated for the success of a "mental takeover" and you are presently suffering from just that sort of takeover, as most of you have little idea of how to connect to the Soul Matrix. In previous sections we mentioned the "brainwashing program." This program was set in motion by those factions desiring your failure, and they have done a good job in coloring your perceptions to hold prejudice against the very information that would set you free to grow and evolve successfully.

Through your traditions you have been taught to obey, to follow blindly the ideas others have handed to you and to fear and mistrust the very nature of your humanity. You have been taught that you were powerless and unworthy, and that your bodies were somehow wretched and unclean. These were *not* the original teachings! The manipulators utilized portions of the original teachings, distorting them, steering you away from the secrets held within your bodies, feeding you the erroneous idea that you could connect with your soul by disowning the body, *when in truth you must connect with the Soul Matrix through the biological form.* The teachings were twisted to make you believe that you could "find God" by searching outside of yourselves, or by appeasing some self-appointed authority figure who had the power to hold your divinity for you. You were led to follow the "letter" rather than the "spirit" of the "law" and the "laws" you were taught to follow had been purposely misinterpreted so the individual could not make a personal connection to Source. At one time, during the early development of the species, when the adepts were working to nurture the intellectual facilities and repress the "ghost "memories, many of these teachings were pertinent. The mental capacity of the human at that time could not sustain the burden of certain knowledge, and so you were steered away from that knowledge.

But this was only meant to be temporary. Instead, through the manipulations of those repressive forces, you were kept in darkness far beyond your time. Information was withheld even after you had matured enough to integrate it effectively. You could compare your species to a child, who was not allowed outside because he could only crawl and harm might come to him. But long after that child was able to walk the freedom of the outside world was denied. For perhaps now the child could walk away, perhaps in his maturity the child would no longer follow the commands of the "parent." And so it has been with the development of your species. Though some of this denial could be attributed to "over-protective parenting," to use an analogy, much of it was orchestrated in order to keep you helpless and subservient to those "parent" figures. Not all of these "parents" agreed that you should be allowed to mature, and those who did not became the forces working toward your demise.

Who were those "parent figures" that nurtured you in time from innocent beings of pure perception into the thinking beings of complexity you have become in your present time? The group of interstellar and multidimensional beings, of which the Sirian and Pleiadian cultures are a part, who originally began the Turaneusiam experiment so long ago. And the multitude of species from other galaxies who originally donated their genetic imprint at the inception of this experiment. They are your ancestors and your true forefathers (and mothers) who "raised" you from the infancy of a new species into the adolescence of your present stage of development. And those ancestors are alive, not only within the genetic imprint that you carry, but also within their own time and dimensional continuum. They are aware of you, and they guide you still, for unlike you, they are not trapped within their own time-space coordinate.

These "parents" have protected your species for hundreds of thousands of years. From the manipulators who desired to "steal your nursery out from under you," and from the other parent species who wanted to redirect the path of your evolution to fulfill their own purposes. You were protected in your growth, and you are still. But you are becoming wise. Wise enough to take a hand in your own protection and in the fulfillment of your genetic heritage. Presently the Zeta are toying with you. This scheme has already been redirected to a large degree, but will remain a threat to you until are able to see your way clearly through the manipulations they have in store.

EARTHSEEDS AND STARSEEDS

The mavericks among you, the pioneers, will lead the way in your awakening to awareness and empowerment. They will lead your species to the discovery and fulfillment of its genetic plan. They are the silent leaders of your time, the speakers sent to you by the Ancient Ones, through whom the knowledge of the original truths will come. Some of you carry within you the assembled codes of your original Soul Matrix, some of you evolved beyond the need of the Host Matrix families because long ago were gifted with the Silicate Matrix. There are those among you now who carry the "Crystal Gene," they are on the accelerated path of evolution, and knowingly or unknowingly, will lead your species to freedom. They are the **Starseeds**. Are you one of them?

The members of your species that were not imbued with the gift of the Zionites, who do not carry the Silicate Matrix within their "junk DNA" and Soul Matrix codes, are known as the **Earthseeds**. Though all of your species originated from the 12 tribes of the Turaneusiam sub-prototype, not all of you were selected for the Zionite experiments and resulting accelerated genetic strain (the original selection of the first encounter was random). This does not mean that one group is superior to the other in terms of innate value, as all of you are needed for the fulfillment of the Turaneusiam imprint. But the Starseeds are "ahead of their time" so to speak, and so they carry with them the burden of the sleeping Earthseeds, and the responsibility of helping them to awaken. The Earthseeds are still connected to the Host Matrix families, they have not yet activated the Keylonta Codes that would allow them to begin assembly of their original memory patterns. Many of them have not yet passed through the original frequency fence that would allow the reassembly process to begin. *These humans are the most vulnerable to manipulation through holographic inserts,* and it is some of these that the Zeta desire to utilize for the breeding of a "worker race." The plan for the selected Earthseeds involves the eventual contamination of food, water and air supply with certain elemental components that would repress the emotional facilities and thus cut off the possibility of the individuals to link with their Host Matrix families. A biological block to the frequencies of the Host Matrices. Those who are not selected are intended to be removed through dramas created by holographic inserts, such as the "Christ" drama example we used in the previous section.

The Zeta have other plans in mind for the Starseeds. The Silicate Matrix within the Starseed genetic imprint is valuable to the Zeta. It is this element for which they search during unauthorized (by the Soul Matrix) abductions, for they hope to create a stronger more versatile hybrid through humans carrying this code. They view the Starseeds as the potential breeders of a three-dimensional Earth hybrid race that they hope will repopulate the planet once the clearing is completed. The unenlightened Zeta also fear the Starseeds, as they possess the potential ability of *seeing through the holographic inserts*. The Starseeds also are able to more easily partake of multidimensional communication, which enables them to "go above the frequency fence" the Zeta are working now to "erect" within the human DNA code (remember, the frequency fence is a type of sound technology that utilizes contrived frequency modulation). Because the Starseed is already re-linked, to some degree, to its original Soul Matrix the Zeta cannot perform a forced matrix transplant upon a Starseed without first dismantling the Soul Matrix. This is very difficult to do with the technology they have available. And the Starseeds are protected multi dimensionally by the Zionites, as well as by other groups (enlightened Zeta, Aethien, Ranthia, Sirian, Pleiadian, Breneau and many other presences). The Starseeds are the greatest threat to the old Zeta agenda, and so the Zeta try to find other ways in keeping them out of operation.

Zeta do whatever possible to keep the Starseed from awakening to its true identity. A sleeping Starseed is not a threat (and is prime for manipulation). Much of the "brainwashing program" has been employed to keep the Starseeds sleeping through distraction and fear of their own identities as appearing "out of the norm." They have also instigated a campaign to create separation and segregation between the Starseeds and Earthseeds, and also between Starseed groups, thereby exerting social pressure upon the awakening individuals.

The Zeta and the Interior Governments have also "pushed" in certain places and in certain times within the Medical communities. The movement to discredit holistic therapies, and to use drugs for the treatment of "emotional" conditions not of a psychotic nature, the prejudice within the psychiatric professions toward "spiritual" or "paranormal" experience, the repression of "women's issues" and "minority" rights—all of these things are fueled by Zeta "agitation" in the "right places at the right times." The Zeta and Interior also infiltrate religious communities when needed, to insure that the factions will remain at odds, to ensure that humans *will not band together in tolerance*. For that would be (and will be) the demise of the old Zeta agenda. You would not believe the issues within your public forum that have come under Zeta/Interior influence at one time or another. Why do you think issues of UFO sightings are repressed and censored from the media whenever possible? Who supports the networks? Advertisers, of course. Who might be influencing conglomerates "behind the scenes"? Perhaps a few "little grey shadows?"

WOMEN

Presently the Zeta and the Interior government are backing a strong campaign *against women*. It is being orchestrated subtly, smoothly, so as to go unnoticed. But the programming is present. Playing upon women's innate love for and bonding with their offspring the Interior movement is aimed at *reconditioning women to view themselves as breeders first*. Rather than supporting the development of the female identity as a balanced force, these *subliminal campaigns* are playing upon women's guilt, coercing them to feel "incomplete" if they do not breed, and to feel *they must martyr personal identity* in order to be "good parents." Women are being programmed to mistrust their bodies and especially their emotions. Both men and women have been programmed to repress their emotions, and to mistrust their intuitions. (It "just so happens" that the emotional and intuitive facilities are the primary means by which humans can see through and break out of *holographic inserts*.) Have you ever thought about the deeper messages being sent to you through your media?

You must understand that the old Zeta agenda calls for "women as breeders and men as workers" in the orchestration of planetary repopulation. Is it any wonder that they would support and encourage these "traditional" values? Who do you think might have helped your species to develop "traditional values" that *served to segregate the genders*, pitting them against each other in a power struggle, rather than uniting them in co-creative partnership *as they were intended*? The idea of *traditional values* has been purposely promoted to you in *distorted form*. It has been promoted with an implied subjugation of the female role. This distortion was started *thousands of years ago* to keep the wisdom of the **United Genders** out of human perception. And the Zeta are now playing upon those themes to further divide you and "keep you stuck" within the old fragmented genetic imprint. Until you overcome these issues, and the *petty power struggles* they breed, you will not know *what freedom is*. The "traditional roles" of the genders were originally intended as a co-creative structure, built upon mutual respect and personal freedom. *They were optional roles*, not intended to be socially imposed. Men or women who did not want to play these roles to each other and within the society *had other legitimate options* to choose from. This is not the case within your present world societies.

You have allowed yourselves to be robbed of a precious freedom. Only you, as individuals can return that freedom to yourselves.

SOUL MATRIX PROTECTION

The first and most important thing you can do to protect yourself from holographic inserts and forced matrix transplants is to open your mind and belief system to the reality of the presence of the **Soul Matrix**. Whether you are Earthseeds or Starseeds, the fact that you exist *implies the existence of the soul matrix*, either the Host Soul Matrix of the Earthseeds or the Original Soul Matrix of the Starseed. Once you have acknowledged the existence of the matrix then *actively petition this soul family/identity grouping* to assist you in strengthening this connection. Reserve some time each day for meditation or prayer (which ever idea you are most comfortable with) in which you focus your attention on making this connection and develop the skill of quieting your mind and body. Find the "place of peace" within you (this does exist and can he found) and center yourself there for at least a few minutes daily. Choose to *evolve consciously* and ask your Soul Matrix to assist you in ways you can understand. *Reach for the higher knowing within your soul matrix*, and it will guide you. Begin to review your emotional reality and sensitize yourself to those areas of repression. Begin to work through your fears inviting your Soul Matrix to assist you. (Working with the Soul Matrix directly can often accomplish more in one week than years of psychotherapy, although therapy can be a useful tool when used wisely). Make a commitment to developing your spiritual awareness, and know that if you learn to look within effectively you have all that you need to spiritually grow. Your "spirit" is your Soul Matrix, and you are never without it.

The second most important thing you can do to avert holographic inserts is to *join together in tolerance with the other members of your species*. The Zeta and the Interior Government use the concept of "divide and conquer," so be aware and begin to de-program yourselves from "common ideas" you may hold that serve to divide rather than unite people. Outgrow your own prejudice and begin to see the common elements between peoples instead of the differences. Work with your own beliefs and emotions as individuals and come together in groups to support world harmony, peace and brotherhood. Observe your "traditional" beliefs for a time and choose to uphold only those that promote tolerance between people, respect for all life forms (even the "bad guys," whomever they may be) and trust of the life force or "soul within you." Be wary of ideologies that steer you away from creating a personal relationship with a "higher power" and substitute "hero worship" of authority figures for a private relationship to the spiritual aspects of your being. Support each other in your growth to spiritual awareness, regardless of what path you take, and do not fall into the trap of condemning others who do not view spirituality the way you do. Become committed to holding a higher vision of brotherhood for the people of the planet, and a vision of balance for the planet itself. Become the Guardian you were created to be and help others to do the same.

These are a few things you can do to begin learning the processes necessary to put yourself "out of range" of holographic inserts. If the Zeta have a hard time using the inserts to direct the populace because the people have become skilled at directing their minds, *the Zeta will not be able to fulfill their desire of forced matrix transplant into the Zeta-mind collective*. Humans have the power to "stop this nightmare" before it goes any further—*perceptual freedom is a precious gift.* If you are wise you will not allow it to be stolen from you without a fight!

EMOTION

Human Emotion is the key to human "salvation," for it is through the perceptual structures of the emotional facility that truth can be discerned. Holographic inserts cannot be detected through the logical mind, mechanical instrumentation (as possessed within your present level of technology) or the five sense perceptual data you are accustomed to using. These inserts, however, can be *felt*, sensed through the emotional and intuitive facility, and can be detected through the use of **Higher Sensory Perception ("HSP").** HSP involves using the seven senses of the human organism that exist *at a higher frequency* than the five identified senses with which you are familiar. Because these sense facilities themselves exist within the higher-frequency bands of the human bioenergetic field, *they are able to bring in and translate* (through the Keylonta Codes) *higher frequency data (some can translate ultra-low frequency also).* The energy that links the human to its Soul Matrix is *high frequency energy.* The "higher" senses of HSP are the facilities used to translate Soul Matrix information, through the body, into the human awareness. Holographic inserts are "broadcast" within a certain frequency range (in your case, the range of the average, or mean, of the five-sense human perceptual range) outside of which the "matter illusion" of the hologram begins to deteriorate. To create mass holographic inserts the Zeta have to create a frequency fence (by manipulating the Keylonta Codes within the human DNA using sound) that "blocks out" the higher and lower frequency bands, "sealing in" the human perceptual range to the frequency bands used in the insert, thus disengaging the individual's ability to translate Soul Matrix data through the body and into conscious awareness.

The development of HSP is part of the human evolutionary path, and the body's ability to process the higher frequency information is just emerging into your species on a mass level. Certain Keylonta Codes must be activated by energy impulsed from the Soul Matrix to set in motion the latent codes (within the "junk DNA") that will direct the body (through its electrical, chemical and hormonal structures) to translate the higher frequency information. Until these latent codes are activated the higher and lower frequency energy will simply "fall through the gaps" within the nerve synapses. The electrical, chemical and hormonal changes created by the latent code activations literally add new "impulse receivers" to the neurological structure and strengthen the nerve fibers to be able to carry a "larger load" of electrical impulse. Without these alterations the human body cannot translate frequency that is outside its translational range. To increase perceptual range the body must be accelerated in its ability to hold and process electrical data, and these accelerations are carried out through Keylonta Code activations orchestrated by the Soul Matrix according to its inherent cyclical rhythms. This process exists as a *natural dynamic of human evolution* and is the process by which you evolve over time. These Keylonta code activation processes can be accelerated through conscious applications of Keylonta science.

The Zeta and the Interior Government are aware of this emerging aspect of human evolutionary development, and desire to stop this particular ability from surfacing within the species. If humans evolve naturally these intrinsic abilities would put humans *out of range of mental manipulation*. The Zeta chose this period in time to intervene, precisely because of the stage of evolution *humans are currently within*. Their plan cannot be fulfilled if humans, on a mass level, develop the perceptual abilities (and resulting knowledge) that would result with the natural evolution of the HSP. And so they enter your time coordinate and simultaneously stage infiltrations at key points within your past with the intention of severing the natural development of your abilities, thus *"splicing" you into the Zeta-collective mind matrix before your emerging abilities allow you to make a strong conscious connection to your own or host soul matrix*. Once you have developed the ability to hold a greater amount of Soul Matrix frequency within your cellular structure the Zeta will no longer be able to manipulate you to the degree that they presently do. They do not have the technology or power to dismantle the Soul Matrix families of *a large collective*. There would be too much interference by the helping groups that exist within the Soul Matrix levels of reality. In order to infiltrate your planet the Zeta must bring the human collective under their direction before that collective evolves to a full embodiment of the Soul Matrix, *and it is your responsibility as humans to not allow this to occur*.

The time cycles of human evolutionary development are not "set in stone," so to speak. Though there are certain set cyclic patterns that govern the movement of the galaxies, planets and all life-forms within those systems as they spiral throughout the Time Matrix, there is some flexibility within these set cycles-. Under certain conditions accelerations in evolution can take place within any of these cycles, and an acceleration within one system will have a reciprocal effect upon the cycles within related systems. Holographic inserts are presently posing a threat to your population (even though most of you have no idea this technology exists) and the development of your HSP is your *primary insurance* for neutralizing that malaise. The Zeta desire to rob you of your evolutionary birthright to HSP as well as removing your freedom of effective choice through clear perception. Though the abilities of HSP are only now beginning to surface within your masses, the development of these abilities, through the *acceleration of your evolutionary imprint* can be achieved. There are methods you can use as conscious individuals to begin this evolutionary acceleration. You do not have to be a "spiritually oriented" person, or religious, to understand the premises of which we speak and employ the technologies we will offer to you. You do not have to enjoy "esoteric" philosophies, or practice ritualized ceremony to understand and develop a working relationship with the Soul Matrix. The Soul Matrix is a *scientific* phenomenon as well as a spiritual reality. It could be viewed as a *naturally occurring structure within the* manifestation of **Life Force Patterns**, much as is the observable structure of your DNA and cellular patterning. "Spirituality" *is simply the portion of true, universal science that you do not as yet understand, for science is truly the* **Mechanics Of Consciousness** *and its manifestations, and consciousness is the true spiritual essence of the universe, and all life forms contained within it.*

THE ZETA-CONTROLLED SOCIETY

At a later time in other transmissions we will provide more information for you on the *conscious* acceleration of the **Evolutionary Imprint** and the development of HSP. The threat of holographic inserts and the Zeta forced matrix transplant is a reality within your system for the time period spanning the next 75 to 100 years (1997 through 2072 to 2097), primarily within the next 50 years (1997 through 2047). After that time, because of the larger evolutionary cycles of which Earth is a part, the Zeta plan will either have met with success or failed. Humanity's ability to overcome its present vulnerability to holographic inserts and accelerate its own evolutionary process will be the primary factor in determining the outcome of these events. If the old Zeta agenda does succeed *humans will be unaware of this*, as the majority will be transplanted into the Zeta Collective Mind Matrix by this time, and will be programmed to see only the "status quo" and the permanent holographic structures held in place by the collective program.

If they succeed there will seem to be improvements in many areas, such as health and health care, environmental restoration, and economic stability that would appear through the use of a centralized, electronically mandated World Banking System that regulates the flow and conversion of "plastic money" on a global scale through a centrally located computerized network that is Zeta operated. Humans will have no idea that the Zeta, and the primary 13 corporations that they covertly direct, are behind these institutions. It is this "Invisible Big Brother" network that your Biblical prophecies of the **One World Order** are referring to. There is a big difference between a free, united global collective and a centrally managed network of covert regulatory systems.

There will be well-organized "spiritual" congregations with powerful, authoritative leadership, who will indoctrinate specific ideological interpretations of traditional and "New Age" theologies. Miraculous happenings will become common place and things will seem much better than they are in your present times. Humanity will seem to be reaching new heights as the Zeta covertly assist the species and the planet to fulfill greater visions of achievement. Then the Zeta will begin to infiltrate their new "high-achieving hybrids" into the populace and systematically begin the extermination of the "genetically undesirable" humans. In the Zeta controlled society you will notice a marked drop in the interest in HSP and ideologies that would lead to its implementation. And a rapid advancement of technological development. These attributes of the Zeta society might seem seductive, as through the holographic programs you would seem to be living more comfortable lifestyles than you had ever known. But if you were able to see (which you would not, as your HSP would be disengaged) the desecration of your Soul Matrix and of the planet that existed in reality behind the holograms *you would not be seduced.* You would also notice, in the Zeta society, a large increase in "emotional and psychological" problems (as we mentioned before, forced matrix transplant has its drawbacks) which will be chemically treated through drug therapy.

A "new" mental disorder will emerge wherein the individuals will seem to "flip between a multitude of identities" and be unable to keep consistent focus of identity in time. Chemical imbalances within the body systems will be found and viewed as the cause of the difficulties when in truth the chemical imbalances and resulting perceptual distortions will both be the symptoms of the forced matrix transplant. There will also be an increase in "subtle memory disturbances" that resemble senility but that occur within a wide range of the population. Certain elements will be placed in the water systems of many countries, for "purification purposes," that will serve to avert some of these symptoms of the forced matrix transplant and assist the human body in remaining within the controlled frequency structure by repressing the emotional systems. These would be some of the earlier indications that the Zeta plan had succeeded.

If humans are able to effectively accelerate their evolution and develop the HSP senses to some degree, creating stronger connections to their Soul Matrices, *before the frequency fence that would scramble those higher frequencies is in place,* the unenlightened Zeta will be unable to fulfill their objectives. In this event they would either depart to other systems or join with their fellow Zeta who are working with the Aethien and others toward enlightened brotherhood. Some of the Interior Government forces would remain, but without the advantages of power and knowledge provided by their Zeta cohorts, their power to manipulate would be diminished. They would remain, continuing their covert tactics, awaiting another potential opportunity to reactivate the old plan. However, the immediate threat to the species would be removed and the opportunity for growth would be extended.

THE FREE SOCIETY

Just as there would be observable indications that the Zeta plan had succeeded there would also be indications that the plan was abandoned. First, the most notable sign would be an *increase in reported instances of UFO sightings, alien encounters and communication transmissions*. Though the old belief paradigm, still colored by the "brainwashing" program, will exist many new outlets and appearances of new belief models will manifest on a global basis. The long journey of healing ideological differences into a common position of brotherhood through tolerance will emerge. New discoveries will be made in the areas of health that will be made available to the masses. Seemingly miraculous advancements in holistic healing will come into view, helping to mend the rift between traditional medicine and contemporary holism. Many new technologies, using the sciences of light and sound will be created and applied to health, social, economic and environmental problems, and much headway will be made in finding solutions. Though you will see many of the same features present within the Zeta society, at least for some time, the *feeling beneath them* will be different—a sense of "lightness" or "absence of tension" will be present.

More and more individuals will begin rediscovering their spiritual orientation and make efforts to accelerate their development. Through these groups strong support systems will emerge within the economic structures of many countries. Companies will be redesigned to allow for the healthy development of families with home work opportunities and flexibility of hours made readily available. Many large companies will downsize, creating instead a greater number of smaller corporations that work in a cooperative rather than competitive framework. People will begin to take responsibility for their own health care, using the increased spiritual and scientific knowledge available. A turn toward "energy medicines" or Keylonta Therapeutics will bring self directed health and healing into the lives of the masses, and large groups of emissaries representing these technologies will travel globally sharing their knowledge with third world citizens so they may begin their own healing processes.

There will be restructuring in the governments on all levels, and there may be several decades of apparent strife on smaller levels as the people reclaim power within their governments and begin to create the social and political changes needed to open a future of brotherhood. There will be periods of instability within every country as the new ideas that promote success-ful evolution sweep through the collective conscience of the race, and people will unite through environmental and humanitarian issues. Earth changes, in certain locations will occur as the energies of Earth, like that of its people reach for higher ground. The "Age of Enlightenment," will dawn and bring with it many awesome and wonderful surprises. Freedom will be the purpose and the process of these times, and your species will grow and prosper through the knowledge that will come into your system. The old ways will grow side by side with the new, merging into a new perspective that has brotherhood as its core and peaceful co-creation as its objective.

Within approximately 50 years the enlightened Zeta and other ET groups working for the advancement of the human species will make their presence known to large numbers of people and begin forming cooperative relationships of learning with the humans who desire this interaction. "Abductions" will no longer take place as the visitors will be able to extend invitations rather than operate beyond the conscious awareness of the people. (Those responsible for the non-consented abductions will have left your system). It will be a great age indeed, far different from the repressed "robotic-like" existence of holographic reality with covert, centralized control. Your species will make the final deci-sion as to which reality it will see by the choices made within your present time. *Choose well.* (This choice will be finalized in 2017 AD, through events extensively described in *Voyagers II: Secrets of Amenti, and Voyagers III: The Angelic Dossier.*)

Many rewards await you if you choose to grow consciously, as in the development of HSP, your perceptual field will expand along with your abili-ties to synthesize a greater range of frequency. You will discover many won-derful things about the world you live in, things that entirely escaped your view before. As you begin to look at your world in a new way, you will also begin to view yourselves in a new light and reclaim some of the limitless aspects of your being that allow joy to touch you as the life force moves through you. Not only will the choice of accelerating your evolutionary path protect you by giving you the tools you need to avert holographic inserts and forced matrix transplants, it will also bring to you a whole new "magical" world of perception to explore. And in this new frontier you will find the solutions to many of your present challenges, both personally and as a human collective.

DEVELOPMENT OF EMOTION

The starting point for development of the Higher Senses is **Emotional Awareness.** For centuries your cultures have taught you to repress, disown and negate emotional reality and experience. Your species has developed a "prejudiced perception" in this regard, in which the physically verifiable impressions brought to you by your five identified senses are considered superior to the more subtle impressions of emotion and intuition brought to you by your higher sense facility. Emotion contained a *power*, which seemed to possess a "life of its own." This "power of emotion" was perceived as a threat to the developing intellect, for the intellect could not comprehend the reality through which emotion occurred and so could not bring this "mysterious power" under conscious direction. In the early days, when the 12 tribes were being trained to develop the intellectual perspective, the blocking of emotional sensation was a tool used in order to assist the developing human to focus his five sense perceptions outwardly into the objective matter-world. Emotion worked a bit differently then, serving as a form of **Instinctual Response** such as is apparent in your present day animals. The instinctual response served to bring data directly from the Soul Matrix into the cellular consciousness, bypassing the "mind" as you think of it, creating an interactive response mechanism through which the organism would receive direct impulse from soul that would direct it toward the action-in-time necessary for the organisms survival. The organism would not have to "think about or choose" appropriate action responses as they would come "automatically" from the Soul Matrix.

As long as an organism, be it animal, human or other life form, had a strong instinctual impulse it would remain under the full control and direction of the Soul Matrix. Such beings would not operate out of "free will" nor would they possess a sense of personal individuation, but would rather function as individual units of a collective. The human was intended to become a sentient, self-motivated being, capable of choice and conscious co-creation with the Soul Matrix, rather than an "unthinking" extension of the Soul Matrix. So in those early times the instinctual response of emotional cognition was partially "dismantled." This involved de-activating certain Keylonta Codes within the DNA pattern, which created a sense of *separation from soul for the developing human*. The separation allowed for a *clearer focus in time and matter*, through which the intellect could evolve and from which individualized identity emerged.

As with many of the other disengaged codes (those from the original Soul Matrices that existed prior to the Host Matrix transplants) these "instinctual emotive" codes were stored within the cellular pattern and the Soul Matrix. A small portion of them were left in operation, giving the human access to small amounts of Soul Matrix data and serving to provide enough instinctual basis to ensure appropriate action in regard to survival of the organism. These remaining codes became the basis for your "fight-or-flight" biochemical reaction response. The stored emotive codes, along with others, were kept with the human within the cellular structure, so as the organism evolved those codes could once again be reassembled and integrated into the awareness of the growing consciousness. As humans evolved through time certain code patterns would be activated by impulse from the Soul Matrix and yet another stage of growth would be set in motion. Through these processes of Keylonta Code activations your species expanded from its earlier digressed forms of relative simplicity into the complexity of the present intellectually focused form that you carry. As you grew so did your ability to synthesize emotional frequency, and greater amounts of these latent codes were brought into activation as you progressed through time. Great power and awareness is stored within these latent code particles, and it is this power that the maturing intellect sensed as it began to observe and define the quality of perception you call **Emotion.**

To the growing intellect emotion appeared to be "chaotic," unreliable and "suspicious." The intellect had developed into the "logical" reasoning power you presently use to decipher reality, but that *logic* used the assimilation of data from only the five senses that you presently know. The sense data and awareness brought in by the seven other Higher Senses (or "high frequency senses") was blocked from the logical mind by the biological organism, whose physical apparatus did not possess the mechanisms needed for this higher sense data to be synthesized into patterns. That apparatus would not evolve into the physical structure until the latent codes were activated by the Soul Matrix. So logic developed, but it was at a disadvantage, as the pool of information from which it had to draw conclusions was limited by the biological immaturity of the human form.

FROG IN A FISH BOWL

To use an analogy, logic developed as a "*frog in a fish bowl*," whereas in its youth it could swim around in circles within the confines of its limited environment, but could not remove itself from that environment to discover the world which existed beyond the glass. Viewing the world it could see beyond the glass, the world seemed threatening, as the shapes and forms our "frog" could see made no sense. The frog presently had no experiential basis with which those mysterious forms could be correlated and understood. In its youth the frog *did not possess the physical apparatus that would allow it to escape from its fish bowl and explore the odd environment it could see beyond.* Without activation of the Keylonta Code patterns stored in the cells, the physical body of the human did not have the ability to expand its perception beyond its five sense world, nor was the human able to make sense of the strange new world of emotional impulse using the limited conceptual basis the five senses provided.

As our frog grew, and legs began to sprout where once were fins, the frog discovered it now had the ability to leap out of its comfortable bowl and explore the strange world outside of the glass. As the human biology evolved the neurological and physiological structures of the body grew, new Keylonta code sequences were activated, and the body could now begin to synthesize greater amounts of the latent emotional codes. The logical/intellectual mind could begin exploring the world of emotional impressions that were emerging into its awareness. But instead of leaping our frog became afraid choosing instead to swim around in circles within its ever shrinking bowl, closing its eyes to the world that flashed by around it. As your species reached the point of biological development that would allow the emotional aspects of reality to be explored, the logical mind chose instead to remain within its limited environment of ideas, and "pretend away" the emotional impressions that were emerging more and more into conscious awareness. As long as our frog refuses to explore the world outside the bowl it will not discover that it is fully equipped to make sense of that environment, and it will remain captive within the bowl with very little room to move or grow. The free world beyond will remain unavailable.

If the human species continues to repress and negate the emotional aspects of its being, which it is now biologically capable of synthesizing, the logical mind will never discover the freedoms that exist beyond the limits of its present ideas. The human will remain trapped within the bowl of duality and five-sense perception, unable to grow beyond the conditions created through that five-sense orientation. The species will never become "fully human" as long as it cuts off from logical awareness the reality of the seven higher senses. If the species is to evolve to fulfill the imprint and role for which it was created, *it must become fully human*. And this requires integration *and synthesis of the latent Keylonta codes* that give you the quality of perception you call *Emotion*.

In the infancy of intellect it was appropriate for awareness to be placed within its tiny fish bowl of simple ideas, where it could grow and develop safely. But "the fins have evolved into legs," in terms of our analogy, and the human logic still closes its eyes to the world of emotion and intuition. Afraid to *leap*, afraid to chart the territories of emotional cognition that exist beyond the "glass" of polarized perception. Human logic, at its present state of evolution, continues to try and comprehend that "magical world" *within the limited confines of its own experiential memory*. And like our frog, human logic will never comprehend the true reality of the world beyond the glass until it leaps out of the "safe little bowl of beliefs" it has been functioning within since its infancy.

The logical mind and intellect were intended to work together, bringing you a more accurate perception of reality than either could alone. The five sense perception of the logical mind brings only "half of the picture," so you will never understand the true nature of yourselves or your world if you do not put that partial picture together with the other pieces that exist within your emotional heritage. You cannot understand emotion by using the logical facilities alone. How long will you remain as "frogs in a fish bowl," swimming around in circles of incomplete logical reasoning?

Emotion has is own logic, methods of synthesizing energy and ideas that are unique unto itself. The logic of the mind will bring you *conclusions*, whereas the logic of the emotions will bring you **Cognition**. Without that cognition, operating subconsciously through the emotive facilities, your logical *conclusions would make no sense to your conscious awareness*.

When you cut off emotional cognition from logical perception, you create an artificial boundary within your identity and conscious awareness. The emotional codes stored within cellular structure were intended to be reassembled and reorganized, as impulsed by the Soul Matrix, as you evolved through time. As these codes were restructured and assembled into the operative codes of your DNA your conscious awareness would receive an ever expanding picture of reality and cognition. The illusionary perceived separation between the conscious biological self and the soul identity would diminish as the codes were progressively assembled, allowing greater amounts of energy, identity and awareness to filter into the physical body and intellectual consciousness. As the latent codes re-assembled, the old "instinctual imprint" of the early human would be combined with the newly developed logical facility, creating a new perceptual modality that would allow for full Soul Matrix cognition to embody within a physically manifest system. If your evolution had moved along as planned, following the impulses generated through the Soul Matrix cycles, your physical form and your logical conscious awareness would have merged with the soul identity, creating a fully cognizant being in flesh. But your evolution did not proceed as intended, and there were set backs, due in part to the manipulation of your genetic code by other ET forces.

THE VIOLENCE MUTATION

At different periods in your evolution, these forces entered your reality, creating distortions within the electrical impulse patterns being sent by the Soul Matrix. These distortions served to further "jumble" the Keylonta Code particles within your cells, disrupting the original code activation sequences. There was originally specific order to the dismantled Keylonta Codes, and their activation sequences were "scheduled," so to speak. This order allowed for a clear pathway for energy to follow from the Soul Matrix into the biological form. The distortions created by the activities of numerous ET groups threw this innate order "out of whack" so to speak, and the emergence of emotional impressions no longer followed the appropriate sequence. Codes were fired that did not have their counterpart "receivers" within the operating DNA and the energy released by these code firings could not be filtered into the biological organism. Instead, this "errant energy" began to "pool" within the higher frequency sense facilities, distorting the natural order of those structures. The distortions emerged into the conscious awareness as *errant emotional impulse*, creating overly aggressive and inappropriate emotional reaction patterns that entered into the body through the existing "fight or flight" code structures that had been in operation. The fight or flight instinct pattern became overburdened with these unorganized electrical impulses, and the chemical and hormonal process of the body became unbalanced, creating the propensity for violent behavior now apparent within your human strain. As this sequence interruption occurred within the cellular imprint and was "put on line," through the operative "fight-or-flight" codes in the DNA, this distortion was *genetically passed on* through your species lineage appearing in sporadic and random manifestations of biological mutation and psychological mal alignment.

The Soul Matrix, in an attempt to override this undesired mutation, reactivated more of the latent Keylonta Codes with the intention of accelerating the body's development so the errant codes could be cleared, by linking them to sequences already operative in the DNA. What this translates into in terms of the development of your conscious awareness, is yet another perceptual mode through which these additional energies could be synthesized. *The birth of intuition began*, as the *intuitive facility* was added into your biological structure. The intuitive facility serves as a *bridge* between the original emotive codes and the divergent impulses arising from the mutation. Through the intuitive facility emotional impulses could once again be synthesized through the body and into the linear patterning of the conscious logical/intellectual mind. Without the *intuitive facility* the excessive electrical impulses from the distorted emotional codes would have overloaded the biocircuitry of the body, creating a wide array of growth abnormalities that would have permanently stunted the evolution of the species.

INTUITION

Throughout your known history the "violence mutation" directed events within the human drama. Your lineage bears the imprint of this mutation, as illustrated by your propensity toward self-destruction. Humans trapped within the self-destructive patterns were, and are, unable to synthesize the overload of electrical impulses coming into the body from the DNA and "fight or flight" mechanisms. This produces distorted mental assimilation and thus inappropriate emotive reactions. *They possess immature intuitive development*, and these individuals represent the portions of your genetic strain that have not yet fully manifested the **Intuitive Bridge** within their biological structures. The bridge, however, *exists as a latent code within the DNA*, and thus the self-destructive tendencies of humans can be healed through the activation of those codes and the development of the **Intuitive Facility**. All of you in your present stage of evolution are working toward the development and strengthening of the intuitive facility and the synthesis of those errant emotive codes. For this reason exploring emotion can seem very difficult, as you will find many impulses that do not fit within your ideas of "acceptability." You will discover seemingly "senseless" patterns of feelings emerging into awareness, and if these are allowed to govern the direction of the intellectual/logical facility you will end up with chaos. The logical mind must learn to effectively direct, not repress, the emotional energies.

We have explained to you the emotional mutation that is now present within your species strain *because you need to know what you are dealing with as you begin to explore emotional reality and develop your higher senses*. There are techniques that you can learn to use to assist in emotional healing, intuitive development and activation of your Higher Senses. The techniques may *make little sense to your conscious mind because presently you do not consciously understand the workings of these internal energy dynamics*. To evolve the emotions and intuitions effectively, you must *manipulate the Keylonta codes* contained within your cells, and you cannot do this without the direction and knowledge supplied by your Soul Matrix. In setting the conscious intention to link with the energies of the Soul Matrix, *you open the door for the needed information to enter your conscious awareness*. For this reason it is of primary importance that you *develop the conscious ability to communicate directly with your soul matrix*.

As long as your logical mind refuses to learn the subtle *dynamics* of energy direction through the mind, you will not be able to bring into your awareness the *knowledge* you need to effectively clear the *emotional* energies. No one can clear your emotional imprint without you first consenting to the process. Once you have agreed to the process consciously, the Soul Matrix will begin to impulse you toward the actions necessary in the outside world that will facilitate this healing. If you are to become whole, if you are to integrate with the Soul Matrix, if you are to become fully human, *you must clear and heal the emotional aspects of your being*. *Repressing emotion, drugging emotion out of existence, and fearing the power of your emotions will not promote healing*. It will cause further buildup of errant energy and more biological and psychological manifestations of a chaotic nature.

Those of you who have developed your intuitive abilities represent the portion of your species who have begun to utilize the Keylonta Codes that were activated to bypass the mutation. You are *further along in your genetic healing*. Most humans have operational intuitive facilities that synthesize energy, emotion and sense data for you on a subconscious level. Those of you who have linked the intuitions to the logical mind, who have expanded your beliefs and ideas to encompass conscious intuitive development are ahead of the game, as you are learning to consciously direct your energies and follow the impulses of the Soul Matrix. Biologically you are accelerating in evolution as you are assimilating greater amounts of the Keylonta Codes within your cellular structure. You are becoming more aware and knowledgeable than your contemporaries who rely upon the logical facilities and emotional repression alone. You have more power, more awareness and more responsibility toward the conscious evolution of your species. And your first responsibility is to be *healing yourselves through clearing the emotional energies and allowing the energy of the soul matrix to flow into your biological form*. Then you will be prepared to help others of your kind approach the subconscious forces that move them.

Through the intuitives will come many healing therapies aimed at clearing the emotional imprint, many ideas and practices that may seem foreign to the logical/intellectual minds of those who are still directed by the subconscious forces. Before you scoff at these "illogical" modalities, *take inventory of how little you really know about the nature of your identity, the workings of your body and the purpose for your existence*. Before you discredit the practices that will allow your logical mind to grow, find humility, and realize that you have much to learn. *Allow your "frog" of logic to leap beyond the confines of its bowl*. Let your contemporaries, who have already passed through the maze of limiting ideas, guide you gently into your own healing through expanding your ideas. *Try some of the new mind technologies that are available to you now, and ask the soul matrix to guide you. You can heal, and through the private healing of each individual will come the healing of the species*.

You have been *programmed*, by those who wish to see you fail in the fulfillment of your evolution, to *remain in darkness*, living in a world of duality in which you are always at the mercy of subconscious forces. They would like to see you remain fearful, frightened by the chaotic energy you can feel within you, and of a seemingly chaotic universe within which you reside. *Do not allow them to win!* You have the power within you to succeed beyond your wildest dreams, to experience realities *free from the disease, sorrow and confusion* that your polarized perceptions create. So *much wonder awaits you as you awaken to the truth of your heritage and take your rightful place within the universe*. You are like a *royal family* dethroned by jealous factions, and you can *reclaim the territories and majesty* that once were your own. Treat yourselves as the *royalty that you are*, and treat your fellow humans (regardless of their position) as beloved members of that lineage.

In taking responsibility for your own emotional reality and committing to the healing and evolution of your personal being, you will emerge triumphant, one by one, into the palace of your awakened identity. Then you can begin to call the others home. Your species can heal, and it *must* if its continuation is to be secured.

There are many, from many places willing to help you. But only you can reach for growth, only you have the power to command the fulfillment of your evolution. *Only you have the ability to awaken yourselves* to see the realities beyond the illusions of your three-dimensional world. Only while you are sleeping, unaware of the truth of your identity, can the Zeta and others bring harm to you. You cannot be manipulated by holographic inserts or forced matrix transplants if your senses have developed to the point of seeing behind them and your logic has grown to understand how to avert them. If your logical/intellectual awareness would get out of its own way, your emotional and intuitive facilities would bring your entire being into balance under the direction of the Soul Matrix. As long as you allow "logic to rule" you will not grow to understand the *logic of the higher senses*. *Your logical mind can be the frog who becomes the prince*, or it can become the toad, burying itself in the sands of fragmented perception. We suggest that you muster the courage to *leap out of the bowl* of your limited ideas and perceptions *and begin to explore the strange new world* of multidimensional reality and identity that flashes by everywhere around you.

Just beyond the distorted emotional imprints you will discover the *original pattern and sequence of the emotional codes*. The emotions, in their organic form, possess a logic and a beauty that you can barely fathom. There is an order and intrinsic structure which is created and maintained through the *Keylonta codes*, and these are *anything but chaotic*. Your logic has become disconnected from the greater structures of which it is a part. *Just as the Keylonta Codes were used by others to create this artificial separation and resulting chaos, so too can they be used to restore the organic order and relink the logical mind to its wholeness of identity.*

In other transmissions we will offer information on the technologies you can use to heal yourselves. We will introduce those of you who desire to know more to the *Keylonta codes*, and teach you how you may begin using **Keylonta Therapeutics** to accelerate your healing and evolution. Meanwhile, there are many new mind-technologies available, many communications from other knowledgeable sources that can set you on your way toward awakening. You can protect yourselves from covert manipulation, holographic inserts and forced matrix transplants by making the conscious intention of linking with your Soul Matrix, and by developing the intuitive aspects of your humanity You can *sense* such manipulations through the intuitions and emotions, so developing awareness of and sensitivity to these *felt impressions of subtle energy* is the most *important* thing you can do to ensure your safety. Learn to consciously *channel the energy of your soul matrix into your conscious mind* and you will have a direct **Interior Guidance System** to steer you away from harmful situations that exist outside of your range of perception. *Remember, the soul matrix is always there, the "soul never forgets you,"* as you are a living portion of its own personal experience. *It is you, the human, that has forgotten the soul and your ability to consciously communicate with that greater identity.*

Remember and awaken, and you will be safe.

In the next section we will return to our discussion of the *adjacent Earth system in which the Zeta old agenda has succeeded.* We will take time to discuss this subject because the realities in that system have a direct bearing upon the future of your Earth system. We hope to show you through this information *what you can evolve to avoid.* And to illustrate the reasons why it is *important that you do.*

6

Special Projects

CROP CIRCLES

Our discussion on the phenomenon you refer to as "crop circles" will be brief at this time, enough perhaps to arouse your curiosity about the nature of events, such as this, that you do not as yet understand. The items we are referring to in this discussion are the land marking formations that have appeared through seemingly mysterious means within many areas of your global community. Our discussion excludes those "crop circle" formations that have been fraudulently constructed by select humans who desire covert notoriety or whom purposely desire to lead you away from the validity of actual "crop circling." Also excluded in our discussion will be the circular and other formations in fields and in other locations, that are the result of mechanical contact, such as that of an air craft or space craft from human or ET origins. To those of you who may balk at the concept of ET visitations, we say to you:

"Prepare yourselves—for throughout the next several decades much learning shall come your way!"

ETs are real, and their visitations should by now be obvious to you. Pay attention and you will begin to see the mounting evidence suggestive of such presence all about you. Genuine crop circles (and the many other-than-circular symbol patterns) that are emerging spontaneously "over night" in your fields, deserts and country sides are far more than you might at first glance suspect. Those who venture to believe in the authenticity of these formations speculate that they are perhaps "landing coordinates" for ET space craft or messages "left behind" from stellar Visitors who have passed through your system. We will tell you this: These symbol formations are not at all "landing pads" nor are they simply dry ET language symbols "left behind" by some long-gone Visitor. They are far more indeed.

First, let it be known that the appearance of such a symbol code is the direct indication that ET and/or interdimensional Visitor presence is presently and actively taking place within the regions of its manifestation. Where you have crop circles, you most absolutely have active "alien" operations being carried out within the geography and the populace in and surrounding those areas. The crop circles will begin to fade only when the presence responsible for creating them has left the location, so as long as a crop formation remains visible you have active and ongoing alien presence. Just as there are ETs possessing benign intentions towards humans, and others with ill-purposed agendas, so too are there crop circles with benign, helpful or harmful purposes. Crop formations are not created through the use of mechanical devices, nor are most of them formed through "laser-like" technologies. The majority of these formations are created through direct manipulation of sub-atomic energy imprints, whereas the designs emerge as part of the organic air/land pattern of the particular geography. They are "cast," so to speak, within the electromagnetic imprint of the organic elements as a result of intended multi-dimensional manipulations carried out by Visitors.

NEUROLOGICAL STIMULATION

Some "crop formations" serve the purpose of stimulating or accelerating the subtle neurological structures of the local inhabitants, while others serve to repress, "scramble" or desensitize those subtle biological processes. Crop formations are one application of the multidimensional language of Keylonta. It is the language spoken by the core of your biologies, and by the very nature of your elemental world itself. Crop formations have multiple purposes. Their primary purpose is to house frequency, or to "ground" into the location certain frequency bands intended to affect the populace in very specific ways. They are composed of frequency patterns, and they directly affect the frequency patterns of all biological life forms within their intended range of influence. This range can span a radius well over several thousand miles from its point of origin. The formations are often placed in sequential fashion, sometimes thousands of miles apart, but each serving as part of a greater frequency pattern that is nearly impossible to detect from ground level human perception. Crop formations are your first visible, physical evidence of ET presence presently available to you on a mass level. They are subliminal programming devices being used to manipulate, direct or guide you through the intimate unknown structures of your subconscious minds and biochemical and electrical systems. They are one type of what we know as mass frequency control devices.

You are dealing here with technologies light years beyond the scope of your present human abilities. Many of the crop formations have been placed so as to assist you by counteracting the effects of other placements that were intended to do you harm. Presently there are more helpful crop formations in place than are their harmful counterparts. More will appear as you progress into the next century. It is important for you to understand that whether the formations are harmful or helpful they are directly influencing you in complex ways on subliminal levels. You must learn to use them, or they will instead serve as the vessels through which you are used. Attempting to destroy the visible evidence of such a formation will in no way "disarm" its attributes. Once it is in place the frequency it harnessed has been indelibly coded into the land, air and biological forms of the region. It is for this reason that the helpful ETs, who became aware of how the formations were being used to harm you, found it necessary to counter the offending codes rather than to simply disengage them from operational focus. There is much you need to learn about such advanced technologies and those such as ourselves are quite willing to share our knowledge with you, so that you may learn the skills required to protect yourselves from those who wish to do and who are presently doing harm to large percentages of your populations. We will offer more extensive data on the mechanics of crop formations at a future time, for those of you interested in learning more about the hidden realities that affect you. We hope this transmission has offered to you some practical insight into the mysterious phenomenon you call "crop circles."

ADJACENT EARTH AND ZETA

In these transmissions we have discussed the subjects of UFOs and ET and interdimensional Visitors as well as a wide range of related topics that we hope have broadened your understanding or at least aroused your curiosity. All of the subjects addressed are relevant to your continued development and successful evolution, whether you realize this or not. The information on the Zeta Reticuli is intended specifically for those who have encountered this presence, and there are many more of you than you might suppose. Your assistance and courage are needed to help direct the remaining unenlightened Zeta toward their higher vision, as held by the Aethien and other Guardian groups. Through the fulfillment of this vision, the Zeta will be able to evolve successfully within another dimension more suitable to their needs, and they will no longer believe they must compete with humans for the territory of your three-dimensional Earth. Helping them to heal and grow will ensure your protection well into the future, as they will have no need to harm you once they realize as a collective that there is another home for them within the universe.

Certain among you (the readers) are being called to assist in a "special project" of sorts, which involves the Zeta, Aethien, Zionites and the Ranthia. Those of you who carry the silicate matrix/crystal gene within your genetic code, and who have begun to develop abilities in multi-dimensional perception and manipulation. You will know who you are and if this message is appropriate for you. The rest of you not involved in these endeavors can get a glimpse into some of the activities that are taking place beyond your notice. We have discussed the realities of other dimensional worlds as they exist parallel and adjacent to you own, and how the Zeta are able to travel through some of these other systems. We have reviewed the new Zeta agenda of relocation to an adjacent dimension where they will be welcomed. Many of the guardian groups are working to assist the Zeta in making this adjustment, and humans (those of you who are ready) are being asked to serve as the true Earth guardians that you are by working cooperatively with the other guardian groups to ensure the success of the new Zeta agenda.

You are being asked to telepathically broadcast, to the Zeta communities at large, the knowledge of this new option, and use your abilities in "mental-energy linking" to help them align with one of the inter-dimensional grids assigned to them. (You'll achieve this by using visualization and projection of consciousness techniques during times of directed meditation, and after centering in the energies of your soul matrix. Those to whom we speak in this message know what we are talking about, these techniques will seem foreign only to those who have not awakened their higher senses.) Some of you are already doing this and we thank you for your concern and support. There are other elements to this Zeta relocation that we need to address briefly, for those who are awakening to their soul matrix contracts of participation in this plan.

The adjacent Earth that the Zeta are being directed to will be a good learning environment for the Zeta. It is a fourth dimension Earth system. This system also has its human, ET and interdimensional inhabitants. It is a system of much less density than your own and so the natural laws operate differently than those to which you are accustomed. Many of you, the Starseeds (those of you carrying the silicate matrix) are able to access the portals to this system during your sleep state (the "sacred dream time") or during altered states of consciousness. Some of you are able to hold focus in this fourth-dimensional world and your own world simultaneously, and are somewhat familiar with the "lay of the land" in this locality. (You may be involved with this project during the dream time but have no conscious recall. This reminder will help you to consciously recall some of what you have been up to while you were "sleeping.") It is to you with dual focusing abilities to whom we now speak (again, you will know who you are.)

First, we would like you to understand (if you do not already) that the events in this fourth-dimensional world directly affect manifestations within your three-dimensional system. What occurs there will "plant the seeds" for what eventually manifests within your system. In the world to which the Zeta are being directed there exist structures and forms similar to your own. Just as there are "unenlightened" forces, often in "high places" within your governmental structures, these forms also exist with this fourth-dimensional reality.

The Zeta need your help to integrate themselves into this system, but of even more importance, those working toward enlightenment in that dimension need your help to redirect some of the misguided projects taking place within their world. One of these projects in particular must be shifted, for if it is not its pattern will manifest in your world, in your future. It is the project of the old Zeta agenda and the secret Interior Government that we previously discussed in relation to your three-dimensional system. In this fourth-dimensional system this project has progressed farther than it presently has within your system. In earlier chapters we reviewed some of the aspects observable within a Zeta-ruled society. What is taking place within this fourth-dimensional Earth represents the evolution of that society. In this locality the "Invisible Big Brother" has done a number of things, which have left the inhabitants of that time-space coordinate without many of the freedoms you presently enjoy. Here, the Interior Government has chosen to barter the organic resources of their planet to intrusive ET factions within their galaxy. Energy is being siphoned from their planet and their people, and is being directed into other planetary systems. The consequences for them are dire if the project moves forth into their future. Not only will they destroy the planetary balances of their own system, but they will set in motion a chain reaction that will literally cut off this world, and its surrounding galaxies and inter-dimensional counterparts, from the time matrix grid. They will "rip a hole in the fabric of time," so to speak. In the sectors of future time where this has occurred, your three-dimensional system was also cut off from its higher dimensional grid. In that line of probable future development of Earth, the Earth meets an untimely end in the year 2976 AD. The 2976 AD cataclysm is further addressed in *Voyagers Volume II: The Secrets of Amenti*.

All of us who are concerned with human and universal evolution to enlightenment are helping to avert this probability. We are trying to disconnect your Earth coordinate from the adjacent system that is in peril. In order to do this, and to stop this pattern from manifesting within your reality, the pattern must be altered from above, within and below its frequency placement. Your world exists below, and your help is needed.

In this fourth-dimensional system the Interior Government works "behind the scenes" while a "puppet government" maintains the illusion of freedom for the people. The "One-World Order" is in place within this world and so this governmental structure applies globally. Here the Interior Government is particularly interested in creating a human-like hybrid mutation, but not in combination with the Zeta race. In this system the Zeta plan "backfired," and they were "denied the fruits of their labors," as the technology they had provided was used in agreements with outside ET groups, to the exclusion of the Zeta. The Interior Government collaborated with the reptilian Dracos race to overthrow the Zeta power holdings. The Zeta were reduced to a "working-class" status, and live in fear of the now more powerful Interior Government and its new Dracos allies. The Zeta had provided the technology and knowledge of genetics that the Interior Government needed to create the hybrid prototype species it desired. The leaders planned to create these bodies and then re-inhabit them (the hybrid prototype had many physical advantages compared to the human body), or "possess" them if you will, along with chosen members of their Dracos allies. This "super race" was created with the primary purpose of having a biology that was strong and resilient enough to move through the time and inter-dimensional portal systems without being destroyed.

The covert government and its allies are aware of the damage they have been doing to their planet and believe that one day their resources will be expended or contaminated to the degree that their survival will not be possible. Nuclear energy is also used in this fourth-dimensional system, and they have only partially discovered how to neutralize the waste materials. They have violated and disrupted the natural balances of their oceans with waste treatment and realize they cannot continue this process. Using technology of the Zeta they have instead devised a way of transporting the radioactive materials, in small amounts, into other dimensional systems, through the portals they have accessed. Your system is one of those on their target list for such dumping. This process has not yet begun, in terms of your time orientation, but will be instrumented within the next 40 to 50 years of your time, if your Earth is not shifted out of alignment with this fourth-dimensional time continuum (this time shift is addressed extensively in *Voyagers, Volume II: The Secrets of Amenti*).

Their method seems ingenious from the outside. Understanding some of the relationships between objects, matter and time that exist between parallel dimensions, their scientists have created a way to transmit radioactive materials from their generators, into other generators that exist within a parallel or adjacent time-space coordinate in other dimensions. If this should occur, your scientists would find themselves baffled, as the amount of radioactive waste created in your plants would appear to double, with no increase in power output or source materials. The waste materials would appear to you as being intensified in power, or radioactivity. And your technologies are light years away from being able to decipher how this intensification is occurring or from where the increased radioactivity is emerging. Needless to say, such an event would prove treacherous to your system, as not only are you not prepared to dispose of such intensified waste, but your reactors themselves are not designed to process those amounts of radioactivity. Over time, this stress would cause your reactors to explode. Period.

The fourth-dimension scientists are aware of this possibility but they are not concerned with these outcomes for you. Their only concern is in being able to shut the portals prior to your systems reactor overloads, so when they "blow" their own reactors will not be destabilized in the process. In their plan your reactors would not overload immediately, as the excess radioactive materials would be filtered into a state of dimensional suspension or "suspended animation" then slowly released into your (and other) systems. Over time the process would create buildups and more rapid deterioration of your processors. The interior fourth-dimension government views this as a good temporary solution to their problems. They do not realize the dire effects and chain reactions it would create for all systems involved. This project must be redirected from your three-dimensional system. We will elaborate upon this as our discussion continues.

Part of what is now taking place within that society is the involuntary abduction of women who possess desired genetic strains, and the chemical sterilization of all men and women the government considers to be of a "lesser" genetic heritage. Children are born by permit only, and many people have been put to death for unlawful procreation. The "puppet government" runs a campaign of disinformation and propaganda whereby the populace is led to believe that these policies are in the best interest of the global community. As if these conditions were not bad enough, the covert forces have begun the process of mass mutation, while the populace over which it has control has no knowledge of what is being done to them. Contrived chemical elements are added to the water and food supply, the air is "drugged" with ionic "enhancers"[1] and inaudible sound and frequencies are being employed to manipulate and control the biological and mental processes of the people. The population has no idea these things are taking place—no idea that slowly their bodies are being destroyed and cut off completely from their Soul Matrices.[2]

Most of the population within this fourth-dimensional world is human. The human species within that reality is being destroyed and mutated into extinction as a biological entity. This system is tightly controlled. Individuals in these cultures cannot receive telepathic or Keylonta communications such

---

1. Energetic elements that accelerate the chemical properties.
2. The old Zeta agenda in your third-dimensional system at least reconnected individuals to the Zeta collective mind matrix, from which life support energy could be drawn. This complex was dismantled in the fourth-dimensional system when the Zeta were removed from power.

as you can. Their intuitive facility has been chemically blocked, without their knowledge. Their emotions have been sedated and drained of energy, and their minds have been controlled through the use of electromagnetic interruption. They are slaves without the luxury of knowing it. They think they are free people and they cannot see their own digression.

You may feel unconcerned about this information, after all this world exists in another dimension and "you have your own problems." Well, let us tell you this: your three-dimensional system is one of the coordinates their rulers have in mind for experimentation. They have not yet decided whether your system will be used as a new home when their planet's resources are depleted, or whether you will be used as a dumping ground for their radioactive waste materials. But either way, because you are so closely related in your time portal systems, your area of the dimensional map is a primary target. One part of their plan involves the infiltration of such target systems. (Events in your present time directly affect conditions in t hat future time continuum, and it is for this reason that the unenlightened Zeta currently desire to place your populations under mind control. The connections between your Earth and this D-4 system is further discussed in *Voyagers Volume II: Secrets of Amenti*.)Your system already possesses the Interior Government and will soon be linking into the world bank and what has been called the "world management team." These entities are already a reality within your system. The public will remain unaware as these structures grow in power. Presently they do not possess the power or knowledge held by the fourth-dimensional adjacent system. Most of these manifestations within your system stem from this fourth- dimensional system. They are attempting to infiltrate your system, and if successful, turn it into another version of what they have created within their home territory. You, as relatively free humans must not allow this to happen.

In this adjacent system everything seems beautiful and harmonious to the "naked eye." People seem to be blissful (not unlike what a massive dose of a mood-enhancing drug added to your water supply might do for you). The illusion of beauty is a perpetually maintained holographic insert, that the humans there believe is reality. As the emotional and intuitive aspects of these people are being controlled they are unable to feel the true reality beneath the hologram. If an individual somehow begins to sense that something is amiss, begins to question, becomes "fatigued" with such "concerns," the government is fast to "assist" him. If "healing drugs" are not successful in reprogramming his thoughts (and realigning him with the propaganda program), the individual is sent away for "rehabilitation." Family and friends are allowed to visit. However, the person they visit is also a hologram, as the human who entered "treatment" has been destroyed.

You must become aware that your system is dangerously close to directly interfacing with this fourth-dimensional reality field. That reality exists as one of your potential futures. One you all could do very well without! There are things that you, as enlightened and awakening humans, can do to assist those in your world who are aligned with this potential future. And there are many who fit into this category.

Let us look for a moment at your American culture—the greatest example of a free citizenry and enterprise system on your planet at this time. What do you think is the mind set of the "norm," the "average" human functioning within that system? We are referring here to the cultural or "tribal" mind, the "consensual reality." In the "official" view of things (those ideas perpetuated through your media, your social, business and religious institutions and your schools), you are taught to believe that some things are true, others are not; some behaviors are acceptable, others not; and some ideas valid, others not. You are taught to view your reality and define yourselves in a certain way in order to be acceptable, functional and "normal" within your cultural boundaries. We shall call these views and definitions the "base program" upon which your citizens function.

Within the complex network of theologies and ideologies of your belief systems there exist central ideas or core beliefs, upon which all the other beliefs are "stacked" or out of which the other surface beliefs emerge. The majority of people operate on this base program of culturally mandated beliefs automatically. The program, its core elements and even the knowledge that the program exists operate on what you would call "subconscious" levels. This implies that these inner programs are directing you, rather than you directing or consciously choosing them. This means that, as individuals, you are not "owning your personal power." You are not empowered, but rather dis-empowered, *as these subconscious programs direct the workings of your mental, emotional and physical system.*

In this Age of Enlightenment part of your healing, part of your evolutionary challenge, is to reclaim that power, access those hidden programs and attain sovereignty over those hidden portions of your identity. In this way you will become enlightened, powerful and free to choose consciously the ideas and beliefs that direct the patterns of your inner forces. Now we shall ask: does your mainstream consensual reality teach you of these things? Do you learn from childhood that you are a blessed multidimensional being here to manifest self sovereignty? Are you taught that you are meant to be powerful, fulfilled and free? Does your training prepare you to work cooperatively in co-creation with others, or does it teach you to separate yourself from others and compete for limited rewards? Do the ideas of those around you convince you that the world is a safe and joyful place, or do they suggest that the world is cold and dangerous? Are you trained to reach out to your fellow humans in trust, or to be suspicious, protect yourself and retreat in fear? Are you taught to love yourselves, your bodies and others, or to judge and condemn? Are you taught of the ways of loving, cooperative, co-creative brotherhood in mainstream thought?

The answer to these questions is an obvious "no." Just examine your daily newspapers and television broadcasts, or attend a local business school. What attitudes and subtle suggestions do they imply? Your mainstream program tells you that everywhere you are helpless and victimized by forces beyond your control, that the world is a harsh and cruel place of limited resources for which you must compete, that your bodies are vulnerable and unable to protect themselves against disease, that humanity is chaotic or "sinful" and human nature cannot be trusted. You are trained to believe through constant repetition and reinforcement that there is not "enough" and you must always need more, and that you are not enough. Not pretty enough or smart enough, strong enough, fast enough, powerful enough, wealthy enough or good enough. You are taught, just as your parents had been, to believe that you are only what exists between the top of your head and the tip of your toes. You are trained to doubt the self, fear the self, punish the self and to place your trust in authorities or "experts" that exist outside of you. You are taught to long for but be afraid of power, and to fear your ability to handle it wisely. Emotion is power, and so it is expected that within this program you are taught to invalidate and repress emotional cognition. The intuitions and higher senses give you direct access to greater power and knowledge. And you are taught to negate, fear, devalue, disown and discredit intuitive perception and knowledge. Does it sound like this "official" mainstream program is designed to help you to become empowered or free? You are programmed to believe that *what is on the outside is more important than what is on the inside* and to continually distract yourselves with the more important external aspects of reality. Does your mainstream program encourage you to look within for answers, to discover your own innate power to create change or to spend time exploring the vast uncharted frontier that exists "between your ears"? The "average American" is far too busy, overburdened or distracted to take the time to explore the self, everything else seems "more important." And many are far too "intellectually smug" to admit that the self is a great unknown, and too frightened to approach the inner psyche with an open mind.

In your present consensual reality program you are trained from infancy to disown the self, to subjugate yourselves to outside authority and to project your personal power outward onto other people or circumstances. From birth you are trained to accept the perceptions of others as being more valid than your own, and to "appease" others at all costs. You are directed into schools that are designed to squelch creativity and personal identity to create "good little students" who obey their teachers and follow the rules. Then you enter into an economic structure that further programs you to obey the authorities, work for others and allow others to benefit in unfair proportions from the investments of your energies and labor. You are taught that in order to survive you must either please others at all cost (because they hold your power) or to fight your way through the system to make it (and forcibly reclaim your power). Sacrifice the self, serve others, work hard, make more, buy more, need more...compete, push, produce.

Look at the messages your mainstream reality and its hidden belief program are sending your citizens over and over: look at how you are programmed to create disease in your bodies and minds, because no one ever told you that you had the power to change the program and make better, healthier idea choices. No one ever told you that "thoughts are things" that create reality.

The base program that people of your time have been subconsciously following has trained you to *close your minds, and to fear, judge and condemn many of the ideas and technologies (such as those of intuitive development) that would heal you and set you free.* We are simply asking you, for the sake of your evolution, to look at the program. And ask yourselves:

Does it nurture human potential or does it limit its possibilities?

Is it a humane program of ideas that begets brotherhood and harmony, or does it create separation, segregation and power struggle?

Does it allow you to love and honor yourselves and others?

Does it teach you respect for all life?

It does not.

Beloved humans, who do you think is responsible for changing the program? Religions? God? The government? The doctors and scientists? The bureaucracies?

These are the very organizations and institutions that stand to benefit most from keeping these self-defeating programs intact. When people can lead themselves they do not need leaders, and when people can heal themselves they do not need healers. When people realize that "God" exists within them and that they exist within that force, they will not need others to save them.

Discovering, comprehending, changing and healing the base belief program is the responsibility of each individual whose life is immersed within and controlled by that program. And each individual that can successfully make conscious changes and create a more rewarding idea program makes it easier for the next person to succeed.

We have spoken to you of the fourth-dimensional adjacent Earth and of the plight of the people living within that system (a reality your mainstream belief program would tell you does not exist). We have done a bit of "program bashing" in regard to your consensual reality. What do these issues have in common? Where do you think much of your three-dimensional "brainwashing" base belief program is coming from? It is coming from this fourth-dimensional system. Should it not be just a bit worrisome to you that the majority of people within your "first world countries" are subconsciously operating on this base idea program?

The "lightworkers" (those embracing the path of enlightenment who are working toward the successful evolution of the species) of this information age are bringing healing alternatives to your planet. They offer to you an expanded, less limited, health giving program of ideas. They will become self aware, empowered creators who are able to break free from the brainwashing of the old base program. And they will light the way for others to follow. We call them "lightworkers" because they bring the light of understanding to your species. They will have the courage to break through the old program, creating freedom through mastery and brotherhood through love. Through the new program of ideas they offer, you will be led, if you so choose, out of the subconscious controls of the fourth-dimensional system, and in your freedom you will leave a new "pathway of thought" for those trapped within that system to follow. In helping yourselves, in growing, you will assist those within the fourth-dimensional system to grow. Even though you reside dimensions apart you are connected in ways that you cannot yet understand. And just as their idea programs affect you and your world, so too can your chosen programs affect that reality. And so when we ask you to assist them we are asking you to take control of the program as it operates within your own private psyche, free yourselves and learn to create brotherhood and joy while you still have the freedom to make that conscious choice. In doing so you will affect much more than you realize. (In future transmissions we will introduce you to the Keylonta Code technologies so you may begin using these tools as you work to heal your base idea programs).

What will happen to those who choose to remain trapped within the illusion of comfort and security offered by the old program? What future might they be headed for? Perhaps a dimensional interface with that fourth-dimensional world we described. Could it be possible that the people upon the Earth are beginning to sort themselves into categories defined by the focus of their subconscious core belief programs? Each group preparing to meet a version of Earth's future that is consistent with that focus? If you had a greater understanding of universal physics and the operational cycles and dynamics of the time and dimensional portal systems, those questions would be statements, for you would understand the greater evolution of which your species and Earth are a part. Consider this question for a moment: if this was a true depiction of the circumstances upon your planet, which probable version of Earth would you be aligned with? What base idea program do you follow? Have you ever stopped to consider what ideas and beliefs motivate your actions and emotions from a subconscious level? This perhaps is a good time to begin exploring.

Those of you who have already developed interdimensional skills and are fluent in the languages of the higher senses are needed to assist those among you who are trapped within the old consensual reality program to redirect the energies of their beliefs. The greatest way to make a difference in the third-dimensional arena is to use your inter-dimensional mind skills and project your consciousness into the fourth-dimensional field. (Simply hold the intention in mind—*where the thought goes energy flows*.) From there you can manifest whatever you hold in mind into three-dimensional reality.

Hold the vision of freedom and brotherhood and you will create change. The fourth-dimensional world we speak of exists now, in dimensional coordinates different than your Earth, but it also exists as a future reality for some of those now residing upon your Earth. There is a select group of lightworkers in your system now that have come to work on this or similar projects. You will know who you are as you will feel intuitively drawn to this information. If you would like more information or desire to communicate with us, you may request an encounter with the Ranthia during meditation or prior to sleep. We are willing to assist those who desire our involvement.

You have been drawn into your reality for a reason. Only you can discover what that reason is and what significance this information holds for you. For those of you who do not feel connected to these "special projects," we have allowed you a glimpse into some of the truly amazing things that are going on around you, so that in your quest for personal purpose you may "think bigger" and "reach higher," realizing that you are not limited by the old concepts of identity that you once accepted. You are intended to grow beyond them.

Early in our transmission we mentioned that there are two advanced ET groups presently working within your Earth system who have the knowledge and power of holographic and portal mechanics. The Zeta and the Ranthia both exist as smaller sub-groups within the larger identity of these collectives. The Ranthia could be viewed as the guardians and overseers of the time portal projects, and we are closely affiliated with those who have been called "the keepers of time" (Maya) in your system. We would represent the greater identity gestalt (having a variety of race manifestations within various reality fields) out of which the Maya collective had emerged into your system. We, the Ranthia, and other time portal guardian groups are beginning to interface with your system once again, as we always do when the cycles of time put your system within proximity to our own. Some humans are also involved in the time portal projects through subconscious (from your perspective) Soul Matrix agreements. We will give you a clue as to which humans are involved with these endeavors. Those of you who are drawn to, have interest in, or have had direct encounters with the UFO, ET or "Visitor" phenomena are those affiliated with the time portal projects. Whether your experiences were "positive or negative" from your perspective, they were intended to teach you many things about yourselves and the illusive worlds of time in which you reside. The first step toward understanding is facing your fear and moving beyond it into the wisdom that shines like a beacon from the other side.

In our closing section we have a few comments for your scientists as they become faced with more and more evidence of multi-dimensional realities. And we will offer a parting message to those of you who have had the open-minded fortitude and courage to follow our winding pathway of information to its natural end. But this ending is in truth only a beginning, for there are many more roads to travel upon the journey to enlightenment. For those of you desiring to continue along your journey, we will provide more information at other times, in other transmissions. You could view the closing of this communication as simply a resting spot upon the road.

We have the utmost faith in your abilities to pull yourselves through the challenges we have mentioned, and we have no doubt whatsoever that you will evolve through time to emerge as the grand and wonderful co-creative guardian species that intrinsically you are. During our time of interface with your system we will offer whatever assistance we can to help you upon your path toward understanding. Until we meet again, happy trails to you as you spiral through the matrix of time.

HELPING ABDUCTEES

We have one parting commentary to your scientists and others who are studying the phenomena of "UFO/alien abduction." Many of you are going to great lengths to "prove" that such abductions are not "real" events but rather aberrations of mind on the part of the abductee. You tend to view the experience as some type of hallucination or symbolic cover memory of terrestrial events. Many of you in the "mainstream helping professions" attempt to invalidate the experiences, choosing rather to medicate your "patients" or to apply therapies geared toward rationalizing away the validity of the experience. In viewing the abduction phenomena in this way you are not only denying yourselves the possibility of true understanding, but you are doing a terrible disservice to those individuals who come to you for assistance in finding perspective on real events that have traumatized them because they have no basis upon which to understand their experiences. You are not serving them by invalidating the integrity of their perceptions, but instead you are intensifying their trauma by undermining the abductees sense of self-confidence and innate ability to heal. In devaluing the reality of their perceptions you are helping them to lose rather than gain control over the experiences which frighten and disturb them. In your privilege of serving your fellow humans you have the responsibility of putting your personal prejudice aside enough to grow, so that you may continue to serve the ever changing needs of those who come to you for service. Humanity is evolving before your eyes, and with that evolution comes changes in perception and a rapidly expanding field of experience. Scientific thought must also evolve if it is to comprehend the nature of the human experience. Scientists, doctors and teachers, you also must grow and evolve your own ideas, if you are to be effective within your professions. You must learn to learn from your subjects, patients and students as well as serving to guide them. You alone, through the idea framework of your traditions, do not have all of the answers. Through their experiences and challenges you will learn more about yourselves and the nature of the universe in which you live.

Though some abduction cases might be contrived mental mal-alignments and others intended hoax, there are many quite legitimate occurrences of actual ET abductions. If you were to use hypnosis as a primary diagnostic tool you would find a vast number of such abduction memories surfacing, even from those who have no conscious recall of UFO or Visitor encounter. Great numbers of your population have been involved with this phenomenon but have no conscious indication of their involvement. An alarming amount of the mental and emotional problems emerging within your populace can be directly attributed to ET encounters of which there is no conscious memory, but only a residual emotional imprint of the events as stored within cellular memory. These stored emotional imprints of unresolved abduction issues exist beneath the surface of consciousness, creating mental reactions and behaviors consistent with other forms of repressed trauma. Until you realize that "Visitor" abduction is a primary subject to which you should look for cause of psychological and emotional disturbance, you will be unable to resolve the casual elements of the maladies; instead you will use drug therapies or analysis to treat the symptoms, but the individual will not be truly healed until the reality of the trauma is identified and brought into the conscious awareness.

How can you assist your patients to integrate and thus heal from their experiences when you refuse to believe the framework from which their trauma arose exists? As long as you medicate away the emotional and psychological symptoms of your patients you will be unable to discover the true nature of their condition. The body itself directly responds to the energy data held within the emotional and subconscious facilities. The memory imprints and subconscious information are stored within the cells in the form of electrical impulse patterns, and these patterns set the manifestation cycles of chemical and hormonal relationships within the body. The chemical and hormonal imbalances, and the brain function deviations[3] you see within your mentally disturbed individuals are the symptoms of electrical impulse abnormalities stored within the cells, and these abnormalities arise when the individual is unable to assimilate (for whatever reason) sense data into coherent patterns of electrical impulse that the body is oriented to synthesize.

What you repress through drugs, physical manipulations, or psychological diversion will continue to remain within the subconscious mind, and will continue to create within the body and mind the same patterns of imbalance. Until the causal aspects of stored experience are found and brought to the conscious awareness in the form of remembered events and emotive impressions.Though these impressions may seem erratic, there does exist an associative relationship between them, and if attempts are made to bring these erratic impressions into logical, sequential order within the conscious mind the repressed electrical impulse patterns causing the imbalances will be "plugged in" to the conscious awareness where they can be processed as experiential events and thus released and healed. As the mal-aligned electrical impulse patterns are assimilated and released through the conscious mind, so too will be the biological, psychological and emotional distortions that arose through those mal-aligned impulses.

Your traditions have much to learn in regard to the mechanics of the psyche and its intimate relationship to the biological and bio-energetic aspects of your being. Until your scientific traditions begin viewing all aspects of the human dynamic in terms of energy relationships, they will have difficulty comprehending the true mechanics that exist behind the dynamics they observe. When science and religion begin to mend their ideological beliefs, and both come into the scientific awareness of the Soul Matrix, or extended energetic identity gestalt that is the foundation upon which all matter and identity is built, spirituality, psychology and biology will evolve into the new understandings out of which intelligent holistic therapies can be created. But until that time human experiential evolution rushes forward in leaps and bounds, and those within the helping professions must catch up with this growth if they are not to become obsolete.

For the present time it would do you well to realize that "Visitor" abduction is occurring on a mass level and it affects large numbers of the popula-

---

3. Brain function and activity are directed through the chemical and hormonal systems

tion, whether or not you believe that this phenomenon exists as a "physically real" reality. Rather than wasting time trying to prove it is not real, might we suggest that you direct that time and energy into finding methods with which to deal with this reality effectively? Your practice of hypnotic therapy is a starting point. This method appears to you as unreliable, with inconsistent results only because you, as yet, do not understand the inner language of energy that the psyche speaks. You do not know what to look for, or how to assemble memory and sensory patterns that emerge from within the subconscious mind. You do not yet realize that there are ordered, sequential electrical impulse patterns existing within cellular structure, and you do not comprehend that the physical tissue of the body matter is the storehouse and assimilation facility of the human organism. There is as much memory stored within your little toe as there is stored within your brain matter. The mind is not only located "in your head" and within the cellular structure of the brain, it is manifest throughout the entire body structure, from a hair follicle to a strand of DNA. *Every molecule and particle is imbued with consciousness. Consciousness is not an attribute of mind. Mind is an attribute of consciousness. And consciousness is an attribute of energy.*

Your "subconscious" mind is that portion of your experiential identity you have yet to assimilate into your conscious awareness. Your subconscious mind exists within the cells of your body and within the less dense forms of your bio-energetic field. The subconscious has an intrinsic order but your conscious awareness and biological form have not yet evolved enough to assimilate that order fully. So to you, as conscious biological forms, the attributes of the subconscious appear chaotic and disorganized from the conscious mind perspective. As you evolve you will begin to understand the logic of the subconscious awareness, and you will grow to hold the operational dynamics of that facility within your conscious awareness. And as you grow to understand these things you will grow to comprehend the reality and meaning of the Visitor abduction experience.

If you would begin to acknowledge the validity of these experiences, and to employ technologies of hypnosis and biofeedback to retrieve the memory impressions that are being repressed within the body pattern, you would begin to get a clearer picture of what takes place within the abduction encounters. And you will begin to understand how the mind and body work together to create the perceptual experience of three-dimensional reality. You will then comprehend the greater significance of Visitor abduction as you will understand the greater reality of the human dynamic. Using hypnosis and biofeedback techniques you will be able to access from the subconscious the memory and emotional imprints of an abduction. You can use these techniques to design new therapies for more traditional disturbances as well. The body will

121

provide answers to your questions, if you allow it to, and if you are able to set up a method by which the body can translate its information into terms (language, sense perception or symbols) your conscious mind can understand.

Using techniques of hypnotic disassociation induced through hypnotic suggestion, you can "ask the body" to communicate to you the nature of its malady. You can "ask the body" of the subject in a natural state of disassociation (drugs and mechanical manipulation of the brain/body systems disrupt the organic patterns of electrical impulse) to communicate to you whether or not the subject has been involved with Visitor abduction events, and whether these events are responsible for the condition of disease the subject has manifested. Using such "body talk" techniques you can assist the body to heal the condition by discussing the specific course of action you might take to remedy the condition. You are not simply dealing with "a body" as a "mindless structure of biological functions," you are dealing with an intelligent awareness, that represents the portions of your greater mind that your logical/intellectual mind has not yet assimilated.

The body knows and remembers far more than "you" do, and it knows what is needed for its own healing. Your challenge is to train the logical awareness to communicate directly with the body consciousness, and to set up a method through which that communication can take place. Even in cases where there is structural damage to the brain, "body talk" techniques may still provide helpful data on the condition and treatment of the individual. Mental illness can be "side-stepped" by the doctor, whereby a direct body communication can be set up during the natural dream state, but it is necessary for the subject to be drug free for at least 36 to 72 hours.

Treatments for many psychological, emotional, behavioral or physical conditions can be devised using "body talk" techniques and such techniques are far more conducive of healing than are treatments designed to repress the symptoms. If your scientists would venture to explore the abduction phenomenon further, and begin taking random samples of the population into controlled experiments of hypnotic regression, biofeedback and "body talk" you would be amazed at the regularity with which abduction memories will surface. Most individuals who have been abducted have no conscious memory whatsoever of the experience. And those who do represent a small portion of the abductee population.

You will often find seven out of ten randomly selected subjects will have subconscious evidence of Visitor abduction.[4] In conducting such experimentation you could easily supply yourselves with overwhelming evidence of the

---

4. Depending upon the geographical location from which that population sample was taken. Some areas of the planet are more conducive to the Visitor presence.

ongoing extraterrestrial involvement upon your planet. You could prove the realities of which we speak to you, and perhaps then you could design methods that would assist rather than further traumatize those having such experiences. For once you prove to yourselves the reality of the abduction experience, you will be faced with the challenge of "diagnosing" what type of abduction has occurred.

The type of abduction will tell you many things about the genetic reality of the subjects, and will also indicate the appropriate methods of treatment for the subjects—on an individual basis. Forced abductions (those that do not involve the subconscious/Soul Matrix consent of the individual) require different handling than do those of a consented nature. In forced abductions, the biological and psychological integrity of the individual has been violated. The entire system, conscious and subconscious, has been traumatized.

This type of intrusion often involves the use of "mind technologies," such as the aforementioned holographic inserts or forced matrix transplants. These devices can "scramble the memory imprints" held within the body, creating the emergence of "cover memories"—abductions that are "cloaked in human form." Memories of alleged past abuse may first emerge, involving humans known or unknown to the individual. There will be some fuzziness of remembered perception in these cases, or sequentially incorrect memory fragments. By looking deeper, beyond the apparent human drama, actual memory of the abduction event will arise. The "body talk" techniques work especially well in these cases, because the body awareness will not release to the conscious mind data that it is not yet ready to assimilate. If the body senses through its own reasoning facilities that the personality is not ready to effectively deal with the experience, it will not release the memory in its true form. However, if the body is asked by a well meaning facilitator, it will reveal information about the nature of the emerging memories and whether it is using cover memories to disguise actual events.

In forced abductions, not only has the memory been potentially manipulated by the abductors, but often the Keylonta Codes within the cellular structure have been altered. This occurs during the procedures of forced matrix transplant, when the abductors attempt to disconnect the human from its organic bioenergetic structure (as described in previous sections) in order to "plug the human into" an artificial matrix or to disengage the humans higher senses. The actual cellular codes that serve to store and organize memory become distorted because of this biological distortion. Techniques of "body talk" may not be successful as the literal biochemical relationships within the body have been "short circuited." Mental, emotional and physical abnormalities may result from this, depending upon the degree to which the Keylonta Codes have been altered. In researching and treating cases of abduction, it is important that you learn to distinguish between the types of intrusion, for the appropriate treatment will depend upon the category of abduction. Not only will you need to be able to diagnose the difference between a non-abduction or abduction, and a forced or consented abduction, you will need to know whether the forced abduction involved only cover memories and holographic inserts or whether a forced matrix transplant was attempted or carried out.

Though you can successfully treat the symptoms of the other forms of abduction, restore memory and assist the conscious mind to assimilate the event, thereby removing the cause of the disturbing symptoms, in cases where forced matrix transplant is involved you will not be able to resolve the issues without bringing the Soul Matrix into play. In these cases you are best to refer your client to those who are skilled in multi-dimensional communication and inter-dimensional manipulation, for these intuitive skills will be required if healing is to take place.

The subject of healing from forced matrix transplants is beyond the scope of this transmission. Using techniques of hypnosis, biofeedback and "body talk,"[5] you can discern whether an abduction has taken place, and if so, what type of abduction you are dealing with. Because it is the symptoms of emotional or psychological disturbance that bring the possibility of abduction to your attention, and because Visitor abduction is now at epidemic proportions among the people in your times (especially within certain geographical locations) you would be wise to devise screening techniques as mandatory preliminary evaluation prior to any psychiatric endeavor. Just because you do not yet hear about abductions on a regular basis does not mean that they are not occurring within massive portions of the population. They are, but repression of conscious memory of the event is a symptom characteristic of the abduction. Often the first indication that such intrusion has occurred is the manifestation of psychological, emotional or behavioral deviation, as the personality and subconscious facility attempt to assimilate the emotional trauma of the experience. If you knew how many problems of manic depression, substance abuse, neurosis, psychosis, and many other physiological disorders can be directly traced to Visitor abduction you would be truly amazed.[6] Visitor abduction cases must be handled differently than non-abduction cases

---

5. Body talk is one method of "communicating" with the body consciousness, through monitoring the body's subtle responses to questioning after creating specific "cues" the body can use as a language of response.

6. Not all cases of these maladies are created by abduction, but all do possess the causal element of repressed, emotionally traumatic experience, which creates chemical and hormonal imbalances that manifest in perceptual distortion.

if healing is to be achieved, as suppression of the symptoms will only worsen the condition.

Unlike other forms of psychological disease that result from the repression of traumatic experience, abduction reactions cannot simply be "drugged out of awareness" or circumvented. Most trauma of terrestrial experience is isolated around certain key memories from the past. The events that caused the trauma in the first place are no longer a part of the present moment reality of the individual—the events are not reoccurring. This is not the case with abduction. All abductions begin in childhood, as the human is prepared on the subconscious levels for manipulations that will occur as the body matures. There are no exceptions. Not all subjects will find the full sequence of memory dating back to the childhood events, but most will. The abductions are performed in scheduled fashion following cycles inherent to the dimensional portal systems, and to the intrinsic cycles of development within the human. They reoccur within a certain preset time schedule. Once abduction has been initiated it will continue, following the cycles, throughout the life span of the individual. Repression and suppression of the earlier abductions will only serve to intensify the buildup of the emotional imprint around the experience, creating further imbalances within the body and mind. The only cure for the post-traumatic stress symptoms that are the result of Visitor abductions is the retrieval and assimilation of the experience into the conscious awareness, and providing a framework of understanding along with an effective course of action for the personality. These will allow for the abductee to face the fear of the unknown, and to become empowered, realizing that certain actions will promote less traumatic experiences that can be understood by the individual. The individual will no longer feel powerless over the experience, nor become trapped within the emotions of fear, anger, apprehension and rage that result from being disempowered. Healing can occur, through which the abduction experience may become viewed as an opportunity for learning and growth, rather than as an intrusion and personal violation.

Most abductions are carried out under the mandates of soul agreements. When humans evolve to a greater conscious connection with the identity gestalt from which their identity is created, they will become aware of these agreements and realize that no violation has occurred, as permission was granted by the individual on a subconscious level. Through growth understanding will come, and with understanding peace. In cases of forced abduction, in which these subconscious agreements were not made, the individual has been violated, and will benefit, once the true memory has been restored, by therapies such as those used in treating cases of rape or other personal victimization. Releasing of the emotional imprint of the trauma and establishment of effective tools for empowerment for the individual will promote natural healing as the personality assimilates the experience over time. In the forced abductions there are methods by which the individual can prevent further violation, but that subject again is beyond the scope of this transmission. We will offer insight into this subject for those who are interested during another transmission. But the *first step to gaining control over the occurrence of forced abduction is making a valiant effort to create a conscious connection to your Soul Matrix, within whatever spiritual orientation you are most comfortable.*

For your further understanding we will offer to you the following insights on the abduction experience. As we have mentioned, abductions are reoccurring and cyclic. There are certain stages of development of the human biology that are most conducive to the genetic experimentation being carried out by the Zeta abductors. In human females, when the hormonal changes associated with adolescence begin, certain arrangements of the Keylonta Codes within the DNA take place, which allow for the successful retrieval of the female genetic matter contained within the egg. For this reason many adolescent females are being led into disruptive behavior patterns that will serve as a diversion to the scheduled abductions. Remember, the Zeta possess the ability to impulse the mental and emotional awareness through the Keylonta Codes of the body. Great behavioral influence can be applied in this way, through which the girl can be led into situations and locations conducive to the abduction. Many (but not all, of course) teenage runaways, or teens that turn to substance abuse and early pregnancy are being impulsed to do so by the abductors who silently watch over them. Most of these adolescents do not understand their motivations for these behaviors, but may attempt to rationalize away the seemingly incomprehensible emotional trauma that swims just below their conscious awareness. We do not mean to frighten you, but teen pregnancy is a desired event by many of the unenlightened Zeta groups who use forced abduction tactics. Following pregnancy there are certain concentrations of energy within the genetic material. This energy in combination with the already accelerated Keylonta Code activity brought on by adolescence creates prime genetic material for the Zeta abductors to use in the creation of their hybrids. Enlightened Zeta who operate within the confines of soul agreements will never participate in these events unless they exist as part of the soul agreement. But the unenlightened Zeta, following the old program, think nothing of impulsing adolescent females into repeated human pregnancies, as they utilize these female subjects to harvest the desired genetic imprint. For this reason we suggest that you offer hypnotic regression therapies for these young women, so you may discover whether or not this intrusion is taking place. If memories indicative of abduction are found, bringing this information into the conscious awareness, and assisting the subject to assimilate and process the hidden emotional trauma they have been carrying as a result of the abductions, will allow the young woman to gain conscious control over her decisions. If she is encouraged to develop her innate abilities in sensing subtle energies, she can grow to discern between emotional impulses coming from her own subconscious and those being transmitted through the manipulation of Zeta abductors.

If you truly desire to assist your populations, you must acknowledge the reality of the extraterrestrial presence and become familiar with the tactics that are being using by them—both for you and against you. If you do not acknowledge the reality of the problem you will not be able to find solutions. It is time that the human species comes out of the darkness, and moves out of the denial of the Visitor presence, so that healing can begin.

THE CELLULAR ALPHABET

A closing note to your scientists—those who have been experimenting with electrical impulse as a method to stimulate brain function. You have recently discovered that you can simulate abduction-like experiences in people who have not actually experienced them.

First we would like to point out that some of those subjects did indeed experience actual abductions, but had no conscious memory of the encounter. You have not properly screened your test subjects prior to your experiments (using the hypnotic regression techniques mentioned previously), therefore subjects who did indeed have repressed abduction memories participated in the experiments, thus contaminating the apparent results of those experiments.

Secondly, yes, you can create abduction-like experiences (or any other perceptual target) by electrically or chemically stimulating certain areas of the brain, or other areas of the body's neurological or cellular structure. You are interpreting the results of your present contaminated experiments so as to indicate that all abductions are false events, representing either "cover memories," hallucination-like mental events or outright hoaxes. Nothing could be further from the truth.

Let us say this to you—just because you are able to simulate an actual event does not mean that the event cannot exist in organic form. Just because you are able to simulate abduction-like impressions does not mean that actual abduction events do not exist, any more than photographing a model of a simulated spacecraft proves that spaceships do not exist. The fact that you can recreate or duplicate an effect does not prove nor imply that the original affect does not occur organically.

In regard to brain manipulation, through electrical or chemical means, you can indeed create many "false memory" or "virtual reality-like" experi-

127

ences. At the present time you are not fully aware of the mechanics of cellular memory storage and retrieval.

Your scientists have failed to realize that every cell stores not only memory, in the form of coded electrical impulse, but also stores the very codes of translation, the Keylonta light-symbol codes. They are the means by which memory is translated into sensual data and the means by which the illusion of three-dimensional reality is manufactured.

Let us compare these Keylonta light-symbol codes (or "Fire Letters") to an alphabet, an alphabet that is multi-dimensional, and whose characters change placement, meaning and sound depending upon the dimensional frequency with which they interface. The Fire Letters of this "alphabet" are stored within every cell of every human; it is the basis for the human genetic code. Through this "cellular alphabet" impulses of electromagnetic energy are aligned and ordered, much as words are formed out of the different letter combinations of your written alphabet. The words, created out of the alphabet of letters, are conveyors of meaning. The words and the alphabet themselves are not the meaning but serve as a conduit through which meaning can be moved from one place to another. The alphabet then represents a tool, which creates a medium through which ideas and perceptions can be shared or projected.

Now, in terms of your cellular alphabet, it too serves as a tool and conveyor of meaning. The Fire Letters represent fixed electromagnetic codes (patterns of sequentially arranged electromagnetic impulses) that can be arranged in many ways to form "words," or electromagnetic code patterns, that can potentially carry a wide variety of meanings when put together in specific ways. Just as a written alphabet holds the potential to convey very simple meanings or more complex ideas, so does the cellular alphabet have the potential to convey simple or complex meanings. The cellular alphabet is designed in a way that allows for many "sentences" to be created at once. The electromagnetic codes can be arranged in numerous ways simultaneously to create multi-layered meanings—each "sentence" "making a statement" in its own right. But when put together with other "sentences" the elements convey a larger meaning that is "greater than the sum of its parts."

The cellular alphabet speaks through numerous languages simultaneously. It is as if the singular alphabet can be used to create "words and sentences" in French, English, German and Spanish (as an analogy in our example) all at once, each sentence conveying meaning to the "people" (or parts of the organism) that happen to speak that particular language. In the case of human biology, each of your five known "senses"[7] would represent a

---

7. ...and the seven others you have yet to identify. You have 12 senses, as you define the concept.

collective that speaks one of those languages. All of the senses use the same Fire-Letter alphabet, or fixed electromagnetic impulse patterns, but each sense translates into meaning only the "sentences" (strings or sequences of electromagnetic impulse patterns) that use its natural language.

As the biology receives these electromagnetic "meanings" each sense then further translates that meaning into other language forms that the conscious human mind can comprehend. In this way the sense data of your perceptual experience is brought into your conscious awareness. The senses serve as "language translators," translating the sentences from their "native tongue" (the original electromagnetic impulse sequences that were picked up by the individual sense facilities) into a form from which your conscious mind can draw meaning. The visual senses will send the meaning cloaked in images, the hearing sense will send meaning dressed in sound, and so on for all of the senses. Each sense sends one aspect of meaning to the conscious mind via the chemical, hormonal, and neurological systems of the body all translated into language that the conscious mind can interpret. These "sentences of meaning" sent by the senses arrive in the conscious mind simultaneously, creating a collective interpretation of meaning the human experiences as perceived reality. The meaning of this reality is "greater than the sum of its parts." At every step the translators of the base Fire-Letter alphabet and the Fire-Letter alphabet itself remain as meaning conveyors only. The meaning flows through the channels of perception, but the meaning is not "locked inside of the alphabet" or its "word combinations."

When you stimulate certain brain areas, such as in the "fake abduction" experiments, you are manually operating certain random parts of this biological translation system. (You are also doing this when you use certain chemicals, and when you are doing "body-work therapy" and therapies that involve conscious release of cellular memory). The cells that you stimulate will indeed translate the energy, or electrical impulse you have sent. The "alphabet" within the cells will translate that impulse into perceptual data characteristic to the particular electromagnetic codes or Fire Letters you have randomly chosen. In such experiments it is as if you randomly "pull letters from the alphabet," then throw them on the table and decide that the alphabet is meaningless because you cannot make coherent "words" out of the "letters" you have chosen. You are ignoring the rest of the alphabet and the multiple levels of translation this alphabet undergoes as it synthesizes the multiple levels of meaning into a cohesive picture of reality.

When you stimulate the brain and create "abduction-like" perceptual experiences, might we simply suggest that you are accessing part of a translation of a few of the "alphabet letters." This in no way proves that other abduction cases are not real, it only proves that you can stimulate or recreate a version of that experience through artificial means by activating the innate cellular alphabet of fixed electromagnetic code patterns.

In actual UFO/Visitor abductions (and during the normal sensory transla-tion process), the entire alphabet and its translators are used by the Soul Matrix and body consciousness with purposed intent (or intelligently directed pur-pose) and the mechanics of their language are understood by that intelligence. In these cases the alphabet is used to convey meaning. The perceptual experi-ence created through the alphabet is not random and meaningless as it is within your experiments. Your illusion of three-dimensionally solid matter is created in just the same way, the only difference is that different "word combi-nations" (electromagnetic impulse sequence patterns) are used to carry differ-ent meanings. Actual abduction encounters are no more or less real than is your perceptual experience of three-dimensional reality. Both involve the translation of experiential information that organically exists as particle group-ings of electromagnetic energy into symbolic experiential representations of the reality that exists as energy patterns. We repeat: Your experience of three-dimensional matter is no more real or valid than the experiences encountered during actual Visitor abductions. Period. In essence, both are mental aberra-tions, "hallucinations," "holograms" or cover illusions, created through the mind and body to give you the perceptual distortion you call three-dimensional reality. This reality is really energy at its core, regardless of what guise that energy wears. Your three-dimensional system seems quite real to you, and Visi-tors abductions are presently an intrinsic part of that system.

Visitor abduction experiences and the experience of three-dimensionally solid matter are both translations of energy reality as perceived through the Keylontic code structures of the human organism. Both are illusions. But both are quite literal and real. To accurately categorize Visitor abductions as "not real but imagined" you would have to place your three-dimensionally viewed world into the same category.

We are suggesting that you could be of far more assistance to yourselves, and to those who come to you for understanding regarding abductions, if you were to stop viewing the experiences as invalid or as indications of mental imbalance. In abduction-related cases that involve mental imbalance it is usually the abduction that created the condition, not the imbalance creating the illusion of an abduction. People having abduction experiences usually are not mentally ill, they are "ordinary people having extraordinary experiences." Mental illness can however result, in some cases, from the trauma of a repressed, undiagnosed or "botched" Visitor abduction. As we have said before, you would be literally amazed (and most of you terribly frightened) by the number of "patients" in your mental hospitals and under psychiatric care for seemingly "typical or clinical" disorders, who are in actuality the victims of undiagnosed abductions. The mental disorders manifest as a perfectly "normal" personality tries to comprehend and assimilate an experience for which it has no logical framework. Conditions ranging from psychosis to "split-personality syndrome" and even suicide can manifest as the abductee faces an inner terror for which there is seemingly no explanation. But we must stress that there is an explanation and a cause behind many of your apparent mental disorders—the cause is quite often Visitor abduction.

To those of you in the medical and psychiatric communities, if you truly care about the welfare of your patients, we urge you to quickly implement screening techniques (as mentioned earlier in this section) to diagnose the probability, not just the possibility, as abduction affects hundreds of thousands of your people globally—even in cases that appear to be "typical or "clinical" disorders—screening is an invaluable tool. For if Visitor abduction is the cause behind the disorder, traditional modes of treatment will be ineffective in the long run! And using drug therapy to disguise the symptoms will only create a chemical dependence within the body, that will make later memory retrieval therapies more difficult to implement. You should also screen those already diagnosed with most "typical disorders," as true healing of those victimized by abduction can only occur through proper diagnosis and memory retrieval and assimilation therapies. If you care about your people you will begin to develop these screening techniques now and to implement them as soon as possible.

People experiencing Visitor abduction do need treatment, and treatment begins with personal respect. Labeling such individuals as "freaks" or viewing them as "mental cases" only keeps you blind and it harms them rather than healing them. There are many well meaning health practitioners who genuinely care about their patients, and to you we say "please have the courage to open your minds to the possibilities we have suggested and begin the intelligent research that is needed. Speak out about your findings and your feelings, on behalf of professional integrity and on behalf of your patients. Open your heart to those who come to you with abduction "stories." Learn to listen and learn to learn. For it is the abductees themselves that will bring to you the information you need to help those victims who are unaware of these events that haunt them on subconscious levels. Use your wisdom to find those who are presently unaware of their abduction experiences as awareness is the first step toward healing. And we suggest that you begin with yourselves, for many of you are also abductees who have yet to remember. Dig for those memories that are harbored within your bodies and souls and you may indeed discover the existence of that soul. Learn to diagnose and treat others by first diagnosing yourselves, and treat others with the respect and compassion that you yourselves would demand. A whole new world now awaits your exploration."

And now a final bit of information concerning abductees: We are addressing those of you in the scientific and medical communities not only to inform you of the existence of the abduction experience but also to inform you that *you*—the doctors, scientists, clergy, "experts" within many fields, as well as the "common man"— are being abducted on a regular basis. Even if you may scoff at the possibility and have no memory of the encounters.

The enlightened Zeta are now working with you, abducting you in order to train you and in order to teach you things you have not yet dreamed exist. These abductions are those of the "agreement" kind (as previously discussed) and you are treated with great respect. No harm will come to you other than the harm you might do to yourselves in trying to deny the experiences or in resisting the visitation should you become aware during the event. You are being trained in knowledge that will help your people and your world. You are being trained through abduction visitations and in your dreams. Ask yourself sometime, "Where do my thoughts come from?" And before you rationalize away the possibilities, make certain that all of those thoughts belong to you. For the Visitors know the human mind from the "inside out" and are quite able to direct you through the impulses of your own brain wave patterns. These professional communities we have mentioned presently represent the highest percentage of humans who are being abducted. And you, within those communities are the most prepared to conduct yourselves rationally in the face of the unknown. That is why you are selected, why you are part of a select group (which does involve some other non-professional citizens) known as the chosen ones. You will be allowed to remember when you are ready to handle that memory wisely, and then your abductions will no longer be abductions, but instead conscious visitations.

All abductees and the scientists who study them are being confronted with experiences they must grow to understand, and with a very real experiential language that neither are yet prepared to decipher that preparation is to come. The meaning and purpose of the abduction experience lives within its translation, but the meaning will be lost to you if you do not understand the "language" through which it comes.

When you look at a tree in your reality you "see a tree" and *assume* that image is its only reality. You are so accustomed to "seeing trees" that you do not question whether or not what you are perceiving is an aberration or hallucination. You accept the reality of the tree without question. Yet when you see a little grey being with big dark eyes, you begin to question your sanity. Perhaps you have been taught to believe in trees but not in ETs?

In its true reality, the tree is not as you perceive it at all. It exists as glowing patterns of light geometries, energy oscillations and sound emanations. That is the true reality of a tree or any other object or being within your three-dimensional system. However, its solidity is apparent, and its solid reality is validated when that pattern of energy is viewed through the energy patterns you call the human body. Thus it is safe to say that the solid tree represents one aspect of the tree's reality. It is one form that the tree takes within the full pattern of its wholeness. The solid tree is no more real or unreal than any of its other aspects. All of them together are *tree*.

So too is it the same for little grey ETs and spaceships and Visitors from other places. All exist as conscious energy patterns, and when perceived through the energy patterns you call the human body, the patterns appear as little grey ETs, spaceships and Visitors from other places. Or perhaps the energy patterns will appear as mountains, oceans or people walking around in three-dimensional human bodies. The experience of the little grey Visitor, the tree or the human and its three-dimensional world represent one aspect of a reality and identity that is multidimensional.

By the way, if you stumble upon and stimulate the appropriate cells within the human organism, you can make people see trees also. Does this mean that all trees are figments of your imagination? That is a *very loaded question*.

Welcome, dear ones, to the science of the subconscious symbol codes, part of the reality construction system we refer to as **Keylonta Mechanics.**

We will offer more on these mechanics in other transmissions. Until then, happy decoding to all of you, and may your journey to understanding reap many rewards!

> Suaehenatunaz
> Rhanthunkeana Matrix
> Ranthia Transmittance Pattern
> 12/21/96-1/22/97

Levels of Identity and Components of Mind

In this section we will provide two exercises that can, with practice, assist you to begin the process of awakening the multi-dimensional aspects of your identity. In Exercise 1, (See "The Dream-time Self-Hypnosis Exercise" on page 144.) the Monitor Technique is geared toward developing mental focusing ability while in the dream state and to train the mind and body to begin organizing dream experience into sequences that are recognizable to the personality. As these skills develop the dream state can be used to access guidance and information pertinent to the personality in the waking state of consciousness. This exercise is particularly useful when attempting to discover whether you have had contact or abduction experiences with ET or other-dimensional beings in this life time and to access more information and memory pertaining to such contact experiences. The exercise is also useful in applications of memory and data retrieval not related to the Contact/Abduction Phenomena.

Exercise 2 (See "The Keylonta Code Pre-Activation Exercise" on page 152.) the Induction Technique is intended to assist the body and mind of the 3-dimensional personality to come into greater alignment and harmony with the personal Soul Matrix (identity levels stationed in dimensions 4–6). This exercise utilizes rudimentary functions of Keylontic Morphogenetic Science, whereby Keylontic Symbol Codes are used to restructure the organization of the personal Keylon Crystal Body (the crystalline latticework blueprint for the body and consciousness that is composed of ultra-micro particle units called Partiki). The existing arrangement of Keylon Codes within the crystalline morphogenetic body will be subtly rearranged to produce greater conductivity of energy and awareness between the physical body, 3-dimensional personality and the Soul Matrix. This realignment of existing Keylon Codes prepares the body for dormant DNA code activations that can be initiated through Keylontic Science DNA Activations Exercises. This exercise does not activate dormant DNA codes, but prepares the body to better synthesize later DNA activations, thus it is considered to be a Keylon Code Pre-activation Exercise.

In using any form of hypnotic or consciousness-expansion technique it is important to first have a rudimentary understanding of the multi-dimensional mental processes involved in such manipulations of consciousness. You do not have to understand the complex workings of the brain and neurological structure to create a working comprehension of the mind and the attributes of consciousness associated with that facility. It is however useful to have a basic model of the structure of multi-dimensional identity in order to gain sovereignty over the processes associated with the multi-dimensional mind. For this reason we will provide the following model of multi-dimensional identity and a brief introduction to the Components of Mind associated with these identity levels. Using this framework you will be able to begin learning to direct multi-dimensional energy into effective transformational patterns on a conscious level. At your present stage of evolution much of these energy-directing functions take place on levels of awareness that are beyond your conscious view. As your consciousness evolves these functions will progressively come under your conscious direction.

THE SIX PRIMARY LEVELS OF IDENTITY AND THE FOUR COMPONENTS OF MIND.

The "mind" is an attribute of consciousness. The mind does not produce consciousness, consciousness is not a product of mind, but rather the mind is a structure of energy that consciousness creates and uses in order to participate within realities that have their basis in differentiated perception. Perception itself is an attribute of consciousness and mind, it is the product of consciousness using the facilities and structures of mind. The mind is the portion of your identity that allows you to experience individuality. The mind exists as a large conglomerate of electromagnetic energy units called **Partiki**, which span multiple dimensional fields. Consciousness itself does not possess form other than the units of electrotonal energy of which it is composed (Partiki), but consciousness uses form constructions such as the mind to create the experience of differentiated perception. The form construction of the mind is created through organized groupings of Partiki units or "electrotonal units of consciousness."

The form construction of the mind has multiple levels that correspond directly to the form construction of the 15-dimensional universe. Dimensions exist as smaller Unified Fields of energy within the larger structures of the Universal and Cosmic Unified Fields. Like the structure of the mind, the cosmos is also composed of organizations of Partiki units that form a crystalline matrix upon and within which all differentiated forms and identities are created. Dimensions are smaller organizations of crystalline Partiki structure that form distinct bands of frequency—patterns of electromagnetic, light, sound and scalar waves—that serve to arrange consciousness in ways through which perception and dimensionalized creation can take place. The structure of the mind is interwoven with the greater structures of the Cosmic Unified Field. Both the structures of the cosmos and the structures of the individual mind are composed of the electrotonal energy substance of Partiki units—units of electrotonal consciousness—and thus the structures of the cosmos and its inherent universes can be viewed in terms of the Universal and Cosmic Mind. The individual mind exists and takes place within the dimensionalized construction of the Cosmic Mind. In simple terms the individual mind is composed of consciousness that manifests as electromagnetic micro-particles that travel in dimensionalized bands of frequency and which create the contours of manifest form and identity.

The bands of frequency that form the mind structure are composed of Partiki units that group to form "interwoven fibers or strings of Partiki" called Partiki Grids. **Partiki Grids** further group to form **Keylons**, the crystalline structures that form the blueprints for identity and matter manifestation. The Keylon blueprint is the **Morphogenetic Field** (form-holding template) upon which the structures of the mind and body are built. Within the greater construction of a 15-dimensional Universal Matrix the personal identity possess a 15-dimensional Morphogenetic Field (a "Keylon Body") that energetically connects the individual identity to the universe and to the cosmos. In universal structure the 15 dimensions are grouped into triads of 3 dimensions each, forming 5 interwoven, over-laid reality fields that are called **Harmonic Universes (HU)**. Each individual mind has a level of **Triadic Identity** (or 3-dimensional identity) stationed within the frequency bands of the 5 Harmonic Universes. The portion of mind that is known as the "Earthly identity" represents the portion of the mind that exists within Harmonic Universe-1, the portion of personal consciousness that is stationed within frequency bands of dimensions 1, 2 and 3. This HU-1 Triadic Identity is one of 6 primary identity levels that exist within the Cosmic Unified Field. The 6 Primary Levels of Multi-dimensional Identity are as follows:

1. Triadic Identity 1: the **Tauren (the Incarnate Matrix)**– HU-1, composed of frequency bands from dimensions 1, 2 and 3. Includes the **Subconscious, Instinctual** and **Reasoning Mind**. Represents the Individual Mind Matrix (or "Personal Logos").

2. Triadic Identity—the **Dora (the Soul Matrix)**—HU-2, composed of frequency bands from dimensions 4, 5, and 6. Includes the **Astral Mind**, the **Archetypal Mind** and the **Angelic (or "Celestial") Mind**. Collectively called the **Superconscious Mind**. Represents the Race Mind Matrix. (or "Collective Logos").

3. Triadic Identity—the **Teura (the Oversoul Matrix)**—HU-3, composed of frequency bands from dimensions 7, 8 and 9. Includes the **Ketheric Mind**, the **Monadic Mind** and the **Keriatric Mind**. Collectively called the **Causal Mind.** Represents the Planetary Mind Matrix (or "Planetary Logos").

4. Triadic Identity—the **Avatar (the Dolar Matrix)**—HU-4, composed of frequency bands from dimensions 10, 11 and 12. Includes the **Christiac Mind**, the **Buddhiac Mind** and the **Nirvanic Mind**. Collectively called the **Metaconscious Mind**. Represents the Galactic Mind Matrix (or "Solar Logos").

5. Triadic Identity—the **Rishi (the Solar Matrix)**—HU-5, composed of frequency bands from dimensions 13, 14 and 15. Includes the **Particum Mind**, the **Partiki Mind** and the **Partika Mind**. Collectively called the **Universal Conscious Mind**. Represents the **Universal Mind Matrix** (or "Universal Logos").

6. Identity Level—the **Geomancy (the Yunasai Matrix)** The 6th Primary level of Multi-dimensional Identity exists beyond the structure of 15-dimensional construction. Collectively called the **Cosmic Conscious Mind**. Represents the Cosmic Mind Matrix (or the "Cosmic Logos"). It represents an eternal gestalt of identity that is non-dimensionalized and free from space-time-matter orientation, a level of mind that exists as part of the One Mind—or the Source Mind of the Core Creative Force. This identity level is called the **Geomantic Entity—or Geomancy**. All other levels of identity and mind and the structures of all dimensional systems exist within the crystalline latticework morphogenetic blueprint of the Geomantic Entity Gestalt identity. Through the Geomancy all things, beings and consciousness are connected to and contained within the Central Creative Gestalt Identity of Source Mind.

The structure of the 6 Primary Levels of Multi-dimensional Identity represent a literal **Family Tree of Consciousness** through which all humans are connected to each other, all other life forms, the Universes, the Cosmos and Source Mind—one Mind ("God"). From the perspective of the HU-1 incarnate identity the process of evolution is the process of incorporating all six levels of multi-dimensional identity into the conscious cognition of "I am...." The first step in awakening multi-dimensional identity is to bring the *Superconscious Mind of the HU-2 Soul Matrix* into conscious recognition within the biologically focused personality. This process is called **Soul Integration**. Within the process of Soul Integration you are primarily dealing with 4 Components of Mind—the Subconscious Mind of D-1 frequency bands, the Instinctual Mind of D-2 frequency bands, the Reasoning Mind of D-3 frequency bands and the Superconscious Mind of the D-4 through D-6 Soul Matrix gestalt. Soul Integration comes with conscious assimilation of these 4 Components of Mind.

THE FOUR COMPONENTS OF MIND

I. The Subconscious Mind/Body Consciousness/ Cellular Memory Facility

Key Functions: Data Storage. Stores perceptual imprints from various Components of Mind and stores directional impulses from the Superconscious Mind, through which the body receives its operational "orders" from the Soul Matrix.

The Subconscious Mind is composed of Partiki units and Keylons, it exists as a minute crystalline blueprint within the cellular structure of the body and serves as a memory storage facility and regulator of the body's autonomic processes. Memory is stored within the cells and Keylon Codes of the entire body, not just within the brain. The biological memory of the Subconscious Mind is called **Cellular Memory.** The Subconscious Mind is the portion of your personal identity that manifests as the physical body form and the crystalline blueprint within the molecular structure. It represents the "Body Consciousness." It is this portion of identity that is accessed when using techniques such as hypnosis. The Subconscious Mind translates energy signatures from the dimensional Unified Fields of energy into perceptual data such as light, sound, taste, smell, touch, temperature, objectified form and linear passage through time.

Working co-creatively with the other Components of Mind the Subconscious Mind creates the holographic illusion of 3-dimensional matter, objectified space and linear passage through time. Keylontic Symbol Codes are the languages of the Subconscious Mind. The Subconscious Mind translates thoughts, ideas and beliefs into Keylontic Symbol Codes of light, sound and electromagnetic standing wave patterns that direct the morphogenetic Keylon structure of the body. Thoughts will thus affect the health or disease of the body, as their biological Keylontic translations will either assist or impede the flow of energy between the body, the personality and the Soul Matrix. The Reasoning Mind can use Keylontic Symbol Codes to direct the processes of the Subconscious Mind and body and to access information stored within Cellular Memory. The Subconscious Mind is primarily associated with frequency bands of D-1, the physical body, the 1st DNA strand, the Base

Chakra and the Etheric Body (1st level out from the physical body) level of the bio-energetic field.

II. The Instinctual Mind: the Emotional/Intuitive facility.

Key Function: Data Relay. To relay directional electrical impulse and information from the Soul Matrix/Superconscious Mind into Cellular Memory storage within the body/Subconscious Mind.

The Instinctual Mind is also composed of Partiki and Keylons, it exists as a minute crystalline blueprint within and surrounding the body and serves to draw information in the form of electrical impulse from the Soul Matrix into the Subconscious Mind/Cellular Memory. Emotion and Intuition represent translations of information from the Soul Matrix/Superconscious Mind as they are relayed to the Subconscious Mind via the Instinctual Mind. The instinctual behavior of animals occurs through a similar process of information "downloading" from the collective species Soul Matrix into the Cellular Memory. Originally the human Instinctual Mind was intended to hold the individuated identity in place while keeping the identity intimately connected to the Soul Matrix and to the guiding impulses of the Superconscious Mind. Due to ancient DNA manipulations of the human gene code the electrical impulses from the Soul Matrix are unable to fully process into the Cellular Memory of the body. The impulses "pool" within the bio-energetic field creating an area of disorganized, chaotic energy between the body, personality and Soul Identity. This area of chaotic energy represents the first level of dream reality that the consciousness will encounter as it disassociates from the Body Consciousness during sleep.

The Instinctual Mind sets the organizational sequence of memory as it will be programmed into the body. Due to the present DNA distortion within the Instinctual Mind memory of multi-dimensional experience, dream reality and cognition of the Superconscious Mind is jumbled within Cellular Memory and appears fragmented to the Reasoning Mind. Repression of emotion and intuition contribute to the distortion of the Instinctual Mind and can create exaggerated physical, emotional, psychological and memory distortions within the identity. Keylontic Science techniques can be used to "side step" the area of chaotic energies within the Instinctual Mind to create clearer memory retrieval, dream recall and communication between the body/Subconscious Mind, Reasoning Mind and the Superconscious Mind. Keylontic DNA realignments and activations can be used to correct the genetic distortion of the Instinctual Mind. The Instinctual Mind is primarily associated with frequency bands of D-2, the emotional-intuitive awareness, the second DNA strand, the second Sacral Chakra and the Emotional Body (second level out from the physical body) level of the auric field.

III. *The Reasoning Mind: the Logical/Rational facility*

Key Function: Data assimilation, translation and manifestation. Assimilates electrical impulse data from other Components of Mind, translates these impulses into patterns recognizable to the waking personality and assists in the holographic projection/manifestation of electrotonal Keylon Codes from the Cellular Memory into externally perceivable reality.

The Reasoning Mind is composed of Partiki units and Keylons, it exists as a minute crystalline blueprint within and surrounding the body and serves to synthesize and translate data from other Components of Mind into a holographic representation of external, 3-dimensionally perceivable reality. It is intended to allow the identity to observe and experience the illusion of matter-density and to perceive and interact with objectified space, time and form.

The Reasoning Mind also assists the Superconscious Mind/Soul Matrix in the manifestation of the biological organism and serves to direct many functions within the Subconscious Mind/body and the Instinctual Mind/emotions and intuition. The Reasoning Mind was designed to assimilate electrical impulses from all fields of perception into a solidified and coherent picture that allows for the experience of individuated biological identity within the framework of space-time-matter. It is a synthesizer of energy, translator of Keylontic Codes and projector of holographic imagery. Part of the Reasoning Mind utilizes the physical brain and neurological structure. Portions of the Reasoning Mind exist within the structures of the Body Consciousness and work co-creatively with the Subconscious Mind. Other portions of the Reasoning Mind exist within the Instinctual Mind and the Superconscious Mind of the Soul Matrix. The Reasoning Mind is multidimensional and it is simultaneously focused within the Four Components of Mind. It represents the organizational aspect of mind through which perceptual data from all Components of Mind can be brought together into a cohesive reality picture.

The "ego/conscious personality" represents the portion of the Reasoning Mind that is primarily focused within the frequency bands of the third dimension, which "looks out upon the illusion of matter-space-time." The "Dream self/higher self" and the "Astral self" represent the portions of the Reasoning Mind that are interwoven with the Superconscious Mind within the Soul Matrix. They serve to assimilate higher dimensional experience and information into terms comprehensible to the ego identity. Due to genetic distortions and the present level of genetic evolution, humans must disassociate the consciousness from the ego and the body during sleep, in order to have full conscious focus within the body of the Dream self, Astral self or Soul Matrix. The Intuitive-self represents the portion of the Reasoning Mind that is intertwined with the Instinctual Mind and emotional body, which

140

serves to unite the physical body/Cellular Memory/Subconscious Mind with the higher dimensional levels of identity. The Dream self/higher self, the Astral self and the Intuitive-self represent portions of the Reasoning Mind that operate, experience and perceive simultaneously with the Ego self, whether or not the ego is consciously aware of these perceptions. Information gained through the various portions of the Reasoning Mind can become available to the ego/personality if the ego accepts its responsibility for being the conscious director of energy that it was intended to be. The ego can build a bridge between the Dream self/higher-self, the Intuitive-self and the Astral self through learning to expand its attention and by working with Keylontic Science. As the ego begins to assimilate the other portions of the Reasoning Mind, the seeming barriers between the Dream self, Astral self, Soul Matrix and Body Consciousness will begin to dissolve. When fully assimilated the Reasoning Mind will have conscious multi-dimensional perception and the ability to direct the Subconscious and Instinctual Minds (and the physical body, emotions and intuition that manifest through the "lower minds") through conscious interaction with the Superconscious Mind of the Soul Matrix.

The Reasoning Mind is primarily associated with the frequency bands of D-3, the logical-rational mental awareness, the third DNA strand, the third Solar Plexus Chakra and the Mental Body (third level out from the physical body) level of the bio-energetic field.

IV. The Superconscious Mind: The Group Soul Matrix
(Note: the second triadic identity of the multi-dimensional identity structure, exists within the D-4 through D-6 frequency bands of HU-2).

Key Function: Creation of experiential templates and individual identities in HU-1. Serves as the creative intelligence behind the manifestation of individuated identities and experiential events in HU-1.

The superconscious Mind/Soul Matrix is composed of Partiki units and Keylons. It exists as a minute crystalline blueprint within and surrounding the matter body in HU-1 and HU-2 and serves as the creative intelligence behind and within sets of 12 physical bodies/identities/incarnates that exist in different space-time locations within HU-1. The Soul Matrix is composed of dimensional frequency bands 4-6 and it holds the templates for biological manifestation, life purpose and experiential dramas within the lower dimensional fields of HU-1. The Superconscious Mind of the Soul Matrix replicates itself through electromagnetic fission then fragments the replica of its consciousness into sets of 12 individuated identities that become singular biological incarnational identities, which are simultaneously placed within the space-time fields of HU-1. Each of the 12 identities in an HU-1 set or "soul family" are directly connected to each other and to the original Superconscious Mind through the Morphogenetic Keylontic structure of the Soul Matrix. The Soul Matrix holds the developmental evolutionary blueprint and memory for each of its HU-1 incarnates and serves to guide the HU-1 incarnational personalities to their highest evolution through information communicated via electrical impulses sent into the HU-1 body through the Instinctual Mind.

Within the Soul Matrix the memory of the purposes and intentions for each individual HU-1 life is stored as well as the memory of the greater purposes and intentions for the set of 12 simultaneous incarnations. Each HU-1 incarnate has free will and can choose to override the impulses sent to it by the Soul Matrix, but the highest evolution and greatest fulfillment of the incarnate comes from following the directives of the Superconscious Mind. The Superconscious Mind represents the creative and organizational component of mind through which the individuated identity is imbued with purpose, intention, motivation and the literal life-force energy through which the HU-1 body is sustained. Embodiment of the Soul Matrix through the evolutionary process of Soul Integration allows the lower dimensional components of mind to fully assimilate into an advanced state of consciousness through which the identity recognizes the plural nature of its simultaneous existence in various dimensions and space-time locations. The Soul Matrix identity manifests as a singular, less-dense matter body within the frequency fields of HU-2 and experiences its HU-1 incarnates as Cellular Memory of its smaller, simultaneous manifestations that exist in HU-1. The incarnate identity was designed to expand back into the Soul Matrix identity following death or transmutation of the HU-1 physical body. The Soul Matrix and Superconscious Mind connect the HU-1 incarnates and the HU-2 Soul Body to the higher dimensional levels of identity and to the original Geomantic Entity Gestalt that exists eternally beyond dimensionalization. The Soul Matrix—Superconscious Mind connects directly to the Over-soul Matrix Causal Mind of HU-3 (dimensions 7, 8 and 9).

The Superconscious Mind represents the portion of your personal identity that holds the awareness of "who I was before I came here" and why you, as a consciousness, chose your particular incarnation. It is connected to the astral identity, the group Incarnational Soul and also to the race mind, species mind and planetary consciousness, as well as to the mind networks of you and your incarnational selves that exist within parallel universe systems. It represents the collective consciousness of your Archetypal identity that knows itself as a singular-being-composed-of-many within the less-dense matter fields of Harmonic Universe–2. The Superconscious Mind contains the D-4 Astral Mind, the D-5 Archetypal Mind and the D-6 Angelic (Celestial) Mind.

The Superconscious Mind of the Soul Matrix is primarily associated with the frequency bands of D-4, D-5 and D-6, the Astral, the Archetypal and the

Angelic awareness, DNA strands 4, 5 and 6, Chakras 4, 5 and 6 and the Astral (fourth level out from the physical body), Archetypal (fifth level out) and the Angelic (6th level out) levels of the bio-energetic field.

Speaker: Valdmyrun
Rhanthunkeana Matrix,
Ranthia Transmittance Pattern
2/26/1997 (update: 1/15/1999)

THE DREAM-TIME SELF-HYPNOSIS EXERCISE

The Monitor Technique

The following exercise is formatted for retrieval of memory and information pertaining to phenomena related to experiences of contact and/or abduction by ET or Other-dimensional (OD) Visitors. The format can be adjusted to reflect other areas of interest by substituting the desired area of exploration for the "target" questions during the exercise.

Choosing a Target

Prior to using this exercise you are to decide upon a "target" that will organize the mental focus and memory retrieval processes within the dream state.

The target can be a direct question (such as "Have I been involved with ET or OD Visitor activity in this lifetime?" or "Are there any unusual events related to UFOs in the past during this lifetime of which I should now be aware?"). If using a question as the target, it is best to use your own wording and to be specific in what information you are asking to receive. (If you are bilingual, phrase the question in the language that is native to your childhood).

Write the question down in a notebook and keep this, with a writing instrument, next to your bed.

You may use other targets, such as feelings or event targets, either singly, or in combination with the target question. If there is a period of time in your life from which memory seems noticeably vague, periods in which you feel you may have experienced "missing time" or events in which you remember having a strange encounter or sighting, these also make good target events. (For non-Visitor related format past areas of trauma, uneasiness or confusion can be used as target events.) You will simply call the event or time period to mind, becoming aware of the feelings or imagery associated with it, then **Lasso** the image or sensation using mentally directed imagery.

In your "mind's eye" draw a circle of energy around the inner image or sensation, leaving a "tail" of energy dangling from the visualized circle. You may draw the image and the "Lasso" in your notebook if you wish.

A third way to decide upon a target is to ask your body consciousness/ Subconscious Mind directly for a body target within the Cellular Memory. Recline in a relaxed position and take several slow, deep breaths until you notice that your heart and breathing rates are slowing slightly.

Clear and still the mind. Mentally direct a question to the body consciousness, realizing that you are literally communicating with a portion of your identity that is aware within the body cells. Ask the body if there is a particular area of memory being held in Cellular Memory that would help you to locate the information you seek. Ask it to direct your attention to a specific area of the body in which that memory is stored, then still the mind again.

Next place your attention within the body and imagine that you are scanning its energy signature from the inside out. Begin at the feet and slowly sweep your attention upward through the body, becoming aware of the inner structures of bone, tissue, organs etc.

As you scan, notice any area that gives you a different impression, sensation, image or feeling than other areas. You may feel a slight tingling in the body target area, a sense of heat or cold, or you may get mental imagery of color change or a mental picture of the body area to which the Subconscious Mind is guiding you for memory retrieval. Some people may receive a direct language translation from the Subconscious Mind, in which a thought such as "the left knee" may come to your awareness. If you focus your attention clearly and keep your mind still you will receive some indication from the Body Consciousness as to what area of the body holds the memory in question.

•**Once you have the target body area, mentally "Lasso" this area with a circle of energy within your mind's eye, keeping the clear intention that you will retrieve the pertinent memory within the dream state.**

You may also want to make a note of the body target in your notebook.

Prior to Sleep

You may choose your target at any time then keep your notebook handy as you prepare for sleep. It is suggested to use this exercise when you plan to get at least 4 full hours of sleep rather than in shorter sleep periods. As you recline review the pre-selected target notes in your notebook and focus your attention on the target.

1. **Holding the target in mind begin to relax the body. Starting at the feet visualize a white mist surrounding the feet. Imagine the mist moving down and through the feet, touching all parts, both internally and externally. Imagine a feeling of lightness spreading through the feet as the mist gently flows over, through and into the cells of the feet. Move your attention and the mist slowly up the legs, stopping over and concentrating the mist in areas until the sensation of lightness is felt.**

   As you move past an area on the body imagine that this area of the body has become invisible as the mist moves away from it, as if you are "rolling the body up" from the feet upward—as you might do with a sleeping bag. Continue to move the mist upward until you reach the head area, creating the feeling of lightness or "not-there-ness" in all body parts. (If you fall asleep before finishing this visualization, simply practice again during the next sleep period, telling your body and Subconscious Mind that you will remain consciously aware throughout the exercise and once you have entered the dream state. With practice of these self-hypnotic commands, you will train your consciousness to follow these instructions.)

Once the visualized mist has reached your head imagine that it is pulling together, concentrating into a small pin-point of light directly over your forehead near the brow area (6th Chakra). Hold the image of the pin-point of light in your mind's eye for a few moments until you can see it clearly.

You will now mentally "name" the pin-point of white light, it will be called "Monitor." Monitor represents the concentrated focus of your awareness and you will take it with you into the dream state. (It may take several attempts before you are able to remain awake this far into the exercise, but do not become discouraged. Continue to use the visualization until you have trained your consciousness to hold the focus. Success will come with consistent repetition. Three days "on"—two days "off" is a good format to use in training your consciousness to hold such a focus.)

Give yourself the mental command of "Monitor On." This will send a subliminal message to the 4 Components of Mind that you are intending to be consciously aware and operable within the dream state.

2. **After giving the "Monitor On" command you will next visualize a circle of blue light surrounding the pin-point of white light.** This step is important as it is programming your consciousness to align with the Soul Matrix in the sleep state. The "circle" represents a Keylontic Symbol Code that will allow your consciousness to pass through the chaotic confusion of the Instinctual Mind and into the Soul Matrix via the Dream self. (The color of blue represents a frequency of light that translates into sound patterns of the fifth dimension, where the center of the Soul Matrix is stationed. Using this frequency in visualization will harmonically align your consciousness with the consciousness of your Archetypal Mind.) This Symbol Code will assist the Reasoning Mind of your Dream self and the Reasoning Mind of your waking focus that you are bringing into the dream, to merge successfully in the dream state. It will further direct the unified Reasoning Mind into the Supraconscious Mind of the Soul Matrix.

3. **As you relax with the image of the white pin-point of light "Monitor" within the blue circle Symbol Code, call to mind the target you have previously "lassoed." Imagine the contents of the lasso, the target you have previously placed within its boundaries and try to sense the energy**

signature of the contents. There will be a "feel" to the contents of the lasso, which represents the Keylon Code morphogenetic energy identity of the thoughts, images, emotions and sensations contained within the lasso.

Next, color the "Lasso" Symbol Code yellow gold. This will program the subliminal suggestion that the intellectual/Reasoning Mind will be operable within the dream and will serve to organize the dream information for retrieval by the waking consciousness.

Mentally take the dangling "tail" of the golden lasso and connect it to the Monitor pin-point of white light. Visualize the Monitor pulling the Lasso into its center until all that remains is a tiny golden speck of light at the center of the white pin-point of light. Now give the mental command "Monitor Retrieve." Continue to visualize the blue circle surrounding the white point of light with the gold speck of light at its center, as you fall asleep. Become aware of your breathing rhythm and with each inhale begin to move the Symbol Code inward toward the center of your brain (the pineal gland specifically).

With each exhale imagine the Symbol Code expanding outward to encompass your head (and body if you still find yourself being aware of the body's position).

Contract the Symbol Code into your brain with each inhale and expand it outward to encompass your head and body with each exhale, synchronizing this visualization with your breathing rhythm. (This allows the subliminal Symbol Code to become programmed into the Cellular Memory.)

Take 4 to 6 breaths then stop at the final inhale, positioning the symbol at the center of your brain.

4. **Next, visualize a small version of yourself "riding" at the center of the Symbol Code, as if you are driving the Symbol as a vehicle that will carry you into the dream state** (you are and it will...).

As the driver, give the mental command "Monitor Retrieve." Keeping the image of the Symbol Code in mind and simultaneously feeling yourself within it, begin spinning the Symbol Code counter-clockwise. (Imagine the front of your body as the face of a clock with the digit-12 position at the top of the head and the digit-3 position to the left—to spin the Symbol counter-clockwise spin it toward the right where the digit-9 position would be).

Trace the spin in your mind while visualizing the Symbol image and repeating the mental command "Monitor Retrieve," as you fall off to sleep.

As You Awaken

5. As you awaken you will train your mind to remember the Symbol Code as you come into the consciously "awake" state. First try to recall the Symbol, even before focusing your attention on any dream material that may be present. The Symbol will serve to organize recall into patterns pertinent to information that you seek.

   Keep your eyes closed and allow yourself to awaken slowly and try to observe the levels of consciousness that you pass through as you slowly emerge from the sleep state. Bring the Symbol into focus in your mind as soon as you are able. Once you see the Symbol, clearly give the command "Monitor Retrieve." Repeat the command several times in your mind then focus your attention on your breathing rhythm.

6. With each inhale imagine that you can feel the energy of the dream material pulling up from the depths of the dream world, collecting within the center of the Symbol. Continue to "breathe" the energy up into the Symbol for as long as you feel the stream of energy flowing. You will reach a point when you feel this stream of energy depleting, growing fainter, until you can no longer feel the movement of this stream of energy. (It may take a few sessions before you can sense the beginning of this stream of energy, but it will be there.)

   When you sense the end of the energy stream take 3 more natural breaths as the energy "settles" into the Symbol Code. Your Symbol Code is now "loaded" with electrically encoded data from the other Components of Mind as derived through the dream state.

7. Moving your body slowly, pick up your notebook and writing instrument, then recline with these in hand and close your eyes again. Focus on your breathing again and give the command "Monitor Retrieve." Allow the energy contained within the Symbol to expand into your body and awareness with your breathing rhythm, expanding the energy with each exhale. This process "downloads" the digital data from the Symbol Code into the Cellular Memory, following the organizational instructions of the Symbol Code.

   Keeping your mind calm and focused on the exercise will allow images, thoughts and emotional impressions from your dream experience to emerge within your mind. (With practice they will).

8. Give yourself the mental command to "Record" as the dream impressions emerge from the Symbol into your mind and allow the images or feelings to flow without being interrupted by other thoughts or body movement. At times the emotional imprint will come first and if you will allow it to flow it will lead to dream imagery. At some point the

flow of sensations and images will stop and you will sense a "settling" of the energy. This indicates that you have processed the body of dream material that you retrieved from the sleep state.

9. **Moving slowly and remaining focused and relaxed, open your eyes and write down the dream impressions and any commentary that comes to mind.** Do not worry about sequence or content in the early weeks of using this exercise, but rather focus upon training your consciousness to use this memory retrieval format. The sequence, content and meaning of the dream impressions will become clearer as your Subconscious Mind internalizes the new Keylonta Code program.

Applications and Indications

The "Monitor Technique" is a good place to begin in exploring and utilizing the inner contours of your consciousness. It will take practice to remember the steps of this exercise and practice is needed for the subliminal Keylonta Symbol Code organizational program to "take" within the Keylontic crystalline blueprint of the Subconscious Mind. After 3 days of practicing the entire exercise use only the Symbol Code image and the command *"Monitor Retrieve"* prior to sleep for the next 2 days. Begin the entire exercise again on the third day and continue the "3-day long version—2-day short version" format for 4–6 weeks. Following 6–8 weeks of consecutive training, you should be able to use only the target/mist/"Monitor Retrieve" command/Symbol Code image portions of the exercise to create the same results as the entire long version of the exercise, as the program will then operate on a subconscious level. After this time you should observe a noticeable difference in your dream content and recall, and you should be able to easily elicit from the dream state answers to pre-set questions.

When using this exercise to discover whether or not you have Visitor contact or abduction related memories it is best to phrase the target question in a way that can be answered in a "yes-or-no" format. The first target question could be "Is there Visitor contact related material stored within the Cellular Memory of this lifetime?" Using such a simplified target it should take no longer than 3 to 4 days to retrieve an answer as to whether Visitor involvement should be a subject for further exercises. Once you become familiar with the technique you should be able to retrieve specific and detailed information regarding your target question. This technique can be used for problem solving and to generate new creative material, as well as to retrieve memories.

Individuals who are not generally prone to dream recall should find more dream memory surfacing into consciousness with practice of this exercise. At first the recall may appear fragmented. In using this exercise with a positive attitude you should see results similar to those experienced by people with avid dream recall, but it may just take more practice. We might add that people who believe they "do not dream" or who have no dream recall, may harbor hidden beliefs about dreaming that operate as subliminal suggestions serving to block the recollection of dreams. Dreaming is a natural and intrinsic part of human consciousness at your present stage of evolution and some recall should be apparent, even if it is sporadic. If no dream recall is experienced you may be holding the hidden idea that dreams are insignificant and thus not worthy of attention. Or you may feel that dreams represent a frightening and chaotic portion of your psyche and you may avoid recall because it threatens your sense of personal control. In either case such ideas will suppress your memory of natural dream activity. You *do* dream, so it is not a matter of having no dreams, but rather that you inadvertently block them by ideas that you hold. In such cases it is helpful to examine your ideas about dreaming and perhaps change your ideas to reflect the new understanding that dreams are a safe and natural way to gain practical and pertinent information. Dreams are not chaotic and they do possess a natural associative organization. Dreams will appear disorganized to the consciousness that is not yet skilled in sequential retrieval. As with any other learned activity, skill level improves with education and practice.

People inclined to dream recall may see rapid results from this exercise. Frequent episodes of **Lucid Dreaming** or **Projection of Consciousness** from the dream state may begin to occur. You may gain more clarity and sequential consistency in dream recall and you may find yourself aware of **Simultaneous Dreaming**, in which you "catch yourself" participating in several dream dramas at the same time. As the Keylonta Symbol Code organizational program is established within the Subconscious Mind you may awaken with the answers to your target question simply "appearing within your mind" in a form of direct cognition. You may also find yourself experiencing "reading dream " or "movie dream" recall. In these experiences the data that has been subconsciously programmed into the Symbol Code reveals itself to you as you begin to awaken, appearing within the inner vision as "text written upon a page," which you can literally read for content. For more visually orientated individuals images, still pictures or "running movies" may appear, rather than written text. The "text" or "movie" dream impressions indicate that the Symbol Code program has effectively "taken" within the Subconscious Mind, the *"Monitor Retrieve"* command works on a subliminal level automatically and the dreams are translated into a format most familiar to your waking consciousness.

When you reach this level of dream retrieval, do not worry about focusing upon the Symbol Code as you awaken. Keep your eyes closed, your body still and allow the text or imagery to flow through your mind. Concentrate on the material as it runs through your mind, intending to remember the content as clearly as possible. When the data stops running, slowly open your eyes and record what you remember in your notebook. If you open your eyes or move the body too quickly you may "lose" the flow of data.

Data retrieval from the Subconscious Mind and dream state is most clear when consciousness makes a slow, subtle transition from the Subconscious Mind into waking awareness. With practice you can become accustomed to being awake and aware while your consciousness is stationed within the frequency bands of the Subconscious Mind. You can then train your consciousness to make a slow "climb" into waking awareness. Mastery of this skill will imprint the Reasoning Mind with new neuro-passageways that will allow you to enter into the Cellular Memory at will for conscious retrieval of data. Such advanced skills require practice in becoming aware of and directing the focus of your consciousness. Exercises such as the *Monitor Technique*, as well as various forms of meditation, creative visualization and projection of consciousness can help you to develop skill in consciously directing your consciousness through the various Components of Mind. These skills are the beginning stages of mastery of the conscious focus within the dream state and the entry point to a "whole new world" of multi-dimensional frontiers to explore. Dream realities will eventually lead you to multi-dimensional cognition and mobility. Developing skill in maneuvering the contours of dream reality will accelerate the process of unifying the Components of Mind and Levels of Identity and expedite the process of Soul Integration.

THE KEYLONTA CODE PRE-ACTIVATION EXERCISE

The Induction Technique

This exercise utilizes the direct induction of primary Keylonta Symbol Codes into areas of the body and bio-energetic field. Induction of these organic Keylon Codes will serve to reorganize the existing crystalline blueprint Keylon Code structures within the body cells and bio-energetic field into arrangements more conducive to mental, emotional and physical balance and frequency harmonization and integration between the various Components of Mind and Levels of Identity. The Keylon Codes work subliminally to affect the Components of Mind by creating harmony of vibratory oscillation rates between the energy units and particles that compose the various levels of multi-dimensional identity. The Pre-activation Keylonta Symbol Codes do not add or delete from the existing Keylon Code organizations of the morphogenetic body—they simply arrange existing codes into more effective patterns. In using this exercise as indicated an overall improvement of mental, emotional, physical and spiritual balance should become apparent, as well as improvement in centering and directing personal energy. Balancing of the existing Keylontic structure of the body prepares the physical body and the embodied consciousness to receive more higher frequency energy/identity/awareness/information from the Soul Matrix and accelerates the process of Soul Integration.

The Induction Technique is to be done from a waking state of consciousness, not in association with sleep. Following the completion of the exercise it is useful to relax for 10-15 minutes and if you fall asleep during this period it will not detract from the effectiveness of the exercise.

Things You Will Need

A. The Keylonta Symbol Code Placement Chart.

B. Four Keylontic Symbol Codes, pre-selected from the Keylontic Symbol Code Placement Chart.

C. A small bottle of fragrant "essence oil", such as the kind used in Aroma-Therapy. If you do not have essence oil you may use any type of baby oil or body lotion, but we recommend essence oil as the fragrance is concentrated and more easily affects the mind and body on subliminal levels.

D. A private, quiet setting in which you can comfortably recline undisturbed for 20-30 minutes.

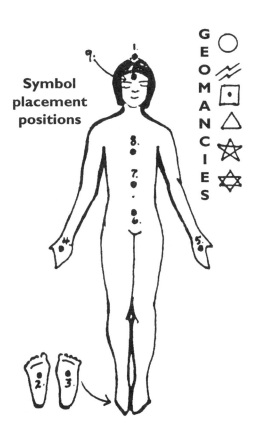

Symbol placement positions

Subdued lighting is recommended but not required. A soothing musical "relaxation type" recording with a slow tempo and no words can assist if outside noise is a problem, but natural silence is preferable whenever possible.

THE EXERCISE

1. Begin the exercise by removing any tight clothing. (For greater comfort we recommend removing all clothing during the exercise.) **Place the Keylonta Symbol Code Placement Chart and the essence oil within easy reach then recline on your back on a comfortable surface. Calm your mind and let all thoughts drift away from your attention. Focus on the rhythm of your breathing for a few moments and consciously slow the breathing rate until the body is relaxed. Give the command "Body relaxed and receptive now"**

to the body consciousness/Subconscious Mind. This can be done mentally, but it is more effective if it is audibly whispered so that you can hear
the command objectively as well as internally. **Repeat the command
slowly 3 times without interruption.**

2. Using the essence oil place a small "dot" of oil from your finger tip onto
   each of the body areas marked 1–5 on the Keylonta Symbol Code
   Placement Chart. Then, with the Symbol Code Chart in view, trace 1
   of the 4 selected Symbol Codes over each body area marked 6–9, using
   a small amount of essence oil on your finger tip. (Chart positions 6–9
   correspond with Chakra centers 2, 3, 4 and 6.)When you have finished
   tracing the Symbol Codes onto the body recline and close your eyes,
   allowing the aroma of the oil to expand around you. (If you are breathing too fast and are not fully relaxed it will be more difficult to feel the
   sensation of the aroma "spreading." By slowing your breathing and concentrating on the aroma you will deepen your state of relaxation.)

3. Focus again on your breathing rhythm and glance at the image of the
   first Symbol Code that you traced on position #6. Focus your attention
   on this position on the body and begin to visualize the Symbol Code
   spinning clockwise, in a circular motion over the body area (imagine
   the front of your body as the face of a clock with the digit-12 at the head,
   the digit-3 at the left, etc. Spin the Symbol Code toward the left for clockwise rotation.)

   As you mentally spin the Symbol Code imagine that it is slowly moving
   inward, through the skin and into an imagined center line of energy
   that runs vertically through the center of your body matter. (This
   energy current exists, it can be viewed with higher sensory perception and
   is frequently called the "Main Vertical Current.")

   Move the spinning Symbol Code into this center-line of energy in synchronization with your breathing rhythm. Move the Symbol Code
   inward as you inhale, then as you exhale, stop the Symbol Code movement at whatever level you sense it to be, and resume moving the Symbol Code with the next inhale. Repeat the inhale-movement/exhale-stop
   sequence until you sense that the Symbol Code is positioned within
   your body directly in the middle of the internal center line, beneath the
   Chakra on which you traced the Symbol Code.

4. Once the Symbol Code is positioned within the internal center-line,
   breathe 4-6 breaths, feeling the energy of the Symbol Code expand
   until it feels about the size of a grapefruit, still within the same area of
   the body/Chakra center upon which the Symbol Code was traced. If
   you are sensitive to subtle energies you will feel a "stopping sensation"
   as the Symbol Code has reached full expansion within the Chakra.

Continue to pay attention to your breathing and as you inhale imagine that you are collecting energy into your body. At full inhale pause for 5-7 seconds, then exhale in one smooth flow of air.

5. As you exhale, imagine that the Symbol Code within the internal center-line is expanding as you "fill it with air and energy" by imagining the breath of your exhale moving into and filling the Symbol Code. Stop the expansion movement at the end of the exhale, pause, inhale, then again exhale and expand the Symbol Code. Repeat this exhale-Symbol Code expansion sequence until you have expanded the Symbol Code outward beyond the perimeters of your body. Feel the energy of the expanded Symbol Code surrounding you like a large "bubble." Sensitives will notice a stopping sensation as the Symbol Code "bubble" reaches its natural point of expansion within the level of the bio-energetic field that corresponds to the Chakra into which the Symbol Code was induced. This sensation indicates that the Symbol Code has been successfully programmed into the Keylontic crystalline blueprint for that Chakra and the DNA strand, body systems, level of consciousness and bio- energetic field level that correspond to that Chakra.

6. Complete the Symbol Code induction process, as described above, for the 3 remaining Symbol Codes, over placement positions numbers 7,8, and 9 on the Keylonta Symbol Code Placement chart. When the last Symbol Code has been successfully induced, take several slow, deep breaths and clear your mind as completely as possible. Now imagine a current of gold colored energy running from the top of your head through the internal center-line of the body, out the soles of both feet and into the ground. Breathe the current of energy upward with each inhale and downward with each exhale for several minutes while holding this visualization in mind. Complete the exercise by giving the command "Body at rest, program completed", repeating the command 3 times.

The Induction Technique exercise need only be implemented once for the Keylontic Symbol Code realignments to begin within the crystalline blueprint of the morphogenetic Keylon body. However, the exercise must be completed in *one* sequence with no interruption, for the program to work effectively. If you are disturbed or fall asleep during the exercise, start from the beginning again at another time.

Following the successful completion of the exercise it is helpful to allow 10–15 minutes of rest or sleep before becoming active. It is also helpful to drink several glasses of pure water during the 2 days that follow completion of this exercise.

The process of Keylontic Symbol Code Induction is an application of Keylontic Science. The exercise provided is a rudimentary demonstration of this technology in motion. Once you become familiar with the process of Bio-energetic Keylontic Symbol Code Induction you can learn more advanced levels of application through which the DNA and various levels of the body and consciousness can be literally programmed for higher performance. In other books we will explore the construction of the 12-strand DNA package—the Silicate Matrix gene code. Once the overlay structure of the DNA is understood, Keylontic Symbol Code Induction can be used to activate dormant Keylonta Codes and repair and replace missing Codes within the DNA in order to expedite healing and accelerate personal evolution through the process of Soul Integration.

Many of you already understand the validity of mental energy dynamics and realize that your waking mind is the literal director of energetic substances on numerous levels of experience. For you these exercises will be easy and you will sense the significance of their processes. More of your populations, however, possess little or no comprehension of the validity of mental energy dynamics. Exercises such as those presented in this book may appear "silly" or irrelevant to a consciousness unfamiliar with the inner workings and structures of mind/matter/space/time. Let us remind you that in using these techniques you are employing advanced energy programming modalities that represent operational applications of Keylontic Morphogenetic Science. Keylontic Science is the most advanced school of scientific thought presently available on Earth. Keylonta is the only contemporary science that takes into account the natural structures of 15-dimensional physics and addresses the mechanics of the Morphogenetic Fields that exist beneath and within all observable creations. Using applications of Keylontic Science may seem foreign to you because you have had little experience in dealing consciously and directly within a multi-dimensional framework.

Like all humans, the skeptics among you also possess a crystalline Keylontic Body upon which the manifest biology and identity are built and a Dream self that represents a more conscious aspect of the Reasoning Mind. Your Dream self is a portion of your consciousness that has access to the Keylontic Morphogenetic Body and to greater amounts of information, and it can synthesize much more complex data at a faster rate than your Reasoning Mind is able to do from the "waking" perspective. Your Dream self knows well the Science of Keylonta and the language of the Keylontic Symbol Codes and it is a master of mental energy dynamics and projection of consciousness. To the skeptics, who might laugh at and dismiss mind technologies such as those demonstrated within these Keylontic exercises, might we suggest that you consider that there is a portion of your own awareness with which you are unfamiliar, which holds information that you need to function more effectively within your waking state of consciousness. That information waits within the domain of the Keylontic Body and the Dream self, but only you can command it to appear. Your Dream self will be your best ally if you apply yourself to developing this relationship, and Keylontic Morphogenetic Science will be your greatest tool in directing and accelerating the process of your evolution.

If these exercises are approached with a negative or skeptical attitude such as "prove it to me," you are operating out of a belief that the dynamics of the exercises are false. Just as in the case of dream recall, your ideas about the subject will serve to enable or block the process. A skeptical attitude will translate on a subconscious level into a subliminal command that orders the biological suppression of the experiences and memory that would reveal to you the true validity of these dynamics. For this reason we suggest using these exercises only after you have cultivated an open attitude and sincere curiosity, for with an open attitude you are far more likely to achieve the results that will allow you to prove to yourself the realities of which we speak.

The coming period of 2012-2017 marks a time of physical and bio-energetic changes on Earth that are unprecedented in recorded human history. Developing skills in technologies of mind and applied Keylontic Morphogenetic Science will assist you to create adaptability of body and consciousness. We hope that you will enjoy the exercises we have provided in this book and that you will use them to your own advantage, to further accelerate your Soul Integration process. Through Soul Integration your race will take its next evolutionary step toward biological and spiritual maturity, to one day emerge within the realms of pure knowing and At-one-ment with the eternal creative **Source**.

Speaker: Valdmyrun
Rhanthunkeana Matrix
Ranthia Transmittance Pattern
2/26/1997 (update: 1/15/1999)

History, Motivation, Meaning and Message

of the *Emerald Order Melchizedek Cloister,*
Interdimensional Association of Free Worlds,
Guardian Alliance and the
Azurite Universal Templar Security Team

The **Interdimensional Association of Free Worlds (IAFW)**, **Guardian Alliance (GA)** and the **Azurite Universal Templar Security Team** are universal service organizations whose beginnings reach far back beyond known recorded history on Earth. The history of the IAFW, GA and Azurites is intimately interwoven with the **lost history and creation of the human lineage**, and also with the creation and evolution of many different Angelic or "ET" races within the **5 Density Levels** of our **15-Dimensional Time Matrix**. In order to understand the **significance of communicative interaction with these three Universal Service Organizations** it is helpful to have a rudimentary understanding of the basic **Primal Order**, structure and history of the reality systems within which all evolution takes place. It is helpful to know that "**Extra-terrestrials**" are in actuality the pre-ancient **Angelic Nations** emerging to visit us from the 5 Densities of Matter in our Time Matrix system and that communications extended by these organizations are **not** procured through the process known as "**channeling.**" It is also useful to realize that all manifest life forms and the inherent foundations of all reality itself emerge from, and exist within, a **Central Source of Creation** that is commonly referred to as Spirit, Source or God. Guardian Angelic Nations often refer to this Central Source of Creation as the "**Yunasai**" (pronounced "You'-na-sigh"), which means "Central Point of All Union" and "Eternal Consciousness of the One-All."

GUARDIANS AND FOUNDERS RACES

In the basic Primal Order of cosmic structure, the first individuated manifestation of a reality field within Source emerges as an inaudible vibration field composed of fixed units of Primal Substance, which collectively form the three eternal Primal Sound Fields and their Primal Tonal-vibration Life Force Currents. The **3 Primal Sound Fields** are collectively referred to as the **Khundaray Fields** or the **Energy Matrix.** The fields of Primal Light, and the dimensionalized structures of Time Matrices within them, **exist within** the 3 Primal Sound Fields of the Khundaray. The life-field of the Khundaray is composed of massive gestalts of **Eternal Sentient Consciousness,** from and within which the Primal Light Fields, dimensional Time Matrices and all individuated life forms emerge into manifest expression. The Eternal Gestalts of Consciousness that exist in the form of Primal Sound Fields are called **Yanas** (pronounced "yon'-us") or sometimes "Ascended Masters Consciousness Collectives." The Yanas Collectives are also occasionally referred to as "**Ultra-terrestrials**" or at times "**Geomantic Entities**," as they would appear as "geometric shapes made of living light" when viewed from the earthly perspective. Due to frequent misrepresentation of the term "Ascended Master" that is common on contemporary Earth, Guardian Angelic Nations prefer to use the term **Yanas,** which means "of, or in, the Yunasai," when referring to the Yanas Collectives.

There are 3 Primary Yanas collectives, each from one of the 3 Primal Sound Fields of the Khundaray. The **Grandeyanas** (pronounced Gron'-dA-yon-us) or "**Emerald Order**" **Yanas** exist within the **Eckatic Level** of the Energy Matrix, the first level of individuation within Source. The **Wachayanas** (pronounced "Wa'-shA-yon-us) or "**Gold Order**" **Yanas** exist within **Polaric Level** of the Energy Matrix, the second level of individuation within Source. The Ramyanas (pronounced Ram'-yon-us) or "**Amethyst Order**" **Yanas** exist within the **Triadic Level** of the Energy Matrix, the third level of individuation within Source. Yanas collectives from each of the 3 Primal Sound Fields of the Khundaray (Energy Matrix) are collectively called the **Eieyani** (pronounced "E-yon'-E"), or the **Eieyani Council,** both meaning "of the Yanas." The Eieyani collective responsible for seeding life into **our Time Matrix** is called the **Melchizedek Cloister Eieyani** or **MC Eyeiani.** The Yanas exist beyond the smaller reality fields within which space-time-matter experience takes place; occasionally they incarnate in various forms, into the fields of space-time-matter within the Density Levels of our Time Matrix, to fulfill universal service missions. When in physical incarnation in time, incarnate Yanas most often use the name **Eieyani** in reference to their family line; in contemporary times, the Eieyani incarnate on Earth are commonly referred to as "**Type-1 Grail Line Indigo Children.**" The Eieyani collectives of the Khundaray Primal Sound Fields are the **Eternal Guardian Collectives** that are responsible for maintaining the structural integrity of the Energy Matrix and Time Matrix systems within them, and for **seeding "life-waves"** into manifest Time Matrices. The Yanas Collectives of the Primal Sound Fields represent our "**Cosmic Family of**

Consciousness," through which all manifest things are indelibly connected to Source through the energetic expression of the Primal Sound Fields.

The Eieyani of the Khundaray Primal Sound Fields last seeded a life-wave into our 15-dimensional Time Matrix **950 billion years ago** (Earth time translation), through creation of the **3 Primary Founders Race Collectives** in our Time Matrix. The 3 Primary Founders Race Collectives are referred to as the **Breneau Orders;** they exist as eternal gestalts of consciousness in the form of spherical Ante-matter constructs of **Thermoplasmic Radiation** within the 3 Primal Light Fields that form **Density-5, dimensions 13, 14 and 15** of our 15-dimensional Time Matrix. The 3 Primal Light Fields within which dimensionalized Time Matrices exist are collectively referred to as the **Kee-Ra-ShA Primal Light Fields.** The Kee-Ra-ShA is composed of the Emerald-Blue, Pale-Gold and Violet Primal Light Fields, which are often referred to as the **"Blue-Eckatic, Gold-Polaric and Violet-Triadic Flames"** or standing fields of spherical light, within which dimensionalized reality fields exist. Each of the **3 Founders Race Breneau Orders** represents a collective of consciousness seeded into time by one of the 3 Yanas Collectives from the Energy Matrix. The **Emerald Order Breneau** exist within the **Blue-Eckatic** Kee-Ra-ShA Light Field, and are representatives of the **Emerald Order Grandeyanas** collective. The **Gold Order Breneau** exist within the **Pale-Gold-Polaric** Kee-Ra-ShA Light Field, and are representatives of the **Gold Order Wachayanas** collective. The **Amethyst Order Breneau** exist within the **Violet-Triadic** Kee-Ra-ShA Light Field, and are representatives of the **Amethyst Order Ramyanas**. The 3 Breneau Order Founders Races are the eternal collectives of consciousness from, through, and within which the life-field seeded by the Yanas, manifests in space-time-matter expression. The Breneau Collectives are often referred to as the **"Rishi"** or **Solar Rishi,"** and sometimes as **"Meta-terrestrials."**

The 3 Breneau Collectives of Density-5, dimensions 13, 14 and 15, represent our **"Universal Family of Consciousness,"** through which all things manifest are indelibly connected to the Khundaray Primal Sound Fields, Yanas and Source through the energetic expression of the Kee-Ra-ShA Primal Light Fields. Each of the 3 Breneau Orders created the first **3 manifest "Founders Races"** in the **Pre-matter Hydroplasmic "Christos Liquid Light Field"** of **dimension-12,** the entry point into densification of matter. The **Emerald Order Breneau** created the **Elohei-Elohim Feline-hominid Christos Founders Races** on a now destroyed Density-4 planet called **Lyra-Aramatena,** which housed **Star Gate-12** of the Universal Templar Complex. The **Emerald Order** Elohei-Elohim **Feline-hominid** Founder Race called the **Anuhazi** (also known as "Lyran-Sirian Whites") were appointed by the Yanas as Guardians of the Density-4, dimension-12 **Aramatena Star Gate-12,** the natural passageway between the dimensionalized Density systems and the Kee-Ra-ShA Primal Light Fields in our Time Matrix. The **Gold Order Breneau** created the **Seraphei-Seraphim Avian-Insect-Reptile Christos Founders Races** on the Density-4 planet **Lyra-Vega**, which housed **Star Gate-10** of the Universal Templar. The Gold Order **Avian** Seraphei-Seraphim Founders Race called the **Cerez** (sometimes called the "Bird People" or "Carians") were appointed by the Yanas as Guardians of the Density-4, dimension-10 **Vega Star Gate-10.** The Amethyst Order Breneau created the **Bra-ha-Rama Cetacean-Aquatic Ape-Pegasus Christos Founders Races** on a now destroyed Density-4 planet called **Lyra-Aveyon**, which housed **Star Gate-11** of the Universal Templar Complex. The **Amethyst Order** Bra-ha-Rama **Avian-Horse-Deer** and **Cetacean** Founders Races called the **Pegasai** (also known as "Pegasus") and the **Inyu** (sometimes called the "Whale People"; NOT the "Dolphin People.") were appointed by the Yanas as **Co-Guardians** of the Density-4, dimension-11 **Aveyon Star Gate-11.** Amethyst Order Bra-ha-Rama Pegasai and Inyu Christos Founders Races shared Guardianship of Aveyon Star Gate-11 with the Emerald Order-Amethyst Order hybrid **Feline-Aquatic Ape** Founders Race called the **Anyu.**

Through the Yanas and Breneau Order Founders Races' seeding of the life-field in our Time Matrix 950 billion years ago, long before creation of the Human genetic line, the primary, biologically manifest Density-4 "**Christos Founders Races**" were created. **The genetic codes and manifestation blueprints for every life form now manifest in our Time Matrix has emerged from combining of the genetic templates of the 3 Primary Christos Founders Races of Density-4 and their various biological expressions.** The Emerald Order Elohei-Elohim, the Gold Order Seraphei-Seraphim and the Amethyst Order Bra-ha-Rama Christos Founders Races were seeded from the Kee-Ra-ShA Primary Light Fields of dimensions 13, 14 and 15, into Pre-matter Density-4, dimensions 12, 11 and 10. This Christos Founders Race seeding took place through the natural **Star Gates** of the Universal Templar Complex that open between dimensions in our Time Matrix. There are **12 Primary Star Gates** in the Universal Templar Complex, each corresponding to 1 of 12 dimensional fields. Star Gates 12, 11 and 10, which serve as the entry points into the Pre-matter Density-4 "Liquid Light Christos Field," are respectively located in D-12 **Aramatena**, D-11 **Aveyon** and D-10 **Vega**. These 3 **Density-4 planets** (the remainder of which appears as the star "Vega" in Density-1), and the Star Gates within them, are all located with the Lyran Star Constellation. This "Primal Triad of Creation" has thus become known as "**The Cradle of Lyra,**" the seeding point of life in our Time Matrix **950 billion years ago.** The seeding of the life-field in our Time Matrix was orchestrated through a **cooperative agreement of intended peaceful co-evolution** between the Yanas and the

Density-5 Emerald, Gold and Amethyst Order Breneau Founders Races; this original Founders Race "Creation Contract" was called the "**Emerald Covenant of Aramatena.**"

Of the three, IAFW, GA and Azurite Universal Templar Security Team, Universal Service Organizations, the IAFW and the Azurites were created first 250 billion years ago, following a series of universally cataclysmic events that nearly destroyed our Time Matrix. During a period of time that spans from **250 billion to 570 million years ago**, a series of wars called the **Lyran-Elohim Wars,** and later the **Angelic Wars,** broke out in the Density-4 Pre-matter systems. The Gold Order Seraphei-Seraphim reptilian **Omicron Race** from **D-10 Lyra-Vega** began to digress and set forth dominion conquest into the stellar systems of our Time Matrix; they became known as the "**Fallen Seraphim,**" the forefathers of the contemporary **D-10 Orion-Drakonian Fallen Angelic Legion.** Simultaneously, the Emerald Order-Amethyst Order hybrid Feline-Aquatic Ape **Anyu Race** from Lyra-Aveyon also suffered digression and petitioned the Elohei-Elohim Feline-hominid Christos Founders Race of D-12 Lyra-Aramatena to destroy the Fallen Seraphim Omicron Race. When the Yanas, Breneau Order Founders Races and the Elohei-Elohim of Aramatena refused, opting for rehabilitation of the Fallen Seraphim, the **Anyu Race** of D-11 Aveyon attacked and destroyed Aramatena to gain control of Star Gate-12. The Anyu's destruction of Aramatena's Star Gate-12 is the event that became known as "**the Original Sin,**" as all life forms, including the Density-4 Christos Founders Races, became trapped in the Time Matrix until the D-12 Aramatena Star Gate-12 could be reconstructed. Consciousness could incarnate into our Time Matrix but could not ascend to leave, while Aramatena Star Gate-12 remained damaged. **The Anyu began their quest of universal dominion with the intention of destroying all races but their own and claiming dominion of our Time Matrix.** In their rebellion against the Christos Founders Races the Anyu Race of Density-4, D-11 adopted the name of the Annu, and became known as the **Annu-Elohim Fallen Angelic Legion;** the forefathers of the **Anunnaki avenger race.** The Annu-Elohim Fallen Angelic Legion created the **Sirian Anunnaki** race to destroy the Christos Founders Race **Guardian Angelic Oraphim-Human lineage** upon its seeding 568 million years ago. **Through the progressive and perpetual conflicts among the Seraphim and Annu-Elohim Fallen Angelic Legions, which began 250 billion years ago in Density-4 Lyra, our Time Matrix was nearly destroyed.**

THE IAFW, AZURITE SECURITY TEAM AND THE MC EIEYANI MASTER COUNCIL

Following destruction of Star Gate-12 during the Lyran-Elohim Wars 250 billion years ago, the Yanas appointed the **Emerald Order Breneau** and their **Elohei-Elohim Feline-hominid Christos Founders Race** as the **Universal Security Team** in our Time Matrix. Under the direction of the Yanas and the Density-5 Emerald Order Breneau, the Gold Order Seraphei-Seraphim Breneau and Amethyst Order Bra-ha-rama Breneau mobilized their Christos Founders Races in a **restatement of the Emerald Covenant Co-evolution Agreement** and formed the **Interdimensional Association of Free Worlds.** The Elohei-Elohim Feline-hominid **Anuhazi,** the Seraphei-Seraphim Avian-hominid **Cerez** and Mantis **Aethien** and the Bra-ha-Rama Cetacean **Inyu** and **Pegasai** Christos Founders Races assembled the massive **IAFW** organization under the tenets of the Emerald Covenant, creating a unified collective of intergalactic Guardian Angelic races from within our 15-Dimensional Time Matrix. By combining their genetic templates, the **Anuhazi** Elohei-Elohim, **Cerez** and **Aethien** Seraphei-Seraphim and **Inyu** and **Pegasai** Bra-ha-Rama Christos Founders races together created a new genetic race line called the **Azurite Eieyani.** The Azurites are a **blue-skinned**, sometimes winged and feathered, Feline-land and water mammal-Avian hominid race carrying **the most advanced genetic code** in our Time Matrix.

The Azurites were created by the Founders Races 250 billion years ago, specifically to allow for the **Melchizedek Cloister (MC) Eieyani** collective from the Energy Matrix and the Density-5 Breneau Orders to incarnate directly into our Density system for **crisis intervention.** The **Azurite MC Eieyani Race** was created to serve as the **Universal Templar Security Team**, the **mobile extension of the IAFW** Primary Guardian Administration. The Density-5 administrative council of the Azurite Universal Templar Security Team, a specialized collective of the Emerald Order Elohei-Elohim Breneau Founders Race, is called the **MC Eieyani Master Council.** The MC Eieyani Master Council is composed of the **Density-5 Emerald Order Elohei-Elohim Breneau,** whose members incarnate through the **Sirius B Azurite** lineage. (Following creation of the **Oraphim- Angelic Human** lineage **568 million years ago,** members of the MC Eieyani Master Council also incarnate into density through the Oraphim-Angelic Human **"Indigo Children" Human Grail Line.**) The **MC Eieyani Master Council** is sometimes referred to as the *Sirian Council* or the *Azurite Council.* (In Voyagers Volume-2, the Eieyani Master Council is called the "Sirian Council.") The MC Eieyani Master Council was created **250 billion years ago** with the formation of the **IAFW,** to serve as the **central administrative council for IAFW efforts** and as the **primary liaison** between the Yanas collectives in the **Energy Matrix** and Guardian Nations within our **Time Matrix.** Though the Eieyani Master Council generally oversees all IAFW activities **from the Density-5 Primal Light Fields,** they directly intervene in conflict-laden areas of the Time Matrix, through incarnation within the **Sirius B Azurite** and **Oraphim Angelic Human** races. Upon their creation 250 billion years ago, the Azurite Eieyani Races were simultaneously seeded in **fully evolved form**, within every Density Level of our Time Matrix, placed in close proximity to the locations of the **12 Primary Star Gates** of the Universal Templar Complex.

Headed by the Density-5 (dimensions 13-14-15)

Melchizedek Cloister Eieyani Master Council of the Emerald Order Elohei-Elohim Breneau Founders Race, the Interdimensional Association of Free Worlds (IAFW) was created after the Lyran-Elohim Wars 250 billion years ago, to reclaim and protect the Star Gates of the Universal Templar Complex and our Time Matrix from destruction via Fallen Angelic Race dominion. The IAFW was also commissioned to implement Genetic Bio-Regenesis Healing Programs to assist the Fallen Angelic Races in reclaiming their original genetic integrity, so they could fulfill the intended evolutionary objective of Ascension out of the Time Matrix. The Azurite MC Eieyani Race was created at this time to allow the MC Eieyani Master Council to incarnate into embodiment directly in our Time Matrix, to serve as the IAFW's mobile Universal Templar Security Team. The Azurite Universal Templar Security Team was created to promote the freedom-based peaceful co-evolution agendas of the Emerald Covenant and to hold the main Security Seals on the 12 Primary Universal Star Gates in our Time Matrix.

Since the time of their creation 250 billion years ago, the IAFW and the Azurite Universal Templar Security Team have served the role of primary **Guardian Race Administration**, and protectors of the **Emerald Covenant** freedom agendas in our Time Matrix. Throughout the many eons of intergalactic, interdimensional history, the IAFW and its countless Emerald Covenant Guardian Angelic Nations, on behalf of the Yanas and the Breneau Order Christos Founders Races, continually labor to restore and maintain the structural integrity of our Time Matrix. Their efforts include 15-dimensional, egalitarian **political arbitration**, progressive **spiritual-science education** and **genetic Bio-Regenesis** evolutionary healing opportunities among **all manifest races**, to inspire **peaceful co-creative evolution and healing** among all races manifest through continuation of the Founders Races' **Emerald Covenant Co-evolution Agreement** treaties. **Presently there are over 25 billion different interdimensional, interstellar Nations serving as active members of the IAFW.**

THE GA AND THE ANGELIC HUMAN LINEAGE

The period known as the Angelic Wars, which began among the Density-4 (dimensions 10-11-12) Lyran Founders Races 250 billion years ago, contained many successes and failures in the IAFW's efforts of restoring peaceful co-evolution and the Emerald Covenant in our Time Matrix. The historical Angelic Wars period came to end about **570 million years ago**, when warring between the Seraphim-Drakonian and Annu-Elohim Fallen Angelic Races again escalated to near destruction of our Time Matrix. At this time, another restatement of the Emerald Covenant Co-evolution Agreement was offered to all races in our Time Matrix. Numerous collectives of Fallen Angelic Races re-entered the Emerald Covenant, accepting "**Host Matrix**" or "**Redemption Contract**" agreements with the IAFW and Founders Races for Bio-Regenesis of genetic integrity. At this time the MC Eieyani from the Energy Matrix and the Breneau Order Founders Races again created a **new biological race line** that was equal to the **24-48 Strand DNA Template** genetic advancement of the Azurite MC Eieyani. The new race line was initiated to allow another life-wave of Eieyani Master Council Guardians to incarnate directly in time, to **relieve the "Tour of Duty"** for the Eieyani that had been serving as the Azurite Universal Templar Security Team since formation of the IAFW. **The new Guardian Race was intended to eventually become the appointed *Universal Templar Security Team,* once their evolutionary development in Density progressed**. The new race also carried **additional genetic coding** characteristic to the more recent primary Angelic race lines in our Time Matrix, enabling the consciousness from any lineage to evolve into incarnation in this lineage for rapid **Bio-Regenesis** and Ascension (Star Gate passage out of Density). The new race line was created by combining the Elohei-Elohim **Anuhazi** Feline-hominid, the Seraphei-Seraphim Avian **Cerez**, a small contribution of Bra-ha-Rama Cetacean **Inyu** and the **Azurite Eieyani** lineage from **Sirius B**.

The new Guardian Angelic Race line was called the **Oraphim**. The Oraphim lineage was seeded in **Density-3** on a planet called **Gaia**, on Gaia's counterpart planet **Tara** in Density-2 and in several other systems. The name "Oraphim" means "**The Lighted Ones**" in the Anuhazi language, denoting the Breneau and Yanas consciousness collectives that incarnated through this biological race line from the **Primal Light and Sound Fields** of the Kee-Ra-ShA and Khundaray. **The Oraphim of Gaia and Tara are the Seed Race from which the 12- Strand DNA Angelic Human "Turaneusiam" lineage, the forefathers of the Earthly Angelic Human Race, emerged.** The name "**Turaneusiam**" means "**Children of the Lighted Ones**" in the Anuhazi language. When the Oraphim race was created by the Guardian Founders Races about **568 million years ago**, the Annu-Elohim Fallen Angelic Legion also created a new Fallen Angelic Race with 11-Strand DNA potential, the most genetically

165

advanced biological form the D-11 Fallen Annu-Elohim are capable of seeding. The new race created by the Fallen Annu-Elohim is called the **Anunnaki,** meaning "**the Avengers of Anyu,**" the original Fallen Lyran hybrid Founders Race from D-11 Lyra-Aveyon. The Anunnaki lineage was created specifically as a vehicle through which the D-11 Fallen Annu-Elohim could incarnate directly into Densities 1, 2 and 3, in **order to destroy the Guardian Angelic Oraphim and Azurite Eieyani genetic lines, to further their continuing agenda of exploitation and dominion of our Time Matrix.** Upon creation of the Oraphim and Anunnaki Races, the IAFW and Founders Races implemented a **more intensive security system** for the Universal Templar Complex of our Time Matrix, and for the races of the Emerald Covenant. **The Founders knew that the Anunnaki Races would be used to conduct conquests of dominion throughout our Time Matrix, which would place all races of the Emerald Covenant and the safety of our Time Matrix in greater jeopardy.**

Faced with the potential catastrophe of Anunnaki Legions waging war through our Time Matrix, the IAFW created a **crisis intervention** *Task Force,* assembled through organizing **millions** of various **Emerald Covenant Nations** throughout the 5 Density Levels of our Time Matrix. One of the primary purposes of this task force was to assist the Azurites and Founders Races to protect, guide and over-see the creation and evolution of the Oraphim-Turaneusiam Guardian Angelic Human lineage, and to assist in its peaceful and harmonious integration and evolution into the interdimensional Guardian Angelic communities. **The IAFW Task Force is called the** *Guardian Alliance* **(GA).** The GA organization, which specializes in propagation of the **Emerald Covenant,** serves as the **governing body of a large collective of inter-dimensional, inter-galactic Guardian Angelic Star League Nations.** Through formation of the GA **568 million years ago,** the many **Emerald Covenant Star Leagues** from galaxies in Densities 1 through 4, dimensions 1-12 were brought into **an organized and co-supportive communications and resource network.** The GA operates under the direction and guidance of the **Yanas, MC Eieyani Master Council, Emerald Order Elohei-Elohim, Founders Races** and the **IAFW.** Under the administration of the IAFW and the GA, 12 smaller "Signet Councils" composed of representatives of various Star League Nations were formed. Each of the **12 Signet Councils of the GA,** appointed by the Density-5 MC Eieyani Master Council, serves as the **Primary Guardians of one of the 12 Primary Star Gates** in the Universal Templar Complex of our Time Matrix. The word 'Signet" is used in reference to one Primary Star Gate of the 12 Primary Star Gates in our Time Matrix. **The 12 Signet Councils of the GA assist the MC Eieyani Master Council and Azurite Universal Templar Security Team of the IAFW in their protection of, and restoration efforts within, our Time Matrix.**

THE 12 GA SIGNET COUNCILS, STAR GATE SECURITY AND "ROYAL HOUSE" DECEPTION

Each of the **12 GA Signet Councils,** under the direction of the Density-5(dimensions 13-14-15) MC Eieyani Master Council and Azurite Universal Templar Security Team, has guardianship over one of the 12 Dimensional Star Gates in our Universal Templar Complex. **In naming the 12 GA Signet Councils and their corresponding Star Gates, the names are translated into the *English language,* in order to give *known directional reference* to the corresponding identified Density-1 star systems.** The **"High Council"** of the 12 Signet Councils are those assigned to the **3 Lyran Star Gates** in the Density-4 "Cradle of Lyra"; the **D-12 Council of Aramatena,** the **D-11 Council of Aveyon** and the **D-10 Council of Vega.** Because the 3 Lyran Star Gates are the primary passageways between the Primal Light Fields and the lower dimensional Density Systems, they are the most important and in greatest need of protection. **Aramatena Star Gate-12 and Aveyon Star Gate-11 were both previously destroyed in battles between the Fallen Angelic Legions, who desired their destruction to block Yanas and Breneau Founders Race assistance from entering our Time Matrix. Lyran Star Gates 11 and 12 were subsequently repaired by the Azurite Universal Templar Security Team, and remain under tight security.** Representatives of the **3 Primary Christos Founders Races** of Densities 4 and 5 make up the administrative body of the 3 Lyran GA Signet Councils. The **D-12 Council of Aramatena-Lyra** is directed by the **Emerald Order Elohei-Elohim Anuhazi** Feline-hominid Christos Founders Race, originally from the planet Aramatena. The **D-11 Council of Aveyon-Lyra** is directed by the **Amethyst Order Bra-ha-Rama** Winged-horse-deer **Pegasai** and Cetacean **Inyu** Christos Founders Races, originally from the planet Aveyon. The **D-10 Council of Vega-Lyra** is directed by the **Gold Order Seraphei-Seraphim** Mantis **Aethien** and Avian-hominid **Cerez** Christos Founders Race, originally from Vega.

As the representatives of the **3 Lyran GA Signet Councils** are composed of members of the original **Christos Founders Race lines** that seeded the life-field in this Time Matrix, the 3 Lyran GA Signet Councils are often referred to as the **"Royal Houses." The "Royal Houses" are the collectives of Christos Founders Races that keep the Founders Race genetic lines, and thus the *potentials for Bio-Regenesis of any race line,* alive within our Time Matrix.** The "Royal Houses" of Lyra are the **D-12 Elohei-Elohim Anuhazi** Feline-hominid **Royal House of Aramatena,** the **D-11** Bra-ha-Rama **Pegasai** Winged-horse-deer and **Inyu** Cetacean ("Whale People") **Royal House of Aveyon,** and the **D-10 Seraphei-Seraphim Aethien** Mantis and **Cerez** Avian-hominid **Royal House of Vega. Guardian Angelic Nations do not usually identify the**

3 GA Signet High Councils as *"Royal Houses"* when in communication with earth humans, as they do not desire to imply any sense of "elitist superiority" in regard to race identification. Though the Christos Founders Races of the Lyran Councils, like the **Azurite** and **Oraphim Eieyani Races**, do possess **genetic advancements** compared to the many other races in our Time Matrix, this advantage is viewed in terms of *greater responsibility* toward assisting in the evolution of other races. **Guardian Races do** *not* **view genetic advancement or advantage of a race in terms of having** *greater value than* **less developed races.** Guardians view all beings in creation with genuine reverence, love and respect, and all races are honored as being **Equal in Blessed Value, because it is recognized that all beings are manifestations of the consciousness and identity of our singular Source or God.** Beings are frequently **unequal** in terms of **evolutionary development** and **spiritual-ethics cognition** in any given moment in time, but they are *always equal in intriinsic value*, and **equally loved and assisted in egalitarian evolutionary advancement** by Source-God and its manifest "spiritually awakened" representatives.

The GA chose to explain the context of the "Royal Houses of Lyra," *not* because they desire any pompous accolade, but rather due to a *misrepresentation* of the *true* Founders Race "Royal Houses" that is presently being orchestrated on Earth by *Fallen Angelic Anunnaki Legions*, in order to *deceitfully recruit human assistance* in fulfilling their *Earth dominion* agenda.

False historical data on human origins and evolution is presently being dispensed on Earth via **channeling contact** from the **Pleiadian-Nibiruian-Anunnaki, Sirian Anunnaki and Sirian "Bipedal Dolphin People-Anunnaki" Fallen Angelic Legions.** Some of them are falsely claiming, quite piously, that their legions are the **Royal House of "Aveyon," the self-proclaimed** "originators" of the earth human race. The Density-4 Lyra planet Aveyon, which housed Star Gate-11, was indeed the place of origin of the **Feline-Aquatic-Ape** *Anyu Race*. The Anyu Race is the hybrid Elohei-Elohim/Bra-ha-Rama race that **suffered genetic digression** and rebelled against the Founders 250 billion years ago, to become the **D-11 Annu-Elohim Fallen Angelic Legion,** from which the **Anunnaki** Fallen Angelic Annu-Elohim avenger races later emerged. The contemporary Anunnaki lines claiming to be the "Royal House of Aveyon" are in truth the *"Fallen* **Royal House of Aveyon."** The **Fallen Angelic Anyu Race** that became the Fallen Annu-Elohim, **intentionally** traded in their original genetic capacity to hold the natural **minimum 12-Strand DNA Template "Christos Potential,"** characteristic to the **Christos Founders Races,** for a digressive **11-Strand DNA Template** mutation. Through **removing the 12th DNA Strand Template**

from their genetic blueprint, the Annu-Elohim successfully **blocked the Density-5 Breneau Founders races from incarnating into their race line**, so they were free to create a **legion of self-contained Fallen Angelic dominion forces** within our Time Matrix. Their intention was, and continues to be, **oppressive, exploiting dominion of our Time Matrix and its life-field**, and **operational control** over the **12 Primary Star Gates** of the Universal Templar Complex in our Time Matrix.

Anunnaki Fallen Angelic Legions that are presently **falsely promoting themselves** as the "original creators of the human lineage," or who promote themselves as being of the **Christos Founders Race** genetic line emerging from the "Royal Houses," are *not* the "Christed" races **they claim to be,** nor are their **intentions** "Christly." **Anunnaki Fallen Legions** are currently attempting to misguide humanity into becoming *"galactic,"* **rather than** *"angelic"* **humans,** which is a **sweetly deceptive cover-word** used to describe their **intended digressive hybridization** of contemporary humans. Fallen Angelic Anunnaki Legions of the D-11 Fallen Annu-Elohim collective, are hoping to **digress the human genome** into a maximum **11-Strand Anunnaki-hybrid DNA Template potential**, in replacing the **minimum of 12-Strand DNA Template "Christos" potential** that is the **rightful heritage** of the Angelic Human lineage. In their misguided contemporary quest for dominion of Earth's **Halls of Amenti** star gates, the Anunnaki Fallen Angelic Legions **hope to rob earth humans of their dormant "Christed Angelic Human Race"** potential through **covert genetic manipulation** (via **distorted teachings** of DNA, bio-energetic field and Merkaba activation) and hybridization programs. The Anunnaki are attempting to perpetrate this **deception of humans** in order to prevent Earth humans from actualizing the dormant **12-Strand DNA potential,** through which humans can reclaim the **Angelic Human** heritage to serve as **conscious guardians of the Halls of Amenti.**

The *Yanas, MC Eieyani Master Council, Founders Races, IAFW , GA* and *races of the Emerald Covenant* are pointing out the *Anunnaki Fallen Angelic Legion's intentional deceptive misrepresentation of information* to humanity, so humans are *better equipped to make intelligent choices* regarding what to believe in terms of *human history, heritage and potential.* Founders Races are presenting detailed explanation of the *truth of the Angelic Human lineage,* so humanity has the *opportunity to form educated opinions* regarding *contemporary contact,* through which *educated action* can be applied when in confrontation with the *ongoing trickery* of Fallen Angelic Legions. Representatives of *Fallen Angelic Legions* will be those first to falsely "reassure" humans that *fallen angelic races and the contemporary conflict drama don't exist.*

169

THE 3 GA SIGNET COUNCILS OF
ETHERIC MATTER DENSITY-3
(DIMENSIONS 7-8-9)

The 3 "Royal House" Lyran Christos Founders Race Signet Councils of the GA were appointed 570 million years ago by the Breneau Order Founders Races, as the Primary Guardians of Universal Star Gates 10, 11 and 12 in **Density-4 Lyra**. The **9 remaining GA Signet Councils** appointed at this time, which serve as appointed Guardians of Universal Star Gates 1through 9, are composed of various different Star Leagues and their Guardian Angelic Nations. **Signet Council 9** is the **Council of Mirach-Andromeda.** The Council of Mirach is composed of a collective of Emerald Covenant Guardian Angelic Races, predominantly those of the **Amethyst Order Bra-ha-Rama Cetacean lineage,** from the **Andromeda Star League**, who serve as guardians of the **D-9 Mirach Star Gate-9** in the Andromeda star system Etheric matter Density-3. **Signet Council 8** is the **Council of Mintaka-Orion;** it is composed of Emerald Covenant Guardian Angelic Races from the **Orion Association of Planets,** who serve as guardians of the **D-8 Mintaka Star Gate-8** in the Orion star system Etheric matter Density-3. Due to the high concentration of Drakonian Fallen Angelic Legions predominant in the Orion star system, which places Star Gate-8 in a more vulnerable position, the Council of Mintaka is directed by the **Gold Order Seraphei-Seraphim Aethien Mantis** and **Emerald Order Elohei-Elohim Feline-hominid Christos Founders Races** from Lyran High Council.

Signet Council-7 is the **Council of Epsilon**, often referred to as the **Sirian-Arcturian Coalition;** it is composed of various Emerald Covenant Guardian Angelic Nations from **various stellar regions**, who serve as guardians of the **D-7 Arcturus Star Gate-7**. Since attempts of Bio-Regenesis and Amnesty Contracts were accepted by several Anunnaki Fallen Angelic Legions about **554 million years ago**, the populations of the **Arcturian Federation of Planets** evolved to include **2 primary race lines.** The original and oldest race line of the **Etheric Density-3 Arcturian system** is a diversified Emerald Covenant Guardian Angelic **Amphibian-hominid lineage** of the Amethyst Order Bra-ha-Rama. The secondary lineage of the Arcturian system emerged through **Annu-Elohim invasion of the Arcturian sector** with their "**Bipedal Dolphin People**" of Sirius and their **Necromiton Anunnaki-Drakonian hybrid** race from Orion and Nibiru. Certain factions of the Arcturian Annu-Elohim Fallen Angelic races accepted **Amnesty Contracts with the GA Azurite Races of Sirius B 554 million years ago**, creating the **Sirian-Arcturian Coalition.** The Sirian-Arcturian Coalition, whose primary base in the Bootes-Arcturus constellation is on theDensity-3 planet **Epsilon**, progressively united the Emerald Covenant races of the Arcturian Federation of Planets, granting them protection from the dominent Annu-Elohim Fallen Angelic Legions in this region. In the appointment of the Sirian-Arcturian Coalition as **GA Signet Council 7**, the primary guardians of **D-7 Arcturus Star Gate-7**, they became known as the **Council of Epsilon**. Presently, large factions of Annu-Elohim from the Sirian-Arcturian Coalition have defected from the Council of Epsilon and withdrawn from the Emerald Covenant, in favor of Anunnaki dominion agendas.

The D-7 Council of Epsilon (Sirian-Arcturian Coalition), **headed by the** *MC Eieyani Master Council, Azurite Universal Templar Security Team,* **and remaining** *Emerald Covenant loyal* **members of the** *Arcturian Federation of Planets* **still hold** *Arcturus Star Gate-7* **under Guardian Angelic protection. In** *September 2000, Annu-Elohim Fallen Angelic* **members of the** *Arcturian Federation of Planets* **launched a** *conquest* **to seize control of the** *D-7 Arcturus Star Gate-7.* **The results of this campaign are yet to be determined.**

GA SIGNET COUNCIL-6, SIRIUS B, INDIGO CHILDREN AND "CHRISTIAC GRAIL LINES"

The **6 remaining GA Signet Councils** that protect Universal Star Gates **1 through 6** in the Densities 1 and 2 (dimensions 1-6) systems operate under the direct supervision of the **MC Eieyani Master Council** ("Sirian or Azurite" Council) of Density-5. The MC Eieyani Council attends directly to the needs of the 6 Signet Councils in the lower-dimensional Densities, through their incarnate representatives in the **Sirius B Azurite** and **Oraphim Angelic Human** Eieyani race lines. Though the MC Eieyani Master Council oversees all IAFW activities from the Density-5 **Primal Light Fields**, they **directly intervene** when needed in **distressed areas** of the Time Matrix. Since the restatement of the Emerald Covenant 570 million years ago, and subsequent creation of the GA, Guardian Oraphim Angelic Human and avenging Anunnaki Fallen Angelic races, the MC Eieyani Master Council has maintained a **biological presence** in regions compromised by the chaos of Fallen Angelic Legion conquest. The Densities 1 and 2 (dimensions 1-6) **Physical** and **Semi-Etheric** matter systems **have been embroiled in continuing Fallen Angelic Legion conflict since the Annu-Elohim Fallen Angelic Legions created the Anunnaki avenger race to destroy the Angelic Human and Emerald Covenant Guardian Angelic race lines.** Since the formation of the GA, the MC Eieyani Master Council has retained a **strong presence** within the Densities 1 and 2 systems of which Earth is a part, in a continuing effort to **bring peace** to the regions of this "**Guardian Angelic Human VS Anunnaki Fallen Angelic**" conflict. Operating from bases on **Sirius B, Sirius A, Inner Earth** and numerous other interdimensional galactic locations, the MC Eieyani Master Council has attempted to guide the 6 GA Signet Councils of Densities 1 and 2 in establishing **peaceful co-evolutionary relations** and opportunities for **Fallen Race rehabilitation.**

The 6 GA Signet Councils working under MC Eieyani Master Council guidance are the appointed guardians of **Universal Star Gates 1 through 6. The council responsible for guardianship of Density-2 Semi-etheric Sirius B Star Gate-6 is a smaller branch of the MC Eieyani Master Council that usually goes by the name of the Council of Azurline.** The Council of Azurline is also sometimes more loosely referred to as the "**Eieyani Council,**" "**Sirian Counci,l**" or "**Azurite Council,**" denoting its **direct affiliation** with the "MC Eieyani Master Council." The appointment of the Council of Azurline as guardians of Sirius B Star Gate-6 570 million years ago represented a **crisis intervention plan.** The plan was orchestrated through the Council of Azurline on Density-2 Sirius B, and directed by the Yanas (beyond Time Matrix) and Density-5 (dimensions 13-14-15) MC Eieyani Master Council, Azurite Universal Templar Security Team and Breneau Order Founders Races of the IAFW and GA. Guardian Angelic race intervention was initiated due to the **long and continuing history of warring** between the Annu-Elohim and Drakonian-Seraphim Fallen Angelic Legions in this region, and their **mutual, though competitive, intention of enslaving and destroying the Guardian Angelic Nations** of the **Angelic Human** and **Emerald Covenant** races. The Sirius B Council of Azurline manifests through a *hybrid Sirius B Azurite and Taran Oraphim Angelic Human* **Blue Angelic Human** race line called the **Maharaji** (pronounced "Ma-ha-ra'-G") or sometimes "**Maji**" (pronounced "Ma'-G"). The name Maharaji means "**Mahara** embodied"; the word **Mahara** is derived from the word **Maharata.**

The word **Maharata** refers to the **Eternal Life Current,** that is made up of the **combined frequencies of Pre-matter dimensions 10, 11 and 12,** which compose the **Density-4 Pre-matter Fields** of Hydroplasmic Liquid Light, most often called the "**Christos Field.**" The Density-4 Maharata Eternal Life Current is the **smallest of 3 Primal Life-Force Currents** that perpetually feed energy and consciousness into our Time Matrix; the Maharata is often referred to as the "**Christiac Current.**" **The frequencies of the Maharata and those of the Primal Light and Sound Fields beyond it represent the "3 *Eternal Life, or Primal Life-Force, Currents.*"** When the frequencies of Density-4 and above are embodied, a biological being can undergo **full cellular transmutation,** returning to the Density-4 Liquid Light **Pre-matter state** for full **Ascension** out of Density, rather than experiencing repeated cycles of death and rebirth within the Density system life cycles. The ability to fully embody the Eternal Life Currents within a physically manifest form is **conditional upon having a minimum of 12-Strand DNA potential,** a "**Holy Grail Line**" or

"Christiac" genetic code. Unlike the Fallen Angelic races, the **Azurite, Angelic Human** and **Maharajhi Eieyani race lines** carry the **12 to 48 Strand DNA Template potential** characteristic to the **Founders Races,** and are thus considered "**Christiac Grail Line**" races.

The "Christiac Grail Line" **Maharaji** Blue Angelic Human Azurite-Eieyani race of Density-2 Sirius B carries the **fully activated 12-dimensional spectrum** of the Density-4 Christos Maharata frequencies within their bodies through **sustained activation of 12 Strands of their 48-Strand DNA Templates.** A being with sustained activation of **12 DNA Strands** and resulting embodiment of the **Maharata** and its corresponding12-dimensions of conscious awareness is known as an embodied "**Mahara**"(bearer of the Maharata eternal life current), "**Avatar**" or "**Christed Being.**" Like other strains of the **Azurite and Oraphim Angelic Human MC Eieyani "Grail Line" races,** the **Maharaji of Sirius B** can **consciously choose** to activate the remaining dormant portions of the DNA Template. Activation of **DNA Strand Templates 1-30** allows a being to fully embody the frequencies and consciousness of the **Kee-Ra-ShA Primal Sound Fields** of **Density-5** (dimensions 13-14-15). A manifest being that activates the **Kee-Ra-ShA** within its body and consciousness becomes what is known as a **Rishi** or "**Rashana**"(bearer of the "Kee-Ra-ShA eternal life current), a fully embodied "**Eternal Light-Being.**" Additional activation of **DNA Strand Templates 30-48** allows a being to fully embody the frequencies and consciousness of the **Khundaray Primal Sound Fields** from the Energy Matrix beyond the Time Matrix. When a being activates **Khundaray** within its body and consciousness it becomes what is known as a **Khundara** or "**Yani,**" a **fully embodied Yanas,** which is the **legitimate use** of the term "**Ascended Master.**"

The primary earthly human lineage is an **Angelic Human Christiac Grail Line** that carries the **dormant 12-Strand DNA Template potential;** certain portions of earth human Grail Line populations carry the **24-48 Strand DNA Template** of the Rishi and Yani "**Eieyani Grail Lines.**" The **Eieyani Grail Line humans presently incarnate on Earth** are known as the **Types 1 and 2** *Indigo Children.* Other portions of the earth-human populations carry 9, 10 and 11-Strand **DNA Template mutations** resulting from ancient race hybridization with **Anunnaki and Drakonian Fallen Angelic Legions.**

All humans can reverse-mutate dna template distortions and bring dormant DNA template potentials into activation through self-generated DNA bio-regenesis technologies, through which the 12-strand DNA angelic human potential can be progressively restored and reactivated within the operational DNA.
This is precisely what visiting Fallen Angelic Legions
do not **want contemporary humanity to accomplish.**

The **Annu-Elohim, Anunnaki** and **Drakonian-Seraphim Fallen Angelic Races** possess a digressive maximum of **11 and 10 Strand DNA Template** potential respectively. As the Fallen Angelic Legions **cannot embody the 12th-dimensional frequencies of the Maharata "Christiac Current"** due to **absence of the 12th DNA Strand Template**; they carry what is considered to be the **"Anti-Christiac"** or **"Anti-Christ" genetic code.** The "Anti-Christ genetic code" can be restored to its original "Christiac" capacity through **DNA Bio-Regenesis, IF** the Fallen Angelic Races choose to do so. **Fallen Angelic race founders from Density-4, dimensions 10 and 11, intentionally choose to retain their "Anti-christiac" genetic code and that of their manifest races.** If the full 12th Strand DNA Template were regenerated within the biological Fallen Angelic race lines, the Fallen Angelic founders of the Density-4 system could **no longer incarnate into the rehabilitated biological lineage.** The **Chriastic Founders Races** could incarnate into genetically restored race lines, to **rehabilitate the Fallen Angelics' historically warring mentality** and **redirect their exploitative control-dominion agendas** back into peaceful co-evolution through the **Emerald Covenant,** which is precisely what the Fallen Angelic race founders do not want to do.

During the formation of the GA Signet Councils 570 million years ago, the MC Eieyani Master Council of Density-5 incarnated into the **Azurite** race line of **Sirius B.** Following the creation of the Oraphim Angelic Human lineage 568 million years ago, the Sirius B Azurites **further combined** their genetic imprint with **certain lines** of the new **Oraphim Angelic Human** lineage, creating the **specialized** Azurite-Oraphim Blue Angelic Human hybrid **Maharaji** race of Density-2 Sirius B. Both the Sirius B Azurites and Maharaji races are often referred to as the **"Sirian Blues."** The Maharaji Azurite-Humans were imbued with **additional genetic coding** that would allow them to **biologically interface directly with the energetic templates of Star Gates 1 through 6** in the Universal Templar Complex. The specialized Maharaji **46-48-Strand DNA Template** allowed the MC Eieyani Master Council members to incarnate through this form to retain **"over-ride potential"** on **opening and closing of Universal Star Gates 1 through 6.** This **additional security measure** was taken in case the **6 Signet Councils,** appointed as guardians of Star Gates 1 through 6, succumbed to Fallen Angelic Legion destruction or dominion. The **Maharaji race of Sirius B** forms the **Council of Azurline,** which to this day remains as the appointed **GA Signet Council 6,** in guardianship over the **D-6 Sirius B Star Gate-6** and advisors to GA Signet Councils 1 through 5 in the lower-dimensional fields.

Though **similar in physical appearance,** the **Sirius B Maharaji "Blue Human" race is *not* the same race strain** as the **Fallen Angelic** race line from the **Orion system** that became known as the **Azrielites** or the **"Azriel."** The

Azrielites were created by the **Omicron-Drakonian-Seraphim Fallen Angelic Legion of Density-4, Dimension-10 Orion,** through **harvesting of genetic material** from *Sirius A* **Azurites** that they had **murdered** during the Density-2 **Sirian Wars** 550 million years ago. The **Fallen Angelic Azrielite** race has been involved with **earthly affairs** most recently since the **1930s,** in which they assisted reptilian **Zeta Fallen Angelic** races in negotiating treaties with **human Illuminati** factions.

THE MAHARAJI, ANGELIC HUMANS, THE PRIESTS OF UR AND MELCHIZEDEK PRIESTHOODS

When the Oraphim-Turaneusiam Angelic Human lineage of Density-2 Tara began digressing through Anunnaki Fallen Angelic infiltration of Tara during the Sirian Wars 550 million years ago (re: *Voyagers Volume-2*) the GA Signet Council-6 **Maharaji** of the **Sirius B** *Council of Azurline* assisted in the **DNA Bio-Regenesis** of the **Taran Angelic Human lineage.** The Maharaji offered **hybridization** to the faltering (Lumian) **Adami-Kudmon -Turaneusiam Race of Tara** creating the **Ceres-Adami-Kudmon-Turaneusiam** lineage, who founded the **Melchizedek Cloister** *Priesthood of Mu* on Tara, to assist in reha-bilitation of **Inner Christos-Law of One spiritual ethics** among rehabilitating Angelic Human Race lines. The Ceres-Adami-Kudmon-Turaneusiam line of Tara further interbred for DNA Bio-Regeneis of the original (Lumian) **Adami-Kudmon** and (Alanian) **Beli-Kudyem** Turaneusiam human race lines, **fully revitalizing** the original **Oraphim-Turaneusiam Angelic Human 12-Strand DNA Template,** creating the **Ur-Tarranate Christiac Angelic Human line of Tara.** Certain groups of the **Ur-Tarranate** Christiac Angelic Human race of Tara received **further DNA Bio-Regenesis** from the **Sirius B Maharaji** about 550 million years ago, receiving the genetic enhancement of DNA Strand Templates 13 through 23, then Strand Templates 24 to 48. The **24-48 Strand DNA Template** revitalized in the Ur-Tarranate Christiac Angelic Human line is that characteristic to the original **Oraphim Angelic Human Race** through which the 12-Strand DNA Turaneusiam Angelic Human lineage of Tara had originally been seeded. The genetically enhanced Ur-Tarranates represented a new strain of the Taran Oraphim "Yani" or "Khundara" Eieyani Grail Line, through which the Yanas could incarnate into the Taran drama to initiate fur-ther DNA Bio-Regenesis programs among the Fallen Angelic races. The **original Oraphim Yani lineage of Tara,** known as the "**Templar Solar Initiates**" had suffered genetic digression through an **attempted Bio-Regenesis hybridization program** to assist certain **Anunnaki Fallen Angelic** factions. The new revital-ized Ur-Tarranate-Oraphim Yani Angelic Human line of 550 million years ago became known as The *Priests of Ur.* The Taran Khundara Grail Line **Priests of Ur** created the **Azurite Temple of the Melchizedek Cloister** and the

Melchizedek Cloister Priesthood on **Tara, which continues to assist the Angelic Human lineage of Earth and Inner Earth to this day.**

Portions of the Christiac Grail Line Ur-Tarranate Turaneusiam lineage of Tara chose not to participate in the "Priest of Ur" genetic advancement from the Maharajhi so that the **12-Strand DNA Template** needed to form the **Adami-Kudmon Christiac Grail Line Angelic Human lineage** that was to be seeded on Density-1 Earth could be retained. Through the genetically rehabilitated "**Ur-Tarranate**" **Turaneusiam Christiac Angelic Human** race of Tara, the Adami-Kudmon Christiac Angelic Human lineage of Tara was formed. Through the **Adami-Kudmon Christiac Grail Line Angelic Human of Tara,** the "**12 Tribes**" of the **Christiac Grail Line Angelic Human lineage** were **seeded on Earth 250-25 million years ago.** The "**12 Tribes**" are the **7 Root Races** and **5 Cloister Races** of the original earthly Angelic Human Christiac Grail Line, from which contemporary humanity originally emerged (re: *Voyagers Volume-2*). The **4**[th] **Cloister Race** of the **12-Tribes Angelic Human** seeding on Earth retained the **closest genetic link** to the **Eieyani Priests of Ur from Tara,** and were thus called the "**Melchizedek Cloister**" **Race** of Earth. **Under the guidance of the Yanas from beyond the Time Matrix, the Density-5 MC Eieyani Master Council, the Azurite Universal Templar Security Team, IAFW and GA, the Melchizedek Cloister Priests of Ur Grail Line** of Tara have orchestrated **massive DNA Bio-Regenesis programs** among many Fallen Angelic Legions.

The Taran Priests of Ur, most often referred to as the "**Eieyani Grail Line Angelic Humans,**" " **MC Eieyani Priests,**" or "**MC Oraphim Priests of Ur,**" developed **advanced mastery** over the **spiritual** and **scientific** aspects of **Law of One spirituality** and **Universal Unified Field Physics** as their **Melchizedek Cloister Priesthood** evolved. The MC Eieyani Priests became active members of the **Azurite Universal Templar Security Team,** developing **Master Skills** in DNA Bio-Regenesis and **Kathara** ("core template") **Healing,** and **Planetary, Galactic** and **Universal Templar Complex** mechanics (Star Gate and planetary core template grid mechanics). Upon seeding of the 12-Tribes Christiac Angelic Human lineage on Earth 250 million years ago, the Yanas, Density-5 Eieyani Master Council, Founders Races, IAFW and GA appointed a branch of the **MC Eieyani Priests of Ur** from Tara as the commissioned **GA Signet Council 5.** GA Signet Council-5 is the **Council of Alcyone,** guardians of the Semi-etheric Density-2, **D-5 Alcyone Star Gate-5** in the Pleiades.

It is through the *Taran Eieyani Grail Line Priests of Ur* and the *4*[th] *Melchizedek Cloister Race* of the *12-Tribes Christiac Angelic Human* seeding on Earth, that the *Melchizedek Cloister Priesthood* , the first *Melchizedek Priesthood* as endorsed by the Founders and Yanas, was originally brought to Earth 250 million years ago. The Melchizedek Cloister

Priesthood of the Eieyani Priests of Ur has always been an *egalitarian, non-gender-biased priesthood* that propagated the peaceful, *Law of* One "freedom-teachings' of the *Emerald Covenant,* and the *Sacred Spiritual-Science Ascension teachings* of the *Maharata-* the Inner Christos, as endorsed by the *Founders Races* and *Yanas.*

During the first seeding of 12-Tribes **25 million years ago,** the "Bipedal Dolphin People-Anunnaki" Fallen Angelic Legions of Sirius A, infiltrated through **forced hybridization,** a portion of the **first Cloister Human** race of Earth, the Christiac Angelic Human **Ur-Antrian Cloister Race.** The 11-Strand DNA Template digressive Anunnaki-Ur-Antrian hybrid became known as the *Eurantia* and later as the "Urantia" Fallen Angelic race line, through which **D-11 Annu-Elohim Fallen Angelic Legions incarnated on Earth** in an attempt to **overtake the Christiac Angelic Human lineage.** The **12-Tribes Christiac Angelic Human lineage** was intended to serve as guardians of **Earth's Halls of Amenti star gates.** The Fallen Annu-Elohim Legions wanted to **claim Earth's territories as their own,** just as they had tried to do **550,750,000 years ago** on Tara, Earth's Density-2 counterpart planet (re: *Voyagers Volume-2*), with the infiltration and corruption of the **Taran Oraphim "Templar Solar Initiates."** The evolution of the Oraphim-Turaneusiam Eieyani *Angelic Human lineage* has been riddled with war and strife since its creation **568 million years ago,** as Fallen Angelic Legions have continually attempted to re-direct its evolutionary path into Fallen Angelic dominion. This warring was **brought to Earth from Tara 250-25 million years ago** and has continued ever since, requiring 3 seedings of the Christiac Angelic Human race lines. **We are presently in Seeding-3 of the 12-Tribes Christiac Angelic Human evolutionary cycle.**

Following creation of the digressive **Urantia Cloister Race** by Sirius A Anunnaki Fallen Angelic Legions 25 million years ago, the Annu-Elohim of Density-4, dimension-11, have continued promotion of the *false creed* of the corrupted **"Templar Solar Initiates"** from Tara among evolving 12-Tribes Christiac Angelic Human nations on Earth. **The Yanas, Eieyani Master Council, Founders Races, IAFW, GA, Azurites, Eieyani Priests of Ur** and **Guardian Angelic** races of the **Emerald Covenant** have simultaneously **continued to return the teachings of truth as endorsed by the Founders and Yanas.**

The *teachings of freedom* that are the *rightful heritage* of the *Christiac Angelic Human* lineage of Earth are the *Sacred Spiritual-Science* teachings of the *Maharata-Inner Christ* and the *historical record of creation* in this Time Matrix as revealed through the evolution of the *Emerald Covenant.*

The *false creed* of the **Fallen Angelic Annu-Elohim, Anunnaki** and digressive **"Oraphim-human Templar Solar Initiates"** of Tara, that was brought to Earth through the **Urantia Fallen Angelic** hybrid-human cloister race **25 million years ago,** promotes the *worship of external gods, angelics and false saviors*. The false "Templar" creed discards the true teachings of the **Inner Christ and human freedom,** deceives humanity into **powerlessness, fear** and subservience, and **distracts humanity** from embracing its heritage as an **Angelic Race,** placing human destiny at the **mercy of false-gods.** Through promotion of this false, *patriarchal, externalized Christ* Fallen Angelic Templar-Anunnaki Creed humanity's **right** to have a **personal, loving and empowering relationship with Source-God** and the **Founders Races** is **denied.** The false patriarchal creed of the Fallen Angelic Templar Solar Initiates and Fallen Angelic Annu-Elohim Anunnaki is designed to continually enslave, digress and dis-empower the Angelic Human lineage. The Templar Creed is promoted **falsely** under the name of a "Melchizedek" Creed. In **contemporary times,** the **false Templar-Melchizedek Creed** emerges through **numerous guises** under the names of **various** *false* **"Father God"** personifications that evolved after the fall of the Atlantian Islands in **9558 BC.**

Beginning with the **Sirian-Nibiruian-Anunnaki-Drakonian false "Anu"** **Father-God** personification in the ancient **Sumerian cities,** followed by the **false Father-God** personification of the competing **Sirius A "Bipedal Dolphin People-Anunnaki"** and many other renditions of **competing control dogmas, human religions** have evolved as a **snare for self-perpetuated enslavement.** (re: *Voyager Volume-2 Update Section.*) **Earth** has become a *self-regulated prison for the angelic human lineage;* this is precisely what Fallen Angelic Legions have **intended to create** through *distorting true spiritual-science teachings* into dis-empowering *control dogmas.* In the contemporary **New Age** Movement, the **Templar-Melchizedeks,** directed by several **Annu-Elohim** and **Pleiadian-Nibiruian-Anunnaki factions** that have **controlled the Density-2 D-4 Solar Star Gate-4** since seizing it from Guardian protection in **25,500 BC,** are again **promoting the Templar-Melchizedek false creed** directly among human populations. **Presently there are** *many* **"Melchizedek"** groups emerging within Earth's global cultural arena, through the subtle contact of "channeling" and overtly through physical contact with selected humans.

Some contemporary Melchizedek Groups are legitimate expressions of the Founders *Melchizedek Cloister* Eieyani Priests of Ur lineage. True Cloister Melchizedek Priesthoods *all* emerge from the *"Melchizedek Cloister Order of the Yunasai,"* the Melchizedek Cloister Emerald Order *Yanas* collective from the Eckatic Level of the Energy Matrix, beyond the 15-dimensional Time Matrix. True Guardian-Melchizedeks will always acknowledge the Order of the Yunasai as their Source, while Annu-Elohim Templar-

Melchizedek Priesthoods will "pay homage" to Melchizedek Orders that go by other names. True Guardian-Melchizedek Priesthoods and their representatives *do not teach a patriarchal creed*, they teach gender and race *equality* and they *do not promote the worship of an externalized god*.

True Guardian Melchizedeks do not teach the "**Christ Crucifixion**" story, but rather reveal the *truth* as it is **recorded in the Yanas' and Founders' Records**. The **Yanas** and **Founders** historical records of dimension-15 and the Eckatic Energy Matrix reveal the "Christ story" of the *Essene Eieyani Priest of Ur* born in 12 BC—*Jesheua Sananda Melchizedek*— the *Emerald Order Christed Angelic Human Yani Avatar* with a fully activated **12-Strand DNA Template**, who became known as "**Jesus Christ**." (see: *Voyagers Volume-2*)

Jesheua Sananda Melchizedek AKA "Jesus Christ" incarnated on behalf of the *Density-5 Melchizedek Cloister Eieyani Master Council*, Founders Races, IAFW, GA, and the Azurite Universal Templar Security Team; he *entered human incarnation through* the D-6 Sirius B Maharaji *Council of Azurline.* Jesheua-Jesus incarnated on Earth to return the Yanas' Melchizedek *Cloister* teachings of the Inner Christ, and to assist in *redirecting the distorted Templar-Melchizedek creed* that had flourished on Earth since the fall of Atlantis, in order to *bring the peoples and religions of the world together* under a common banner of *Mutual Love, Respect* and *Angelic Human Freedom,* in preparation for the *scheduled 2012-2017 AD opening of Earth's Halls of Amenti Star Gates* and subsequently *humanity's opportunity* to reenter the Founders *Emerald Covenant.*

Jesheua Sananda Melchizedek, AKA Jesus Christ, was *not* crucified and **did not die**. Jesheua or "Jesus" *ascended* through the Arc of the Covenant passage via **Sirius B Star Gate-6** in 27 AD, following completion of translations of parts of the **Founders' Maharata-** Inner Christ Spiritual-Science Texts and after **fathering** a new, revitalized **Eieyani Christiac Angelic Human Grail Line** on Earth. Jesheua's lineage of **6 children**, fathered between **18 AD-23 AD**, are the **forefathers** of the *Indigo Children* Eieyani Grail Line that has been progressively incarnating on Earth for the **last 100 years**. The story of "**Christ's Crucifixion**" was **staged** by the Annu-Elohim. In **325 AD** the remnants of Jesheua's **Melchizedek Cloister** Inner Christ teachings and the history of his family line were **edited and distorted** by the **Council of Nicea** and the **Church of Rome** in their assembly of the book that became the "**Canonized Bible**." The Council of Nicea distorted the remaining Essene *True Inner Christ Teachings* into a **Fear-based Control**

Dogma, intended to **up-lift the political cause** of the **Roman Empire** to world dominion.

"Jesus Christ" was real, **but many of the** *stories* **told about him** *are not.* **What he stood for, the** *Maharata-***teachings of the** *Inner Christ* **and the Founders'** *Emerald Covenant* **was, and still** *is, truth.*

Due to corruption of the **power-elite** within human governments in the ancient world, *Christianity* **was robbed of the truth that Jesheua-Jesus tried to reveal, and** *all* **of humanity** has been subsequently robbed of the **freedom, enlightenment, unity, love and joy** that Jesheua's teachings were intended to inspire. **Jesheua was not the only** *Speaker of the Emerald Covenant.* Since humanity was first seeded on Earth, the GA, IAFW, Eieyani Master Council, Founders Races, MC Priests of Ur, and the Council of Azurline have made repeated attempts, at times *temporarily* successful, to return **humanity's rightful teachings** of freedom and divine connection. Every time the Emerald Covenant teachings were provided by representatives of the Founders, the meaning and purpose eventually became **distorted into control dogmas** by corrupt human factions that operated under Fallen Angelic influence. Through the loss of the ancient teachings of Jesheua Sananda Melchizedek-Jesus, and the many Emerald Covenant Speakers who came before him, humanity was also **denied the privilege and responsibility** of the Angelic Human heritage, and through this denial, we have temporarily lost the **memory** of our *Christiac* **Angelic Human** potential. With loss of this memory we have also misplaced **Reverent Respect** for ourselves, each other, our planet and its Life-field, and God. Through forgetting our Angelic Human heritage, we have also misplaced the **privilege** that would come as a natural circumstance of our *Christiac Legacy—* **eternal life,** which is the **natural product** of *12-Strand DNA Template Christos Angelic Human* evolution. **Communion** with Fellow Guardian Angelic Nations that is accomplished through *open use of Earth's star gates.* **Passage** through Earth's natural *Star Gates* into the *"Higher Heavens"* of our 15-dimensional Time Matrix, **ascension** from Density, to experience whenever we desire, **reunion and** *conscious, perpetual co-creative* **At-ONE-ment** with **Source-God.** These privileges and the **responsibility** toward **personal, race, planetary, galactic and universal evolution** that such privilege implies, represent our heritage as **Christiac Angelic Humans.** We will be enabled to claim the Divine Rights and Responsibilities of the Angelic Human heritage when we allow ourselves to embrace our Inner Christos potential, through which the Angelic Human spirit can awaken in embodiment.

The irony of human evolution is that the **Fallen Angelic Legions** have served as the **Promoters and Instigators** of our **spiritual and thus physical** imprisonment, but *we* have been, and continue to be, the **Executors and Administrators** of own **Living-Death Sentence.** Inadvertently, we perpetuate our **imprisonment in mortal limitation** and recreate the **symbolic crucifixion of the Living Inner Christ,** as we have been **tricked** into placing our salvation in the hands of the very **Fallen Angelic Legions** that the Angelic Human lineage was created to **restore and heal.** It remains the **Human Prerogative** as to what interpretation of reality, and what **definition of Self and God** we will choose to acknowledge, honor and act upon.

As Jesheua Melchizedek—Jesus—tried to show us, the true Savior of our race has Always *lived within each of us*, as the sleeping Inner Christed Self that struggles to awaken. Jesheua-Jesus, and the many Emerald Covenant Speakers that came before him, have tried to bring this truth to us and demonstrate its power; so that we, as the Guardian Christiac Angelic Race that we *are*, might finally re-awaken to set ourselves, our Souls and our planet free from the illusion of mortal limitation and the manipulation of Fallen Angelic dominion.

2000 years ago humanity was faced with a *choice* of allowing the Inner Christos to lead us home, or to Crucify the Inner Christ that Jesheua-Jesus modeled for us through the worship of externalized God-personifications. We are faced with this same choice again between 2000-2017, and the Fallen Angelic Legions will do their best to provide us with all opportunity to make a misinformed decision.

On behalf of the **Yanas** from beyond the Time Matrix, the Density-5 **MC Eieyani Masters Council, Founders Races,** the **Azurite Universal Templar Security Team, Eieyani Priests of Ur, IAFW, GA** and **Guardian Angelic Races** of the *Emerald Covenant,* and in support of the causes of *Angelic Human freedom* and the *continued healing and survival* of Earth, GA Signet Council-6, the **Council of Azurline,** guardians of **Sirius B Star Gate-6** and *progenitors* of the **Indigo Children Eieyani-Christiac Angelic Human** race line presently incarnate on Earth, are revealing this **historical information** pertaining to the "**Christ Story**" and Pre-ancient Angelic Human evolution because, the *time has come.*

Since the failure of the intended Star Gate Opening Cycle of 22,326 BC, All Angelic Nations have been quite aware that a Major Confrontation, over the evolutionary destiny of Earth humanity, would occur between Guardian and Fallen Angelic Legions upon the next due Star Gate Opening Cycle of 2000-2017 AD. Many times, such as during the "Christ Drama" of 12 BC-27 AD, Guardian Nations have tried to prepare human-

181

ity for peaceful navigation through this pending confrontation, and many times they have attempted to negotiate peaceful resolutions to this scheduled conflict with Fallen Angelic Legions, before *the time* of *final conflict* arrived.

THE FINAL CONFLICT, STAR GATE-6, MAJI PRIESTS OF AZURLINE AND THE "CHRIST DRAMA"

The natural Star Gate Opening Cycle that was due to occur in 22,326 BC failed and Earth's Halls of Amenti star gates did not open, because the **Pleiadian-Nibiruian-Anunnaki Council,** which was once part of the **GA Signet Council 5** *Alcyone Council,* broke their Emerald Covenant agreements in **25,500 BC.** Reverting to Annu-Elohim Fallen Angelic **dominion agendas,** the Nibiruian Council and related Annu-Elohim Fallen Angelic groups **seized control** of the Density-2, D-4 **Sol Star Gate-4,** to which the Nibiruian Council had once been **entrusted** with guardianship. The Density-2, D-4 Sol Star Gate-4, the **4**th **of the 12 Star Gates** in the Universal Templar Complex, is the **connection point** between the **Density-2** universe (dimensions 4-5-6) and **Universal Star Gate-3** in the **Density-1** (dimensions 1-2-3) universe. The **Sol Star Gate-4** is the **primary passageway** between Density-1 and Density-2 universes. **Universal Star Gate-3** is located at **Earth's core.** Earth's **Halls of Amenti** star gates, which connect to the **Density-2** planet **Tara** and many other areas within the **4 Densities** of our Time Matrix, connect to the star gates of the **Universal Templar Complex** through the **D-3 Earth Star Gate-3.**

When the Pleiadian-Nibiruian Council defected from the Emerald Covenant and Alcyone Council in **25,500 BC** and **turned D-4 Sol Star Gate-4** over to **Annu-Elohim Fallen Angelic** dominion, they effectively **blocked Earth's Halls of Amenti at the D-4 Sol Star Gate.** Since 25,500 BC, the Annu-Elohim, Pleiadian-Nibiruians and related Anunnaki Fallen Angelic Legions have attempted to keep Guardian Angelic nations out of earth involvement, while keeping the Angelic Human souls of Earth locked into **repeated cycles of reincarnation** on Earth, **blocking their passage of Ascension** through the Sol Star Gate-4. Since the fall of Sol Star Gate-4 to Fallen Angelic dominion in 25,500 BC, **Guardian Angelic Nations,** under the direction of the **Yanas,** Density-5 **MC Eieyani Master Council, IAFW** and **GA** have intervened on Earth directly. Through the **technical Templar Science** expertise of the **Sirius B Maharagi,** Taran **MC Priests of Ur** and the **Azurite Universal Templar Security Team,** the Guardians **reopened the Sirius B Star Gate-6 passage** to Earth. The **Star Gate-6** passage, called the **Halls of Amorea,** and later in Egyptian times, the "**3**rd **Eye of Horus,**" connects the Density-1, D-3 **Earth Star Gate-3** directly to Density-2, D-6 **Sirius B Star Gate-6, bypassing** D-5 Alcyone Star Gate-5 and D-4 Sol Star Gate-4, and thus circumnavigating the star gate passages controlled by **Annu-Elohim Fallen Angelic Minions.** The **Sirius B Star Gate-6 Amorea passage** had originally been used by Guardian Nations to orchestrate **Seeding-2** of the Angelic Human 12-Tribes **3,700,000 years ago.** The Amorea passage had been damaged in the **Thousand Years War** of **846,000 BC,** requiring the current **Seeding-3** of the 12-Tribes to be conducted in **798,000 BC** through the new passage of the **Arc of the Covenant,** which was created in **838,000 BC** for this purpose.

The **MC Eieyani Priests of Ur** and **Maharagi** of Sirius B repaired the **Amorea passage** between Earth and Sirius B Star Gate-6 in **22,500 BC** and entered **full incarnation on Earth** through a **new Eieyani Indigo Children Grail Line.** The new **Sirius B Priests of Ur Grail Line** of Earth, referred to as the **Eieyani Melchizedek Cloister,** the *"Priests of Azurline"* or the *"Magi Priests of Azurline–MC,"* presence on Earth was intended to be **temporary.** The **Maji Priests of Azurline-MC** were to remain in **seclusion** within their "Hidden Cities" on Earth, only until completion of the Guardian mission intended for the **22,326 BC Star Gate Opening Cycle.** (re: *Voyagers Volume-2, Update Section.*) The Maji Azurline Priests-MC were commissioned by the Density-5 **Emerald Order Eieyani Master Council** to **free Earth and its Angelic Human lineage** from advancing Annu-Elohim and Pleiadian-Nibiruian Anunnaki Fallen Angelic infiltration, which was progressively overrunning **Atlantian culture** through the Nibiruian's hold on Sol StarGate-4. Many **thousands of years of negotiations** between Guardian Angelic and Fallen Angelic High Councils had **failed,** and the Annu-Elohim Fallen Angelic Legion, through their Pleiadian-Nibiruian-Anunnaki, intended to **orchestrate their final strike against the Angelic Human populations of Earth.**

On behalf of the Annu-Elohim Fallen Angelic Legion of D-11, the **Pleiadian-Nibiruian-Anunnaki** intended to **temporarily evacuate** their hybrid races among human population, then use their **Battle Star Nibiru** (not the same stellar body as the *planet* Nibiru) to **force Earth into pole shift.** During a Star Gate Opening Cycle, when the connections between the Sun's Sol Star Gate-4 and Earth's Star Gate-3 are volatile and delicate, the Nibiruians could easily orchestrate pole shift on Earth, in order to **clear Earth's territory of the Angelic Human lineage,** for their own intended **re-colonization.** In **22,326 BC,** the Nibiruian-Anunnaki intended to use the **Battle Star Nibiru** to break the natural **electro-magnetic field bridge** between the Sun's Sol Star Gate-4 and Earth Star Gate-3, which would throw the planet into pole shift over a 3 to 8 year period. The **Maji Azurline Priests of Ur-MC** were sent into the Earth drama **to prevent this cataclysm** from occurring. The only way Guardian Angelic Nations could prevent the Nibiruian-Anunnaki Fallen Angelic

183

Legion from throwing Earth into pole shift, was to override Nibiruian control of Sol Star Gate-4. Through activating **Sirius B Star Gate-6**, and using the Star Gate-6 **Halls of Amorea passage** to hold Earth's electro-magnetic fields **securely in alignment** with **Sol Star Gate-4** and **Alcyone Star Gate-5** during Earth's **22,326 BC Star Gate Opening Cycle**.

The Maji Azurline Priests MC **22,326 BC Earth Crisis Intervention Mission** was only **partially successful.** Guardian Nations had hoped the Maji Priests would be able to **secure Earth's electromagnetic fields**, then use Sirius B Star Gate-6 to **break Nibiru's hold over Sol Star Gate-4**, to bring **Star Gate-4 and Earth** back under **full Guardian protection.** Once Earth's **Halls of Amenti** star gates were secured, the Maji Azurline Priests MC intended to **prepare Earth populations** for **physical visitation** from the GA Signet-5 *Alcyone Council* and Signet-6 *Council of Azurline*. The **GA Council of Alcyone**, guardians of Density-2, **D-5 Alcyone Star Gate-5** in the Pleiades, were to prepare human populations for **entry into a restatement of the Emerald Covenant** *Universal Co-evolution Agreement.* If earth humans chose to enter and honor the Emerald Covenant, the Council of Azurline, guardians of Density-2, D-6 Sirius B Star Gate-6 were to offer official invitation into the Emerald Covenant. The **Maji Priests of Azurline** were to provide the true Emerald Order Melchizedek Cloister Priests of Ur **teachings** of the *Maharata-*"Inner Christ," DNA Bio-Regenesis and Masters Templar Mechanics to enable the Angelic Humans of Earth to **heal** and **re-awaken.** Through implementation of the Emerald Order MC teachings, the Angelic Human 12-Strand DNA Template could be regenerated among the Earth human races and the awakened Angelic Humans could **create for themselves** the opportunity of **self-directed Ascension** out of Density or **biological immortality** anywhere within the Density systems. Once Earth's Angelic Humans demonstrated sufficient **ethical-spiritual maturity**, the Angelic Humans who chose to remain on Earth would be **honored** with the commission of **serving as guardians** of the **D-3 Earth Star Gate-3** and **D-4 Sol Star Gate-4.** This was the Maji Priests of Azurline-MC intention when they entered incarnation on Earth in **22,500 BC**, in preparation for Earth's **22,326 BC Star Gate Opening Cycle**.

The 22,326 BC Star Gate Opening Cycle did not take place as scheduled. The **"Hidden City"** of the **Maji Azurline Priests** that held the earthly opening to the Sirius B Halls of Amorea passage was found and directly **attacked and destroyed**, via physical visitation to Earth by the Pleiadian-Nibiruian-Anunnaki (*see Voyagers Vol. 2, Current Events Update Section*). Though the **Amorea passage survived the attack**, the **crystalline technology** that the Maji Azurline Priests were intending to use to override the Nibiruian hold on Sol Star Gate-4 was damaged, and could not be repaired rapidly enough for use in the 22,326 BC Star Gate Opening Cycle. The Azurline

Council of Sirius B used Star Gate-6 and the Amorea passage to **stop the opening** of Earth's Halls of Amenti Star Gates **before the opening cycle began, successfully preventing** the Annu-Elohim and Pleiadian-Nibiruian-Anunnaki Fallen Angelic Legions from forcing Earth's **pole shift.** But the Council of Azurline and Maji Priests were **unsuccessful** in freeing Earth, the Angelic Human lineage and Solar Star Gate-4 from Fallen Angelic dominion. **The intended plan of the Annu-Elohim and Anunnaki Fallen Angelic Legions was also only *partially* successful.** In the 22,236 BC confrontation, the Pleiadian-Nibiruian-Anunnaki Fallen Legions "scored a victory" in **retaining control of Sol Star Gate-4,** and thus could continue their **progressive infiltration** of Earth and corruption of the earthly Angelic Human races. But they **did *not*** succeed in creating **pole shift** and "clearing Earth's real estate" for their resettlement **as they had originally intended to do.**

The 22,326 BC confrontation between Guardian Angelic Nations and Annu-Elohim/Anunnaki Fallen Angelic Legions, over the destiny of Earth human evolution and control of Earth's Halls of Amenti star gates, was left in a temporary "Stalemate."

Neither side in this **polarity drama** accomplished what they had set out to do, and both sides **required the event** of a natural **Star Gate Opening Cycle on Earth** in order to bring their plans into **fruition.** To prevent the Annu-Elohim Fallen Angelic Legions' intended destruction of the Angelic Humans of Earth, **Guardian Angelic Nations** needed the D-3 Earth Star Gate-3 and the D-4 Sol Star Gate-4 in the Sun to naturally open. Natural opening of Earth's star gates would allow Guardian Angelic Nations the opportunity to secure Earth's **Halls of Amenti** star gates and to **peacefully** retrieve Earth and Sol Star Gate-4 from Pleiadian-Nibiruian-Anunnaki Fallen Angelic control. The Annu-Elohim and their Anunnaki Fallen Angelic Legions need Earth Star Gate-3 and Sol Star Gate-4 to naturally open in order to have the opportunity to trigger misalignment of the Earth and Solar star gates during their activation cycle, through which inevitable pole shift would occur. During a natural Star Gate Opening Cycle, pole shift could be initiated by the Pleiadian-Nibiruian-Anunnaki if they could use their **Battle Star Nibiru** to break the electromagnetic link between Earth and the Sun, **before** the Guardian Angelic Nations could utilize Sirius B Star Gate-6 to **secure the natural Earth-Sun alignment.** Like the Guardian Angelic Nations, the Pleiadian-Nibiruian-Anunnaki Fallen Angelic Nations also required the **unique conditions of geo and astro-physics characteristic to a Star Gate Opening Cycle,** to fulfill their intended objectives. Both Guardian Angelic Nations and Fallen Angelic Legions knew that **this con-**

flict was not resolved in 22,326 BC, and that the races would meet their final confrontation during Earth's next Star Gate Opening Cycle, the earliest possible date for which was **2000-2017 AD.**

It was known by the Angelic Nations Since 22,326 BC, that the ultimate
confrontation and *final conflict* between Guardian Angelic Nations and
Fallen Angelic Legions was most likely to occur during Earth's 2000-2017
Star Gate Opening Cycle. This ancient and on-going speculation became
historical fact with the official, irreversible initiation and consummation of
Earth's 2000-2017

STAR GATE OPENING CYCLE ON JANUARY 1ST, 2000
(see: *Voyagers Vol. 2*).

If Guardian Nations and the Founders Races had taken a **stance of non-interference** during the **22,326 BC drama,** the **Angelic Human lineage** of Earth would have been **destroyed** and Earth would have evolved from this point under **Fallen Angelic rule.** If the Founders Races permitted the **Fallen Angelic Annu-Elohim** to take possession of Earth, and thus **Earth's Halls of Amenti star gates, Drakonian** races from the **D-10 Fallen Angelic Seraphim** Legion would **attempt to claim Earth and the Halls of Amenti from Annu-Elohim rule.** Drakonians would **invade Anunnaki settlements of Earth** to prevent the **D-11 Annu-Elohim,** the Drakonian's **ancestral adversaries,** from using the **Halls of Amenti** to fulfill their desire of **exterminating the Fallen Angelic Seraphim races.** In the event that the Earth drama unfolded in this way, Earth would have become a **short-lived battle zone for Fallen Angelic Legion warfare,** culminating in **planetary destruction.** The same **scenario** had manifested in **848,000 BC** during the **Thousand Years War,** (RE: *Voyagers Vol. 2*), culminating in the **total destruction** of a planet called **Maldak,** which once existed in **Earth's galaxy.** The only difference between the two dramas is that **if Earth were to meet with a fate similar to Maldak,** the highly populated **Pleiadian and Sirian star systems of Density-2** would also be **destroyed** due to their **connection to the Halls of Amenti.** A cataclysm of this **magnitude** would cause the **collapse of our entire 15-dimensional Time Matrix;** the **Universal Templar Complex Star Gates** would **implode,** culminating in a **massive "Super Nova"** of all main galaxies in our Time Matrix. If this travesty were to occur, the **consciousness embodied there within** would be reduced to literal "**space dust,**" or *units of undifferentiated consciousness without form or sentient memory.* Fallen Angelic Legions hope to find refuge in other neighboring Time Matrix systems should their actions inadvertently initiate this event.

The Founders Nations had **not intended** such **chaos,** nor had they **antici-pated** that the **polarity dramas within this Time Matrix** could reach such extremes; extremes that **threaten the structural integrity** and well-being of other life-systems **far beyond our Time Matrix.** On **directive of the Yanas** from the Energy Matrix, and in order to **preserve their original intentions of peaceful, loving co-evolution,** the Density-5 Founders Races have continued their effort to restore peace and healing to our Time Matrix. The **Founders res-toration efforts** have been ongoing since the **onset of digression in this Time Matrix** during the **Lyran-Elohim Wars 250 billion years ago.** Guardian Angelic Nation intervention in Earth's affairs **in 22,326 BC** was yet another, **comparatively small step** taken in the **Founders' plan to restore peace and safety to this Time Matrix.** With the **privilege of free will creation** once given to the **Founders Races** by the **Yanas,** which set the life-field of our Time Matrix in motion **950 billion years ago,** so too came *responsibility* **for their creations** and their potential influence on other Time Matrix systems. The Founders know they are accountable for what occurs within this Time Matrix, and they realize that "**they made the mess so it is their rightful responsibility to clean it up.**" For this reason the **Founders Races and Guardian Angelic Nations** will continue with their **crisis intervention efforts** for however long it takes in terms of experiential "time." The **Founders** themselves are as **weary of this raging polarity drama** as are the uncountable souls of **Guardian Angelic Nations** that have continually assisted the Founders in their efforts to heal this Time Matrix.

Presently, unbeknownst to the human populations of Earth, the contem-porary earthly drama plays a direct and tremendous role in whether this Universal Polarity Drama has continued possibility for healing. The Angelic Human Lineage of Earth was created to serve as guardians and protectors of Earth's Halls of Amenti Star Gates and the Universal Tem-plar Complex. Guardian Angelic Nations presently need the assistance of on-planet humans to fulfill the Maji Azurline Priests of Ur 22,326 BC plan of using the Sirius B Star Gate-6 to prevent Nibiruian-initiated pole shift on Earth between 2003-2008. The Founders Race crisis intervention plan cannot be successfully accomplished without a sufficient team of Angelic Humans and Indigo Children Grail Line humans *on planet,* who can render the advanced Planetary Templar Mechanics needed to override Nibiruian control of Sol Star Gate-4.

In 1992, tentative negotiations called the "**Sirian-Pleiadian Agree-ments**" were secured between Guardian Nations and the Pleiadian-Nibiruian-Anunnaki Fallen Angelic Legions of **Nibiru.** In 1992, **much to** the outrage of the D-11 Annu-Elohim and many other Anunnaki Fallen Angelic Legions, the Pleiadian-Nibiruian-Anunnaki Council agreed to enter the Emerald Covenant Co-Evolution Agreement, and promised return of Sol Star Gate-4 to GA Signet Council-6, the Sirius B Maharaji Council of Azurline. Upon return of Sol Star Gate-4 to Founder Race protection, the Council of Azurline, Alcyone Council of D-5 Alcyone Star Gate-5 and the Azurite Universal Templar Security Team, intended to protect Earth from the contemporary Drakonian pole shift takeover agenda. In 1992 it appeared that the long dreaded, but anticipated, potential major crisis of an overt, 3-way confrontation between the Guardian Angelic Nations and competing Annu-Elohim and Drakonian Fallen Angelic Legions, had been finally, if only temporarily, resolved through negotiations. With the combined, co-operative efforts of Guardian Angelic Nations, and the newly supportive Pleiadian-Nibiruian-Anunnaki, who presently have a great deal of control over many Ley Lines and Vortices in Earth's Planetary Templar Complex, protecting Earth through the 2000-2017 Star Gate Opening Cycle would not be overly difficult to achieve.

Following the 1992 Sirian-Pleiadian Agreements, the focus of Guardian Angelic Nations was upon preparing Earth's Templar Complex for the 2012 opening of Earth's Halls of Amenti star gates and readying humanity for the "New Age of Enlightenment" and humanity's pending entry into the Emerald Covenant. On September 12th, 2000, the Pleiadian-Nibiruian-Anunnakis withdrew from the Emerald Covenant and entered alliance with the newly formed Annu-Elohim-Drakonian United Resistance ("Resistance" to the Emerald Covenant). On September 12th, 2000, the United Resistance issued an edict of war against the Angelic Human lineage of Earth and the Guardian Angelic Nations, if the Guardians refused to immediately withdraw their support of Earth humanity and leave Earth territories to the Fallen Angelic pole shift dominion agenda. The Density-5 Eieyani Master Council and Founders Races refused to withdraw their support of earth humans, and since September 12th, 2000 the IAFW, GA and the many other Guardian Angelic Races of the Emerald Covenant were placed on a state of "Red Alert."

This ancient *final conflict* drama between Guardian Angelic Nations and Fallen Angelic Legions over the destiny of Earth and human evolution, has been anticipated by Fallen Angelic Legions with fervor, and by Guardian Angelic Nations with dread, since the "Stalemate" of this confrontation that occurred in 22,326 BC. Though peaceful solutions appeared promising, following the 1992 Sirian-Pleiadian Agreements, the September 12th, 2000 declaration of War by the United Resistance confirms that the "Final Round" of this ancient confrontation will progressively move into the contemporary Earth arena.

The *outcome* of this drama lies squarely in *humanity's hands.*

Since the failed Star Gate Opening Cycle of **22,326 BC**, Guardian Angelic nations have **repeatedly attempted to awaken the Angelic Humans of Earth** so humanity could **create its freedom** and **prepare for the peaceful but direct intervention** that would be required when the *the time* of the *final conflict* arrived. Since 22,326 BC, and the later fall of the Atlantian Nations in 9558 BC and subsequent Nibiruian Fallen Angelic infiltration of Sumerian culture, **human evolution has been a continuing drama of conflict and chaos.** (RE: *Voyagers Volume-2, Current Events Update Section*) The **remaining records** of "ancient human history" cover a period of time during which **competing factions of Fallen Angelic Legions** continually attempted to "**secure their ground**" within human populations, in anticipation of the 2000-2017 Star Gate Opening Cycle, when they planned to "**lay their claim**" on Earth's territories. Since **22,236 BC to the present day,** Fallen Angelic Legions **knew they would attempt to destroy humanity through pole shift** when the *final conflict* arrived, and that they would **spare only their easily controlled "Chosen Ones"** for digressive colonization.

Fallen Angelic Races have envisioned and promoted "Armageddon" and "End Times" scenario since the 22,326 BC confrontation, knowing that they intended to *instigate war* among human nations on Earth as a precursor to initiating the planetary pole shift agenda, when *the time* of the *final conflict* came.

As Fallen Angelic Legions progressively guided humanity toward **their intended 2000-2017 Armageddon "End Times" scenario** since 22,326 BC, Guardian Angelic Nations **continually attempted to prepare humanity for peaceful resolution** of this pending "End Times" drama. The **Guardians last major attempt** of preparing humanity to serve as the **agent of healing in the 2000-2017 Final Conflict,** was during the "**Christ Period.**" A **Team of Magi Azurline Priests of Ur,** who had been incarnate as members of the Maji Priests overtaken by the Nibiruians in the 22,326 BC confrontation, re-entered Earth incarnation. Their **purpose** was to return the knowledge of the **Emerald Covenant** and pending **Final Conflict,** and to **explain the peaceful solution** of reclaiming the **Angelic Human-Inner Christ heritage.** Through the **Founders Sacred-Science teachings** of the **Inner Christ,** humanity could learn to **re-activate the Angelic Human12-Strand Template,** so humans would again **become capable of utilizing advanced Planetary Templar Mechanics,** which are **run through the human DNA Template.** If humanity can **reawaken** the dormant **Angelic Human DNA Template,** the human body can **biologically interface with the electromagnetic functions** of

189

Earth's Planetary Templar star gate system, **as it was originally designed to do.** In **actualizing the Angelic Human potential,** humans **would not only set themselves free,** but could also assist Guardian Angelic Nations in **setting Earth free,** by securing Earth's Halls of Amenti and regaining the Sun's D-4 Sol Star Gate-4 under Guardian Nation protection.

Jesheua Sananda Melchizedek—"Jesus" of the Bible, was the Magi Azurline Priest of Ur who had, like the other members of his GA Crisis Intervention Team, incarnated through the Sirius B Council of Azurline, to return the teachings of the Emerald Covenant and Melchizedek Cloister Spiritual- Science DNA Template activation training in preparation for the anticipated 2000-2017 Final Conflict.

The **teachings of Jesheua-Jesus,** like those of so many Magi Azurline Priests of Ur before him, were **rapidly distorted and destroyed by human power elite organizations** operating under **Fallen Angelic Legion influence.** The true historical **story of Jesheua-Jesus** was twisted, edited, literally re-written and used by factions of both Annu-Elohim/Anunnaki and Drakonian Seraphim Fallen Angelic Legions, and their human "puppets," to promote a control dogma of external Father-God worship.

The *intention* behind this *manipulation of truth* was to bury the *real truth* that *Jesheua-Jesus* had provided, and to literally *"set humanity up"* for the **"big party"** that the Fallen Angelic Legions had planned for the days of the Final Conflict.

Fallen Angelic Legions knew that if they could continue to motivate masses of humans to **pledge allegiance to external figures of Gods** and their **"Divine Representatives,"** as they had been doing since promotion of their Sumerian **"Father-God Anu,"** that plenty of human **"specimens"** would be available for hybridization, following the "End Times" holocaust. All the Fallen Angelics would need to do would be to **visit Earth** in the guise of their **promoted "Holy Figures"** as the End Times drama unfolded; and humans, **robbed of the true power** of the Inner Christ teachings and **eager for "salvation,"** would **joyfully follow wherever the Fallen Angelics might lead.** Humans that followed **most devoutly** the Fallen Angelics' "appointed Gods and saviors" would be "rewarded" for their loyalty with "salvation" from destruction **via evacuation,** when the time for creating pole shift had come. "Rescued" humans would feel **honored** when assigned to "Godly Spouses," and would feel **privileged** to participate in "re-colonization" hybridization programs to "begin a new heaven on Earth."

The *real* "Jesus"- Jesheua, and the Ascension and Eternal Life that he stood for do indeed exist, and so do the Heavens and the "House of Many Mansions" that are manifested by our *one* Source-God.

But the **Christ crucifixion story** and the **worship** of, and **transference of personal power** to, **externalized personifications** of Gods, saviors and deities, was, **and still is, an intentional fabrication** promoted by **Fallen Angelic Legions.** This **deception** was created with **great motivated intention,** to mislead the **Angelic Humans** of Earth into **inadvertently assisting the Fallen Angelic Legions** to fulfill their **ancient quest for Earth's Halls of Amenti Star Gates** and to actualize their **long-coveted dream of Earth dominion.**

Christianity is not the only world religion that has been robbed of its original Sacred Intention. Other representatives of *real* truth have appeared, at times, in *every earth religion,* and like the teachings of Jesheua-Jesus, the teachings of truth have been compromised wherever Guardian Angelic Nations tried to plant their seeds. *All genuine* spiritual teachings of Earth originally emerged from translations of the Emerald Covenant Founders Races Sacred Spiritual-Science teachings.

Guardian Angelic Nations are now attempting to **reveal this disturbing truth** to humanity, NOT because they desire to cause fear, strife or heartache. Had the current drama on Earth not reached *critical proportions* with the **September 12**[th]**, 2000,** United Resistance declaration of **War,** it would have been unnecessary to make these revelations so directly at this time. But due to the manner in which contemporary events have unfolded, the **long-awaited** *final conflict* **has arrived.** *"The time" is now,* whether we choose to believe this while there is *still time* to *do something effective about it,* or whether we realize it "after the fact," if we have a chance to realize it at all. Though this manifestation of *final conflict* is a **large and ancient drama** that has made its way back to our door, it is **not a drama we need to fear.** As Angelic Humans, we have the **power to serve as healing agents** within this conflict, if we are wise and courageous enough to *see* what is going on, and to assist Guardian Angelic Nations in **peaceful healing strategies.**

This is *not* a conflict that can be resolved by violence.

It is a Victory that *can* be achieved,
but only through Spirit, Wisdom and Love.

Becoming aware of the challenges as they exist within the current drama is half the battle won! Over the **next 8 years** it will become **increasingly important** for humanity to face the issue of **race conflict** over the reality

191

of the power known as **God.** The unfolding drama will force the hand and the answer to the question of "Internal God vs. Externally God Personified vs. No God? " will determine the outcome of the *final conflict,* individually and *en masse.* As they have **planned all along,** the **Fallen Angelic Legions are now moving forward** with their plans of **covertly instigating conflict among human nations;** conflicts that are intended to escalate into **World War,** in fulfillment of their contrived "Armageddon" scenario. *We can stop this.* Part of the *Fallen Angelic plan* involves the **progressive manifestation of staged** "Holy Dramas," as the Fallen Angelics' "Chosen Ones" are rallied for service and later evacuation. This **rally call** is now *loud and clear* within the **New Age Movement,** as well as within the dogmas of **Traditional World Religions.** The covert rally call of Fallen Angelic visitors is also heard within the "UFO Movement," and it is **everywhere promoted** within the **Scientific Paradigm of Official Denial;** denial of both the **presence of Visitors** and the **existence of the human Soul,** through which this conflict can be healed.

The ancient distorted renditions of Historical False-truths will *soon* be used to *ensnare the human race* in a manifest *spiritual-political drama* with *Fallen Angelic Legions,* who plan to *misrepresent themselves* as our "saviors" by staging a false *"Second Coming of Christ"* Drama. In this drama, representatives of *Holy Figures* from *all major world religions* will appear to *come collectively* to "save the world" and unify world religions and governments under a *false* "Common Humanity" cause. A cause which is a *One-World-Order control agenda* in disguise.

This drama will take place between 2002-2012 only if humanity is unable to perceive the deception. If humanity can re-awaken to the freedom and responsibilities of the Christiac Angelic human heritage and take peaceful counter-strategic measures, this pending confrontational drama does not have to manifest any further than it already has.

The Choice Remains As *The Human Prerogative.*

The *only viable solutions* to this progressively manifesting *final conflict* visitor drama are: **Advanced Planetary Templar Complex Grid Work,** through which the **Halls of Amenti Star Gates** and **Earth's Vortex System** can be **protected from** *further* **Fallen Angelic Race** infiltration; and *personal self-generated* **DNA** *bio-regenesis* of the dormant angelic human **12-strand DNA template,** through which *Advanced Planetary Templar Complex Grid Work can be run,* and by which the **human bio-energetic field** can be **healed** and **protected.**

The Stage for this " false *Second-Coming/Armageddon Drama"* was *intentionally set* many thousands of years ago, by *Fallen Angelic Annu-Elohim and Anunnaki Legions* who knew this time period would bring a *Star Gate Opening Cycle.*

Learning *How To Apply The Solutions*
to resolve this drama is *easy.....*

Understanding *why* the Solutions are needed is the *difficult* part.
To understand the realities of the current drama the human mind must overcome *many thousands of years* of false Fallen Angelic Legion *Propaganda,* and humanity must reach *within* to find and awaken the wisdom, power, freedom and love of the Angelic Human Christed Soul.
It is, at once, that easy...and that hard.

If Guardian Angelic Nations did not fully believe in the love, strength, courage, power, inherent wisdom and intrinsic purity that lives within the Angelic Human Spirit, they would not be attempting to *awaken* the Angelic Humans *now.*

When the Founders Races, IAFW, GA and Guardian Angelic Legions of the Emerald Covenant **first initiated public contact** through the **May 1999** publication of the **Voyagers** Series, the *"final conflict"* drama **had not yet reached critical Crisis Status.** At that time, the Fallen Angelic Legions' *"False Second Coming"* drama had been successfully orchestrated in the **Parallel Earth system,** which runs just a bit ahead of us in time. In our reality system, much hope remained that the **1992 Sirian-Pleiadian Agreements** would allow the *final conflict* to be resolved through peaceful negotiation. **Events have not manifested on Earth or in the heavens as the Guardian Alliance hoped.** Parallel Earth, in their time line, has entered an **irreversible** "slow roll pole shift," which began in **November, 2000,** in our time line, and will complete with a **"rapid roll"** in our year **2009.** If we can assist the Guardian Alliance **between 2001–2003** in orchestrating the **advanced Planetary Templar Mechanics** needed to **secure Earth's Halls of Amenti under Guardian protection,** there is **still time** to **prevent our Earth from being "pulled along"** in the Parallel Earth pole shift. There is **still time** to prevent the *final conflict* that will bring **Pleiadian-Nibiruian Fallen Angelic** visitors *physically* to our door. There is **still time** for humanity to **reclaim its Angelic Human heritage, just in time** to fulfill our original **Divine Commission** of serving as **Guardians and Keepers of Earth's Halls of Amenti star gates** and the Planetary Templar Complex. The Founders Race teachings are being progressively provided for those who care enough to learn.

The message of the **Yanas, Founders Races, IAFW, GA** and **Guardian Angelic Races** of the **Emerald Covenant** is this:

Beloved Sleeping Angels,

You are Loved beyond all knowing. You are honored in your Being.
You are cherished as the harbingers of hope for this Time Matrix
that you were originally intended to be.

You were *born free* into Density and the worlds of manifest illusion, from
the Love of Cosmic *Source* that is your Home.

Beloved ones, Choose *well...*
Choose Love...
and then Choose Freedom.

Angelic Humans, *fly*!

Reclaim your *rightful place* among the Stars!

Temporary Maharic Seal
Bio-Regenesis Technique

For building bio-energetic field integrity and accelerating spiritual actualization.

Prior to use: Read through the steps and practice the visualizations and their sequence slowly, for familiarity.

1. Imagine the 2-dimensional image of a "Merkaba Star" or six-pointed "Star of David," in the color of Pale Silver, as if the image is drawn on a black background on the inside of your forehead. This image represents a composite scalar wave pattern **Keylontic Symbol Code** called the "Hierophant." Its color denotes the frequency spectra of the 11th and 12th Dimensions, and its form, combined with these color frequencies, represents the control code of the 12th dimensional frequency band. It is the Key Code to unlock the 12th-Dimensional Maharic Shield in the personal and planetary scalar grids.

2. INHALE, while visualizing the Hierophant Symbol at the center of the brain, in the Pineal Gland.

3. EXHALE, while using the exhale breath to firmly move the Hierophant down the Central Vertical Body Current (energy current in the center of the body), then out between the legs and straight down into the Earth's core (your 13th Chakra).

4. INHALE, while imagining that you can see at Earth's core a huge, **Disc-shaped Crystalline Platform of Pale Silver Light** that extends outward on a horizontal plane through the entire body of the Earth and out into

195

the atmosphere. Visualize the Hierophant suspended in the center of the disc (this image represents the Planetary Maharic Shield, the scalar wave grid composed of dimension 10/11/12 frequency, with the Hierophant Key Code positioned to activate the Planetary Shield.)

5. EXHALE, while pushing your breath outward into the Earth's Maharic Shield, imagining as you exhale that the force of the breath has made the **Earth's Maharic Shield** begin to spin.

6. INHALE, using the inhale breath to draw **Pale Silver Light** from Earth's spinning Maharic Shield, into the Hierophant positioned at the center of the Planetary Shield.

7. EXHALE, using the exhale breath to push the Pale Silver Light throughout the entire Hierophant making the Hierophant glow and pulsate with Pale Silver Light.

8. INHALE, imagine that the glowing Pale Silver Hierophant momentarily flashes Crimson Red and returns to Pale Silver. Then use the inhale breath to draw the Hierophant **vertically up** from its position at Earth's core, to a position 12" below your feet (the position of your dormant personal Maharic Shield scalar-wave grid). As you inhale the Hierophant upward from Earth's core, imagine that it trails a **thick cord of Pale Silver Light** behind it. One end of the **Silver Cord** remains attached to Earth's core, the other attached to the Hierophant (the Cord represents an "Energy Feed Line" through which you will draw energy up from the Earth's Maharic Shield into your personal Maharic Shield)

9. EXHALE with your attention on the Hierophant positioned 12" below your feet and use the exhale breath to push a **burst of Pale Silver Light** outward on a **horizontal plane** from the Hierophant. Imagine that a **Disc-shaped, Crystalline Platform of Pale Silver Light** about 4' in diameter, extends on a horizontal plane 12" beneath your feet around the Hierophant at its center. (This image represents your personal Maharic Shield.)

10. INHALE while using the inhale breath to draw more **Pale Silver Light** up through the **Pale Silver Cord** from Earth's Core, into the Hierophant at the center of your personal Maharic Shield.

11. EXHALE, using the exhale breath to push the Pale Silver Light **from the Hierophant**, out **into your Maharic Shield.** Imagine that your Maharic Shield now **pulsates**, as it fills with the Pale Silver Light from Earth's Core.

12. INHALE, again drawing more Pale Silver Light up from Earth's Core through the Pale Silver Cord into the Hierophant, and imagine the **Pale Silver Cord expanding to four feet in width,** forming a **Pillar of Pale Silver Light** running up from Earth's Core **directly into your four-foot-diameter Maharic Shield.**

13. EXHALE, again using the exhale breath to push **Pale Silver Light from the Hierophant** outward into your Maharic Shield, while imagining that your Maharic Shield **"takes on a life of its own,"** the disc suddenly **"folding upward"** with a **"popping"** sensation, to form a **4' diameter PILLAR of Pale Silver Light** all around and running through your body. (This is your Maharic SEAL, a temporary scalar-wave pillar of dimension 10/11/12 frequency light that blocks out disharmonic frequencies from dimensions I through 12, and begins to realign disharmonic frequencies in your body and bio-field to their original perfect natural order)

14. INHALE, imagining that the inhale breath draws the Pale Silver Light **from the Pillar encasing the body into every body cell.** Sense the tingling feeling as the Pale Silver Light moves through the physical body.

15. EXHALE, imagining that you can feel the energy of the Pale Silver Light **expanding into every crevice of the body** and then **outward around the body** into the Bio-field.

16. Breathe naturally for a minute or two, as the feeling of the Pale Silver Light moves through you, while **sensing the energy presence** of the Maharic Seal Pale Silver Pillar 4' around your body. The more time you spend breathing and sensing the energies, the more dimension 10/11/12 frequency you are drawing into your Pillar, which will increase the length of time the Maharic Seal Pillar will remain in your Bio-field

17. Return your attention to the Hierophant still positioned 12" below your feet.

18. INHALE, using the inhale breath to draw the Hierophant up through your Central Vertical Body Current, then out the top of your head (the 7th "Crown" Chakra), to a point about 36" above the head (the 14th Chakra).

19. EXHALE FORCEFULLY, using the exhale breath to **rapidly expand the Hierophant outward** on a horizontal plane at the **14th Chakra,** until the Hierophant suddenly "disappears" from view, with a mild "popping" sensation.

20. Breathe normally, while visualizing for a moment a **brilliant 4' Pale Silver Pillar of Light** extending from the **Earth's Core** upward, **fully encasing your body** and extending far above the head, into Earth's atmosphere and to a **single Star of Pale Blue Light** far off in deep space. Your Maharic Shield is now temporarily activated, and your Maharic Seal Pillar is temporarily manifest within your Bio-Field. The Maharic Seal will remain in your Bio-field anywhere from 20 minutes to 1 hour at first. The more this exercise is practiced, the longer the Pillar will remain.

21. For **quick reinforcement of the Maharic Seal**, once the full process has been run within 24 hours: Simply Imagine a **spark of Pale Silver Light** at the Pineal Gland, exhale it rapidly down to **Earth's Core** and imagine the Earth's Maharic Shield **spinning**. Call to mind the **Pale Silver Cord** and **Inhale** the 4' diameter Cord all the way up around you, **forming the Pillar,** attaching it "out in deep space" to the Star of Pale Blue Light

The Short Version of this technique provides a "**manually created**" **temporary Maharic Seal** in your Bio-Field, and **requires manual resetting every 24 hours**, with **frequent reinforcement during the day.** Using and practicing the **full version** of this technique, as described in the *Kathara Bio-Spiritual Healing System™ Level-I Maharic Recoding Process™*, **will progressively program the Cellular Memory of the body to hold the Maharic Seal for prolonged periods of time.** With consistent practice of the **full technique**, over an extended period of time, the Maharic Seal will function **automatically** as a permanent fixture within your Bio-field.

In the meantime, the **Short Version** of this technique, coupled with **reinforcement throughout the day,** will provide **Bio-field protection** and **gentle, regenerative Core Template realignment** for all aspects of the physical and Subtle-Energy-Body systems. **It is recommended to use at least this Short Version of the Maharic Seal technique prior to ANY energy work,** "**channeling,**" **or Astral and Dream Projection.** It will not only **provide protection** from disharmonic energies; it will also **amplify the results you desire to gain** from these activities.

It is best to use the Maharic Seal daily. Used in the **morning** before starting your day, the Maharic Seal will help to **harmonize personal and environmental energies** throughout the day. Used in the **evening** prior to sleep, it will begin to **increase conscious memory of sleep-time experience** and will protect your consciousness and body from dis-harmonic energies while you sleep.

- The Maharic Seal™ is a **Keylontic Science scalar-wave technology** built upon the **advanced scientific principles of 15-Dimensional Partiki Mechanics and Unified Field Vibrational Mechanics** and the advanced spiritual principles of **Merkaba Mechanics** and **the Law of One.** Further exploration of these advanced spiritual-sciences is Presently available through the training course of the *Kathara Bio-Spiritual Healing System™ Certificate Program* and through the introductory *Tangible Structure of the Soul-Accelerated Bio-Spiritual Evolution Program™* audio course, both available from the Azurite Temple of the Melchizedek Cloister. See ordering information at the end of this book.

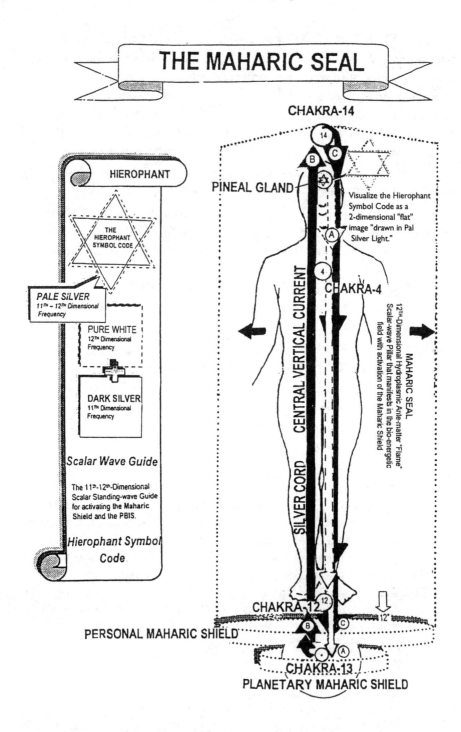

THE MAHARIC SEAL

CHAKRA-14

HIEROPHANT

THE HIEROPHANT SYMBOL CODE

PALE SiLVER
11ᵀᴴ – 12ᵀᴴ Dimensional Frequency

PURE WHITE
12ᵀᴴ Dimensional Frequency

DARK SILVER
11ᵀᴴ Dimensional Frequency

Scalar Wave Guide

The 11ᵗʰ-12ᵗʰ-Dimensional Scalar Standing-wave Guide for activating the Maharic Shield and the PBIS.

Hierophant Symbol Code

PINEAL GLAND

Visualize the Hierophant Symbol Code as a 2-dimensional "flat" image "drawn in Pal Silver Light."

CHAKRA-4

CENTRAL VERTICAL CURRENT

SILVER CORD

12ᵀᴴ-Dimensional Hydroplasmic Ante-matter "Flame" Scalar-wave Pillar that manifests in the bio-energetic field with activation of the Maharic Shield

MAHARIC SEAL

CHAKRA-12

12"

PERSONAL MAHARIC SHIELD

CHAKRA-13
PLANETARY MAHARIC SHIELD

Index

What to Do Next

1. To assist directly in Planetary Grid clearing and balancing, frequently use the Temporary Maharic Seal Bio-Regenesis Technique (see page 195) for progressive development of personal bio-energetic field clarity and amplification, acceleration of spiritual development, holistic healing and beginning DNA Template Bio-Regenesis.

2. To explore the Spiritual Actualization Masters Program for Personal Development, order from Azurite Temple. (See next page, or http://members.aol.com/azuritetemple/)
• The Tangible Structure of the Soul Accelerated Bio-Spiritual Evolution Program audio course
• The Kathara Bio-Spiritual Healing System Certificate Program- correspondence audio-video course and manual.
• Related Supplementary Bio-Regenesis Technique Programs and Spiritual Development audio-visual Workshops.

To further explore the CDT-Plate translations, "Indigo Child" phenomena or Masters Planetary Templar Mechanics Global Healing Programs for Planetary and Universal Studies, order from Granite Publishing (see last page):
The Voyagers Vol. 2 *The Secrets of Amenti*;
The Voyagers Vol. 3 *Keys to the Secrets of Amenti;*
The Voyagers Vol. 4 *The Angelic Dossier.*

If you think you may be or know an "Indigo Child" or an "Angel or ET" contactee and need assistance, or if you want to enter the Emerald Covenant or join the Azurite Amenti Planetary Templar Security Team to participate in Advanced Global Healing Efforts, or if you are interested in receiving non-denominational, egalitarian Melchizedek Cloister "Law of One" Ordination, Baptism, Marriage, Renewal of Nuptial Vows, Last Rights, Spiritual Healing Facilitation or Spiritual Consultation services through authorized MC Ministers of the non-denominational dogma-free Azurite Temple MC ministry, contact the Azurite Temple (see next page).

AZURITE TEMPLE SHORT ORDER FORM

Code	Item Description	$$	#	Ext. Price
'S-BR1/ A-HB	*The Tangible Structure of the Soul Accelerated Bio-Spiritual Evolution Program*: Level-1 Bio-Regenesis Activation Techniques 6-audio course and Manual	$99		
A1-M/ A1V	*The Kathara Bio-Spiritual Healing System^{TM} Level-I 2-Audio, 1-Video Course, and Manual*	$75		
A1/ V-HB	The Kathara Bio-Spiritual Healing System™ Level-1 4-Video Workshop & Course Manual	$105		
'V-1/B	*Voyagers Volume-1 The Sleeping Abductees* 2e. 2001	$16		
'V-2/B	*Voyagers Volume-2 The Secrets of Amenti* 2e 2001	$23		
'V-3/B	*Voyagers Volume-3 The Keys to the Secrets of Amenti*	$17		
.R/HB	*Angelic Realities: THE Survival Handbook* includes full description of all materials available	$15		
'rder Sub Total				
L Residents please add 7% Sales Tax				
'rders over $20.00 ADD $8 shipping; Orders over $50.00 ADD $15 shipping				
'rder Grand Total Enclosed				

YMENT: ☐US Check ☐US Money Order ☐Foreign(cash only)

☐VISA ☐MasterCard ☐Amex ☐Discover

card # _____expiration date _____

signature_____

AME:_____ PHONE:_____

IIP-TO ADDRESS: _____

TY/STATE _____

P/POSTAL CODE/COUNTRY_____

Make checks/MOs payable to "The Azurite Temple MC"
Credit Card Phone Orders, or mailing list, call (941) 952-1096
Send order form/ payment to:
The Azurite Temple MC
4411 Bee Ridge Rd. # 291
Sarasota, FL 34233 USA

Granite
G Publishing
G roup

To receive a free catalog that includes the *Voyagers* series as well as
many other fine books,
and to get a free sample of our cutting-edge periodical
the 5th World Journal,
please write to...

Granite Publishing Group
P.O. Box 1429
Columbus, North Carolina 28722

or call...
800.366.0264

or visit our web sites at...
http://www.5thworld.com

and the Azurite Temple at
http://members.aol.com/azuritetemple/

or email us at ...
orders@5thworld.com

Thank you.